Shatter the Darkness

When Ingrid Seymour is not writing books, she spends her time working as a software engineer, cooking exotic recipes, hanging out with her family and working out. She lives in Birmingham, AL with her husband, two kids and a cat named Mimi. She can be found on Twitter Ingrid_Seymour

www.IngridSeymour.com

www.facebook.com/IngridSeymourAuthor

Also by Ingrid Seymour

Ignite the Shadows
Eclipse the Flame

Shatter the Darkness

INGRID SEYMOUR

HARPER
Voyager

HarperVoyager
An imprint of HarperCollins*Publishers* Ltd
1 London Bridge Street
London SE1 9GF

www.harpercollins.co.uk

This paperback edition 2018

2

First published in Great Britain in ebook format by
HarperCollins*Publishers* 2017

A catalogue record for this book
is available from the British Library

ISBN: 978-0-00-818150-5

Set Sabon by Palimpsest Book Production Limited,
Falkirk, Stirlingshire

Automatically produced by Atomik ePublisher from Easypress

Printed and bound by CPI Group (UK) Ltd, Croydon, CR0 4YY

Chapter 1

The Kevlar vest is tight and uncomfortable around my chest. I push it from the side, trying to find a perfect fit, wondering if I'll ever get used to wearing it and, more importantly, if I'll ever understand this new, vicious world in which my life hangs from a thread every time I take to the streets.

My black military boots thud against the concrete sidewalk as I move away from Pacific Place and Elliot Whitehouse's headquarters. We haven't moved, in spite of IgNiTe's attack a month ago. We're still in the same building. Moving would signify fear, and Elliot is too proud for that.

The late May sun warms my face, and it's a welcomed feeling that shows me the world has kept its normal course in at least one way.

In the last month, many of the major streets have been cleared by the Eklyptor "government," but not this one, which is exactly why I prefer it. I don't have to walk among the invaders who pretend Seattle is theirs and us, humans, the vermin who infest it, and not the other way around. The biggest Eklyptors factions in the city, Whitehouse and

Hailstone, are still not seeing eye to eye, but that hasn't gotten in the way of their Takeover efforts, at least not nearly as much as I'd like. They have divided the city among themselves as if it were a big cake, and each is taking care of its slice diligently enough. Damn them!

I pass a burnt Metro Transit bus, its frame charred and many of its windows melted away by the intense fire that consumed it. Orange traffic cones and pedestrian safety fences lie strewn all over the street like forgotten relics from a faraway past. I skirt around them, then walk ahead, looking over my shoulder every few steps to make sure no one is following me.

My heart flutters, restless. I can't wait to meet James and confirm he's okay. I haven't seen him since he took a bullet trying *and* failing to kill Whitehouse. He's been too busy fighting other Eklyptor factions, and this is the first chance he's gotten to meet me. A month ago when I last saw Aydan, he said James was recovering quickly thanks to his accelerated healing powers. Sometimes it pays to be a Symbiot. Still, I want to see him with my own two eyes.

With a certain skip in my steps, I cross 9th Avenue and continue down Pine Street. I'm eager to reach the van where I stash my motorcycle after each use. I'm dying to ride, to wrap my legs around the rumbling engine, and zip around the city streets on my way to hope.

That's what IgNiTe, James and the crew are to me: Hope with a capital "H".

As I pass in front of a gutted deli, I'm startled by my own reflection on one of the few window fronts that survived The Takeover riots. My features look so etched and angular that I hardly recognize myself. I've lost weight which is natural considering the stress of living under Whitehouse's roof and the loss of appetite caused by dining around semi-human creatures all the time. But hey, no one can blame me, not when eating at a trough with a team of pigs would be an upgrade. My brown hair is well past shoulder length, curling slightly at the tips. My skin is sallow—not the healthy golden shade it used to be. I don't spend much time in the sun anymore, which I sorely miss. Only my brown eyes seem the same, sharp and wide. Though, if I'm honest with myself, the sadness that used to live in their depths seems more profound now.

As I stare at my barely-recognizable image, something moves behind the window. My heart skips a beat. I jump back, hands snatching the gun at my hip, a Glock 22 with its 15-round magazine in place. I aim the weapon, hand shaking. I struggle to focus on whatever is on the other side. It takes me a few seconds to make out a shape huddled under a table. Slowly, my brain processes the information: a dirty sneaker, blue jeans, a puffy blue jacket and long, blond hair under a gray wool cap.

A girl!

A perfectly human girl, judging by the lack of buzzing inside my head.

Her face is obscured, but I can still see her wide blue eyes, brimming with fear. She's clutching a yellow bag of chips close to her chest. Her hands shake as much as mine. Her face is contorted in a grimace of the worst kind, a mask of terror I know all too well. I've felt it on my own face one-too-many times. And why shouldn't she be terrified?

She thinks I'm an Eklyptor.

I'm walking the streets in plain daylight, as if I have nothing to fear. Only our enemies do that these days. She has no idea of the courage it takes to pretend you're one of them.

I put up my left hand in a pacifying gesture and slowly lower my gun. The grimace on her face deepens, letting me know she's aware that when Eklyptors show mercy, they'll make you wish they'd shown you death.

She pushes further under the table.

I should help her, but it would be a mistake. She wouldn't trust me. There isn't an explanation I could offer that would satisfy her. Not that I would fault her for that.

If she's stayed alive this long, she must be doing something right. I carefully holster the gun. Without breaking eye contact, I step back to the edge of the sidewalk.

A horrible sadness fills me and, suddenly, I feel like crying. How many like her are out there? How much longer will they be able to hide? Something passes between us. Her grimace softens an infinitesimal amount.

I look away and, fighting my rising shame, I continue down the street. My heart seems to shrivel in my chest, shame wrapping itself all around it and squeezing, squeezing, squeezing. I take a deep breath and stuff my hands in my pockets, shoulders to my ears, eyes on my boots.

She's better off without you, Marci. You'll just get her killed or captured, and how are you gonna feel then?

A hell of a lot worse; that's how.

I'm almost to the parking lot where I've kept the van ever since that first night I hot-wired it when I notice two moving black blotches against the blue sky.

I stop, all my senses on alert.

Scouts!

With measured steps, I continue down the road, more aware of my Kevlar vest and my .40 caliber gun. I don't like that they're flying in my direction and that I have nowhere to go but toward them. I'm in the middle of the block. Turning back or hurrying ahead would simply bring them here much faster.

And what about the girl? God, what about the girl?!

As their monstrous, dark shapes move closer, losing altitude, I keep wishing they'd spot something more interesting on another street and leave me alone.

No such luck.

Their enormous aquamarine and yellow wings flap in unison, making a rhythmic *thwack, thwack* sound. The sun shines on their colorful membranes and the sight is almost beautiful. Flying Eklyptors aren't common. It takes them years to morph their hosts into air-conquering beings. Even from a distance, it's obvious these scouts are older than old. They move too gracefully, almost as if they were born this way.

Within seconds, they cover an entire block and descend onto the middle of the street, about twenty-five yards away from me. I stop and hold their gaze. They size me up, then walk forward and get within buzzing distance. My head drones as I know theirs do. The one I judge to be the leader walks a few steps ahead of the other one.

He or she is tall—well over six feet—and, on the ground, moves clumsily on leathery talons tipped with ebony curved claws several inches long. Its legs are tall and spindly from ankle to knee but widen into muscular, smooth thighs covered in dappled yellow and aquamarine skin. The wings spring from its sides and are now folded neatly behind its back, extending well above its head. Its torso and arms are still human in shape and proportion, but covered in the same bizarre skin and voided of any markings that may identify it as male or female. Neither one wears any clothes, just a belt around their waist with a weapon, extra bullets and a standard issue scanner attached to it.

They stop about ten feet away, looking wearily at my gun. They both tip their bald heads to one side as if to listen better. Their eyes have no whites. They're round, orange marbles with small black pricks in the middle, like hawks'. They watch me for a moment. Their long, beak-like noses twitch and make snuffling sounds as they scent the air.

"Faction?" the leader asks in a slithery voice that is almost feminine. I decide this one was once a woman.

"Whitehouse. Yep, yep, Whitehouse it is." I treat them to *Azrael's* crazy talk. Ever since my agent took over me and revealed its deeply disturbed behavior, I've kept up the pretense that the creature is still in control. It is a useful tactic that helps me keep a low profile—no one wants to deal with a nutcase.

They frown their huge brows. I've never met these two before, but I need to stay in character in case I see them at headquarters or anywhere else with Eklyptors who know me.

Slowly, I pull out a pair of dog tags from behind my shirt. After Zara Hailstone's death at what was supposed to be a friendly meeting with Elliot, hostilities between Eklyptor factions have intensified, creating the need for a way to easily tell friend from foe.

"Toss them," She-Bird says, putting out a long-fingered hand.

I throw them. She catches them in one hooked claw, examines them for a moment, then passes them to her companion.

"Check this, Griffin."

Griffin pulls the scanner from the belt at its waist and

plugs one of the dog tags into a thin slot. An instant later, there is a short double beep.

"Clear," the second scout says, tossing back the dog tags.

I catch them and put them back on. "Seen much action today? Huh? Huh?" My tone is casual enough. I should have nothing to fear from any Whitehouse Eklyptors, but I think I'll never stop being unnerved and wary of them, no matter how deeply infiltrated I am.

"There's some fighting going on in the west side. Around White Center," the leader says with a squawk. "Igniters, I think. That's all we've heard. You?"

I shake my head. "I just left headquarters. Haven't seen a thing. Nope, not a thing." An image of the scared girl in her blue jacket pops into my head.

The scouts nod. She-Bird looks down the street. "Where are you headed?"

"Just . . . uh . . . repurposing. Looking for a new ride. Something fun." This is common enough. There are so many abandoned vehicles I could drive a new one every day. "A motorcycle, maybe. Yeah, that would be fun." I make engine noises with my mouth, sputtering saliva like a toddler.

The leader scoffs, looking disgusted. "Not graceful," she says, giving its wings a quick shake to demonstrate how much she thinks of motorized means of transportation.

"Best I can do right now." I shrug and point a finger down the street. "Need to go. Gotta be on my way."

They look about as ready to get away from me as I am to get away from them. A great benefit of my crazy Azrael act.

I give them a military salute, then march forward, sensing their eyes on the back of my neck. It takes all I've got to ignore the feeling and keep moving without looking over my shoulder. With every step, I wait for the flap of wings, instead I hear the retreating *click, click, click* of claws against asphalt.

Finally, I give into my curiosity and look back. They're walking away from me, their unusual shapes swaying from side to side, their noses pointed upward as they sniff the air.

"Shit!" I murmur under my breath and slip into the recessed entrance of The Paramount Hotel.

Suddenly, the leader turns its head sharply toward the deli and gestures Griffin. They take their guns out and clamber toward the small restaurant on their leathery talons.

The girl's luck has just run out.

Chapter 2

I pull away and press my back against the wall. "Shit, shit, shit." I slap my hands to the sides of my head and squeeze.

What do I do? What do I do?

I have to help her.

Yeah? And get yourself killed?

No. Can't risk that! Getting rid of Elliot is my priority.

I'm still deliberating when I hear a loud shattering sound, followed by a shrill scream. In an instant, I make my decision.

This fight is *for* every human being, not only *against* every Eklyptor.

If I lose sight of that, I may as well let my crazy agent take over again.

Before doubt creeps in, I jump out of my hiding place and run the way I came. What I see sends a jolt of adrenaline into my veins, electrifying me.

She-Bird is holding the girl by the neck as if she's nothing more than a doll. Her legs kick in mid-air while she scratches her attacker's forearms like an enraged feral cat.

9

My boots slap the pavement and catch the scouts' attention. Their heads snap my way.

I stop, chest pumping, mind reeling with possible things I could say to prevent this disaster. With no other option and little hope, I go for the crazy, stamping a maniacal grin on my face and clapping with happiness.

"Ooh, you got one. You got one!"

The scouts stare down at me with their big, orange eyes. She-Bird's mouth twists and tightens. "We've got this under control. Move along."

The girl's legs continue to kick, though not as forcefully as before. Her face is turning pale and her screams weak and hoarse.

"Can I have her? Tell me I can have her!" I say, as if the girl is a bug, and I'm a sadistic child with a magnifying glass and ideas fit for a summer day.

"Why would you want her?" Griffin asks, giving She-Bird a sideways glance.

The girl's arms fall limply to the side as her attacker gives her a shake and a tighter squeeze around the neck. Her eyes widen for an instant, then roll to the back of her head.

Do something, Marci! She's gonna die.

"Uh, she could be my pet. Yes, my lovely pet," I say.

"There's no room for pets," She-Bird says. "They either die or they join the ranks. Except without *Spawners*, the second option isn't really possible, is it?" she asks the question as if the lack of reproductively-capable Eklyptors is my fault. If she only knew.

I almost laugh, but I'm too scared for the girl. The truth is: I'm responsible for the extermination of Whitehouse's Spawners. I was the one who found out where he kept them hidden and gave IgNiTe the intel so they could kill every single one of them.

"So the girl dies," She-Bird says, then slams her against the blacktop and leans into her, putting all her weight into a killing chokehold.

"No!" I scream, unable to help myself.

As if my word was a threat or a punch, Griffin crouches into attack position. "You're a fuckin' *Fender,*" he says, the word rolling off his tongue the same way the word Eklyptor rolls off mine.

"Take her!" She-Bird orders. "Alive, if possible."

So much for lying my way out of this one.

Heart, blood, lungs automatically pumping into action, I spin to the side just as Griffin lunges. Like a raging bull, the beast charges past me, staggers to a stop and spins to face me again.

Their plan might be to take hostages, but mine is not. I go for my gun. Inhumanly fast, Griffin gets his weapon first and, in the same motion, aims and shoots before I even have a chance to lift my arm.

Two hammer blows hit me in the chest. My body jerks twice. Pain blossoms from a pinprick into a huge mushroom cloud and drops me to ground. I fall on my back and blink up at the blue sky, fighting for breath.

"Alive, I said, you asshole," She-Bird scolds.

"I wasn't about to let her shoot me," Griffin complains.

"Go check on her," she growls.

Get up. Get up. Get up.

Gun still in hand, I roll to the side, shooting. One of my bullets strikes its intended target, piercing She-Bird strangling forearm. She growls, lets go of the girl and cradles the wound to her chest.

Pain still burning under my vest, I keep rolling until I

reach one of the many abandoned vehicles that litter the street. I take cover behind it and jump to my feet. Crouched low, I scurry to the back end of what turns out to be a large SUV. I press my back to the vehicle and thump my chest three times.

God, it hurts.

I'm panting, wishing I could rip the vest right off.

Bullets pierce through the back windshield and zip past my head. I duck, run around to the front of the SUV, and shoot at Griffin over the hood.

My aim is true.

Griffin's inhuman eyes go wide. In slow motion, he looks down at his chest. Blood squirts out from two round holes on a yellow patch of skin. He drops the gun and falls to his knees, wearing a dumbfounded expression.

Eyes roving from side to side, I look for She-Bird. She's nowhere in sight. I whirl, thinking she might have sneaked up behind me, but there's no one, just the trashed sidewalk and the once-trendy brick buildings.

Breathing in overdrive, I pull away from the SUV, spinning, the gun sweeping wide circles around me. Slowly, I make my way to the girl, my head snapping this way and that as my imagination conjures shadows in every possible hiding place. I look up, trying to spot a flying figure in the sky or up in the buildings. I find nothing but feel watched. Thoroughly watched.

"Hey!" I nudge the girl in the ribs with the tip of my boots, afraid to let down my guard and check if she's breathing. She doesn't respond.

God, was this all in vain?

I poke her again. She moans. I point the gun to the ground and slowly squat, my gaze still jumping from the street to the sky and the top of the buildings.

"Hey, hey! Can you get up?"

The girl rolls to her side and curls up, grabbing her neck and sobbing in a weak, broken voice.

"C'mon, you have to get up. We have to get out of here!"

My heart is racing faster than ever. Images of monsters dropping from the sky flash in and out of my vision. God, what if She-Bird went for backup? We're not that far from headquarters. If she did, my cover is blown. *Shit!*

"C'mon!" I growl in my most commanding voice. "If you don't get up, I'll leave you here, and you know they'll be back."

She rouses at the threat. Her eyes blink open. She swallows audibly and winces. After a moment, she looks up. Our gazes meet. Her blue eyes are bloodshot and terrified.

"Do you want to live or not?" I ask.

She nods but looks so doubtful it makes me think she might rather die. Well, screw that. I didn't risk my life to have her give up on me, so I hook an arm around hers and force her up.

"Follow me. We have to get out of here. C'mon!" I push her toward the SUV, then move that way myself.

I give the car a quick inspection, checking its tires and general state. It looks drivable. It'd better be.

I run to the driver side door and try the handle. No such luck. Holding the gun with both hands to steady my nervous grip, I take a couple of backward steps and shoot at the window. The girl yelps, startled by the sound.

The bullet drills right through the glass, creating a large spider web of cracks that spreads outward.

Teeth clenched, I slam my elbow against the fractured glass. It takes a couple of hits before the window collapses inwardly and I'm able to pop the lock. After tossing the sheet of broken glass onto the street, I hurry inside and unlock the passenger side door.

"C'mon, get in!" I command the numb-looking girl. She doesn't move. Instead, her eyes dart from side to side as if looking for a place to run.

"Don't be stupid. You'll never outrun them," I say as I smash the butt of the gun against the plastic that wraps around the steering column. The cover snaps off, revealing a bundle of wires.

My heart races like a ticking clock in overdrive. We have to get out of here. Stat!

I set the gun down on the seat and get to work. I've just finished pulling the bundle of wires loose when the girl shrieks and takes off down the street at a full pelt.

Jolting upright, I go for the gun but, before I get a hold of it, there is a *whoosh*, and I fly away from the car and land in the middle of the street with a bone-shuddering thud. My lungs empty themselves at the impact. I wince in pain but force myself into action.

In one fluid motion, I bring my knees toward my face then kick-up to a standing position. Just as I get back on my feet, She-Bird tackles me to the ground. I land on my back once more and lose what little oxygen I'd managed to take in. The scout straddles me. Her hawk-like face is twisted in fury. She balls her hand into a large fist and pulls it back. I throw my arms over my face and manage to block the blow.

"Thought I'd let you get away, you little shit?" She-Bird tries another jab. I block it, too. She growls in frustration and tries to get my arms away from their protective position.

Pulling hard, she grunts between pointed teeth. "Whitehouse pays extra for Fenders and doesn't care if they're bruised up or not. Not as long as they're alive."

Her tall wings blotch the sky above, shining, translucent. It's a beautifully cruel sight.

With the high-pitched cry of an eagle, She-Bird digs her sharp claws into one of my wrists and pries the arm away from my face. Through the opening, she uses her quick, avian reflexes to sneak in a powerful blow. I growl between clenched teeth, feeling as if a boulder has smashed against my cheekbone.

But there is not time to wallow, not when the punch has unbalanced her, and countless karate sparring matches taught me the required moves to escape this sort of situation.

The technique comes to me as second nature. In a brisk, strong move, I thrust my knees into She-Bird's butt. The unexpected thump unbalances her further. She lurches forward. Her hands move to brace the fall and land right above my head. I follow up by sweeping her arms from under her and pushing her sideways with all I've got.

To my surprise, all I've got is too much. She-Bird is lighter than I thought, surely a trait required by all flying creatures. We tumble over and over and, when we stop, the scout ends up on top of me again.

Shit!

With a jerk, she pulls out her gun and aims it at my forehead. I freeze.

"You sure are more trouble than I thought you'd be," she says between sharp breaths. "Maybe too much trouble to take you in alive." Her face twists grotesquely as she seems to ponder what to do with me. Her orange eyes pierce mine, hatred burning in their depths.

I see the instant she makes up her mind to kill me. A cold shock bursts in the middle of my chest with the knowledge that I'm about to die. I close my eyes and, for a moment, regret my decision to fight for the girl. The regret only last for an instant, though. Confronted with the choice again, I'd do the same thing. Any other decision would be one I couldn't live with.

The shot explodes with a deafening bang that sends a jolt through my body. I jerk, startled by the loud crack and a wet splatter on my face. My eyes blink open. She-Bird wavers over me, her forehead blown open, brain matter dangling from a jagged hole. She tips forward and crashes on top of me.

I lie still for a moment, uncomprehending. All of a sudden, She-Bird's dead weight turns into a suffocating force. Desperately, I push her off me and sit up, swiping at my face over and over. My heart thumps in my ears. I spit blood and wipe my tongue on my sleeve, vomit rising to my throat.

I don't know how long I sit there—wild and horrified by the fact that I'm wearing someone's death all over my face—before I realize I'm still alive. Eventually, I come to and look around, wondering how come *my* brains are not the ones splattered all over the pavement.

A pair of blue eyes looks down at me from behind the barrel of my own weapon. The girl I planned to rescue stands in front of me, legs shoulder-width apart, gun gripped tightly between trembling hands. The SUV sits behind her, the driver side door thrown open. Two parallel streaks run down each side of the girl's face as tears spill freely down her face.

Her mouth trembles. She looks scared out of her mind and doesn't seem willing to aim the gun in any other direction but the bull's-eye between my eyebrows.

In a shaky voice, she asks, "What . . . what the hell are you?"

Chapter 3

I snake the SUV between abandoned cars and debris, expecting to run into an impassable section of road sooner or later. Still, I don't dare take the viable roads Eklyptors cleared for their purposes, not while carrying strictly human cargo.

"What's your name?" I ask the girl.

"Hannah," she says from her crouched position at the foot of the passenger seat.

I can't afford to let her sit where an Eklyptor might spot her. If they see two people but sense only one, they'll give chase. Our chances are precarious enough riding on these roads. My hope is that the Igniter battle She-Bird mentioned will keep the skies and streets clear for now.

"I'm Marci," I say.

"Where are you taking me?" Hannah's question is full of suspicion, as if I didn't just save her life and she decided to repay the favor.

"To safety."

"Why had they let you go?" She's surely having second

thoughts about putting herself in my charge. Her eyes are wide and scared. She looks as frightened and paranoid as a mouse. But who can blame her? Only God knows what she's been through, what she's had to do to survive. Very likely it's the paranoia that's kept her alive this long.

It's a heck of a good question, anyway, one I cannot answer. I got her in the car with a promise to tell her everything, but now that we're on our way, I don't have to tell her jack. The situation is too complicated to explain. I can't tell her I'm a Symbiot. Not when I'm hoping James will take her with him. There are very few Symbiots among James's ranks, and their identities are revealed on a need-to-know basis. I know only three others: James, Aydan and Rheema. If there are more within the ranks, they're hidden from me as well. I doubt IgNiTe, the group of human rebels who openly defy Eklyptors, would appreciate the news. Everyone is doing their best to keep their spirits up; there is no point in giving them more to worry about.

"Well, um . . . I'm a spy." I can't think of anything else to tell her. Besides, it's not a lie.

She shakes her head, looking as if I just told her I'm a hungry werewolf with rabid thoughts of taking a chunk out of her.

"I'm with IgNiTe," I add, hoping this will ease her fears.

"IgNiTe?!" she exclaims. From the excited ring of her voice, it seems I have quickly risen from werebeast status to saint. "Are you serious?!"

Man, I feel like a celebrity. I nod and keep driving north. The further away from downtown we go, the clearer the streets become and the slower my heart beats. Scouts keep closer to headquarters. Their numbers are limited, and Elliot likes to keep them close. He won't be happy to learn that two of them are dead. It's not like he can easily replace them—not when it takes years to morph and grow additional appendages.

Hannah seems content for a few minutes, then the questions begin again.

"But how does that work if . . . if you're human?"

Smart girl. Surely another reason she's still alive. She should make a nice addition to James's ranks. This fight can use every person we can get, especially if they're intelligent.

"Uh, some of them like to keep humans around, like pets." My stomach twists. The simple idea of being a traitorous, Eklyptor pet makes me want to retch.

Hannah's nose wrinkles with a disgusted grimace. "That has to be horrible. How can you stand it?"

I shrug.

"And what if they decide to turn you?"

"It's a risk, but these are desperate times."

She puts a hand over her mouth. "I couldn't do it. I would just . . ." She muffles her words and shakes her head, looking horrified.

"It isn't easy. I assure you."

We don't speak for a few blocks. I've managed to take us completely out of downtown, and I'm well on my way to my rendezvous spot with James.

Hannah hugs her legs to her chest and rests her chin on her knees, looking pensive. "Will IgNiTe take me?"

"If you're willing to fight. If you're not, they'll find a safe place for you. One of the underground human communities."

"They really exist?!" she asks as if I just told her Sasquatch is real, and she can't wait to meet him. "We heard rumors, but we never saw them."

"We?" I ask, then immediately regret it.

She stares down and pulls at her jacket as if it's out of place, which it isn't. You'd think I would have learned by now. I've lost enough people in this fight to understand the touchy subjects.

"I'm sorry. I shouldn't . . ." I trail off. There's nothing to say.

The silence between us is heavy for a long moment, then Hannah speaks, "Mom, Dad, my sister, Josephine, and Mack, our dog." She worries at a hangnail, pretty much obliterating it.

I don't want to hear this. I don't. If she expects wise words from me I have none. If she expects sympathy—I have plenty of that, heck, I even have empathy—but I've never been good at expressing it.

"We lived in a condo right on Olive Way. We were at home when all hell broke loose. We stayed holed up in there until the food ran out. About two weeks." Hannah pauses and takes a deep breath.

The Eklyptors never bothered searching people's houses. A good number of citizens just came voluntarily in the beginning of The Takeover, believing the lies the beasts spread through the news channels, the ones that said the authorities would provide answers and help. They were like mice crawling inside the lion's mouth. They never stood a chance, because Eklyptors took control of everything that was important: hospitals, government, police. They had their infected monsters in place, ready to assume power as soon as hostilities began. As for the humans who stayed hidden, Eklyptors knew they would soon have to come out in search of food. The creeps are in this for the long run. So why hurry?

21

"We tried to talk to the neighbors," she continues, "but the few that were still there wanted nothing to do with us. One guy even threatened us with a gun, saying we wanted to steal his provisions. The empty units had already been raided by them. We found a few cans of soup, but that was it. So Dad . . . he decided to go out to find stuff to eat. He took Mack with him and made us stay back. It was so hard waiting for him, not knowing if he was all right. We were so relieved when he came back. He ran into no trouble, was even able to fill a backpack with enough food for a few days. Stuff like canned tuna, crackers and Slim Jims."

A vivid image of her family huddled together, dividing up the few items, pops into my mind. How many families went through the same? How many are still together?

"Of course, the food didn't last," Hannah continues. "Dad felt confident he could go out and get more. He hadn't run into any problems the first time, so he assured us it would be fine. We still didn't like it. He had no idea how awful waiting for him had been. I told him we should stay together, but he wanted to make sure we were safe. He said that was his priority."

Hannah doesn't need to say what happened next. Her story is charged with the power of an awful punch line.

Her father never came back.

She cries silently. Her hands flutter to and away from her face as she wipes tears off her cheeks and jawline.

I clench the steering wheel and look straight ahead. I doubt there's a human left on Earth who doesn't have a nightmare story to recount. I have my share of them, but I'm not burdening her with mine, am I?

What does she expect me to say?

Apparently nothing, because she goes on, oblivious to my

discomfort.

"We stayed there for two days, eating little more than cracker crumbs and crying ourselves crazy. Finally, I convinced Mom we had to go out and look for him. In case Dad came back, we left him a note that said we'd be back every night. We packed what we could. Flashlight, matches, first-aid kit, stuff like that.

"We were terrified, but at least we were doing something, instead of just waiting like useless fools. First, we went to the convenience store where Dad went the first time. He'd said there was nothing left there, so it was unlikely he'd gone back, but it was all we had to go by. It was so hard moving through the streets. We kept expecting someone to jump us from every door and alley." She gives a dry laugh. "I saw people watching us from their condos. They just stared at us from behind their curtains. No one offered to help. No one."

She lifts her chin and looks over at me. I throw a quick glance her way. The wonder and gratitude in her eyes let me know how surprised she is that someone, namely *me*, gave a damn and risked everything to save her life.

Yep, it was nuts. Even I can't believe it, so she should shut up before she makes me regret it.

But Hannah is on a roll, and I don't have the heart to tell her to stop. Maybe she needs this, maybe it's therapy. Too bad I'm not a shrink.

"I used my cell phone to navigate us, snapping pictures of the areas we had checked. It's so odd that phones and TVs and all that crap still works when everything else's gone to hell." She shakes her head. "Anyway, it was slow going. We hid and crouched more than anything else. We almost got spotted a couple of times by . . . *people* driving past.

23

Then, just when we were about to go back home, we . . . we found Mack. He was Josephine's dog, a good-hearted black Labrador. He was dead. Shot in the head and laying by the side of the street.

"Josephine lost it. She went hysterical, screaming and crying, clinging to Mom. We tried to calm her down, but we couldn't. 'If Mack is dead. Dad is dead,' she kept saying over and over again.

"Then, all of sudden, this man comes out of one of the buildings. He looked furious and dangerous. At first, I thought he was one of *them*, but he was mad because of the racket Josephine was making. Not like he made it any better by yelling at her to 'shut the fuck up unless you want the Eklyptors to show up.'

"When Josephine wouldn't shut up, he tore her away from Mom and slapped her across the face. He looked like he was ready to kill her. Mom and I pulled him away and that's when he pulled out a gun and he just . . ." Hannah trails off, too choked up by her tears to continue.

The corners of my eyes prickle. I think of Dad, Mom, Xave, all gone. The pain of their absence smarts like a wound freshly opened. It always rides right under my skin, but it hasn't resurfaced is some time—not when hatred and revenge-lust are my prevalent emotions while living among Eklyptors.

I want to curse Hannah, want to blame her for pouring salt on the wound and reminding me of my own misery and loneliness, but she's gone through enough as it is. The last thing she needs is my brand of bitterness undoing the little comfort she's found in pouring her heart out.

After her tears run out, Hannah takes a deep breath and shifts in her spot, one hand digging inside her blue jacket.

I look sideways at the exact moment she pulls out a small revolver from the depths of her puffy top layer. I nearly slam on the brakes, expecting her to point the gun at me, but she just lets it dangle between her thumb and index finger.

"I killed him," she confesses, though not with regret. She sets the gun on the seat at her side, mouth twisted in disgust. "He shot Josephine and Mom, but I . . . I fought him. I took the gun from him and . . . I used every single bullet. I'm still waiting for the guilt to keep me up at night, but the only regret I have is killing him too fast. I wish I'd made him suffer. I wish I'd let him linger, knowing he was gonna die. I'd have loved to see the fear on his face. Does that make me a monster?"

This a rhetorical question, right? She must know the answer. Except she looks up at me, her blue eyes full of fear for what my answer might be.

"You might be asking the wrong person." I take the next right and notice a car ahead of us. The way is fairly clear on this road. The obstructing debris—shattered glass, broken down cars, chairs and tables from the nearby restaurants— have been moved to the sides. I don't warn Hannah or remind her to stay low. She's scared enough as it is and wouldn't risk even a small peek out of the window.

"Why do you say that?" she asks.

I sigh and bite down my response. *Butt out*, those are the words that come to mind first, but I make an effort to be civilized. The fact that I live with animals doesn't mean I should act like one. I would have answered her that way before The Takeover, but only because at the time she would have been able to find someone else to *bond* with. Post-Eklyptors, not so much. The going is tough. People who love you and understand you drop like flies at your feet. Now it sort of feels like any stranger you meet can be your friend, as long as they're the human kind, that is.

"Because I happen to know real monsters. To me, you're just a girl."

The car ahead of us turns onto another road. I don't get to feel at ease for long, though, because another one appears; this one headed in our direction in the opposite lane. It's a couple of blocks away, so I still don't say anything. Instead, I look for a way to turn, but the intersecting streets are barricaded. I clench my jaw.

Hannah rests a cheek on her drawn-up knees. Blond hair spills to the side, tangled and dirty. She looks like she hasn't showered in weeks and, judging by the red circles under her eyes, hasn't slept much either.

"I keep thinking maybe Dad's out there, somewhere." Hannah closes her eyes as if she's having a daydream. I think she is.

"Stay down," I say behind my hand. "A car is going to pass by. Don't freak out."

Hannah holds her legs tighter, going rigid with tension. I keep my left hand on the wheel and the right one on the gun on my lap. When the car passes—a red BMW—I exchange a glance with its passenger. From here, he looks perfectly human, but my head buzzes, letting me know he's an Eklyptor. He nods and keeps on his way. I breathe a sigh of relief.

As long as we don't encounter any morphed creatures with super noses or thermal vision, they won't detect Hannah. If we run into more scouts, however, we're screwed. I worry at the leather steering wheel with a sharp thumbnail, leaving marks behind.

We ride in silence for a few blocks. We run into a few other cars, but we pass them without problems, although not without considerable heartburn. For the most part, the drivers look perfectly human, except for one with colorful, butterfly-like patterns on her skin.

The older Eklyptors who have managed to develop useful traits are higher in the pecking order. They were the commanders for the different factions during The Takeover. The newer Eklyptors are the regular "citizens." They are the ones keeping things going, showing up to work to make sure the cities they stole from us don't fall apart. So the further we move away from downtown, we should be less likely to run into enhanced beasts. I relax a little.

Finally, I turn onto 15th Avenue East, the road that leads to Lake View Cemetery and my rendezvous with James.

"We're almost there," I say.

I stop at an intersection. A car comes to a sudden stop on the opposite corner. My gaze locks with the driver's. I wait for the buzzing to begin. It doesn't. I judge the distance between us. The guy is close enough. My head *should* be buzzing.

He's human!

My eyes widen in surprise. When he notices my startled expression, his eyes grow as wide as mine and, in the same instant, he steps on the gas and sends his tires screeching and smoking. His car, a white truck, seems to sit still on the spot for a moment, revving, then tears down the street, going from zero to sixty before I blink. I watch him fly by the front of my SUV and disappear down the intersecting street like a bat out of hell.

"Wow." In spite of everything I've seen since I learned about Eklyptors, I'm surprised by this. It's too terrible an example of what our once-trusting society has become. It makes me wonder about how it used to be. Did we really use to sit next to each other at the movie theater? Dine in crowded restaurants? Shake each other's hands and say "nice to meet you"?

"What is it?" Hannah asks in a trembling whisper.

"Nothing. It's fine. Just another used-to-be dying in front of my eyes."

I move forward, knowing that guy is feeling pretty stupid right about now, though he's probably also breathing a sigh of relief.

We arrive at the cemetery a few minutes later. The main gate is open. I drive through it slowly, the speedometer needle barely moving from zero. I stop by the same statue of a virgin where I met James once before, the day he took me to The Tank for the first time. I look around but don't see him anywhere.

"Stay put," I tell Hannah, then open the door and step out of the car.

A few clouds float above. They are gray, full of the threat of rain. The sun hides behind one of them, and I wish it wasn't so. A cemetery has enough gloom as it is. A heavy silence seeps from the tombstones and saturates the air. My soul goes quiet and still with respect for the dead. My heart finds a certain peace at the thought of at least some of us being in a better place.

The peace doesn't last that long. Only until a gust of wind whirls around the SUV and ends up right behind me.

I stiffen. "Hello, James."

"Guerrero," he says, pressing one arm around my neck and a gun to my temple. "Hands up."

Chapter 4

"Who's that?" James demands, gesturing toward Hannah.

I'm sandwiched between the open door and the fastest human being on the planet, as far as I know, anyway. Hannah is still huddled on the passenger-side floorboard. She looks up at us, arms wrapped around her knees, visibly shaking.

I take a deep breath to calm myself. A gun to my temple is a new threat. I wonder if James is serious and took the safety off and everything.

Of course he's serious, Marci. Don't be stupid! A heart attack is nothing.

"Um, just a girl. Her name is Hannah." I remember hearing somewhere that if an assailant knows your name, he's less likely to kill you. Since he already knows mine, I give him the girl's. "I was on my way here when I saw her. I wouldn't have brought her, but two scouts spotted her, too. I couldn't let them take her."

"It's hard enough to trust you already. This is pushing it."

"I know. I know. But what would *you* have done?"

James says nothing to that.

"It's . . . it's true," Hannah says from within the SUV, her voice so weak and shaky it's barely audible. "She saved my life."

"Don't make any sudden moves." James removes his arm from around my neck and proceeds to relieve me of my gun. When that is done, he steps back and moves his own weapon from my temple to the back of my neck. "Now, step away from the car."

I do as he says. He sidesteps with me, staying at my back. When we are about ten feet from the SUV, he says, "Hannah, I'm going to need you to get out of the car. Hands up in the air."

There are no signs of movement within the SUV. I think of the revolver she was carrying and hope she doesn't try anything stupid. James almost strangled me once. I doubt that, under the circumstances, it would be hard to get him in a trigger-happy mood.

"Did you hear me?" James's voice goes up a notch. The kind of deep tone a father might use on his daughter.

"I did. I'm coming out. I'm coming. Please don't shoot," Hannah says shrilly.

She wriggles herself out of the tight space and pushes onto the passenger seat, her hands up in the air.

"Now, slowly, open the door and come around the car, hands where I can see them," James instructs.

Hannah follows the instructions closely, keeping her hands above her ears as she rounds the front of the SUV. She stops about ten paces away from us and gives James a small nod as if saying: "See, I'm just a girl."

"All right, now take off your jacket and throw it aside," James says.

Hannah frowns at the request but does as she's told. It *is* a puffy jacket. Much could be concealed under it. She's left in a tight fitting t-shirt that barely hides her thin frame.

"Now both of you, move away from the car." James gives me a slight push.

Hannah and I walk side by side down the middle of the road, James following but staying a fair distance away.

"All right, that's good. Turn around."

We stop and face him. James reaches into his back pocket and tosses me a pair of handcuffs. I catch them in midair. I get my first good glimpse of him since the attack at Elliot's headquarters. James looks harried, the crow's feet around his eyes more pronounced than before. His normally well-shaved head is sprouting a few hairs from the sides, and his shoulders appear narrower. He's never been a big man, just average height and build, but he always looked fit. I guess this war is getting the best of him. I'm sure getting shot didn't help either.

"Cuff her," James says, his gray eyes as intense as ever.

"Is that necessary?" I ask, though I know it's a stupid question. We can't trust anyone.

"I'm taking no chances."

I face Hannah. "I'm sorry. He has a lot to safeguard, but I promise he won't hurt you if you don't cause any trouble."

She nods shakily and lowers her arms. I clamp one cuff to her right wrist, then walk behind her and secure the other at her lower back. As soon as I'm done, I put my hands up again.

"Sit on the sidewalk and stay put, Hannah," James says in a voice that is sounding kinder by the minute. "Like Marci said, just do as I say and everything will be fine."

"I will, Mister . . ." Hannah sits with some difficulty. She lowers her head and sniffles a few times, but quickly composes herself.

"You can call me James."

"Thank you, Mister James."

He smirks and shakes his head. After a pensive moment, he jerks his head and the gun to one side, signaling me to move away from Hannah. As we walk toward the opposite sidewalk, I notice James's ultra-firm grip on the gun. It seems he's taking no chances with my telekinetic powers either. *Ha!* Like I've learned to control them. I can only wish.

James's gray eyes drill into mine. "So . . . still Marci?"

I cock my head to one side and nod.

He sighs. "It's a damn thing. I want to trust you, but . . ."

"Don't feel bad. I've given you plenty of reasons not to."

An image of my bloody hands after I failed to stop Azrael from killing Oso flashes in front of my eyes. My heart tightens with the regret that assaults me every time I think of that kind man, and of the way that petty creature took his life. A wave of disgust runs through me as I imagine the parasitic agent lodged, seething, lurking, inside my brain.

"Report," James says.

I take a deep breath, trying to remember everything that's happened since the last time I met with Aydan—too long ago for comfort. After IgNiTe's attack at Whitehouse head-quarters and the eradication of his Spawners, things have been busy for the Seattle resistance. Without Spawners the Whitehouse faction can't grow its base—an advantage IgNiTe must fight to maintain.

"Well, everyone's still in turmoil," I say. "Lyra says Elliot has been busy doing damage control. He has been meeting with his captains, making plans few are privy to. He's being extremely paranoid. He had his tech people check the network, but I made sure they didn't find any of my hacks. So I've been able to watch the security system closely and have seen very little going on in the building. Whatever meetings he's holding, they must be happening elsewhere. I suspect he has gone low tech. He's taking no chances. The bastard. I wish you would just let me put a bullet between his eyes."

"Stick to your orders, Marci. Killing Elliot would make his faction unpredictable. I know you've sworn revenge but, take it from me, you should strive to live for more, find a worthy reason. Revenge will blind you to the things that truly matter."

"I know. I know." Maybe James is right, but, at the moment, nothing sounds better than making Elliot pay.

James grunts and casts a quick glance in Hannah's direction, frowning.

I continue, "Anyway, Lyra suspects he's planning a trip to England, something in the next couple of months. She thinks he's going to get the Spawners who survived the attack in the Glasgow safe house. The one the London IgNiTe cell couldn't destroy entirely."

"Yeah, that was unfortunate. The Takeover was more effective there, and our IgNiTe cells are weakened. I wish they'd been strong enough to carry out the job." He runs a hand over his bald head. "But I can't blame them, I suppose. They did their best. I wonder how many Spawners survived."

"Don't know."

"At least we've slowed down the rate at which they're infecting people." The way he says this lets me know he thinks it's not enough. "I wish we could destroy Hailstone's

Spawners, too." A muscle jumps in his jaw, showing his frustration. "Anymore on Whitehouse trying to reach out to Hailstone to form an alliance?"

"No. That's not going to happen. Lyra killing Zara Hailstone took care of that possibility. I doubt Luke would be up to working with his *mother's* murderer." The bitterness I feel is obvious in my voice.

Zara was not Luke's biological mother. Her faction kidnapped him right from the NICU the day he was born, sending my family into lifelong turmoil. Karen is his real mother. The woman who, in spite of raising me and supposedly giving birth to me, isn't my genetic match. Talk about an identity crisis. I don't even know where the hell I come from. It turns my head and stomach just to think about it, and something tells me I don't want to find out.

God, what a freakin' soap opera.

"Even if Luke was game, Elliot would rather destroy them for daring to attack him. He's dying to find out where they are hiding. He even has a task force dedicated to it, a small one, but still."

James rubs his chin. "Is that so?"

I nod.

"We definitely need to keep an eye on that situation in case we can take advantage of it. What else?"

I pull out a thumb drive from my jacket pocket. "I've found some info I'm sure you'll find valuable. Every day there's less and less going through the network, especially this type of stuff, but I caught this."

James holsters his gun and takes the thumb drive. I give him raised eyebrows as if asking "so you trust me, now?" He shrugs. It's not like he really has anything to fear from me. I don't have a weapon, and he could run a million circles around me in the time it would take to make up my mind to attack him.

"So what is it?" He gestures toward the thumb drive as he slips it into the breast pocket of his brown leather jacket.

"Weapon and ammunition delivery dates and routes," I say, a huge smile spreading over my lips.

James's eyes go wide. He puts a hand over his breast pocket protectively. For a moment, he looks on the verge of saying something but, instead, he presses his lips into a tight line. I know he can't trust me with any details, but it's better this way.

"It should be a win-win all around," I put in. "Fewer weapons for Eklyptors, more for Igniters."

His gray eyes narrow in assent, and I suppose that's the best I'm going to get. If IgNiTe is hurting for weapons, that's not something I need to know—not when I sleep in the lion's den every night, and I'm prime candidate for "Deranged Agent Takeover Syndrome."

"We'll check it out thoroughly. Thank you. Now . . ." He sticks his hand inside his jacket and pulls out an orange zip bag. "I need your blood."

I frown. "What for? Kristen's tests don't work on me. She must be checking for antibodies, so I'll always test positive after that crazy fucker took over me." I gesture toward my head.

"We know that, but—"

"Look, I'm not an Eklyptor." I know the conviction in my tone is useless after all the trouble Azrael caused for IgNiTe, but it's there nonetheless.

"You can't blame me for wanting more proof than your word," James says firmly, though not unkindly. "Kristen wants to take another look at your blood. Maybe there's a marker that sets you apart from Eklyptors, and she can develop a test that puts you in the clear. Wouldn't that be nice? For all of us."

I scoff. "Sounds too good to be true, but yeah . . . it *would* be nice." I dare not think of what could happen if James and the crew were certain that I'm human. Would they let me go with them? Would my stint with Whitehouse come to an end?

James gestures to my arm. I take off my jacket and let it fall to the ground. He pulls out a thick elastic band from the bag and wraps it around by bicep. With surprising practice, he prepares the syringe, finds a vein and sticks the needle in the crook of my elbow. I wince, watching as he presses a glass vial into the cartridge and blood begins to flow and fill the tube. He removes the elastic band and draws two more tubes of blood.

"Done." He pulls the needle and stuffs everything back in the zip bag.

"It didn't hurt," I say, surprised.

"Yeah, I'm a regular old nurse these days. Been getting lots of practice."

I can only imagine all the people they've had to test. Aydan told me there are camps where the elderly, children and those humans who can't fight are kept safely. As is to be expected, everyone is tested carefully before being sent there—buzzing or not. Of course, those who can fight are also scrutinized. In their case, it's actually a daily thing, to ensure no one is infected while out on duty.

Suddenly, I remember Hannah and wonder how all of this looks from her perspective. I glance over her way. She's sitting still as if frozen, her eyes wide and full of questions.

"I'll have to test her before I take her with me. We all

carry a handful of tests for emergencies. There's no buzzing coming from her, but one can never be too careful." He pulls another bag from his jacket. This one is blue. "I'll keep one and give you the rest. Maybe there's somewhere you can hide them just in case." He takes one small packet out of the bag and hands me the rest.

"Thanks." I doubt they'll be of any use to me, but you never know. I pick up my jacket and put the tests away in one of its pockets.

"Did you at least kill the scouts?" James asks, gesturing toward Hannah.

In way of answer, my mouth twists into a satisfied smirk.

"Good. I hate those bastards. Well, we'll be in touch. I should be heading back." He gives me an apologetic smile.

"How's Aydan . . . and the others?" I add the last part hastily. I got used to meeting with Aydan, having a more frequent link to the crew, but I haven't seen him in a while. I don't even know why. Things are more secretive than ever.

"They're fine. Busy. Fighting."

Just as I expected, he doesn't give me much. "I'm glad. Well, thanks for coming out to meet me," I say, staring at my boots. "I know you're too busy to deal with the likes of me."

James sets a heavy hand on my shoulder and gives me a gentle shake, forcing me to look at him. "If we had more like you, we'd be in better shape."

I blink slowly, shake my head and, suddenly, find my vision blurring with tears. "If it wasn't for me, for my weakness, Oso would still be alive. Also Xave."

Crap! Get it together, Marci.

I can't come undone in front of James. I need him to see me as a balanced person, someone who can control her emotions and doesn't fall apart while begging for misery-canceling sedatives. Been there, done that. I sniffle and fight to keep back the tears. They spill down my cheeks in spite of my efforts.

"Look at me. Look at me!" he orders as I continue to stare at my boots. I can't lift my eyes to his. My guilt is too heavy.

He puts a finger under my chin and forces my face upward. "It wasn't your fault." His tone is firm, but no matter how convincing, I don't believe him.

"I need you to understand that, Marci," he continues. "If you need to blame someone, blame me."

I blink and search his troubled gray eyes. For a moment, I think he must be saying this for my benefit, but he's never been the kind to engage in idle talk.

"I've been fighting this evil for a long time." He breaks eye contact, turns sideways and lets his eyes wander over the many tombstones. They dot the grassy area like dominoes. "So long that I forget how difficult it is in the beginning, how disjointed and disorienting life becomes. All I seem to remember is the strength needed to overtake the threat, the will necessary to stay ahead and remain in control. From the beginning, all I saw in you was that strength, your determination to fight.

"I forgot how young you are. It was unfair to expect so much from you. When I finally tried to protect you, it was too late. After Xave died, I thought being with your mother and away from us would help, but . . ." He shakes his head. There's really nothing else he could add. There was no way he could have known Luke had turned Karen into an Eklyptor or that The Takeover was imminent.

He shakes his head. "If I'd focused more on *us*, the team,

rather than my blind desire for revenge, Xave, Oso and so many others would still be alive. Marci, I . . . I failed you." James's voice breaks. And it undoes me even further. He's never talked to me like this. I never imagined he felt this way.

"So blame me." He turns and faces me, his gray eyes as intent and decisive as ever. "Only me. For what has passed and what is to come. Because I shouldn't expect you to go back and continue to put your life on the line, except that. . . I do. Because we need you. We need everyone willing and able to fight, especially if they're as strong as you are. And for that, I'm sorry."

I shake my head, emotions crashing against my chest like massive waves.

He doesn't blame me. He doesn't blame me.

For weeks, all I've known is despair and nightmares, both driven by the purest guilt imaginable. Xave and Oso's faces live in my mind in their most ghastly forms: twisted in shock and pain as they died. Xave passed on my watch. Oso, at my own hands. In the end, they're both casualties of my inability to control my agent and abilities, casualties of my weakness.

Tears flow freely, but I buckle down and manage to cry silently, even as sobs rise to my throat, desperate to get out.

James looks down at me, his gaze brimming with sympathy and emotion. "I hope you really are Marci or I'll feel like a real fool after this." He puts a hand on my shoulder again and, to my surprise, pulls me into his arms.

I thud against his chest, rigid, arms at my sides. He presses a hand to the back of my head and pats me gently, as if I'm but a child who in a different lifetime might have been his daughter.

"Whatever wrong you think you might have done, it's forgiven." He rests his chin on the top of my head. His breaths come in and out, heavy and quite audible.

I squeeze my eyes as waves and waves of emotion wash over me.

"I hope you can forgive me, too. Because I can't forgive myself."

Chapter 5

I make the drive back to downtown in a lonely daze. Hannah went with James after she tested 100% human. I watched them walk away, wishing I could switch places with her. My legs trembled as they disappeared over the crest of the steep street, and I heard James's Harley roar to life on the other side. It took everything I am not to run toward them, begging to let me come.

Now, I'm headed south on Pacific Place, almost back to the place where She-Bird and Griffin lie dead—if no one has found their bodies, that is. If they have, I'm sure the situation at Whitehouse HQ has gotten pretty interesting.

When I get to the parking lot where I stashed my Kawasaki, I pull in and park the SUV next to the delivery van I stole several weeks ago. I hop out and check the van. It looks untouched besides the four punctured tires and busted headlights I personally inflicted on it—which so far have been enough to keep anyone from repurposing it.

Nervously, I peek through the driver side window to confirm my bike is still inside the windowless delivery area.

I spot the tip of a handlebar and breathe out a pent up breath. It's ridiculous how relieved I am at the sight of it, especially when I could repurpose something much better out of the thousands of abandoned vehicles throughout the city. But I don't have much from my previous life, especially things that link me to Xave the way my bike does.

He helped me make the choice when I bought it. Afterward, we worked on the custom details and adjustments I wanted, then rode it through Seattle together. I can still feel his arms around me when I take it for a spin and close my eyes against the wind. He's been gone for some time now, but the way my chest tightens at his memory makes it seem as if it was only yesterday that I lost him. I miss him so much. I turn, press my back to the van and throw my head back. Shutting my eyes against the now-gray sky, I inhale and try to regain my composure.

I pull myself back into the moment and remember James ad how his words dismantled me. I don't know why I thought having his acceptance would make things easier.

It doesn't.

On the contrary, I feel as if the strength that has fueled me all this time just ran empty. Puff, gone up into the atmosphere, much like the air from the van's tires. From the beginning, a big part of my drive against Eklyptors has been the desire to prove myself to James, to show him I'm good enough to be part of his team. Now, it seems I've been wasting my time and, all along, he's considered me worthy, capable.

I exhale, unclench my fists which have tightened of their own accord, and find myself feeling sort of . . . aimless. I don't need to prove myself to James anymore. I never did, it seems. I chuckle at the irony.

Could I leave now? Could I abandon this side of the fight and go back to IgNiTe? I think of the test James talked about, of the possibility of regaining my humanity in the eyes of my Symbiot friends. Would they blame me for wanting to go back? Would they accept me in spite of everything?

Or could I quit altogether? Lay down my weapons and let others do the fighting? Could I do that without disappointing James and the others, without feeling I failed them? Would they understand I've already given so, so much?

I laugh a short, derisive laugh.

Who am I kidding?

I may not have to prove myself to James anymore, but he did say he needs me and asked for forgiveness for what he still expects of me. But even if that wasn't the case, there's that small promise of revenge I made to myself. I have a score to settle with Elliot Whitehouse and Luke Hailstone. I'm not going anywhere.

Yes, James's acceptance is satisfying, but it will pale in comparison to the pleasure of making Elliot and Luke pay for all they've taken from me.

For that, I can be courageous.

For that, I can be strong.

Chapter 6

As soon as I enter the mess hall, I sense a charged mood in the air. Everyone is talking animatedly, hardly touching their meals. I move to the food line, ears perked to the many ongoing conversations. I catch words, but nothing definite.

Captains. Trip. Scouts. Shot. Igniters.

I snatch a red tray from the pile, place it on the metal rails and slide it forward. As I point at the braised pork chop, steamed vegetables and rice pilaf, I think of Hannah clutching a bag of chips to her chest, her face gaunt and pale. My stomach turns to stone.

The server—a tall, blond guy with a face as smooth and white as a toilet bowl—hands me a plate full of food. I force myself to take it.

"Good deal. Good deal, Narcissus," I ramble in my usual Azrael fashion.

"I've told you a thousand times my name is not Narcissus," he barks.

"Yeah, whatever," I mumble.

He'll never convince me he doesn't spend hours in front

of the mirror, looking for wrinkles and blemishes so he can zap them with his Eklyptor morphing powers.

I turn and give him a backward wave. My gaze sweeps the dining area looking for Lyra. She's not here. My boots tap against the chevron-patterned linoleum floor as I practically march in place. Briefly, I consider dumping the food in the garbage can and leaving. My appetite has vanished, and eating among these beasts isn't likely to improve it.

Except not staying might appear fishy, so I find a spot on an empty table and set my tray down. Dozens of Formica tables are lined up in rows, most occupied by camo-clad Whitehouse members. The place never fills to capacity, since people eat in shifts based on their scouting and fighting duties. Though it's always seems crowded enough for my taste, especially when some of the diners are too big for the narrow chairs.

I stare at the pork chop and can't help myself but wonder how many people are starving to death, hiding in vacant buildings, too afraid to go out and look for sustenance. I stab my fork into the center of the chunk of meat.

"Both shot dead. I knew Griffin, but not the other one," Hounddog says as he and Gecko Man take a seat at an adjacent table.

I perk up and surreptitiously watch them, eyes on my plate most of the time.

Gecko Man's tongue flicks in and out of his mouth so fast that he leaves me no doubt he could catch flies in a snap. The fleshy appendage flicks out a few more times before he gets it under control and says, "Fuckin' Igniters! They're getting bolder. But let them keep venturing closer. We'll show them."

So they found the dead scouts and think Igniters killed

them. Well, they're not wrong. No wonder everyone seems more irritated than usual. I press my lips tight to repress a grin. It's nice to see my efforts giving the beasts some heartburn.

On my way back to headquarters, I avoided passing by the deli, fearing no one had found the bodies and trying to avoid being spotted anywhere near the scene of the *crime*. I wonder who found them.

Gecko Man's protruding eyes blink with lids as big as napkins. God, someone needs to tell him he's taking the bug-eyed look way past gecko and well into giant bullfrog territory. If he doesn't watch, he'll poke an eye out with his fork one day.

"Have you heard the rumors?" Hounddog leans forward and, from where I sit, I can almost see his features reflected on Gecko Man's eyes.

"You mean about Lyra and the tailed one, what's her name?"

I frown and lean slightly forward, wondering what sort of rumor could involve both Lyra and "the tailed one." He's talking about Lamia, the lizard-looking woman who's had it in for me ever since I killed Tusks.

Food twists in Gecko Man's mouth like laundry inside a washing machine. Gah, talk about an appetite killer. Come on! It's not like I need extra help with that.

Hounddog lowers his voice to a whisper and, once more, I find myself wishing for enhanced hearing. I wonder how I'd go about modifying my body to gain that ability. I really need to find out. My accidental telekinetic powers are cool but completely unreliable. A skill developed on purpose and, therefore, dependable would be better—even if less awesome. If only I could handle those stupid meditation sessions, but

I'm useless at them.

I catch nothing of what Hounddog says. Not one word.

Seething, I take a bite of broccoli and chew it listlessly. I'm about to cut a piece of pork chop when a rippling murmur begins by the mess hall entrance. I try to see what is causing the commotion, but people jump to their feet, obstructing the view. I push my tray away and stand, too. I still don't see anything.

"Damn damn damn," I say under my breath and climb on my chair for a better view.

Even on the chair, I see nothing, except the double doors swinging closed.

Hounddog's black, dog nose twitches. "I guess the rumors are true." The upper lip of his slowly-growing muzzle lifts in a sign of dissatisfaction.

"What rumors? Damn it!" I say, louder than I intended.

Hounddog gives me a nasty glare. He normally acts as if I'm not here, so much that I'd started to believe he was *unannoyable*. I'm glad to see he's not. I wave at him and give him my fakest smile. At least I don't have to pretend to like any of these jerks. If that were the case, my life here would be infinitely harder than it already is.

I stretch my neck to look past the mass of monsters lined up at the entrance. From the way they're standing—so straight and proper—I'm certain Whitehouse just walked in the room. I think of turning on my buzz-o-meter to confirm I'm right but decide against it. These days, I only do that if I have to, like when I roam the streets. Most of the time, I keep it down to a one-way channel. My life is a lot easier without rank signals droning inside my head.

A moment later, Elliot Whitehouse—flanked by Lyra and Lamia—moves into my line of sight and climbs the raised dining area at the end of the mess hall. It's his favorite spot. He loves to get up there to tell us what to do and *not* to do.

He faces the crowd, his unnatural golden eyes surveying his subjects. My fists clench. My vision tunnels. His gaze locks with mine for a moment, then moves on. Lyra spots me and frowns. Her round, yellow eyes flick downward almost imperceptibly. I think she's trying to tell me to get down from the chair, but the view is too good to relinquish it.

Lamia spots me, too. Her mouth curls up, the way it always does when she sees me. Her long, barbed tail twitches from side to side, something I've discovered is a sign of irritation. I smile at her, trying to convey a message.

So glad to have that effect on you, Little Godzilla. She looks away first. Score!

"Good evening, everyone," Elliot says as if he's dealing with respectable people and not a mild upgrade from the inhabitants of the Woodland Park Zoo.

"Good evening," everyone repeats. If parrots can sound polite, so can this bunch. That doesn't make them decent, though.

I, for my part, choose my words with sincerity. So I mouth "screw you," instead.

"Let's get straight to the point. As you well know, IgNiTe's vile attack on the reproductively mature members of our faction was an unexpected, low blow that has hampered our ability to grow our numbers."

Elliot sounds as if he just swallowed a giant frog. I almost laugh out loud. It must be hard for him to eat his pride and admit these things.

"We did not go into this battle lightly," he continues after

48

clearing his throat and adjusting the sleeve of his jacket. "We knew Seattle would not be easy to occupy. Our pre-takeover analysis told us as much. So we went in expecting the fight to be fierce from the beginning. However, the city's IgNiTe cell is strong. In spite of our most conservative prediction, it seems we . . . underestimated them."

God, it's so hard not to laugh out loud.

"These human rebels combined with our hostilities toward the Hailstone faction have cost us dearly. So much that now, as hard as it is to believe, our numbers are dwindling compared to those of our opposition. Every day, the casualties chip away at our faction, reducing the advantage we worked so hard to build.

"We. Cannot. Allow. That. To continue." Elliot's voice rises with every word along with the redness on his face. Maybe he'll blow up. That would be nice.

The crowd assents, echoing his sentiment by nodding, stomping, and repeating his words.

I huff.

Elliot holds a hand up. The crowd quiets. "In spite of that, Seattle is still under our control and I intend to keep it that way. Humans will not get in the way of our faction's success. And once they've become nothing but a nuisance, the strongest Eklyptor leaders around the world will get their chance to campaign against the weak and undeserving factions. In the end, the winners will take the spoils and will control *everything*. As of now, our faction is poised to be one of the strong, if not the strongest, contenders in that final race.

"However, that will not be the case if we do not focus on eradicating IgNiTe first. We have to stabilize our hold over the city. Then we can worry about our faction's position."

Well, that's new.

"To accomplish that, we all must do our part. Directed by you, my elite, our troops continue to fight bravely against our enemies. For this, I commend you. Your efforts won't go unnoticed when our faction rises to the top.

"This war is far from over, and we need you and every single one of your soldiers in order to win."

He pauses and slowly lifts a fist over his head. "We shall be victorious. IgNiTe and their rumors about a cure do not scare us."

"No, they don't!" several voices echo.

"This is a minor setback, one we will all help overcome. For my part, I've already been hard at work, devising a plan that will ensure our success. The details are on a need-to-know basis but, rest assured, the wheels are already in motion.

"Today, I'm here to inform you about a hierarchical change that will ensure our efforts go as planned. As of this moment, two of our most effective and loyal members, Lyra and Lamia"—Elliot demonstrates to his right, then to his left, inclining his head; both women stand firmer and practically click their heels, *Hail Elliot* style—"have been promoted to my first and second in command, respectively."

Gecko Man makes a grunt of disapproval in the back of his throat. In truth, most of the men seem to echo his sentiment with similar signs of discontent. That figures.

"I trust," Elliot says, raising his voice and staring down anyone who seems to disagree with his choice of leaders, "their orders will be respected and followed as if they were coming from me, because, indeed, they *will* be, whether I'm here or not. Do I have your understanding?"

A loud "Yes, Sir!" rumbles through the room. Even Gecko Man adds his voice, louder than everyone, it seems. They all fear Elliot too much to risk being singled out for lack of proper support.

"In the upcoming months, my absence might be necessary, and I can't stress enough the importance of following the chain of command."

"So it's true," Hounddog says under his breath, a low growl of discontent vibrating deep in his chest. Not a few weeks ago he was at the same level as Lyra and Lamia. He certainly isn't happy to find himself outranked, not when his buzzing vibe is the same as theirs.

My thoughts reel. Were Lyra's suspicions right? Is Elliot traveling to England to bring his London-based Spawners here, to tip the odds back in his favor by stealing our human soldiers and turning them into monsters that will fight for him instead?

At the idea, my blood begins to boil, bubbling and rising all the way to my head. Getting the list of Whitehouse's reproductively capable members and convincing James to trust me on the matter was no easy task. All the Seattle IgNiTe cells fought, at great peril and loss, to exterminate every single Spawner. I can't allow Elliot to fetch more of those creatures to replace the ones he lost here. The scales are slowly tipping in our favor. We can't lose this small advantage we've gained.

My hands shake at my side. I imagine a gun between my fingers, my grip tightening around its cold handle. But I don't have a gun. I'm not allowed to carry one in here. There's only me and a crowd of people between us, and I would never get to him. I'd be ripped to pieces before I'm able to pull one hair off his miserable head.

But you don't need to get to him, Marci. You could just . . .

Suddenly it's not a gun I imagine in my grip. It's Elliot's heart, supple and fragile. My body tingles with a strange energy that should, by now, be familiar. My powers are surging. For once, I let my instincts guide me, willing the energy to find its way to the surface.

Elliot's mouth continues to move, but I don't hear the words. I'm in a vacuum where nothing can reach me. My eyes focus in and out, and I'm pulled forward as if sucked through a giant straw. There is a flash. I see Elliot for an instant, then he's gone, obscured in a sea of black and red. A part of me urges me to pull away, but I ignore it. Like sand slipping through fingers, my mind falls away from the moment and into that strange reddish darkness.

The world thuds around me, making a rhythmic *whooshing* sound. I am bone and tissue and *heart*. In a detached way, I'm aware of my body, still standing on the chair. But, at the same time, I'm here, just where I want to be.

Blood rushes in and out, relentlessly. I'm strong and feel as if I could go on forever, except, maybe, that's a bad idea. Actually, a terrible, terrible idea. What if I just stop. What if I refuse to go on.

There's a cough, followed by another and another. There's pain, the brutal, arresting kind. I sense it, taste its bitterness as if from a distance. I will it to grow, to paralyze this black, cruel muscle that I've become, except something fights me, but what? I can't tell.

I gather my will, pack it as tightly as I possibly can, then release it.

Stop.

Beat no more.

I stretch and stretch and stretch. I have no end and no beginning. The effort to impose my will tugs in both directions and my center becomes thinner. I'm a piece of chewing gum pulled to the point of breaking apart.

A shadow rises in front of my eyes, followed by a hundred more. They take me by surprise, swarming my thoughts like starved piranhas. They haven't attacked in weeks, and I think they've been hiding, waiting for this chance.

Everything is thrown into a deeper darkness. My heart, my own heart, thuds out of control.

No. No. No.

I've been eclipsed. Azrael bided its time, made me think I had defeated her for good and I was safe. But that was never the case.

My heartbeat escalates, reaching its peak. I'm at the sharp edge of no return when my defensive mechanisms engage, and my thoughts begin to jump like never before.

Greasy hands.

Chalked hands.

Cues and billiard balls.

Another life. Not this life.

A better one. A lost one.

My chest spasms. My eyes spring open as I take a deep breath and resurface. Miraculously, I'm still standing, feet planted on the chair, even as I sway and put my arms out to regain my balance.

My eyes dart desperately in all directions. Did anyone see? Does anyone know what I was trying to do, what I was going through? Has the mole been unearthed?

The first thing that registers through my addled senses is the uneasy silence that hangs over the room. Sweat and fear slide down my spine, turning my courage to pulp. I've been discovered I'm done for.

But, as my senses settle back into place, I realize no one, and I mean absolutely *no one*, is looking at me. Instead, everyone's attention is still glued to the front.

Shaking my head, I grab on to the moment and process the situation. My gaze snaps forward like everyone else's, taking in the sight. Confused, I wonder why Elliot isn't talking anymore and, instead, is standing slightly bent over with a hand to his breastbone. Lamia hovers over him, touching his back, wearing a worried expression.

He coughs and thumps his chest. I stare at the top of his head, shocked with the realization of what I've manage to do. I press trembling fingers to my mouth. To anyone, I may look like a scared Eklyptor, anxious about her leader's wellbeing. But what I am is a traitor full of expectation and hope.

God, what if he dies? James thinks his death would mean chaos. What if he's right?

Elliot coughs a few more times, then straightens suddenly, slapping Lamia's hand from his back. His face is pale and twisted in a hideous grimace. He takes deep breaths and rubs his left arm, eyes darting around the room, examining the upturned faces of his followers with something that looks like hatred, as if he blames them for this lapse, for this display of weakness and vulnerability.

Does he suspect one of us did it? Can he tell?

His golden eyes scan the room. I fear the moment they'll meet mine to discover it was I who supplanted his heart and tried to steal everything from him—just the way his kind supplants us and steal everything we hold dear. But when he sees me, propped high on my chair, a hand pressed to my mouth, he doesn't pause—not even for an instant.

And why would he? He thinks I saved his life. I couldn't possibly be trying to kill him now. I'm his loyal Azrael.

When he's done with his inspection of the crowd, he jerks his jacket down and squares his shoulders with determination. He takes a step, falters. Lamia's hand flies to his elbow to steady him. He shrugs from her grasp and throws a nasty glare in her direction.

Head held high, he takes another step, then a third one. Finding himself steady, he descends the two steps in front of him, then strides resolutely toward the double doors, Lyra and Lamia following at a respectable distance.

I almost killed Elliot. The thought soaks through me like a downpour, chilling me to the bone. Would meditation bring me that kind of power? Would I want it?

Chapter 7

After Elliot leaves the mess hall, I jump off the chair and sit down, feeling dizzy. The din of cutlery and conversation returns by degrees. I rest my elbows on the table and hold my head, thoughts still jumping, shifting away from the shadows that still loom over my mind.

Damn you, Azrael!

I almost killed Elliot. I shake my head, thinking how easy it would be to be rid of him if I could fully control my powers, how quickly I could end this war if I systematically killed every Eklyptor leader. If only I could practice meditation every day, but I haven't seen Aydan in weeks, haven't had his help, and I'm still too scared to do it alone.

Could someone else help me? Lyra, maybe? She must be a master at meditation. She's morphed herself into Cheetara, after all. Could I trust her?

I bite my bottom lip, considering the other side of this coin, the morality of having the power to kill someone with a mere thought. The idea sends a chill straight into my bone marrow. No one should have that kind of power, especially not a sixteen-year-old with a temper.

The chill deepens when I think of all the people I might have killed during my lifetime if that skill had manifested early on. God, I almost did the same thing to Aydan right after Xave died—rage and my desire to push him away nearly turned me into . . . what? A murderer? Or something far worse I can't even name?

Elliot deserves to die. He's a monster, and I've promised myself to make him pay. But what about others just like him? Eklyptors and humans alike. What would stop me from killing them? What would give me the right, make me the judge?

Would anyone feel comfortable around a person who could do little more than blink to render you inert? Hell, *I* wouldn't want someone like that near me.

I drive stiff thumbs into my temples as a headache throbs to life. This philosophical debate combined with keeping the reawakened shadows at bay is giving me a migraine.

Shakily, I stand and take my tray to the conveyor belt, food cold and stiff on the plate. I leave the mess hall, turning my back on the black-uniformed Eklyptors, trying not to think what it would be like to snap my fingers, then turn to find every single one of them lying on the floor, clutching their chests.

Some part of me thinks it would be wonderfully easy to end this war that way, while another part feels almost certain I'd be unable to live with that kind of god-like power and the guilt of being able to impart instantaneous death—no matter how well-deserved.

When I make it to the barracks, I crash on my bed and put a pillow over my head. The large room is blessedly quiet since everyone's still at the mess hall. I want sleep to take me away, to erase my twisted thoughts and give me fluid dreams the shadows can't chase. But sleep runs in the opposite direction, totally mocking me.

"Azrael," a voice says right next to me.

I sit up with a start and send the pillow flying to the floor.

Lyra, in all her black-furred glory, is standing between her bed and mine, looking down at me with her round, green eyes. They are intense, angry even.

"Shit! You need a bell around your neck. What the hell?!" I stand, pick up the pillow and throw it back on top of the gray covers.

She ignores my little quip and drops the satchel she's carrying on the floor. "What happened in the mess hall?"

I frown. "Huh?"

Is this about Elliot? No, it can't be. She doesn't know about my powers. I've never mentioned them to her. And even if I had, making the leap from knowing someone can move objects with their mind to suspecting they can crush someone's heart is pretty extreme. Maybe she's asking something different. Maybe something else happened after I left.

"What are you talking about?" I ask, deepening my frown.

Lyra narrows her eyes, which doesn't quite have the mean effect she's probably going for. The gesture just makes her look like a friendly, content kitten.

"I'm talking about Elliot, and his . . . episode," she says.

"Episode?"

"Don't play *stupide*."

"Are you talking about him coughing in the middle of his speech? Maybe he has walking pneumonia."

She snarls deep in her throat.

"You're acting weird," I say with a dismissive flick of my

hand.

Nope. No chance in hell I'd let her help me with meditation. She might be IgNiTe, but I don't fully trust her. One, I met her as an enemy and first impressions are hard to erase. Two, she openly threatened me, said that if I'm part of Hailstone's grand plan to get rid of the need for human hosts, she would be against me—a nice way to say she'd put a bullet in my brain. Three, I'm not sure I want to make anyone aware of my monstrous potential. This feels private, like a reason to slick my hair back, don horned-rim glasses, change my name and pretend to be harmless and adorably clueless.

"I'm acting weird?" she asks. "This from someone who channels a creature like *Azrael* and sneaks through the ventilation system doing who knows what."

"Someone who channels Azrael?! That's not fair. I do what I have to do."

I rub circles into my temples and sit on the desk chair, wondering how she knows about the ventilation system. I haven't even used it since I planted a bug in Elliot's PC, the day I discovered I could switch off my buzz-o-meter in both directions when he almost caught me spying. Why is she bringing that up anyway?

"The ventilation system is a thing of the past," I say, figuring there's no point in denying it. "I can go in and out as I please, now." I pat the access card that hangs from my belt loop.

"So you didn't put poison in Elliot's food or through the vents in his office?"

I laugh. I can't help it. This is what she thinks I did? It's kind of sordid. My kind of idea, really, but so far off the mark. "I don't know the first thing about poisoning. Though, maybe I should set my mind to learning the task."

Lyra's beautiful emerald eyes regard me for a moment longer. Finally, she seems to believe me and sits on her bed, looking puzzled. She scratches her head with a sharp feline claw, then preens her fully-grown whiskers. "He says he's in top health. There should be nothing wrong avec son cœur."

His what?

"His heart," Lyra says when she sees my confused frown.

"I'm all for learning French, Lyra, but it's at the bottom of my priorities at the moment. Surviving sort of puts a cramp in my personal improvement goals. Capisce?"

She rolls her eyes. "Americans."

"Hey, you'd better watch it. You're starting to sound like Elliot."

Lyra shudders as if I just compared her to a street dog.

"I don't get it." I sit on my own bed across from her. "The old fart might be, um, sick, and you're upset? Wouldn't that be a good thing if he croaks?"

"It'd be a good thing if they all *croaked*." She makes air quotes. "But if *he* dies, someone else will take his spot, someone less sophistiqué et more hungry for carnage."

"Hungrier," I correct.

She gives me the finger.

"Hey, just trying to help." I put my palms up, recline on my pillow and look at the false ceiling. "I guess you're right. James says the same thing."

"Elliot cares about keeping the status quo and infrastructure. He doesn't want to inherit a world in tatters."

"Well, you're his first in command, now." I prop myself on one elbow and face her. "Wouldn't you take his place if he's gone?" I've many times asked myself why Lyra, who, early on, infiltrated the faction and managed to earn trust, didn't just kill him at the first opportunity, but instead, continues to work alongside him.

She scoffs and gives me a contemptuous look that lets me know how naïve, stupid—or both—she thinks I am. "Haven't you been paying attention? No one is happy Elliot is leaving Lamia and me in charge. Do you doubt challengers would present themselves if Elliot dies? It would most likely cleave the faction into smaller groups."

"Well, that should make it easier to bring them down, right?"

"It is hard to predict exactly what would happen, but I fear—and my superiors *and* yours agree—smaller factions would be much harder to control. We would have guerrilla warfare on our hands. Eklyptors going into hiding never to be rooted out. Non, we can't allow that. Our focus is elsewhere—on a cure." She adds the last words in a hushed tone, even though there's no one in the room with us. "Capisce?"

"Yeah. I get it." It seems to me Lyra's more worried about getting to Hailstone than the cure, but whatever.

We lie quietly for a moment, both lost in our own thoughts, staring at the ceiling as if a magical solution will flutter down on us. Finally, Lyra sits, picks up her satchel from the floor, and tosses it onto my lap.

I startle, instinctively, curling my body away from the bag. "What's this?"

"Some things that might be useful. We got a new shipment of weapons today. Surveillance equipment came with it. Spy stuff. Trackers, tiny cameras, microphones. That sort of thing."

"Oh, yeah?" I start to open the bag.

Lyra shakes her head. "Better not be too obvious with those. Remember, everyone still thinks *tu es folle*." She winds a finger around her temple. "And *I* wouldn't give a crazy person those kinds of things."

A heavy sigh pushes past my lips. I'm so sick of this place, of hiding and pretending to be someone I'm not.

With my desire for revenge against Elliot stifled at every turn, my presence here feels more useless every day. Add to that the fact that most communications have gone low-tech, making my hacking skills about as useful as roller skates at a nursing home.

Grumbling, I stash the satchel under my bed and lie back down. As soon as my head hits the pillow, my mind races away from this place, a common occurrence, lately.

As is most often the case, my thoughts drift to a small neighborhood north of here. There, I find a two bedroom/one bathroom house with a small porch and green siding. Across the street, a one-story rambler sits quiet and empty. A boy with red, fireman boots used to live there years ago. I don't know why I revisit these places so often. There's nothing left there for me, just old things and fraying memories. Yet, so much more than what I find here every day.

I long to go back.

Chapter 8

I stand in the middle of the street, eyes shut. The silence is overwhelming, unnatural, so unlike all the memories I have of this place. Evenings like this one used to be noisy with kids chasing balls or riding their bikes, neighbors playing their stereos too loudly, and noisy mufflers announcing the passage of the *tough kids* from down the street.

Now, there's just the wind rustling the trees and crickets chirping louder than they ever have, two sounds that will never make me think of home.

Turning right, I face my house and open my eyes. At the sight of it, a hook embeds itself in my heart and tugs so fiercely that my knees tremble. Xave's house is at my back, and I fear that laying eyes on it might hit me with an emotional blow that will knock me to the ground. I don't look. Not yet, at least.

There are bad memories in my old house too. Last time I was here, Luke was inside, waiting for me. I had come home, reeling from Xave's death, still believing I could count on my family. Instead, dear Luke tore my already-broken

63

world into smaller pieces, stealing my mother in the worst imaginable way. An Eklyptor. They turned her into an Eklyptor. Bastards!

And even though some time later DNA evidence proved that Luke and Karen were nothing to me, that day, I lost my family and was left utterly alone and confused.

I lace my fingers behind my neck and squeeze my head between my arms, wishing I could evict those ugly memories and leave only the good ones. Karen brought me home from the hospital, thinking I was hers. She used to smile and feel proud of me. I was safe under this roof. I was happy, at least until Dad died when I was five.

Dad.

He's a big reason I risked coming here. Traveling alone through the streets of Seattle is risky even for a Symbiot who can pass as an Eklyptor. Running into a member of a different faction—Hailstone in my case—would be a death sentence. They blame Whitehouse for the death of their leader, Zara Hailstone. I wonder what they would do if they knew it was an Igniter who shot her point blank.

I take one slow step at a time until I reach the white-painted door I remember so well. I'm aware of just how heavy it will feel when I push it open and how much force I'd need to slam it shut. God knows I did that enough.

I think of the narrow table in the foyer and the shoebox I placed on top of it. I wasn't strong enough to open it then. But today, I'm ready to see the things Xave left at The Tank, things Oso gathered for me because the kind man thought I'd like to have them. I swallow and fight back the tears brought on by their memories.

My hand shakes as it moves toward the door knob. The key is in my pocket, but I'm certain Luke and Karen didn't bother to lock last time they were here. A sinkhole could devour my home, and they wouldn't bat an eye.

The metal is cold in my hand as the knob gives without opposition, just as I thought it would. Slowly and reluctantly, I turn it all the way, fearing what I may find inside. Human squatters? Eklyptor beasts? A ransacked mess? My heart picks up its pace.

As the door swings open one inch at a time, my right hand moves automatically to the gun at my hip. I hold my breath. Trapped air burns my lungs and throat as I wait. A gloomy interior reveals itself in stages. The house seems totally empty. I step inside. A musty smell greets me, making me feel I've walked into a foreign place, not the only home I've ever known.

My first instinct is to close the door behind me, but I don't. An old habit makes me flip the switch on the wall, and when the lights don't come on, I'm not surprised. Eklyptors control the power plants, and make sure only the necessary ones run. Only enough electricity is generated and delivered to downtown Seattle and its southern suburbs, where the bulk of Eklyptor factions are concentrated.

Without removing my eyes from the dark depths of the house, I switch my backpack to the front, take out a flashlight and click it on. As the empty hall reveals itself, I exhale in relief. My heart quiets a bit, enough to let the thought of that shoebox jump to the forefront. I swing the beam of light to the foyer table to find nothing but a decorative set of candles and a thick layer of dust.

A stab of sharp pain goes through the middle of my chest. *Where is it? Where is Xave's box?!*

I shake my head, trying to recall. Did I put it somewhere else? Maybe it's in the kitchen or my bedroom. I wasn't thinking straight that day. Yeah, that must be it. I'm not remembering correctly.

I take two more steps forward and shine my light into the living room to my left. The sofas and bookshelves cast elongated shadows on the floor and the wall. Everything looks undisturbed, just the way it did the last time I was here. I press forward, but not without casting a quick glance over my shoulder. Past the front door, the evening melts into a deeper darkness.

On the right, the master bedroom door is closed. I have no desired to open it—none whatsoever, but I have to check every room if I want to keep my heart from hammering its way out of my chest. I push the door open and peer inside. After a quick inspection, I walk in and check the closet. For added peace of mind, I even check under the bed. Only dust.

Of its own accord, my hand points the flashlight to the night table. I inch closer toward the circular beam of light that spotlights a picture frame. I pick up the photo. My index finger caresses the side of the metal frame as my eyes drink the familiar image: a snapshot of Karen, Dad and me at the beach.

"Dad," I say in a shaky murmur. There's a broad smile on his face and his brown eyes sparkle as if he holds the secret to happiness. I stand in the middle, wearing a pink bathing suit, my smile so much like his. Karen looks happy, too, but out of place—more than ever before. Her wind-blown, light hair and blue eyes don't belong. She never felt like my mother because she wasn't. I wonder if she knew. I'm sure she felt it, but did she *know*?

Overtaken by a desire to set things right, I set the flash-light on the night table, hastily take the picture out of the frame, and rip Karen out. A tear rolls down my cheek. I wipe it off on my shoulder and try not to think about what Dad would say. Karen was the woman he loved and chose to marry. How can I blame her for being so much less without Dad? His loss was a blow that would have ruined better women. She was supposed to grow old beside him. Without his love, she grew bitter instead.

I let the torn piece flutter to the floor and slide the other into my jacket pocket. Having a picture of Dad gives me a strange sense of calm, like I could pull it out at any time and say: "See, that's my Dad," and people would reply "Oh, gosh, you look just like him." It feels like insurance to my dogged resolve to call Brian Scott Guerrero my father, even when my origin has become a big question mark and I sometimes doubt I'm his daughter.

With a jerk, I press a hand to my breast pocket and affirm, "You *are* my father."

Being no DNA match to a mother who never loved me and a brother who was nothing but fake doesn't mean I'm no match to Dad. This whole situation is so convoluted anything is possible. Besides, if I was capable of seeing Karen and Luke as family when they gave me little reason to love them, I can definitely claim Dad. He at least cared for me the way only a real father can.

Hand pressed to my chest, I leave Karen's room and shut the door behind me. If I ever get to live here again, I will gut this bedroom and leave no trace of her behind.

Pushing those thoughts aside, I move further down the hall. Next, on the left, is the kitchen. The flashlight shakes in my hand, casting a trembling light onto a fallen chair. Images of my fight with Luke and Karen flash before my eyes.

We want to help you, take away the pain. Give us a chance.

My teeth grind. What do they want with me? What is this "grand plan" Hailstone has? And how does it involve me? The questions whirl inside my head, even though I don't want to know the answers.

The sweet smell of decay registers faintly. Dirty dishes in the sink? Spoiled food inside the fridge? Dead mouse? I don't really want to know. Methodically and without stepping into the kitchen, I shine my light onto the table, the counters, the floor, looking for the shoebox. Not here either.

At the end of the hall is my bedroom. Directly overhead is a small attic with a pull-down ladder and a padlock to keep it off limits. I look at the dangling cord, wondering what might be left up there, maybe things that used to belong to Dad and Karen didn't get rid of. I put the attic in the back of mind for now and, instead, step toward my bedroom door.

The jamb is splintered. Luke chased me in here and kicked in the door as I escaped through the window. I barely made it out with my laptop, a few hundred dollars in cash, and Dad's copy of a Neruda book of poems. I blink the frantic memory away and sweep my bedroom with a quick arch of the flashlight. It's empty. The hammering of my heart slows to a subdued drumming I can live with.

Again, I search for Xave's shoebox, on the desk, the bed, the floor. It isn't here.

Damn!

Luke must have taken it. It's the only explanation. He probably threw it away out of spite. My spirit withers. I don't even know what was in the box, surely nothing important, but they were Xave's things.

For a long moment, I sit at the edge of my bed, moving my light from one spot to another, regarding, in wonder, all the things that once seemed so important to me. A pair of scuffed Harley boots. A top of the line gamer keyboard. Several pairs of protective motorcycle gauntlets. Xave was with me when I bought half those things.

I press a fist to my mouth until the pain distracts me from it all. I can't think of the past. Not if I want to be able to put one foot in front of the other every day—even if my only reason for doing so is vengeance. Maybe it's a good thing the shoebox is gone. I'm not strong enough to think of all those I've lost without disintegrating to pieces.

Shaking myself, I stand. I'm not here to dwell in the past. I'm here for a very different reason. I came to search the attic, to find something, anything, that might have Dad's DNA on it. It's a long shot after all these years, but I need this answer.

I go back into the hall and stand under the trap door. After setting my open backpack on the floor, I take out my gun, aim carefully, and shoot the lock. It comes apart with a metallic ding and thuds to the floor.

Good aim, Marci. I've gotten better. Target practice with Lyra has helped.

After holstering my gun, I jump, snatch the dangling string and pull it down. The trap door opens with a squeal as the springs stretch. I tug on the ladder, let it unfold to the floor, then take the steps two at a time. I stop halfway in and shine the flashlight into the small space. It reveals nothing but inch-thick layers of dust and cobwebs.

My heart sinks until I spot a lonely cardboard box in a dark corner. Hope surging, I climb the rest of the way and step lightly in its direction. The plywood groans under my weight, but it holds.

I shine my light on the box. I crouch and wipe a hand over the dusty top to expose the handwritten label. A million dust motes fly into the air, in and out of the light beam. I squint and pull the edge of my collar up to my nose. As the dust settles, block words etched in Sharpie take form: BRIAN'S THINGS.

My throat tightens, and it isn't only from the dust that has worked itself in there. "Brian's Things"? This is what Dad's life is reduced to? What Karen deemed appropriate for the few belongings he left behind? God, I hate her more than ever. I should have had this box. She should have given it to me.

I take a knee, thinking of Xave's shoebox and how it parallels to this. The two men I've loved the most are gone, and all I have left of them are two cardboard boxes.

With a fingernail, I work at the corner of the tape that keeps the flaps together. It comes off easily, its adhesive quality obliterated by years of heat and cold exposure in this space. After a deep inhale, I open it and shine my light inside. At first glance, the plainness of the contents is underwhelming. Dust has seeped inside and covers what seems to be a stack of manila folders. They look like medical records and probably are. Dad always brought work home. He cared that much about his patients.

I dig past them and discover a few other things underneath. My spirits lift. I take the files out and set them aside. A smile stretches over my lips as I do a quick reconnaissance. This is more like it.

I'm itching to take it all out and inspect it right there and then, but I stop myself. I want to savor this. I want to take my time and look at everything under better lighting.

The feeling that I've regained something—I'm not sure what—swells in my heart. It's stupid, I know, but I can't help it. All I have from Dad is that book of poems, when I've always wished for so much more, something to connect me to him. And, now, this might be it.

Quickly, I stuff the medical folders back into the box and, with some difficulty, take it down the rickety ladder. I set it down next to my backpack, fold the ladder into place and push the trap close. The spring whines again. The door clanks shut.

I'm about to pick up my stuff when the sound of steps freezes me on the spot. My heart takes a leap and a surge of adrenaline bursts through my system like jets of fire.

Without thinking, I drop the flashlight and let my hand fly to my hip. My gun goes up as I turn to face the danger.

Chapter 9

I've only turned halfway when someone kicks my arm so hard that my hand opens on reflex. The gun crashes against the wall and clatters to the floor, right on the path of the fallen flashlight. The loss of my weapon sends my already surging adrenaline to new levels, spurring my survival instincts to the max. If my powers were reliable, I would order my attacker's brains into next week, but for the moment, I have nothing but my own fists to defend myself.

I jump back, doubling the distance between us, giving me a fighting chance.

The flashlight illuminates the gun and casts a faint light on a pair of man boots. I squint, trying to see a face, but all I see is a dark silhouette.

"Hello, Marci."

Recognition thrills through my body in a sickening wave.

"Luke!" My voice is a hateful growl.

"I knew you would find your way here sooner or later," he says in a conversational tone that could make someone think we're friends. Except we are not. What little used to be between us, whatever that was, never even came close to friendship.

My eyes dart around, looking for his Hailstone cronies. He seems to be alone, though I highly doubt it. They've probably surrounded the house by now.

Careless. So careless and stupid.

He must have left a trigger behind, something to let him know the second someone crossed the front door. I should have guessed that, but I clearly underestimated how badly he wants me.

Now, how the hell do I get out of this one?

I look to my backpack, which is closer than the gun. I try to remember what I packed. Could any of it help me escape? Extra bullets, a few of the surveillance gadgets Lyra gave me, and some food. That's it. Shit! Why didn't I pack a grenade? That would have been useful. Now my only hope is to club him to death with a protein bar, then snatch the gun and run out of here, bullets blazing.

"How have you been?" he asks.

"Screw you, Luke!" If words could kill, mine carry the weight of an Avada Kedavra.

I wish him dead and reach for his heart with my powers. I wait for my vision to tunnel, for that clarity and awareness to flood. Nothing. I quest for the gun next, imagine it flying into my hand, but it's the same. Nothing happens. I feel empty, as powerless as an infant. There isn't the slightest surge of energy within me. I'm useless.

He chuckles sadly. "I know I'm not your favorite person, but it can't be *that* bad. Can it? I've never harmed you, Marci"

"Your faction killed Xave. Trust me, it is much worse than you think."

"Him?" he scoffs with dry amusement. "That was an accident. He was in the wrong place, at the wrong time, *and* with the wrong crowd. Besides . . . you must know, he wasn't good enough for you."

"Shut up! *You're* the one who's not good enough, even to speak his name."

Fuck this! I don't have to sit here and make small talk just because I'm a good-for-nothing Symbiot whose powers won't kick into heart-crushing mode. I have my own hands to do the job.

I crouch low, a smile suddenly stretching my lips as I realize something. He doesn't want me dead. If he did, I'd already be lying on the floor with a bullet hole between my eyes. I guess that means he needs me.

For my part, I have no intention of falling into his web, plus I *do* want him dead. And, I'm not afraid of him. He might be big and muscular, but he has no sparring training, at least not at my level. I can take him.

Without warning, I sprint at his dark shape, accidentally kicking the flashlight. Shadows revolve in the narrow hall as it spins.

Dark. Gloom. Dark.

It's like fighting my agent. My thoughts begin to jump as I close in, slamming my shoulder into Luke's stomach.

He staggers back, hands flying to his middle, bending forward, gasping to catch the air I just forced from his lungs.

The spinning flashlight and shadows slow down.

Dark . . . Gloom . . . Dark.

It stops and goes out.

Pitch black.

Quickly planting my feet on the floor, I throw a front kick to his head. He surprises me by lifting an arm and blocking it—quicker than I thought he could move.

Damn! Where's the gun? Eyes flickering downward, I search for it. Luke finds it first and, again, moves faster that I expect him to. He kicks the heel of his boot backward, sends the weapon spinning into the darkness.

In the split second it takes me to consider what to do next, Luke's huge, dark figure lunges forward and tackles me. I stagger backward, trying to keep my balance, but he's too heavy.

My legs give. We fall to the floor, knocking my backpack on its side. My neck snaps. My head hits hard tile. Pain. Specters awaken in my mind, ready to take advantage of this awful moment.

Agony crawls up my spine. I desperately shake my head. I can't fight the agent and Luke at the same time. I can't. The fear sends my mind into overdrive, and I imagine Luke's Eklyptors outside the house, swarming like fluid shadows, swaying and shifting, creating shapes more monstrous than Azrael can.

They're swallowing the house whole, their inky essence climbing up the siding, covering the windows until there's no light left in the world.

God, no!

I need a light.

A flame.

Anything to shatter this awful darkness.

Luke tries to pin me down.

I jam a knee against his crotch. He rolls off to the side, groaning. I wriggle out of his grasp, scramble to my feet, and desperately reach for the flashlight.

Luke clasps my ankle, and I go down. Both hands out, I brace my fall. The side of my face hits something. I panic for an instant until I realize it's my backpack.

Terror still scratching its way up my throat, I jerk my leg to yank it free, but Luke's grip is strong. I try again, this time twisting my body and, at the same time, kicking at his knuckles with my free leg. He lets go.

"Would you stop?" Luke says between his teeth.

With a furious growl in the back of my throat, I jump to my feet again, the backpack in my clutches. Making a big show, I dig inside of it, causing the impermeable fabric rustle.

"Stay where you are or I'll shoot you," I say, my voice firm in spite of the lie. I squeeze the handheld surveillance receiver in my hand and point it at him. It's too dark in here for him to realize I couldn't kill a roach with this thing.

"Call your men off or I swear you won't make it out of here alive." I take a few steps back, feeling for the real gun with my feet, but it's hopeless.

"My men?" Luke moves. I squint at his dark silhouette. He just sat up, I think.

"Don't move," I yell.

"I won't. I'll just sit here. I promise. I'm just . . . ow . . . seeing if my balls are broken."

"I sure hope so." My breaths pump in and out.

Calm down, Marci. Calm down. Think!

My fear subsides a notch, but I'm drunk on adrenaline. My body tingles. My fingers twitch, and I'm sure that if I really had a gun, Luke would be dead by now.

"Don't be so mean. I'll need them one day." Luke moans.

I ignore his revolting comment. "You're gonna tell your men to leave unless you want me to kill you," I repeat. "I'd have no problem facing them, knowing you're nice and dead."

He sighs. "I'm alone, Marci. There's no one else here."

What? Is he serious? There's no one out there to stop me from racing away on my bike. Why would he come alone?

"I don't believe you," I say. "You're a coward. You wouldn't come here on your own."

"A coward? That's what you think of me?" He sounds genuinely surprised.

"That's just the tip of the iceberg."

Another sigh. "No point in arguing your misconceptions. But I did come alone. You can go check if you want. I'll wait right here."

Something in the tired and resigned tone of his voice lets me know he's telling the truth. I relax a little more, but don't let down my defenses by any means.

"All right, don't move. I'm going to pick up the flashlight." I take a sideways step and snatch it off the floor. I'm afraid it's broken, but it's only switched off. I flick the button and light pierces through the darkness, creating looming shadows too similar to my own specters for comfort. Better than the alternative, tough.

I shine the light on Luke. He turns his face away and places a hand in front of his eyes. "Do you mind?"

Taking advantage of the deer-and-the-headlights effect, I shine the light to the floor and quickly look for the gun. Nothing.

Where the hell did it go?

I bring the light back to Luke's face, just out of meanness.

"Seriously? Don't be childish?" He places his hand over his eyes, blocking them completely. In this light, his features look strange, too sharp and savage.

I ignore his comment and take several backward steps to the still-opened, front door. The evening outside has fallen into full night. I lean backward, stick my head out and look right, then left. No one is out on the porch, so I move outside to take a better look. The street is empty, and the only difference since I came in is the large car parked behind my bike.

"Satisfied now?" Luke calls from inside.

For a moment, I weigh my options. I could turn tail, hop on my bike and leave Luke's ass sitting there in the dark. The thought is fleeting, though. I can't run, not when there's a chance to find answers to the questions that have plagued my mind since Kristen ran those DNA tests. Besides, there's Dad's box. I can't leave without it and have it *disappear* like Xave's.

I crack my neck, square my shoulders and go back inside.

"Glad to have gained some of your trust," Luke says.

I laugh, really laugh. "You have some nerve. Trust is a severed road between us. The kind that can never be rebuilt."

"Forgive me, if I disagree."

"Well, let's not waste our time in hopeless conversation. What do you want to talk about?"

"Everything."

"I said let's not waste our time. Why don't you begin by telling me who the hell you are and why you destroyed my home?"

"May I stand? I want to talk about that and more, but not like this. Maybe somewhere else, somewhere with light and a hot drink. A coffee with ten packets of sugar, just how you like it."

I scoff. "What are you, now? A comedian?"

This is not a world for conversations and shared cups of coffee. This is a world where hungry girls cling to bags of potato chips, and friends don't trust friends without blood proof.

"If you want to talk to me badly enough to do this, then talk here and now. If not, I'll be on my way. I don't share drinks with *beasts*."

"Clearly, you've spent too much time in Whitehouse's company. I am not like him. Not in the least." Luke pushes to his feet.

"Don't move, I said!"

He ignores me, stretches to his full height, then steps out of sight into the kitchen.

Marci, you idiot.

He probably has weapons stashed in there, just for this sort of occasion. And even if he doesn't, there are knives in there—much more effective than a handheld receiver at making people dead.

The sound of a drawer opening breaks through the silence. I back away and stop at the threshold, shining my light all over the floor.

There!

I spot then gun, rush to it and replace it for the tracker. Shuffling backward, I move to the threshold once more and raise the weapon, heart still thundering but considerably tempered by the very real, very deadly thing in my hand.

A match strikes to life in the kitchen. The glow of a warm light follows. Candles.

I watch in disbelief as, gradually, the hall grows brighter and brighter.

"See, I don't have to be a comedian. Just a bit smart," Luke says from around the corner. "Come sit with me." He pulls a chair—making the sound of its dragging legs obvious—and, presumably, takes a seat.

I consider the possibility that he's waiting, weapon in

hand, then come to the conclusion that if he'd wanted me dead or trapped, he wouldn't have come alone.

Inhaling resolve from the air, I take long, quick strides toward the kitchen and go in ready to shoot. What I encounter under the candlelight, however, sends an eerie shock into my veins and freezes the very bullets inside my gun.

Chapter 10

My jaw hangs open as I stare in disbelief at the person sitting at the kitchen table. I blink, doubting my eyes, then doubting my recollection of the last few moments out in the hall.

Yes, that was Luke I just fought, not this guy. Yes, that was Luke's voice I heard. So where did *this* creature come from?

"Please, sit." He extends a hand toward the chair across from him.

The sound of Luke's voice in this person's mouth makes my insides twist with a mixture of horror and surprise.

"What have you done?" My words shake with incredulity.

Even if he looks different now, the basic frame is the same, and, deep down inside, I know this is the boy I've known since Kindergarten. We shared classes, recess, lunch. We faced each other in challenging games of chess, and played brother and sister for a short while. And that weird connection I've always shared with him? It's still there. I feel it like an invisible tether between us.

He shrugs. "Nothing drastic."

The fact that he doesn't think it's drastic shows me how disconnected he's become from humanity.

Luke was always handsome. His blue eyes and blond hair like Karen's. His tall, muscular physique like Dad's. Such a perfect combination of their best features.

Now, however, he is . . . godlike in his perfection.

His eyes shine azure and full of life. His head is covered in silky strands of hair that look almost unreal. His cheekbones are higher and every angle in his face more chiseled. His once blond, pale lashes and eyebrows are now darker and thicker. The redness that used to lightly mark his chin and forehead have been replaced with the smoothest, most even-toned skin I've ever seen. But most striking of all is his posture, and the lithe and graceful way he moves. *Not human.* It's the only description that comes to mind.

He inclines his head to one side. "Do you like what I've done?"

His question reaches me, but its meaning eludes me. I'm too entranced by the smoothness of his small gesture and the flawless curve of his neck and jaw.

"You . . . you look *inhuman*."

His eyes tighten at the word, a slight expression that doesn't reveal much through his perfect, baby-like skin.

"That is because I am," he says with a smile more dazzling than a ray of sunshine piercing your eyeballs.

In spite of the smile and his nonchalant answer, I can tell my words bothered him. He doesn't want me to see him as anything less than human. He wants me to see him as more. But why would my opinion matter to him?

"I changed my DNA, you know? Not just my appearance," he says in a deeply satisfied tone.

My shocked skepticism turns to total disbelief.

"I can pass this on to my *offspring*," he adds, saying the last word with something close to reverence.

The hairs on the back of my neck stand on end, and my stomach twists in disgust and horror. If he can pass these changes down to his children, does that mean he can also pass down the infection? Eklyptors' offspring are born fully human. The hosts' DNA is never altered no matter how grotesque the agent manages to transform its vessel. This is why they need Spawners, why adult Eklyptors grow those tentacle-looking things that inject parasites into their victims' spines. Could this ability to transform his DNA and pass it down be part of Hailstone's grand plan to get rid of the need for human hosts? It has to be.

Questions swell inside my head. How did they figure it out? Are they already giving birth to infected babies or, more accurately, giving birth to Eklyptors? Do they plan to share this knowledge with other factions?

God! IgNiTe needs to know this!

Luke regards me with interest, waiting for me to say something. Instead, I'm horrified into silence. After a moment, he runs a hand through his hair and shifts in his seat. The change in position is smooth, like the gentle flow of a river, like the terse passage of the wind over a meadow. It's hypnotizing.

"Tell me something, Marci. Are you happy?" There is legitimate interest in the question. "Is this," his hand slides through the air demonstratively, "enough?"

"Better than the alternative." I lower my head and clench my teeth. I could kill him now. I have the gun, and we're face to face. No morality should stop me, not like that day

I had the chance to shoot him and Zara, but I couldn't bring myself to do it because their backs were to me.

"The alternative?" he asks as if we're talking about something that doesn't exist, like brain-eating zombies or blood-starved vampires.

I humor him, but only because it gives me the chance to insult him. "Living trapped inside my own head, you butt wipe."

He seems taken aback at my colorful words, then says, "Ah, that." He makes a movement with his hand as if he's tossing something up in the air.

"Yeah, *that*. Don't play stupid," I say. "It may still seem like I live in a trap, but nothing compares to what your parasitic cousin wants to do to me." I poke a finger into my temple.

Azrael and its shadows stir at the mention of its stupid name. My thoughts jump in circles, then spiral down and out of the way, quickly leaving the specters behind.

Luke shakes his head, looking puzzled. "When I first came to you and Karen, I didn't have any idea Symbiots existed. No one did. And the fact that you're one of them, it's just . . . so unfortunate. I've wondered many times why *you*, of all people, had to be one of them. It has made everything so complicated." He sighs, sounding as tired as an old man.

Me, of all people? What the hell is he talking about?

"Of course," he continues, "if your agent took over now, you would know it and would, unfortunately, be aware of your exile."

"My exile? Is that what you call it to make yourself feel better about what you do? It's not an *exile*. It's theft, imprisonment, and torture. Worse than death. Worse than anything

I can imagine."

"In some cases, yeah. But it shouldn't have been like that for you. It isn't like that for my host. That consciousness never developed. It didn't have a chance. So I've made no one suffer. I'm not sure you can make the same claim."

"If you're suggesting I've made my agent suffer, I'll have you know it's been a pleasure. Nothing but payback, at any rate. This is *my* body, and I would do anything to keep it from falling under the control of an intruder."

"Intruder, huh? I'd say it's all a matter of perspective for people like you and I. All cells were there from the beginning."

"How dare you compare who I am with *what* you are?"

Luke sits forward and lays both hands on the table, one next to the other. The delicate quality of his movements draws my attention to his fingers. They are longer and more slender than I remember, wrapped in smooth skin with hardly any creases around the knuckles.

I don't know why, but his flawlessness—more than the monstrous shape of Eklyptors like Tusks or Lamia—brings my primal fears to the surface, jump-starting my fight-or-flight response. My heart speeds up. My hands sweat. And I swear the curve of the trigger under my finger feels like an inevitable solution.

Except I can't—not the way he's talking, sharing things I would never have imagined.

"We're not that much different, Marci."

"Is that what you tell yourself so you can sleep at night?"

"There's little that could help with that particular problem."

His candid answer, although satisfying it's also surprising. "That makes two of you. You and Elliot should exchange medication names. A bullet between the eyes would also help. Permanently."

"It amazes me how easily humans forget that *nature* also applies to them. You're not above its laws." He cocks his head to one side in a quick jerk, much like a bird. The movement still appears inhuman, but much more digestible than his even, fluid motions. "Are you?"

I clench my jaw. My teeth grind. I know this argument all too well. We, humans, have stayed on top and made this world our own with our savagery. We have killed and destroyed in the name of progress and science. We have driven countless creatures to extinction and continued to do so until the day we met our match.

Yes, the laws of nature—survival of the fittest—apply to all.

My argument is flawed and, in this ongoing chess match of ours, Luke still seems to have the upper hand.

Check.

"I guess we're not," I admit, speaking through the knot in my throat. "But that doesn't mean we'll go down without a fight."

"Certainly not. This is what prey does, it flees, hoping to outrun the predator. But we all know how that turns out in the end."

Even though at times I've felt that we are nothing but helpless prey, he knows well we're more than that. "I don't know if you got the memo," I say with a curt laugh, "but it's not *us* running scared at the moment. Could be part of the reason you're having trouble getting some shuteye at night?"

Luke's satisfied expression sours.

Who's in "check" now? I smile crookedly.

"Setbacks were taken into account when we drew our plans," he says. "We are prepared. Don't doubt it. Seattle is only one city. The overwhelming majority of the world has offered no problems. As expected."

Anger thrills through my body and, with an involuntary jolt of electricity, my right hand jerks up. The gun trembles in my grip as my forefinger gently caresses that tempting "solution."

"The truth can be upsetting, can't it?" He raises his eyebrows to the gun.

I take several shuddering breaths to calm myself. Our gazes lock. His eyes offer no signs of fear, like he doesn't care if he lives or dies, if his perfect body thuds to the floor in the sad, abandoned kitchen of the home he so easily and thoroughly destroyed—like he knows the "laws of nature" will continue their course, with or without him.

I tell myself he doesn't look scared because he senses my empty threats. But that's not it, is it? He's too sure of their plan, too confident of their success to worry about failure. If he dies, another leader will take his place as head of Hailstone, and it will be business as usual. But if I kill him, *our* success, the answers we need, might die with him and he understands that.

If I want to win this game, I have to be smart. Smarter than him. Something that, to this day, seems to have eluded me.

Control yourself, Marci! There are answers here.

With a growl, I put the gun down and demand, "What do you want from me?" My voice betrays the anger that still roils within my chest.

"Ah, you're finally ready to listen. Good." Luke stands, the chair scraping the tile floor as he does so.

I take a step back. The jitters attack me again, making my trigger-happy finger tingle. I curse inwardly. *He has no weapon. He's no threat. So toughen up, big girl!*

He heads my way, his every step exact and even, as if decided by some complex, split-second mathematical equation that calculates precise shoe-to-floor pressure, leg angle and distance. When he gets close, I step aside, attempt to come up with my own calculations where "X" is the safe distance between me and this alien creature I once thought I knew.

Luke stops, his shoulders perpendicular to mine. He stuffs his lithe hands inside his front pockets and looks straight ahead. His profile is breathtaking. I think of smooth marble statues, regal and undisturbed by anyone who might gawk in their direction.

"I have much to reveal to you," he says without looking at me, "but you'll have to come with me if you're interested. We can't talk about these matters here."

"Go where?" I demand.

"Hailstone headquarters."

I burst out laughing. "You've gotta be kidding."

"I'm not," he calmly says, then walks out of the kitchen and heads for the front door.

I move into the hall and stare at his retreating shadow. As he moves away from the candlelit kitchen, the angles of his shoulders appear less sharp, more human.

"Hey!"

Luke doesn't stop. He just walks on, utilizing the same mathematical perfection.

"So you came all this way for nothing?" I yell.

Still no reaction.

An idea sparks in my mind. I dig in my jacket and retrieve

a small disk from a compartment in the handheld surveillance receiver, palming it.

Just then Luke stops and gestures toward the small table in the foyer. "I have your shoe box, thought I should keep it safe." He starts walking again.

"You bastard! That was Xave's. How dare you?" I rush him.

Even though he hears me approaching, he doesn't look back. When I reach him, I slap my hand to his back and push him. He staggers forward but catches his balance with little effort. He turns slowly, his annoyed gaze swiveling to mine. My eyes snap to his, away from the tiny tracker stuck to his jacket.

"Give it back!" I command, letting anger take over me. Still, I feel certain he'll see my guilt instead and will reach over his back to snatch the tracker off.

"Come with me and you will get the box and more."

"Why do I need to come with you?" I work myself into a bout of hysterical anger—not that it's hard. "So you can force me to stay against my will?"

"I'm giving you a choice, in case you don't realize it." Luke's words are calm, almost reasonable. My hatred for him redoubles. "If you want answers to your questions, you must come with me. If you can live without the answers, you can continue as you are. This is the one kindness I will show you, even if *everyone* disagrees I should give you that much."

So he's here against his faction's wishes? Why?

"It's your decision," Luke adds.

It's déjà vu all over again, like the day James asked me to follow him if I wanted to understand the buzzing inside my head. Except, I'm sure the answers I got then were harmless compared with whatever Luke has to offer.

"Well," I run a hand over my mouth, trying to look conflicted, "I doubt these answers will be worth my while. I'd tell you where you can stuff them, but I'm sure you already know that."

Luke blinks very slowly, lowers his head. "For what it's worth, I think you would like my plans for the future. But if I tell you about them and then let you go, I don't even know who you'd share them with first. IgNiTe? Whitehouse? I'm sure you can understand my reservations."

I have no answer to that.

He nods, then turns to leave. When he's facing the street, he speaks in a barely audible voice. "I have always cared for you, Marci. If you search within yourself, you will realize it's true. I am not a monster. Just a consciousness inside a body, like you, like everyone else." With that, he walks down the porch steps, heads toward his car and melts into darkness.

Chapter 11

As soon as Luke leaves, I pull the handheld receiver from my jacket and turn it on. During the few seconds it takes for it to come to life, my heart freezes, afraid the tracker won't work. But soon a blinking, red light on the screen assures me that my fears are uncalled for.

I hurry back inside and blow out the candles in the kitchen. I might not ever have a chance to live here again, but just in case, I don't want the place to burn to the ground. Back in the hall, I use my flashlight to find my backpack and Dad's box.

My mind races, trying to figure out how to carry the box on the bike. No way in hell, I'm leaving it here. *Bungee cords!* I bought a set when I first got the bike. I run to my room and dig in the closet for a couple of minutes before I find the unopened pack at the bottom of a pile of books. Backpack secured to my shoulder and Dad's things in tow, I trot outside and secure the box to the back of my bike, using all the cords, except one.

I straddle my Kawasaki and, with the remaining cord,

secure the handheld receiver to the middle of the handlebar, where I can easily keep track of the little flashing dot on the screen. I put on my helmet and, in a couple of minutes, I'm following Luke's electronic trail, weaving through southbound streets.

He's moving at a considerable speed. I twist the accelerator, trying to maintain a constant distance between us—enough to keep track of him and still stay out of sight.

The traffic on I-5 is light, nothing like pre-takeover levels, but I'm surprised to see the way Eklyptors are gaining confidence every day in spite of the rebellion's constant attacks. I keep my body low and tight against my bike, glad for the protection of my helmet and visor. It's stupid, really. The only thing that offers me protection is the buzzing signal transmitted by my brain, but I always feel as if something in my eyes will give me away.

We stay on I-5 for about twenty-five minutes, then exit on Highway 518 toward Tacoma International Airport. After only two miles on 518, Luke veers right and actually takes the exit that leads to SeaTac. I follow the road warily, wondering if Hailstone actually set up their headquarters at the airport or if Luke is headed elsewhere.

He could very well keep driving south and out of the airport service roads, but passing through this area to reach any destination other than SeaTac would make no sense. So he must be headed there. Too leery to follow, I pull into an abandoned-looking rental car facility while Luke follows down Airport Expressway.

From the many rows of lonely rental cars, I pick two and park between them, keeping a close eye on the receiver. The electric poles are working here, so I make myself small, pressing my body close to the bike, to avoid being seen.

After a minute or two, the blinking dot that indicates Luke's location stops. According to the map, he parked in Departure Drive which, as the name indicates, is where people get dropped off to board their flights—not that any travel goes on these days. From what I understand, keeping airports functioning isn't an Eklyptor priority at the moment. Securing things on land has been and continues to be their focus, especially in Seattle. Owning the skies is certainly part of their plans, but they have to win this fight first.

I sit tight for a few more minutes, watching the dot for any movement. It stays in place. Biting my thumbnail, I try to decide what to do. Should I leave and bring this piece of intelligence to James? I scoff at that idea. IgNiTe must already know about this place, just like they knew about Whitehouse headquarters. I'm just not privy to that type of information. Regardless, I'll still have to tell James, on the off chance this is news. I wish I could give him something juicier than a mere location, though. I itch to find out more.

I ponder my options and decide to wait for at least another hour to see if Luke stays or leaves. I look around for a more comfortable place to stake him out other than perched on my bike. The rental car building seems like a good place, but I decide against it, in case I set off an alarm trying to break in. The cars would also be equipped with alarms, but maybe . . .

I get off my bike, hang the helmet on the handle and start testing doors. The first three cars are locked, but I finally luck out with a white minivan. I figured I'd find one. I'm willing to bet most of the cars are actually unlocked. Before The Takeover this place would have been teeming with people 24/7, travelers and workers driving cars in and out. The probabilities that they bothered to press the lock button are small.

Hunched low, I move my bike next to the minivan. I open the sliding door and throw the receiver and my back-pack inside, turning off the inner lights for added stealth. Before going in, I turn back and decide to also get Dad's box. After sliding the door shut, I let my eyes adjust to the gloomy interior. The nearby lamppost shines good-enough light on the passenger side, so I push my stuff that way and, folding the backseat out of the way, clear a nice space for myself.

I set the receiver right in front of me and place Dad's box to my right. Luke's tracker blinks away around the same general area as before. I assume he's somewhere inside the airport now, but the tracker is only so accurate.

For the next ten minutes, I watch the dot until my eyes cross and boredom hits me like a sack of bricks. I eat a protein bar and drink a bottle of water, throwing the garbage on the back seat. All the things that Luke revealed tonight whirl inside my mind, drawing my attention to Dad's box.

"It isn't like that for my host. That consciousness never developed. It didn't have a chance." Luke's mind was never human. Always an Eklyptor. How? He implied it should have been that way for me, too. Why wasn't it?

Different DNA, you idiot!

But whose? Not Karen's. Not Brian Scott Guerrero's.

I tear at my hair. *You look just like him. You* have *to be his daughter, damn it! God, I can't lose Dad, too. I can't!*

Before I know what I'm doing, I'm digging into that box, desperately and unreasonably trying to find the hope I've lost. He *is* my father. I feel it in my heart and, so help me God, there will be something in here that will help me prove it.

Chapter 12

Pulling the medical files out of the box, I set them aside and shine my flashlight on the rest of the contents. The next layer reveals two textbooks *Atlas of Anatomy* and *Principles of Internal Medicine*. They are both heavy and well-worn. I take them out and set them to the side. I need more than just these remnants of Dad's medical career, but I'm fearful that might be all I'll find.

Under the textbooks, things are more promising, more personal. I pull out a golden stethoscope. An image flashes before my eyes . . .

The stethoscope hanging off Dad's neck as he presses it to my chest. He listens for a minute, then goes on to tickle me.

A smile stretches my lips, my heart aching at the memory. I turn the chest piece and find Dad's name engraved on the back. After a good look, I stick it in my backpack and check the receiver to confirm Luke's position hasn't changed. It hasn't.

I go back to the box and pull out a wallet. I open it and

find Dad's driver's license still in the ID compartment. I ache at the sight of his young face, younger than I remember it.

"Dad," I murmur. "I wish you were still here."

In an effort to keep it together, I tear my eyes away from the image and, instead, search the other compartments. All I find are a few, old business cards and an even older two-dollar bill. I've never come across one of these before. If I had, I'm sure I would have saved it as well. I put the wallet in my backpack too and check the receiver again. No change.

The next items in the box are three sealable plastic bags with what looks like t-shirts inside. I move them closer to the window to get a better look, but it doesn't help. I'm about to open one of the bags when I decide against it. Maybe they hold some of Dad's DNA. It's a long shot, but not impossible. They go in my backpack as well.

I find other things in the box that also go in my fattening pack. Dad's dog tags, his wrist watch, a Seahawks cap, an old photo album with pictures of people I don't recognize—most likely his Chilean ancestors—and a set of nice pens with his name engraved on them.

In spite of the treasures I've found, I feel vaguely disappointed. The box contained nothing definite to help clear up my questionable paternity. I stare at my hands for a few minutes, lost in thought. Distractedly, I reach for the medical files and set them on my lap.

There are four folders with colorful letter and numbers stickers on the side tabs. I frown.

The letters are: GUE.

So not just any files but *our* files. It makes sense. A doctor would keep a close eye on his family's medical records. But why are there four of them? The question is stupid, and the answer obvious. Dad must have gathered "Max's" information from the hospital, however little there was, anyway.

I open the first folder, the thickest, and confirm my suspicions. It reads:

First Name: Karen
M.I.: B.
Last Name: Guerrero
Date of Birth: 09/30/1976

I thumb through the pages and find a detailed medical history, blood test results, prescription copies for antibiotics and flu medications. All very standard stuff.

The second file is Dad's.

First Name: Brian
M.I.: S.
Last Name: Guerrero
Date of Birth: 08/05/1974

The contents of this file aren't very different from the first. There's some additional stuff about his military service and veteran status, but little else.

The third folder is light in my hands. It has to be Max's . . . Luke's. I open it with a sense of dread, thinking of the pain Dad must have felt at handling the scant medical data the doctors collected from that infant boy before he was kidnapped.

First Name: Maximilian
M.I.: V.
Last Name: Guerrero
Date of Birth: 12/03/1999

There are only two pages. The first one contains extra data like time of birth, length and weight. There are also hemoglobin, and oxygen and blood sugar levels. Things they check as standard procedure in all newborns, I presume. I turn to the next page, expecting much of the same, but my heart takes a tumble when my eyes zero in on a circled section of the page.

Probability of Paternity: 0%
The alleged father is excluded as a biological father of the tested child.

My lungs freeze. My mind reels for understanding. This doesn't make sense.

The alleged father.

Alleged. Alleged. Alleged.

The word hammers against my heart the way it must have hammered against Dad's.

Luke was not his son.

I shake my head, more confused than ever. What the hell is going on here? How is this possible? How can Luke be Karen's son but not Dad's? It's not like Karen was cheating. She was artificially inseminated for the love of—

A knot of disgust twists itself inside my stomach as, for the first time, I look at this from the right angle.

God! I turn away from the awful realization.

I press a hand to my stomach in an attempt to hold back the rising vomit.

Dad suspected something grave enough to order this test. The pages shake in my hand as I look over them. The test was performed on January 20th, 2006. Five years after the birth? What? Maybe I'm looking at this wrong. Maybe these are someone else's files, and I'm having some sort of delusional episode. Where would they have gotten Luke's DNA at that point? Did they save his blood? His umbilical cord? Maybe they had to after he was kidnapped, as a precaution. Makes sense.

The file falls from my hands as my mind takes a leap into a sea of possibilities. Ideas wash over me, like battering waves. One particular possibility taunts me, but I refuse to look at it.

It's too sick, too sick!

Desperately, my fingers fumble for the last file. This is thicker than all other three combined. My heart beats, beats, beats as if it will drill a hole through my chest and tumble onto my lap.

First Name: Marcela
M.I.: V.
Last Name: Guerrero
Date of Birth: 12/03/1999

I flip the pages in a mad dash, looking for one in particular. They rustle and wrinkle under my nervous touch. For a moment, I fear there will be no DNA test for me, but it's there, waiting patiently at the very end of the file. There, circled in a similar manner as Luke's page, is the result. My heart stills. I shut my eyes and allow myself a moment of satisfaction.

Probability of Paternity: 99.9998%

My eyes close. A hot, exhausted breath breaks through my lips. Tears spill past my lowered lids and down my cheeks. Slowly, something like pride or truth rebuilds inside of me, restoring certain strength into my bones that I didn't know had been missing.

I was right. I was right.

Brian Scott Guerrero is my father. I am his daughter, and no one, *no one*, will ever be able to take that away from me.

The word *relief* isn't enough to describe the feeling that washes over me. I am whole again. Vindicated, somehow. It's ridiculous how little it hurt to lose Karen compared to the dread of losing Dad. I guess it's impossible to mourn what you never had.

After a steadying inhale, I open my eyes. Almost by accident, my gaze falls on the receiver, and I'm reminded why I'm here. I blink at it, the feeling that something is wrong not quite registering. It takes me a paralyzed moment to comprehend what the problem is.

The dot is gone!

I curse at myself. Damn, I should have waited to go over Dad's things. Now I have no idea if Luke left or the tracker just blinked out of existence. If the latter, I'm screwed because that would mean he discovered it.

Stupid. Stupid.

Hurriedly, I gather the medical files and zip them securely into my backpack. The only things left on the minivan's floorboards are the empty box and medical textbooks. I'm trying to decide whether to take them or leave them when the sound of approaching engines makes the decision for me.

I leave the books behind, strap the heavy pack on and jump out of the van. I crouch next to my bike. Are the cars just passing by on the adjacent road? Or are they closer? I listen intently.

Closer. Definitely closer.

Adrenaline shooting through my veins, I hop on my bike and hit the ignition. The engine roars to life and I race forward. I'm almost to the exit when a large SUV pulls up in front of me. I brake and, planting one boot on the ground, turn on a dime. I head back the way I came, the SUV hot on my trail. I drive between two long rows of cars, twisting the accelerator to the max. I'm almost clear of the lined-up rentals when a truck sprouts out of nowhere and blocks this end of the street. I squeeze the front brake. Tires squeals, rubber burning. I veer to one side, hoping to drive between two of the parked rentals, but I lose control of the bike.

I fall sideway, feel my bones break into a million pieces. The Kawasaki slides away from me, scraping the road with an ear-splitting screech.

I struggle to my feet, ignoring the pain. Headlights shine directly on my face. My vision blurs. I put an arm over my eyes and glance to the side, looking for an escape. I'm about to take off running when a voice booms through the air, splitting the night in two.

"Don't move or I'll shoot."

Fear and shadows clog my vision. I freeze on the spot.

Chapter 13

I stand surrounded by cars on all sides. Halogen lights shine brightly on me, rendering me bare. My eyes water as I look around, assessing my situation. Several dark figures stand silhouetted in front of the harsh headlights. I take a step toward my fallen bike, more out of concern than out of an impulse to escape.

"I said don't move!" the booming voice reminds me. I stop and squint in that direction. I shake on the spot, both from fear and anger.

My hand inches to the gun at my hip.

"Don't even think about it." The warning is quiet and sends a chill across my back. Some basic instinct I've managed to ignore other times holds me in place.

The owner of that powerful voice steps away from the SUV and its blinding lights. His steps are unhurried and confident. By degrees, his features reveal themselves under the light of the lampposts overhead. My head begins to drone as if a jet engine swallowed me whole.

The sight of him sends my anger skidding straight into

its accompanying fear. Here, in front of me, is another creature that shouldn't exist. My spirit, my very essence, recoils inwardly, more horrified than when confronted with half-crocodiles and oversized, humanoid bats. Though, in this case, it's not the hideous quality of the features that sends primal shivers up my spine, but—as in Luke's instance—the unsettling, inhuman beauty.

"Ms. Guerrero," the man says in an exquisite baritone. "That was a nasty fall. Did you hurt yourself?"

My first instinct is to throw a curse at him. He just threatened to shoot me and now he's worried about my fall. I say nothing. My throat is dry and no words make their appearance. I'm still too enthralled by his aspect, trying to process all the ways that make him different—other than the long set of pointed horns that sit on top of his head, that is.

"My name is Tauro," he says, taking a step closer, as if willing to satiate my curiosity.

He gives me a crooked smile and a perfect raised eyebrow. I gasp as I get a better look at his eyes. They're dark as the night. No whites. No irises. Just black and shiny like the purest obsidian.

My arms break into a million goose bumps. Logic dictates he's looking at me. He's standing just a few paces away, talking to me, so he *must* be looking in my direction. But the truth is, I can't be certain. His attention could be on something else entirely.

Tauro stands in silence as I drink him in. His eerie eyes look immobile under a high, chiseled brow. Like Luke, this man's face is fashioned of flawless angles, calculated in perfect mathematical proportions. His smooth, taut skin makes it impossible to guess his age. He has no laugh lines or creases that may suggest his temperament. He is elegantly tall with wide shoulders and narrow hips. Black hair sits in a casual tussle on top of his head, giving way to a set of polished horns that, instead of making him a monster, grant him a strangely regal air. He's dressed simply in a pair of dark slacks and a gray shirt rolled up to his elbows.

He clears his throat. "Ms. Guerrero, my colleagues and I are here to take you to Mr. Hailstone."

Mr. Hailstone? I nearly burst out laughing, but something about this man makes me stop and reconsider. The respect in his words feels genuine, and laughing in his face feels like an insult. Not that insulting seemingly educated jerks has ever been a problem for me. Elliot can attest to that. But I don't feel on even ground with this man. I feel out of balance, in desperate need of a firm grip of the situation before I do anything stupid.

"Please, will you come with us?" Tauro extends a hand toward the SUV behind him.

I hesitate, casting a regretful glance toward my bike.

"Don't worry about your motorcycle," Tauro says in a reassuring tone. "I'll send someone to retrieve it and make repairs, if necessary. This way, if you would."

I take a slow, reluctant step forward, seeing no way out of this.

"First, your backpack, please," Tauro says, extending a hand in my direction.

I practically bare my teeth at him.

"Don't worry. I promise I will return it."

Shrugging the pack off, I hand it over.

He herds me toward the SUV, an arm curving over my shoulders, never touching me. Two men flank the vehicle, weapons held securely across their chest.

"Gentlemen, put your weapons away. I'm sure Ms. Guerrero has no intention of causing us any trouble tonight."

"Marci. Call me Marci," I say almost compulsively.

The men eye my gun distrustfully.

"Oh, yes. You're weapon, too." Tauro gingerly reaches forward and unholsters my gun so quickly I barely have time to blink.

Damn it!

"You might get it back. It all depends," he says.

If he knew I want to shoot him between his creepy eyes, he wouldn't be saying that.

Tauro opens the SUV's back door and ushers me inside. I climb in, heart in my throat, thoughts of torture chairs and torn fingernails flashing through my mind. I slide all the way across the seat. My gaze flicks to the door handle. I'm considering slinging the door open and fleeing, but the idea is cut short when Tauro presses his cold fingers to my wrists.

"You don't want to do that," he says in a tone that suggest I would regret it. But not because he would make me pay for daring. No, it's not a threat, but an admonishment that suggests I would wish to be back if I actually managed to escape.

I intertwine my hands over my lap, lower my head, and make myself as small as possible. The other two guys take the driver and passenger seats. They look straight ahead, not saying a word. They look perfectly human, and their quiet, stern attitudes scare me more than any outward hostility might.

My hands sweat. I place them face down on my thighs and take a deep breath to gather myself. Certain that my head will explode if I don't, I turn off the incoming buzzing, but let them sense mine. I don't want these Eklyptors freaking out if they stop sensing me. Besides, no one needs to know I'm capable of doing that.

We drive down Airport Expressway in silence until we park by the curb in the departure area. Tauro gets off, and the driver opens my door to let me out.

"Watch your head," he says.

I give him a dirty look, but manage to hold back a sarcastic comment. I go around the back and meet Tauro who waits for me with a smile beautifully drawn on his perfect mouth.

"This way." He leads me through a set of sliding doors guarded by a score of guards dressed in khaki camouflage. They nod respectfully at Tauro. We step into the carpeted lobby. Against the far wall, the different airline counters lie deserted. Cords delineate narrow corridors for nonexistent passenger lines. The sight of these things waiting for life to resume its course unsettles me. What if their wait is fruitless? What if it goes on forever?

I shake myself when Tauro calls my name. I've been standing frozen on the spot without realizing it.

We walk further in, past the TSA checkpoint. It's now-useless metal detectors ignore the armed Eklyptors who walk behind me, as if they're carrying lovely teddy bears and not deadly assault rifles.

Moving down the wide, long hall, we pass restrooms, duty-free shops and magazine stands. I'm surprised to find that everything inside is still in order, not pillaged and destroyed like everywhere else in the city. I'm also surprised the place looks empty, not many soldiers walking around.

"If you would like a novel to read or a new t-shirt," Tauro points toward the stores, "you're welcome to anything in there. Just make sure you put the book back once you're done with it."

Is he serious? I scrutinize his face, trying to find the glint of a joke there. There is none. I've never seen an Eklyptor reading a book. All Whitehouse soldiers ever do is go out on raids, eat, sleep, and bitch about IgNiTe. Maybe Tauro is offering me a book because he knows I'm still human. But if nobody else if going to read it, why would he care whether or not I put it back?

After the stores, we come into an area with three fast food restaurants. It is here that the first signs of faction life begin. Several people sit at small, round tables enjoying burgers, fries, pizza, chips—all sorts of junk food. They chat in relaxed tones while others stand in line, placing their orders. The smell of oil and grilled meat suffuse the air, making the situation feel eerily normal. They could have fooled me, if not for the furry faces and vibrant skin patterns on a few of them.

When they notice us, the chatter stops abruptly. Everyone's gaze turns our way. At first, I think they must be looking at Tauro and his hypnotizing appearance, but they're looking at me. I stare back at them, even though the weight of all their curious gazes makes me want to turn away.

Fingers point in my direction. Whispers are exchanged. To my surprise, a few people smile and wave, as if I'm some sort of celebrity they recognize. My gaze finally snaps to the floor.

"What the hell?" I murmur.

"They're glad to see you are finally here," Tauro says. "But let me say no more. Mr. Hailstone will explain everything."

"When you say Mr. Hailstone, you mean Luke, right?"

"Yes, Luke Hailstone."

"You realize he's not a 'Mister.' He's just a snotty brat who never even finished high school."

Tauro chuckles. "Much like you, I suppose."

"I would say touché, but there's a big difference. I don't go around letting people call me *miss* anything."

Tauro presses past the restaurants and into the area dedicated exclusively to the terminal and its numbered gates. "Well, we believe in respecting our leader."

"He wouldn't be anyone's leader if Zara hadn't been murdered by Elliot's faction," I say, hoping the comment will be salt on a fresh wound.

"An unfortunate incident that has granted our new leader quite a bit of sympathy from our faction members."

"What do you call that? A win-win?" The edge of sarcasm is sharp in my voice.

Tauro makes a small sound in the back of his throat in disapproval of my cynical streak. He looks down at me, eyebrows slightly pinched in the middle. I try to read his expression, but his all-black eyes make it impossible. I wonder if that's why he changed them.

Further down, the waiting areas around each gate are occupied by a few more Eklyptors. They are watching television, playing games on their phones, reading, some are even sleeping curled up on the floor, their heads resting on rolled up jackets or book bags, as if their flights have been delayed and they're simply waiting to get to their final destinations. They aren't even wearing uniforms like everyone does at Whitehouse's. Again, several faces turn in our direction. This time, I follow my instincts and stare straight ahead.

After passing most of the gates, I begin to get impatient.

"Where exactly are we going?"

"We've actually arrived." Tauro points toward a sign that reads *Gate B14*. "Ladies first."

Panic settles in the pit of my stomach. "I'm not getting on a plane," I say, planting my feet firmly on the floor.

Tauro laughs condescendingly. "Don't worry. We won't be taking off. I assure you. Mr. Hailstone simply likes privacy."

He seems sincere enough. Still, I'm not taking any chances. "He can come out here and talk to me. That would work just as well, don't you think?"

Tauro takes a step closer and leans into me. "I haven't given you any reason to distrust me, so please don't make demands, Marci. Be a good girl."

His quiet, almost gentle words seem to brush over my skin, sending a spider creeping up my spine. I get the feeling this is the kind of person you would deeply regret upsetting.

It's not easy, but I swallow my pride, step through the gate and walk down the narrow jet bridge, hoping Luke isn't about to fly me across the world.

Chapter 14

"Hello, Marci," Luke says from the comfort of an armchair.

I look around, unsure of whether I've stepped into a plane or someone's living room. Luke's *lair* occupies the first class compartment of what seems to be a 747 jumbo jet. The aisles have been gutted of their uncomfortable seats, and the space has been completely remodeled into what could be called a welcoming space—*if* the blond, lying Eklyptor was removed, that is. There are lamps, two more armchairs, a small refrigerator with snacks on top, a Bose stereo, even a few well-supplied bookshelves.

"Been to IKIA lately," I ask.

Luke chuckles good-heartedly. "It's one of the spaces I keep. Not the main one, but my favorite."

I stash that information in case it later becomes useful. I guess this is why I didn't see many soldiers roaming around. I wonder where he houses the majority of his faction.

"You have to admit it's pretty cool," he says.

"It would be if certain *props* could be removed." I give him a look, then extend it to Tauro who stands behind me.

"Fair enough." The warm glow of a lamp shines above Luke's head, illuminating the book he was reading. He sets the paperback down on top of the bookshelf. "We can do something about half the problem. Thank you, Tauro. I can take it from here."

"I'll be right outside, in case you need me." Tauro inclines his head. I make an unnecessary show of getting out of the way of his horns. He ignores me and, somehow, manages to make me feel childish. He leaves silently, as if he has levitating powers or something.

"Sit, please." Luke points at an armchair across from his.

I plop myself down, acting unimpressed and unafraid. I'd hate to admit I'm neither one of those.

"Great minds think alike." He smiles.

I frown at him. What is he talking about?

Luke leans forward very slowly, his hand reaching toward my boot. Gingerly, using thumb and forefinger, he picks a small piece of something attached to my shoelace. He places it on the palm of his other hand and offers it to me.

I move close to take a better look. It's different than mine, but similar enough: a tracker. *Crap!*

Check. Or is that checkmate?

Is this how things will always go between us?

"Where is Xave's box?"

"Not now."

I bite my thumbnail, trying to disguise my frustration.

He sets it on top of his book which happens to be *Lord of the Flies*. I try to think of something snippy to say about his choice of literature, but I can't. I've read the stupid book and enjoyed it, too.

I shift in my seat, "You said you wouldn't force me to come."

111

"I didn't. You came of your own accord."

"That's bullshit. Let me go!"

"Can't do that. I'm sure you understand why."

"So what? I'm your prisoner, now?"

"Yes," a simple, unequivocal answer.

I push to the edge of the armchair, fists clench.

"My hope is that, soon, you won't look at it that way, though," he says.

My breath catches midway down my throat. My entire body tingles with the urge to run, though I hold no illusions I would get far. Panic soaks me through and through. He means to release my agent, to help it take over once more. That's the only way I would ever stay in this place. Will they torture me? Do they know that's a sure way to break me, to weaken me so Azrael can shove me out of the way?

"I'd rather die," I blurt out.

Luke regards me with concern, his iridescent blue eyes shining under the lamp light. They're shockingly beautiful.

"Die?" he says the word as if he's never heard of the concept. "There's no need for death when there's a consensus."

"It wouldn't be me. *I* would never see things your way."

He rubs his chin in a manner that looks too deliberate, except all of his movements are like that now, so it may be quite accidental.

"Oh!" he exclaims, some sort of understanding coming over him. "You think I mean to bring your agent forward." To my surprise, his mouth twists with distaste. "No! I would never attempt that!"

For a moment, I think I should pinch myself. This must be a bad dream or a joke of some kind. That, or Luke is seriously high. What could make him think that Marci

112

Guerrero, a human, would ever see things the way he does?

Luke straightens and adopts a very serious expression. "I . . . I like you as you are." He holds my gaze for a short instant, then looks down at his hands so shyly that it makes me think it's an act. He's never been the shy kind. Never.

And what the hell does he mean, anyway?

I'm speechless and not about to spur this conversation in any way, so I zip my lips and make sure my body language says it all. I push away until my butt hits the back of the armchair and tightly cross my arms over my chest.

He doesn't get the hint and goes on. "You are the Marci I've known for over ten years. I wouldn't dare change anything about you."

"Yeah," I say nonchalantly. "That's great. I like me this way, too. There's one thing we can agree on. Just don't get your hopes high on us agreeing on much else."

His head bobs up and down as he nods several times. His expression is sad and, something about his smooth skin going through the tremendous effort of forming downward lines around his mouth and eyes, makes his sadness look epic.

"I can understand your hostility," he says. "Our situation was greatly mismanaged."

"If you're referring to the callous screw up of pretending to be my brother, that's gotta be the understatement of the century," I say, then open my eyes wide and put on a shocked expression. "Gosh, something else we can agree on. Hell must have teleported to the Arctic, and Satan's balls froze solid."

Luke sighs. "Do you think we could have a civil conversation?"

"What? Am I getting on your nerves or something? I

thought you said you liked me just as I am." I don an innocent expression and bat my eyelashes.

"I guess we can't. Not that I blame you." He rubs the back of his neck. "Well, let me start with an apology."

"Don't be ridiculous. Apologies are for spilled milk, not long-lost-brother shenanigans. And don't get me started on the blatant murder and attempted extermination of an entire species. Oh, and there's also that time you *stole* the person I thought was a mother. Good one, by the way! That was extremely classy."

He cocks his head to one side. "So you know about Karen?"

I nod, wondering where she is. Somewhere in this airport?

As if reading my mind, Luke says, "She . . . um, I'm sorry to say that she's dead, a casualty in a battle against Whitehouse."

The words feel like a blow to my chest. I do my best to harden my expression. "No, you killed her when you put an Eklyptor in her brain. She's been dead to me ever since." I have buried her deep inside of me, and I don't plan to exhume what remains of her—not even at this news.

"I'll never forgive myself for that mistake."

"It makes no difference to me," I blurt out, trying very hard not to care. "I also know you're not my father's son. So tell me, how the hell does this mess work? I can see only one possibility, one I have a feeling you'll have no trouble explaining." One that makes my stomach turn with an explosive mixture of disgust and rage.

Luke runs his forefinger across the arch of one of his eyebrows. He looks like someone who's trying to gather courage. He doesn't want to talk about it which means it must be as repulsive as I imagine. A pang of denial hits me straight in the middle of the chest. I jerk to my feet and walk to the small refrigerator at the opposite end of the cabin and stare at the snacks piled on top.

How could they do that? How could they?!

Suddenly, I don't want Luke to explain anything. I don't want to hear him apologize, grovel, justify. Confirmation is all I'll ever be able to take from him, so I ask, "Did Karen give birth to you?"

"I would like to—"

"Just answer the question!"

He gives a deep inhale. "Yes, she did."

"Where did *I* come from?"

"You—"

"No, stop! Wrong question." I pick up a small packet of cheese crackers, try to focus on the yellow letters written on it. Yes or no. That is all I need from him.

"Did Karen give birth to twins?" It's a stupid question. The hospital records say she did. She said she did. Dad said she did. I guess I'm just prolonging the inevitable.

"Yes." Luke has caught my drift. He's smart like that.

I throw a glance over my shoulder. His chin is on his chest, his eyes focused on his shoes. I look back at the crackers and fold my fingers around them.

"Did she give birth to me?" My voice shakes with the question. I know the woman isn't my mother, our DNAs don't match. This, under normal circumstances, would be an absurd question. But Normal died months ago, leaving us with Ludicrous who, besides being deranged, also happens to have a cruel sense of humor.

The crackers fall to the floor and my hands are halfway to my ears before I stop myself. I don't want to hear this, but it's not like I'm five years old and I can refuse to listen, singing *la la la*.

"Yes, Marci. Karen gave birth to you."

Chapter 15

Before I know what I'm doing, my arm is sweeping across the top of the small fridge, knocking chip bags, candy bars, granola packets out of the way. A terrible growl builds in my throat and tears through my lips. My clenched fists shake at my side. The tendons at my neck stand like ropes. My ears are full of something—rage? horror?—and feel as if they're about to erupt like tiny volcanoes.

Tauro is in the room in an instant, barely making any noise as he rushes into the cabin. I sense him out of the corner of my eye as he joins the shadows that quickly whirl to life in the wake of my distress.

My mother didn't give birth to me.

My mother didn't give birth to me.

My mother didn't give birth to me.

The inane thought runs through my head over and over again.

"Everything okay?" Tauro asks.

"Yes. Please leave, Tauro. Just go!" Luke pushes him out the door.

My head in my hands. I dig my fingernails into my scalp.
Zero percent maternity . . . Zero percent love.
False. Fake. False.
Lives.
Destroyed.
My thoughts jump, avoiding dark hurdles that do their
best to trip them. I curse at Azrael, at Luke, at the world.
Finally losing it, I whirl, slam my hands against Luke's chest
and send him sprawling backward. He stumbles and conven-
iently falls on his armchair.

"Monsters! How could you do that?!"

"I was part of their game, too. I didn't do anything."

"Why?! Why?!" It makes no sense.

Why would Doctor Dunn impregnate Karen with
mismatched embryos? He was supposed to make a couple
happy. He was supposed to take the wife's eggs and the
husband's sperm to make a baby that was all their own.
Instead, he used only Karen's egg to make Luke, and only
Dad's sperm to make me. Where the hell did the rest come
from?

"Monsters!" I scream again, this time at Luke's face,
spittle flying from my mouth.

Monsters playing god.

God turning a blind eye.

"Calm down, please." Luke moves his hands up and
down, as if I'm a spooked horse.

"Neither one of us should be here. We should have never
been."

Karen and Brian Guerrero wouldn't have been able to
make *us*. No. The kids they would have made and raised
would have been normal and adapted. But they never got
a chance. Instead, the once-happy couple became part of a

heinous plot that destroyed their lives and crushed any chance at happiness and normalcy without compassion.

"We have no right being here," I yell, trying my best to reign in my temper, but finding it impossible.

"But we are, Marci, and through no fault of our own. Now we have to make the best of it." Luke's own anger begins to rise.

"Is that what you're doing? Is this your version of *making the best of it*?!" I demand.

He gives me a defying glance but says nothing.

"Guess what? You're freakin' failing!" I growl.

"Not as dismally as you."

I flip him the bird. "Did Karen know I'm not her daughter?" Suddenly, this seems like a crucial question.

"How should I know?" Luke gets to his feet.

I take a step back, hating how he towers over me. "Dad knew," I say.

I expect him to look surprised, to ask how Dad learned the truth, but he doesn't. Instead, he paces to the opposite end of the cabin, a hand pressed to his forehead.

My next realization washes over me like a bucket of ice-cold water. In an instant, my boiling rage disappears, leaving behind nothing but numbness. I collapse on the armchair, tears finally free from the cage I tried to build around them.

"You killed him," I say in a monotone. "He found out, and you killed him."

In my peripheral vision, I see Luke turn to face me once more. "*I* didn't kill him."

"You stole his wife from him. You stole his children from him and, finally, you stole his life."

Dad, I'm sorry. I'm so sorry.

I bury my face in my hands and cry. The knowledge of

his death sweeps through me the way it did the day Karen told me he was never coming back. I feel like a small girl torn apart from the too-few worthwhile things life ever let her borrow. Nothing was ever meant to be mine for very long, not my happy childhood, my father, Xave. It seems Dad and I are the same in more ways than one. Everything was taken from us.

"Maybe this is enough for tonight." Luke's voice is quiet and soothing. He sounds closer.

My jaw clenches. My teeth grind. I inhale deeply and squeeze my eyes behind my hands. Emotions burn in my throat, building an impossible knot.

Stop. Stop. Stop.

I don't want to cry anymore, not in front of him. All I want is to utterly eradicate my capacity to feel anything, so these heartless monsters can never hurt me again. It takes me a few heart-rending moments, but I gather myself and build a thick wall around me. With several deep breaths, I regain my focus and center myself in the now—away from what it was, could have been, and never will be.

I raise my face from my hands and stare at Luke. He's sitting back in his armchair, regarding me with something that looks like regret, except beasts like him aren't capable of such feelings. I narrow my eyes at him, understanding things better than ever before.

"Enough?" I say. "But why stop? We haven't gotten to the best part yet, have we?"

Because the rub is in the *why*. It has to be. They went through a lot of trouble to make Luke and me. I'm sure everything I've heard so far will pale in comparison with whatever he's yet to say.

"So go on, Luke. Make my day even better."

"No." Luke refuses to go on.

"But I thought you were dying to tell me all these wonderful things that would eventually open my eyes. I thought you said you'd make me see things your way. Well, news flash, I still don't, so don't stop on *my* behalf."

"I knew this conversation would be hard on you, I just didn't realize how hard. It would be best if we stop and continue tomorrow. It's late. You must be tired."

"You were never considerate before. Why start now?"

Luke ignores me and walks to the plane's entrance. "Tauro, could you come in, please?"

Tauro walks in, ducking his head to avoid impaling the plane with his pointed horns.

"I think we've had enough for tonight." Luke speaks to his henchman in a low, confidential tone, as if he'd like to pretend I'm not here.

Tauro nods.

"Take her to one of the second-floor offices, get her some dinner and post two guards by her door." The last bit is spoken louder and accompanied by a pointed look in my direction. He expects trouble. Well, the least chance I get, I'll oblige.

I stand, because I know there's no point in arguing. Even though I want to forever rip this Band-Aid, the discussion is over for tonight, and it's my fault. I lost it. I allowed myself to get emotional in front of Luke—a side of me he'd never seen. I was always good at concealing things from everyone. But this new world has torn me open and, now, my insides keep spilling like the stuffing of some ruined teddy bear. Now, all it takes is one good jab in the wrong place, and all my emotions come flying out.

"This way." Tauro extends a hand to indicate I should

walk first.

Nice little butler, I think, but say nothing. I suddenly find myself exhausted and can't think of anything better than to get away from everyone, even if it is to a locked office with monsters for guards.

I walk ahead of Tauro with firm steps. We get past a few gates, past the relaxed Eklyptors with their phones and casual conversations. My eyes rove around all the faces, hatred ballooning inside my chest. I think of their hearts flattening into thin slivers, but they go on as if I don't exist.

Then my eyes stop. My feet stop. My lungs stops.

"Keep going," Tauro says.

But my body is a nail and shock is the hammer.

"What's the matter?"

I blink and stare at the ground. Tauro regards me for a moment, then begins to turn toward whatever stole my breath. Not knowing what else to do, I let out a loud kiai, jam my elbow in the pit of Tauro's stomach and take off running.

I don't get very far before two guys dressed in khaki tackle me. I crash to the floor, bones rattling. But it's okay, I don't mind. All that matters is I didn't give away the fact that I recognized one of their residents.

Aydan is here.

Chapter 16

Two guards yank me to my feet. They flank me, their heavy hands squeezing my upper arms, making my hands throb from lack of blood. I struggle, but that only makes their grip more vicious.

Tauro joins us. His smooth features and black eyes are unreadable. He looks at me without saying a word. I drop my gaze, unable to withstand his scrutiny.

At least he doesn't know what caused me to freeze on the spot. I'm dying to look in Aydan's direction, but I stare doggedly at Tauro's lace-up shoes. Questions fly like confused bees inside my head.

Why is Aydan here?

Did James send him?

Is he here on an IgNiTe mission?

God, he has to be. He has to be!

The alternative it too horrible to contemplate. Damn, if only IgNiTe didn't have to keep me in the dark, I would know what's going on.

Out of the corner of my eye, I perceive Aydan. He's

moving through the food line, along two other guys. He's in civilian clothes, like most of the people lounging in the terminal. He wears his customary black jeans and t-shirt.

"Well, let's go," I say, desperate to move on.

If Aydan's here on a mission, I don't want to risk giving him away. If he's here as an actual member—

My throat tightens with sudden fierceness. I don't . . . I don't think I could take that.

"Why so eager to leave?" Tauro says in a suspicious voice. "Mr. Hailstone said I should get you dinner, remember? What would you prefer? Hamburger?" He gestures toward the fast food area. "Pizza?" He slowly turns to face the line where Aydan stands.

"I'm not hungry," I blurt out.

Tauro ignores me and carefully surveys what lies in front of him, which includes a glass counter stocked with greasy pizzas, a young server and three customers, counting Aydan at the front of the line.

"Get your hands off me, would you?" I fidget in hopes of calling Tauro's attention back to me. It doesn't work, and all I manage to do is piss off the living vice grips that clasp my arms. "Assholes," I mumble.

Aydan pulls away from the counter, a plastic tray in tow. A large slice of pepperoni pizza and a drink sit on top. My heart hammers out of control.

He walks to a supply area and gets a set of plastic utensils, a straw and a handful of napkins. I can only assume he's seen me and is deliberately ignoring me. Regardless, he's going to have to look this way sooner or later. Tauro is obviously staring at him. From such a short distance, not noticing us at all would be a dead giveaway that he's pretending. Others have noticed us as it is. He would have to be blind not to wonder why he's suddenly become the center of attention.

My stomach climbs to my throat. Tension ripples across my shoulder.

Aydan turns away from the supplies, takes two steps, then stops. He does a slow double take at Tauro and frowns. His gaze drifts in my direction. His frown deepens. There's no recognition in his eyes. None.

I try to tell myself this is good. This means he's still Aydan and not a full-fledged Eklyptor, but that's not necessarily true. He could be a new, promising member who doesn't want to associate himself with the tainted Symbiot his host used to know.

"Do you know this girl?" Tauro demands of Aydan.

"No, sir," he responds.

His familiar voice sends a thrill down my back. I feel betrayed, somehow, even though it's stupid because this is exactly what I want from him, full-fledged or not.

"And you?" Tauro flags the other two guys in the line. "Do any of you know this girl?"

They give me the once-over and shake their heads, their expressions as blank as Aydan's. Tauro grunts, not pleased at all. He knows someone's lying. He just doesn't know who. He turns away without a word and orders the guards to follow. They drag me away.

In spite of my desire to find out if Aydan's still in control or has become a prisoner in his own mind, I move away with quick steps and no backward glance.

I debate whether to stay silent or say something, wondering which option would help confirm Tauro's suspicions. In the end, I decide to continue my initial cynical pattern. "Paranoid much?"

Tauro ignores me, pulls out a radio and talks rapidly and quietly into it. I make out enough to realize he's ordering someone to keep an eye on three men, one of them a new member by the name of Specter. I recognize one of Aydan's user handles, the one he preferred before permanently changing it to "Dr. V." Does the use of this name mean he's still himself? I guess not. His agent could be using it in some messed up ironic twist.

I wonder if Tauro knows everyone's name around here. Or has Aydan made himself notorious enough to be remembered?

Shit!

It takes a major effort to swallow the curse words that flood my mouth. As if the nightmare Luke just unloaded on me isn't enough, now I have to worry about Aydan too?

Fifteen minutes later, I find myself sitting on a desk chair with a pizza dinner in front of me. I eat without appetite, because I need the energy. It's been a long, freakin' day. When I finish, I wash everything down with a cold soda, clean my mouth with a beige napkin and push the tray away. This fills you up, but it pales in comparison to what Onyx serves. Elliot's army's cook and only decent Eklyptor I know occupies the body of a guy who used to be a five-star chef, and she's using his culinary skills to the fullest, even she hates the *maleness* she also inherited from him.

My watch reads 11:46 P.M. I stand and look around at the small, windowless office once more. There is a calendar on the wall above a set of metal filing cabinets. The page is stuck on March—the month of The Takeover. On the opposite wall, the print of a landing plane hangs within a cheap black frame. There's nothing else on the walls and nothing personal on the desk or filing cabinets. I suspect those things were removed and thrown in the garbage. Mementos of that sort mean nothing to these creatures. At least the beasts can't rid themselves of their hosts' memories. I find some satisfaction knowing that, in a small way, those trapped consciousnesses live on.

I walk to the door, put a hand on the nickel-plated door knob and turn it ever so slightly. I've barely twisted it when a loud thump from the outside makes me jump back.

"Stay away from the door," an angry voice says on the other side.

Oddly, my anxiety settles a little. This is the type of treatment I'm used to from Eklyptors—not Tauro's courteous demeanor. This makes my hate flow like hot honey, just like it should.

I lower my head and try to look under the door, but there's nothing to see, unless I count the black, sealing strip that covers the narrow gap to the floor. Restless, I search the office, opening drawers in hopes of finding something that can be used as a weapon. Nothing.

Willing my powers to the surface, I stare at one of the metal cabinets and imagine it crashing through the door, crushing the guards in the process. It doesn't move. I curse and plop on the desk chair.

Looking for an escape, I focus on my breathing and thought jumping. I don't want to stay in this moment, this place, this life. I want to be elsewhere. Maybe in front of Lake Union under a moonlit sky.

Almost without thinking, I reach for my backpack, which was brought back along with my dinner and a note: "The Hailstone faction keeps its word." I hug it to my chest and rest my cheek on it. Everything *not* resembling a weapon is still inside. I checked as soon as they left me alone.

The edge of despair draws nearer, pushing me toward self-pity, which isn't far, all things considered. I wish I could sleep and quiet down the thoughts swirling through my mind, but that type of rest has evaded me for some time, even given the best of circumstances. And tonight isn't even close to "the best" of anything. If I switch the perspective to "the worst", however, today gets a medal.

I close my eyes and listen. There's a heavy silence that, for a moment, makes me think I'm truly alone, maybe the only person left in the world.

A strange, vaguely familiar feeling brushes my skin. The hairs on my arms stand on end. My eyes spring open. My ears tune into silence, listening, listening, listening . . .

Thud.

Thud.

I jump to my feet, send the rolling chair flying against the wall. Backpack tight in my arms, I stare at the door knob. It turns very slowly. My breath catches as expectation builds in my chest.

I don't blink.

The door opens one inch at a time.

A familiar face pokes in. Our eyes lock. I press my lips together—doubt heavy on my shoulders—and hold back the wave of relief that wants to crash against me. I can't trust him. Not yet.

"Marci?" Aydan pronounces my name exactly the way I would pronounce his, if I could speak.

Marci, is that still you?

Marci, can I trust you?

Marci, are you still human?

All those questions inside a single utterance of my name. It's hard to fathom. Maybe this doubt in his voice should serve as proof that he's still my friend. No Eklyptor could ask this in quite the same way, could he?

Yes, he could! Yes, he would!

Aydan stands there, well aware of my own conundrum. His face is pale against his red lips. They stretch into a sad smile that doesn't reach the depths of his black eyes.

"I guess you're just gonna have to trust me and the fact that I haven't killed you." He offers me the same words I gave him the first time we met after I betrayed The Tank's location to Whitehouse.

I don't know why, but something breaks inside of me. I let the backpack fall to the desk, cover the distance between us and wrap my arms around him.

At the verge of tears, I press my face to his shoulder and hold on tight. He doesn't say a thing, just holds me back until I grow back a skeleton and feel I can stand without his support.

When I pull away, our eyes meet. We exchange no words, but they're not necessary.

I'm not alone anymore.

He lets me get my backpack, then interlaces his fingers with mine and pulls me out of the room.

We step over two fallen bodies, then run.

Chapter 17

My hand is tight in his, I follow Aydan to the end of the hall, then down a set of stairs. Our steps are hurried but quiet against the carpeted floor. As we descend, Aydan slows his pace and straightens.

He reluctantly lets go of my hand. "Look normal."

I do my best not to peer around like a hunted mouse and, instead, focus on the directional signs overhead. *Luggage Claim*, left. *Rental Cars*, right.

"The front is better guarded," he whispers as we walk down. "And alarms will sound if you use any emergency exits—not that you'd be able to outrun them, anyway. You need wheels." He presses a set of keys into my hand. "You'll have to use one of the walkways to the parking deck. You can use the fob to find my car in the lower level."

I'm shaking my head as I listen to his rushed words, my brain unable to process them due to my growing denial. From the instant we ran out of that office, I had imagined us leaving this place together. It's illogical, I know. He's here for an important reason, a mission James must have assigned to him. He can't abandon everything because I stumbled into this. He's already risking too much by helping me.

"There are a couple of guards by the walkway, but I can take care of them." His dark eyes flash back and forth as we arrive at the bottom of the stairs.

We see no one.

"Guards make rounds, so let's move. Not too fast. We don't want to appear suspicious." He takes a left and begins a leisurely walk down a wide, dimly illuminated corridor.

My heart thumps four times per every step we take.

"What are you doing here?" I ask.

"Ah, she still remembers how to speak," Aydan says. "I was starting to wonder if you'd gone full-fledged, and your agent was afraid its craziness would give it away."

I think back and realize I haven't spoken a word. Aydan has never had the *pleasure* of meeting Azrael, but I had explained how nuts my agent is and how its speech pattern is nothing like mine. I had to warn him about it in case I'm ever eclipsed again.

He looks over at me. "Or maybe it was my awesome rescue that left you speechless."

"So far this doesn't qualify as a rescue. I'll hold my judgment." I could tell him it was relief that stole my voice, but it would lead to questions and the need to admit that I was afraid.

"You're welcome." He gives me a sideways glance and a raised eyebrow. I match his smirk and, just like that, things fall into place.

"So, what are you doing here?" I ask again.

He shrugs. "You should know. You invented this."

"What?"

"You know . . . the Symbiot spy thing."

"Huh, that's news to me."

"Well, it seems to work pretty well." He slows down suddenly and cocks his head to one side, peering toward an intersecting hall.

Steps.

He looks all around. There are no doors, no big pieces of furniture, nowhere to hide. The few planters and benches would conceal nothing bigger than a cat.

Aydan grabs me by the waist and pushes me to the wall until my back is flush against it. He presses his body to mine and leans his head down. My eyes go wide and stare into his. His lips part and, for a moment, I think he's going to kiss me, but he only gets close enough to hide my face from whoever just turned the corner.

"Get a room," someone calls as they pass by.

Aydan's warm breath brushes my lips. My heart thuds with the fear of being discovered and the fear of something I can't define. My eyes fall to his lips. They tremble. His chest moves up and down. His normally pale cheeks are pinker. He moves a millimeter closer. The reflex to wet my lips assaults me, but I manage to repress it.

The idea of kissing Aydan had never entered my mind, but it has now. This closeness, the intensity in his eyes, the quivering of his lower lip are all too suggestive, too . . . self-explanatory not to plant the seed. And somehow, those things also help me realize that *he* has thought of it.

Aydan wants to kiss me.

My chest tightens with the strange realization.

Aydan wants to kiss me?!

Suddenly, the thought seems ludicrous. Aydan hated me just a couple of months ago. As a matter of fact, he couldn't stand me, couldn't be bothered to help me or say a decent thing to me. When James asked him to teach me to meditate, he acted like he'd been asked to babysit a wild hyena. When he was expected to work with me hacking the security system to Elliot's fertility clinic, he thought I would be a hindrance and behaved as if my hacking skills were on par with a script kiddie, even though he already had proof of my abilities. And during the mission itself, he cut Xave's communications to keep him in the dark and to, ultimately, aggravate me.

My out-of-control tallying stops.

Shit!

My mouth goes dry.

Aydan likes me. He has always liked me.

No. That's just crazy. It's all because of this messed up situation, this unexpected need to act like we're . . . making out when all we're trying to do is find a way out of here, a way to stay alive and defeat this evil.

But no matter how much I deny it, the knowledge sticks and, suddenly, I'm seeing all of his actions, all of his behaviors toward me, under a different light.

He never hated me. He never thought I was stupid or a waste of time. He never thought I was weak even when he called it to my face after Xave died and all I wanted was mind-numbing sedatives. When he asked me to prove that I was strong, he knew I wouldn't be able to resist, knew the challenge would bring me back to the world of the living.

I remember how, using his powers, he scattered beautiful fireworks over the surface of Lake Union, and the way his glow enveloped me when he hugged me, relieved that I had survived the battle at Whitehouse headquarters.

Emotions war against each other in the middle of my

chest. Inexplicably, a tear slides down the corner of my eye. There's too much inside me trying to push its way out, and there's no way I can hold on and no way I can let go—not when there's so much of Xave I need to keep close, not when I'm unable to decide if caring for others is a blessing or a curse.

Aydan stops the lone tear's descent by pressing the back of his forefinger to my cheek. He never breaks eye contact, and I'm surprised to discover how expressive black eyes can be, how much can be said without words.

"I know," he says in a low, resigned whisper, then pulls me close and presses a soft kiss to my forehead.

We stand there for a long moment. I relish the contact in an almost primal way. The touch nearly convinces me that I'm not alone and don't have to be. There's someone who cares about me, someone who can selflessly set his own feelings aside with two simple words.

I know says he understands what I'm going through, how I feel. *I know* tells me he doesn't care I'm still hung up on the past, on a love that could never be. *I know* shows me his feelings are what they are, even if mine are inaccessible, behind thick layers of guilt, what-ifs and broken dreams.

He pulls away reluctantly. "Let's get you out of here."

We walk to the end of the hall without a word and stop before turning the corner. He presses a finger to his lips and peeks around the edge of the wall. I peer around him and see two armed guards flanking the walkway entrance.

A low hum fills my ears. The hairs on the back of my neck stand on end. Suddenly, the air crackles and a delicate slice of near-invisible lightning flies out of Aydan's fingers and shoots straight toward one of the guards. The precise volt hits the man right between the eyes. He hovers for a moment, then goes limp and collapses to the floor, face first.

The second guard gives a startled yelp, runs to his companion and kneels next to him. He calls his name and pokes him. After a dumbfounded moment, he goes for the radio at his hip, but never reaches it. Instead, he falls forward and topples over the other guard. Their fallen bodies form an "X" on the floor.

So this is how he immobilized the other two guards without leaving any outward signs of injury.

"Your skills have improved," I say, a bit of envy coloring my voice. This is how far I could be with my own skills, if I learned to handle meditation on my own.

"You'll get there. I've told you that with each meditation you grow leaps and bounds. Leaps and bounds, Marci." Aydan steps from behind the wall and walks to the fallen guards. He takes their guns from their holsters, hands one to me and heads into the walkway at a clipped pace.

Just as we make it across, an ear-splitting alarm begins blaring.

"Shit! Someone took notice. My car's that way," he points toward the section marked with a letter C. "Go. I'll make sure no one comes this way. Just drive, don't stop. And if you have to run someone over, do it!"

He takes a step backward.

I catch his wrist and hold him back. "Come with me." The irony of the request doesn't escape me. He asked me to leave Whitehouse several times, and I went back every single time.

"You, better than anyone, know that I can't." His gaze is full of sadness and deep understanding. He knows exactly how it feels to let someone go, to allow them to head straight back into the beast's jowls.

I release my hold of his wrist one finger at a time.

"Be careful," he says, then turns away and runs back the way we came.

For just a moment, I watch his retreating figure. Something seems to shiver inside of me as he moves away. I struggle with the sensation for a moment, trying to decipher what it means, then snap out of it and turn in the direction Aydan indicated.

Gun pointed at the ground, I run out onto the parking deck and weave through a few lines of cars. I press the fob once and hear a short double beep over the din of the blaring alarm. I cut slightly to the left and quickly spot Aydan's VW Jetta.

I'm almost to the car when a guttural sort of purr stops me short. I hold the gun up in the direction of the sound, but all I see are cars. I whirl, the gun making a semi-circle around me. I peer behind every car, behind every concrete column.

Nothing.

In spite of that, I still know I'm screwed.

Chapter 18

Walking backward toward the Jetta, I take two careful steps, peering between two cars. A large shape emerges from behind a large SUV and my blood runs cold.

A lion!

Or, more precisely, something that is trying to look like one.

The animal is huge, much bigger than any feline I ever saw at the zoo. The top of its massive, mane-lined head is as tall as a small horse. Its paws are the size of soccer balls and move as silently as if they were walking on air. Round, quicksilver eyes stare at me with intelligence and a sort of wicked pleasure. The creature's mouth stretches in a macabre smile.

Its slick body comes away from the car, revealing a musculature so massive and perfect it makes me think of a chiseled, marble statue. This is no overgrown lion. Its coat is perfectly white, pure as snow. Nature never made anything so beautiful and flawless.

"Stop or I'll shoot you." I shuffle back toward the Jetta

and throw the driver side door open.

Certain that *Mega Simba* understands English, I jerk the gun, hoping he's at least a little bit afraid of the weapon. A strange, low chuckle sounds in the back of his throat. A cold chill seeps into the depths of my soul. No, he's not afraid, and his confident, unconcerned air tells me the bullets would do little more than tickle him.

Damn!

My eyes flash toward the inside of the Jetta. I consider how long it would take me to jump inside, key the ignition, start the engine and tear out of here.

Too freakin' long.

Certainly longer than it would take Mega Simba to bend his hunches and take a leap straight for my throat.

The huge feline takes another step forward just as I hear shouts coming from the walkway. Time is running out. I sharpen my aim to the center of Mega Simba's head and lock my gaze with his.

Let me go or I have no other alternative but to shoot you, my eyes tell him.

Practically shrugging, he throws his head back. His mane sways ever so slightly. He doesn't give a flip. Shooting this thing should be easy, after all I've been through, but I don't think I'll ever get used to it. I clenched my teeth, take a deep breath and, closing my mind to the guilt, pull the trigger. I blink with the loud shot. In the split second my eyes are closed, Mega Simba leaps out of the way and avoids the bullet.

The slapping sound of boots against pavement sharpens my sense into a thin blade. Since killing the beast seems to be out of the realm of possibilities, the car is my only option. Before I over think things, I leap into the Jetta, fumbling with the key. Mega Simba leaps with me and clamps his jaws around my ankle. I collapse on the driver seat, one leg in, the other one in the beast's mouth.

I flinch, waiting for the stabbing pain of the animal's huge canine teeth and the bone-crushing pressure of his bite. When they don't come, I jerk my leg back in an attempt to release it. Mega Simba gives me a sideways, amused glance.

"What the hell? Let go of me!"

Mega Simba rolls his eyes.

Seriously? What—who—is this creature?

I key the ignition and start the car.

Mega Simba make a noise in the back of his throat that sounds like "uh-uh."

"There!" a voice shouts.

I look up to find a group of men running in my direction.

"Let. Me. Go!" I pull my free leg back and jam the heel of my boot straight into Mega Simba's right eye.

The sudden kick catches him by surprise, and he lets me go. Clawing the seats, I scramble inside, shift into reverse and step on the gas. The engine revs and the tires squeal as the car lurches backward. The open door slams against a still-recovering Mega Simba. He staggers sideways until he manages to get out of the way. I go too far and crash into the car behind me. My door slams shot with the lost momentum. Hands shaking, I shift into drive and floor it. The car speeds forward with a loud screech of tires.

I speed down the lane, cars blur by, left and right. I search desperately for the exit sign. When I spot it, I head in that direction without hesitation. My hands are both on the wheel, but I don't let go of the gun, even if my thumb and forefinger are the only ones engaged. I direct a quick glance to the rearview mirror. Four or five men run behind with no hope of catching up. For an instant, I think I've won. Then Mega Simba rushed past them, his strides as long and fast an ostrich on steroids.

Crap!

My eyes snap forward. Ahead, I see the exit. It's a simple gate with a wooden arm painted in yellow and black strips. Nothing even the small Jetta can't break through. I can almost taste the free road beyond.

I'm only about thirty yards from the gate when someone suddenly steps in front of the car. In the split second it takes extra adrenaline to shoot into my veins, I recognize him.

Luke.

He plants himself in the middle of the lane, legs spread apart, arms at his side like some stupidly brave cowboy. I keep my foot on the gas. I'll call his bluff, and he'll have to jump out of the way. Our gazes lock. My vision suddenly tunnels, and the determination of his features comes into focus. There's no doubt whatsoever in his expression, no fear. I clench the wheel with white-knuckled strength.

He'll get out of the way. He will.

I'm certain until, abruptly, I'm not. My certitude flips on a dime and, out of the blue, I just *know* Luke will not move out of the way. Something, that weird connection we've shared since we were kids, lets me see his intentions as plain as day.

I should kill him. I *need* to kill him.

With every piece of who I am, with all the awful things he's done to me, with every promise of revenge I've made to myself, I should have all the fuel needed to ignite my desire to kill him.

But I don't. I just don't.

James asked me to find a worthier reason to live, something other than revenge. I didn't want to listen, but maybe I should. If this is how my revenge efforts will go, I desperately need to focus my energy on something I'm actually good at.

A loud roar fills my ears at the same time that I slam on the breaks. They lock. The acrid scent of burnt tires fills the air. The Jetta starts to slow down but, in a panic, I realize it won't stop in time. Sixty to zero won't come soon enough. I push on the break harder, thrown my weight back against the seat for more leverage. It makes no different. Luke is only ten feet away, showing no signs of appreciation for his soon-to-be-over life.

I grind my teeth and growl as if that will make the car stop.

It doesn't.

Unable to watch, I shut my eyes but, just as I do, the car comes to a sudden stop. My body whiplashes forward. I scream. My gun falls on my lap as I instinctively cross my arms over my face. I slam against the steering wheel. My neck bends violently forward, then back. Pain shoots down my spine, making my legs tingle and go cold.

I groan and throw my head back against the headrest, face contorted in pain. As the sting of the impact subsides, I blink to clear my eyes. My chest pumps up and down with difficulty. It feels as if my bones have crumbled to pieces.

It takes a long moment for my eyes to see straight. When they do, I find Luke still standing in front of the car, a mere couple of feet away. Deep concern etches his face but disappears when he sees I'm not seriously hurt. My thoughts do cartwheels, trying to figure out how I came to stop with such abruptness.

It all becomes blatantly clear when I catch sight of a huge, maned head in the rearview mirror. The creature looks immense, so much more than it did a moment ago. At first, I think I've really hurt my head, or my eyes, then I realize he's standing, his huge paws pressed tightly to the back of the car. That's when I notice the Jetta is tilting backward.

Mega Simba stopped the car, a giant stepping on a cockroach.

I shake my head and snatch the gun from my lap. My hand trembles as I open the door. I take a huge inhale and throw my feet onto the pavement. My knees wobble like thin blades of grass, but I manage to stand. I push away from the car and make sure I can keep an eye on Luke in the front, and his men and overgrown kitten in the back.

Tauro is among the men and so is Aydan, looking paler than ever. They don't know he helped me. I hope. I look at all of them with the same level of hatred. It is extremely hard to do when my gaze brushes Aydan's, but I manage. I hope he doesn't try anything stupid. We're outnumbered here. Like a thousand to two, if one counts the feline in terms of muscle mass.

I clear my throat and turn to Luke. "I really, really wish I could've obliged you on that death wish of yours. Too bad I haven't managed to become a murderer . . . yet."

They all watch me coldly as I squeeze the gun and do mental cartwheels, trying to figure out how I'll get out of this one.

Chapter 19

Luke walks around the car and moves closer. "Are you okay?" He looks genuinely concerned and, for some reason, his distress makes my blood boil.

As if this wasn't his fault!

If he's so worried, why doesn't he just let me go? But oh no, forget that. He would have me practically break my neck instead.

"No. Of course I'm not okay. The blond boy's beast stepped on the car I stole and nearly broke me in half."

"Glad to see you're still your normal self," Luke points out. "C'mon. Let's go back." He extends an arm in the direction of the walkway.

"I'm not going back!" The words rumble out of my chest. The gun trembles in my grip.

Luke's eyes flicker to my hand, then back up to meet my gaze.

Tauro takes a step forward. "Let's not do this again, Marci."

"You stay out of this. Go join a rodeo or something." I

143

don't even look at him. My gaze stays leveled with Luke's. He's the one who calls the shots here anyway, as unlikely as that still seems to me.

"Marci, be reasonable," Luke says.

"Be reasonable? Be reasonable?! You tell me you want to talk to me, reveal only half of some disgusting truth you think I'm supposed to care about, then lock me up in an office when it pleases you, and now you ask me to be reasonable? Screw you! Either tell me what you need to tell me, or let me go."

"Okay, fine. Let's go inside. We need to discuss this in private."

"I am not going anywhere." My voice is firm. I grip my gun with both hands to help deliver the message a little better.

Mega Simba gives a tired snort and lowers his huge paws to the ground. The Jetta's front tires settle with a squeak. He leisurely strolls to the side, plops his massive body down and begins to lick his paws. I watch dumbfounded. Everyone else, including Aydan, ignores him, as if they're used to this type of domestic behavior from such a wild-looking beast.

Luke gives a resigned exhale. "All of you, leave!" he orders with a wave of his hand.

"Are you sure it's safe, sir?" one of the men behind Tauro asks. He gives a meaningful glance toward my gun.

Tauro turns and faces them. "Do as Mr. Hailstone says. Stay nearby, in case we need you."

They nod and begin to retreat. Aydan hesitates. I catch his gaze and try to convey a reassuring message. He walks away with the rest of the men—his steps a little shorter, a little slower.

"Well, talk," I say.

144

Luke brushes blond hair off his forehead in a tired manner. It's clear he doesn't know where to begin. The information he's already shared with me is unsavory enough. How much worse can the rest be? I have a feeling what I've heard so far will be nothing compared to what comes next. I square my shoulders and armor-plate whatever sensibilities this world hasn't managed to steal from me.

No matter what, I won't give him the satisfaction of seeing me upset.

Not again.

"Just spit it out, Luke. I don't care at this point. We both know it won't be pretty."

"No, it won't," he admits. "I have struggled with this myself, especially with my parents' decision to do what they did, the way they did."

"Your parents? When you say that . . . would you mind telling me who the hell you're talking about?"

I know—based on what Lyra has told me—that Zara and Tom Hailstone were responsible for Luke's kidnapping from the NICU as well as his subsequent "pretend" adoption. They raised him as their son, even if biologically he's Karen's and . . . who else's? Dr. Dunn's?—the man responsible for impregnating Karen with a pair of infected, mismatched embryos.

"Zara and Tom Hailstone," Luke answers, his blue eyes filling with sadness at the mention of the names.

"But Dunn was your real father, right?" I still remember him crying at the funeral and stupidly comforting him, believing he was my long, lost brother. Such a crock of lies.

"No. Tom was. Tom and Karen. Dunn was just a front. He worked for my parents, performed the in-vitro fertilization and implanted the embryos. He conducted the . . .

experiments that led to *us*," he says the last few words so very carefully that I feel as if I'm made of glass, and he's afraid this truth will crack me into a million pieces.

We are experiments.

But of course.

My vision grows blurry. If I had a soul, would it have died at this revelation? I shake the thought away, swallow hard.

Now the rub is . . . What was the purpose of these experiments? And did they work?

I take a deep breath and ask the million dollar question. "And my mother? Who is she?" I think I already know the answer, but I want to hear it from his perfect, inhuman lips.

"Your mother was Zara."

The image of the woman dying at Luke's feet rises in my mind. Lyra shot her point blank. Luke tried to save her, carried her out of Whitehouse's headquarters and called for help. They didn't get there in time. She died on the concrete, in the middle of the battle, while Luke begged her to be strong and I wished her to died. Something twists inside my chest. It's ugly and misshapen, like a tumor no one will ever be able to root out.

"Go on," I say, my voice as cold as shards of ice.

Luke exchanges a glance with Tauro who is still standing to the side, immobile as a statue. Mega Simba is also still there, his huge head resting on crossed paws.

"Okay." Luke seems puzzled and relieved at the same time.

He's expecting me to fall apart again. But this one is not hard to digest. I could never see that woman as my real mother. I knew nothing about her. I only ever had one parent, anyway. My other half could have sprung out of the air, for all I care.

"For many years," Luke continues, "my parents' goal was to figure out how to allow our kind to . . . procreate. I'm sure you're well aware of our limitations."

I say nothing and think of the only Spawner I've ever seen, that hideous, tentacled creature at Elliot's party.

"Well . . ." Luke pauses, lowers his head and paces in front of me.

"Well what? Are you saying this experiment . . . *us* . . . was supposed to help with that?"

Luke stops and looks at me sideways, his expression as sad as any I have ever seen. "Yes. My parents' goal was to create two Eklyptors who could procreate."

Two Eklyptors who could procreate.
Two Eklyptors who could procreate.

The words get stuck on repeat inside my head. They flash like traffic signals, guiding my thoughts down a brightly-lit street where all the pieces of the puzzle come together in perfect clarity.

Two Eklyptors.

Luke *plus* Marci *equals* two.

"But I'm not an Eklyptor!" It's the only thing that bears saying, the one thing I hold on to—a drowning person on a life raft.

I'm not an Eklyptor. I'm not.

I. AM. NOT.

And I would never procreate with one of these beasts.

The angry thoughts tear through my mind, like war tanks bent on destruction. They are so loud in my head that I barely hear Luke's next words.

"You are supposed to be my mate."

Chapter 20

I don't know if I've gone crazy, but the sudden and uncontrollable way I'm laughing makes me wonder.

I have to make a concerted effort to hold on to my gun, because this laughter is too much, and my hands want to fly to my stomach to contain the wild attack.

Luke stares at me dumbfounded. He looks to Tauro who also seems to be wondering about my sanity. Mega Simba raises his head for a moment and lets out a bored yawn when he realizes the situation hasn't changed one bit since he went to sleep.

"That is priceless," I say between ill-contained chuckles. "I am supposed to be your mate?!"

Luke's clear blue eyes darken. A muscle in his jaw jumps. He thinks I'm having a laugh at his expense. And maybe I am, but it's not just him. It's the entire situation. It's ridiculous. Who in their right mind thought up this absurdity?

"I'm sorry, Luke, but really, I'm supposed to be your mate? How did we go from being brother and sister to this? I mean, who the hell thought of this? Because surely, this entire experiment is a hopeless failure."

Tauro sighs and exchanges a knowing look with Mega Simba, as if they totally agree with what I'm saying. I scowl at them.

Luke gives me a tired answer, which makes me think he was expecting my question. "My parents had their reasons for doing what they did. I didn't always agree with them, but I tried to understand."

"And did you? Understand, I mean."

As ridiculous as this sounds and as hard as I'm laughing, the idea of being Luke's mate slowly burrows into my brain, an insidious worm that makes itself comfortable, even as I try to keep it away.

"It all made sense when it began. You see, my mother, Zara, tried to get pregnant from an early age, but her host was somehow defective. She couldn't carry a pregnancy to term, so by the time Dunn was ready to test his theory, my mother already knew they'd need a surrogate mother.

"Several viable candidates were chosen. Given that two genetically unrelated embryos were needed for the experiment, their partners were also carefully selected. In the end, eight couples made the list. Two embryos were implanted in each woman. One male, one female, each carrying one half of Zara or Tom. He did it this way because he expected the pair to adapt to each other's presence, hopefully erasing the bothersome rank messages." He gestures toward his head. "He was wrong about that, of course. I suppressed mine at an early age, though. We expected you to do the same, but . . ."

The worm burrows deeper and deeper. My stomach twists with the possibilities the little pest slowly unleashes inside my head.

"From that experiment, only four of the women carried to term. One of them gave birth to one child only who died within hours, the second embryo never developed. The second woman gave birth to stillborn twins. The third gave birth to a boy and a genetically . . . inviable girl. The fourth gave birth to a perfect set."

Luke's words echo inside my head.

Stillborn.

Inviable.

Perfect.

The worm feeds on the words and gets fatter and fatter.

"In simple terms, Dunn spliced Eklyptor DNA into those human embryos. And from all his attempts, only you and I were a success."

My breathing speeds up. To stop myself from hyperventilating, I take one long inhale and let it out slowly through my mouth. *I will* not *freak out.* I made myself a promise. Luke will not see me fall apart again. Never mind the fact that I'm more of a monster than I thought. Never mind that I'm not only infected, but my DNA is actually spliced with that of a monster.

I'm not human at all.

I'm a new species.

"When we were born," Luke continued, "our faction was under attack. A French group, now part of IgNiTe, had followed my parents from Paris, where my father was from. He wanted to leave us with Karen, thought it would be safer if no one knew we existed. But my mother wouldn't have it. She wanted us by her side. Dunn was supposed to take the two of us away, but Karen and Brian kept you in their room, while I was in NICU, so he could only take me.

"After that, there were police around the hospital and,

once you were sent home, your father wouldn't let you out of his sight. Zara still wanted you with us, but my father's sudden death made her reconsider, and she decided to let you be. To let Karen and Brian raise you. It wasn't easy for her. You were her daughter while I was Tom's."

"Spare me," I say as my teeth grind in fury. "Zara's sensibilities mean nothing to me. I'm not her daughter. I have no mother. Never did. Don't forget that."

Luke nods and concedes.

"She wanted us to grow up knowing each other. That's why she enrolled me in your school since the beginning. But I didn't know. Not until I turned fourteen. That's when they told me. I mean, I knew what I was. They never hid that from me. I just didn't know about you, about our connection.

"You might remember I stopped talking to you for a while when we were in eighth grade."

I shake my head, even though I do remember. Because shortly after he stopped talking to me, he also started asking me out.

"Then I asked you out." He shakes his head. "You probably thought I was crazy."

Crazy? No, all I remember is my stomach churning at the thought of going out with Luke *Smith*. Something inside of me rebelled at the idea of getting romantically involved with him. When he made me believe he was my brother, I thought I'd figured out why the idea of being his girlfriend gave me the creeps. Now, it seems, there are other, far more twisted reasons for my revulsion.

"Zara couldn't understand why you rejected me. She thought you should be attracted to me, should feel the connection between us, the way I did. She kept insisting I ask you out, and I did, but I could only take so many *nos*. After that, I resented you, though I kept telling Zara I was doing my best to win you over. I was angry and felt . . ." he looks skyward, licks his lips, ". . . used. For a while, I decided that Hailstone's plans for us weren't my own. I mean, that's quite a thing to unload on a couple of kids: *the furthering of a new species.* I hit quite a rebellious streak, for a time."

"Aw, you poor thing. But it seems you've had a change of heart, hmm? I bet mommy was proud."

"A lot has happened since then," Luke says angrily, his blue eyes flashing with rancor.

"Not on this side of the world. It's still all just a bunch of *nos* over here."

"Maybe when you stop and think about the situation, you'll change your—"

"Fat chance!"

Luke ignores me and keeps going. "Your mind. This world is not as it used to be and *nos* aren't what'll help you survive."

"Is that a threat?"

"No." Luke shakes his head. "It's not a threat, just reality. You have little chance of survival out there, Marci. You need our protection."

"I'm doing swell on my own, thank you."

And there's no way in hell I'll make babies with you, you sick bastard!

Just then it hits me, if I'm a different species wouldn't all the DNA tests Kristen ran on me have shown that? My mind reels, trying to remember the different analyses she's performed on me since I joined IgNiTe. If she'd found something wrong, she would have mentioned it, right?

Right?!

They've kept so many secrets from me lately that I have to wonder. Would they share such findings with me? Or would they save the information to themselves?

"Things could be better for you," Luke says.

"They *were* better, and your kind screwed that up."

"Zara, Elliot and all The Takeover leaders belong to a different generation. Eklyptors have craved for this for a very long time, longer than you and I can understand. They have struggled to survive, to take a foothold. They rose from nothing and built their numbers at an excruciating pace, while humans reproduced faster than rabbits."

His comment angers me, but it's hard to argue with our reproduction rate, so I take a different approach. "And you think that gives you the right to do this?"

"It's not about having the right to do anything. It's about being able to do it. Humans know that very well. So they want to make shark fin soup . . . then why not catch a bunch of sharks, cut their fins and throw them back into the ocean to die? So they can sell ivory for a huge profit . . . why not hunt elephants to near extinction? So they can pollute and destroy the planet . . . why not dump chemicals into rivers and kill the rain forest? So they can cage specimens of every species for their own amusement . . . why not open a zoo or a circus and charge for admission? I could go on all night, and you know it."

How can I argue with any of this? How can I say "it wasn't me, I didn't do any of those things"? It was our responsibility to stop it, and we didn't.

Luke takes a step closer. "So we can take residence in human brains and make better use of their bodies . . . then why not take them over? Why not cage them and save them from their self-destructive behavior?"

"All right, I don't need a biology lesson. Survival of the fittest and all, I get it. Just don't count us out so easily. We're not going down without a fight. There are people with their own brains working to find a solution, and they will. It's just a matter of time."

"You are not one of them, Marci." Luke's mouth stretches with an almost imperceptible smile of satisfaction. "That is where you go wrong. And we're not Eklyptors either. We are the best of both species. We can create a new world, a better world. I can alter my DNA to get rid of disease. Did you know that? We could have new generations with no cancer, no genetic inequalities of any kind. No more blind or deaf people. Everyone could develop whatever skills they want, anything that makes them happy. They could look however they wanted. Just imagine that for a moment."

"It sounds mighty boring."

Luke gives me a court laugh. "Is that the best you can do? Boring? All that means is you don't have an argument against the eradication of disease and the utopia of equality. And who would? Aren't those the things the most altruistic humans have been trying to achieve for a long time?"

"Fine, whatever. Go and try to build your new world, but leave me out of it. I'm not like you. I *am* human."

"There's no denying it. Something is different, but you are definitely not human."

"Bullshit!"

"Dunn conducted several in-utero tests, Marci. Our DNAs are unique."

"No. That's a lie."

James would have told me.
James would have told me.

Luke's eyes fill with sympathy as if I'm a child and he's just stolen my lollipop. "I'm sorry you have to learn things this way, but if you give it time, I know you'll come to terms with it."

"You say you don't want me to change because you like me as I am. Well, let me tell you something, you don't know me at all. I would never come to terms with this. It's unnatural, wrong. One twisted man made this happened. He played god and went and messed with something he had no business messing with. I will not be part of this. You and whoever else Dunn managed to *GMO* can go give your boring utopia a try. You can count me out."

Luke's face tightens ever so slightly. I watch him closely, trying to figure out what the subtle expression means. His face is so smooth it's hard to tell. Is he hiding something? Did some part of what I said hit a sore spot?

Something dawns on me. "There aren't any others." I intended it to be a question, but it comes out flat. He made it sound as if there were more experiments after the one that created us, but they must not have worked. We're the only ones!

Luke's silence serves as my answer.

I laugh. "So you're basing this whole scheme on two people. One of them being me? You have got to be kidding me!"

He doesn't look amused in the least.

"Talk about poor planning."

"It's not a simple matter. Dunn kept trying up until the day he died, but it appears we were an accident. Not much different from humans or any other species that has ever been," he says this with a hint of pride in his voice.

"Not different from Frankenstein either," I say.

"Or you might compare us to Adam and Eve, if you're into fiction," he says.

"You're insane."

"For wanting a better world than what Eklyptors can create? We are better than them. Better than humans."

"No, for believing this scheme will work. It won't." My face flushes with the effort of containing my emotions.

"Is it that bad, Marci?"

"Bad and impossible. I will never be part of this."

"You will see the good in it. You just need time to think about it."

His arrogance makes him blind.

My hand clenches around the gun. The tips of my fingers relish the handle's pitted surface. I could shoot him between the eyes and his precious dream would disappear. It would all be gone in the blink of an eye.

His little science experiment would never go anywhere without him or . . . without me.

I lift the gun to my temple. "I'd rather die."

Chapter 21

For the first time, the expression on Luke's smooth face tells me something with clarity.

He's terrified.

"Marci, what are you doing?! Put the gun down."

"Stay out of the way. I'm leaving."

Luke moves both hands in a pacifying gesture. "Please, the gun could go off by accident. This isn't a game."

"Who says I'm playing?"

Tauro and Mega Simba perk up and move closer, also looking concerned about my choice of escape plan. Well, will you look at that?! It seems being willing to die has its advantages. They're finally taking me seriously.

"Tell your hench-creatures to stay out of the way." My gaze remains locked with Luke's, trying to make him understand this isn't a joke. If he's not getting the message loud and clear, he's not only too pretty he's also blind *and* deaf. In the past, I've been willing to die for much less than this.

For a moment, he just stands there, his blue eyes searching my face. Finally, he says, "Tauro, Leo, move back. Marci

157

and I still have things to discuss."

I wait until they step back before saying, "I have nothing more to discuss with you. You either let me go or I'll stay right here . . . forever." I stamp a boot against the pavement and press the gun into my temple a little harder. The end of the barrel digs into the tender area in an all-too-enticing manner. What would be so awful about dying? What is there to live for in this new, terrifying world?

Aydan's dark, intense eyes come to mind. I blink, surprised, and push the notion away. He's not a good enough reason to stick around. No one is. People leave, die or get turned into Eklyptors. And when they're gone, you're worse off than before, wondering why the hell you bothered to keep on fighting.

"You wouldn't hurt yourself," Luke says in a reasonable tone that implies he knows me.

I laugh. "Try me." I begin to squeeze the trigger. A shiver slides down my spine, enticing me further.

Luke's face goes pale. "Okay, okay." He steps back and extends a hand toward the Jetta's open door. His eyes flick to Tauro in a desperate plea. I have no idea what he expects him to do, but I don't hesitate. I move toward the Jetta, gun still angled against my head.

"It's a risk to let you go. You have to realize that," Luke says.

"I won't tell anyone where you are." It's the fattest lie I've ever told, but I make it sound very convincing. Luke seems to believe me.

"We are not gullible, Marci," Tauro says.

I bet Luke would miss his little plane. Maybe his trust for me is enough to keep him here. He's the boss, after all. If they leave, it doesn't matter. This excursion already proved worthwhile.

Wasting no more time, I angle my body to get into the Jetta, but I don't get far. A strident shot blasts right next to my head. My ears ring. The gun flies from my hand, skids across the hood and clatters to the ground on the other side.

In spite of the jolt, my instincts respond with cold precision. Lighting fast, I jump into the car, slam the door shut and start the engine. The car lurches forward. Luke jumps forward and bangs his fist against the window and yells at me to stop. I ignore him and, instead, concentrate on the barrier ahead as well as the huge, leaping feline with a taste for imported coupes. Through the rearview mirror, I can see that Mega Simba is already on the move, his long strides cutting the intervening distance between us without effort.

Shit!

What made me think this would go any better than the last time?

Same car. Same Mega Simba.

Only crazy people expect different results when the input variables are the same.

As I speed past the exit, foot to the metal, the Jetta crashes through the gate and sends it flying up in the air. I check the rearview mirror again and see that Mega Simba looks twice as big now. I lean more heavily on the accelerator, but it's useless. I've already floored it.

The engine strains. The odometer already reads thirty and climbing. But this is no sports car, and it's struggling.

"C'mon, c'mon!" I shake the wheel as if the car's asleep, and I'm trying to wake it up.

Desperately, my gaze flicks back to the rearview mirror. My heart leaps as I see Leo flying through the air in his final leap to stomp me to a halt for once and for all. With a sudden jerk, I twist the wheel to the left. In spite of the maneuver, I still expect to feel a thump against the Jetta, but there isn't one.

Again, I look for the beast in the rearview. Nothing. I glance back through the side mirrors. Still nothing. I crane my neck, peer over my shoulder, and finally spot him. He's on the ground, lying on his side, inert. My thoughts bend out of shape, trying to figure out what just happened.

Nothing comes to mind. The loud thumping of my heart, the revving engine, and blurring lampposts at my sides fill my senses—not to mention the darkness in the small rectangle of the rearview where my eyes are glued, expecting to spot pursuers.

I'm not sure why, but they don't come. Maybe they can't retrieve their cars fast enough. Maybe they're too busy helping their pet lion. Maybe Luke ordered them to leave me alone. This last possibility stands out from the rest. I imagine he still thinks I'll come around after some time processing the news. Good thing he's so deluded!

It isn't until I'm a few miles away from SeaTac that I think of a logical explanation for Mega Simba's collapse.

Aydan!

Aydan and his magic electroshock must have happened. But does that mean he gave himself away to help me? God, I hope he didn't.

Chapter 22

"Repurposing, I was repurposing. Wanted to get me some cool wheels. Yep," I say in my crazy Azrael speech. I'm back in the barracks at Elliot's headquarters, trying my best to keep it together while Onyx practically interrogates me.

"And did you?" Leaning against one corner of my desk, Onyx pulls up the tube shirt she's wearing. Her boob-growing efforts are paying off. She's graduated from mosquito bites to golf balls, much like a prepubescent girl. She still hates the male body she got stuck with and is bent on morphing herself into a curvaceous vixen. She's nothing but determined.

I dig in my backpack and take out the sealable bags with Dad's t-shirts in them. I set them on my desk and lovingly lay a hand on them. The plastic crinkles.

"Nope, nope. Didn't find what I wanted. Won't rest till I do, though."

I have to go out again, have to talk to James, have to know if he's been lying to me, have to find out if Aydan is all right?

161

Aydan, what did you do?!

No one came after me, not another beast, not another car. Wondering what happened is killing me. I almost turned around a million times as I drove out of SeaTac but, instead, I kept my foot on the gas and told myself I had no other choice. I can't fall in Hailstone's clutches again—not after learning what I've learned. This has never been about me or Aydan or any one person. And now that I know their plans, much less so.

"What exactly are you looking for?" Onyx smacks her purple-painted lips and dabs a finger against the corners of her mouth. She adjusts her top again. It's stripped with hot pink and white horizontal lines.

"A Harley. Supped up, shiny, no scratches." My answer is clipped as I sit in front of my computer. I need to send James a message, but I can't do that while Onyx sits here wiggling inside her blouse and using me as entertainment to relieve her boredom. It's not my fault her life as the head cook of Elliot's private army has lost its luster, and she'd rather spend the day learning new make-up tricks to hide her stubborn mustache.

I wake up my computer and fire off *Space Invaders*. Hoping to send a clear bug-off message, I begin playing the game, banging on the keyboard at a frantic rate and making inane shooting sounds.

Onyx tries to make further conversation, but I ignore her. After several attempts, she huffs. "You and that stupid game." With a hurt expression, she gets up and walks away, her four-inch heels clicking as she exits the barracks.

Just as I get ready to send James's message. Lyra strolls in. I notice her out of the corner of my eyes, her strides confident and lithe. I curse inwardly and pull up the video game once more. I wouldn't normally hide my IgNiTe related activities from her, but this is different.

If she finds out what I now know, she would make good on her promise to kill me. She's been working for years to defeat Hailstone and discover their grand plan. If she gets even a whiff of the role I play in that stupid scheme, she'd slice my throat before I have time to count her whiskers.

"Where have you been, Cher?" Lyra asks, sitting on my bed and flicking her penetrating green eyes to the game on the computer screen.

"Out and about," I say.

Her ears flicker, which I've learned happens when something bothers her.

"I met James," I add in a low voice, choosing to give her a bit of the truth before she decides I'm up to something. She has a very suspicious nature. So cat-like of her!

"What about?"

"I hadn't seen him since the battle here. He wanted to thank me . . . for saving him, you know." It's true enough. I saved James from that curly-horned Amazon after she shot him in the chest. He would have died under her gun if I hadn't intervened. Come to think of it, I also saved him from Tusks, and his crazy jeep stunt. It took that much to convince James that I was still me and not the crazy Eklyptor who killed Oso.

"Ah, oui."

Just to make sure Lyra stuffs her questions, I give her a bit more information. "He took my blood. They're going to try to develop a test so they can tell whether or not I'm still me."

Lyra makes a very French dismissing gesture with her hand. "Why bother? You're the only one of your kind. I'm

163

fairly certain no one has come back from full-fledged. You are a freak." She laughs, her pointed canine teeth touching her lower lip.

"Says the human kitten." I flip her the bird without even deigning a look in her direction.

"Well, try not to disappear again. Lamia has been riding mon derrière, asking where you are. You know she doesn't trust you. Today she pointed out that you were out when those scouts were killed. You didn't have anything to do with that, non?"

"Umm . . . I might have."

"Oh, mon Dieu! Tu es folle?!"

"Yeah, you too, lady." I have no idea what she just said, but it sounded like an insult. For good measure, I flip her the bird again. "Just FYI, the scouts had captured a girl. I couldn't let them take her. Maybe you would have, but not me."

Lyra drops her angry expression, and her eyes become rounder and bigger. She almost looks cute. "I would not. Every human life is worth a battle. Je suis désolé." Head lowered, she stands and lets me be.

Her contrite reaction and apology surprise me and make me wonder if there's a person she wished she could have battled for.

I watch her leave. Her back is slightly hunched and her nose pointed to the floor. She's so dejected she doesn't even notice Lamia as they pass each other by the door. The lizard woman gives Lyra a contemptuous look, but her worthy effort is wasted. Lyra exists as if her steps will take her into a different dimension, one very far away from this one.

Finding herself ignored, Lamia's eyes search the barracks for another victim. Her toxic levels of disdain are too highly curated to go to waste. Unfortunately, I'm one of her favorite targets. Her gaze flies directly to mine, even though my bed is at the very back of the large sleeping quarters.

Her long, barbed tail goes up behind her in a sort of threat or challenge. Which? It makes no difference to me. I don't have time for her ass. I turn to the computer and ignore her, even as I feel her mean gaze like a poke on my side.

Quickly, I type a message for James, send it, and go back to playing my game.

I hope he'll understand the urgency in every word of my short message.

WE. NEED. TO. TALK. IMMEDIATELY!

Chapter 23

An hour later, I come to, thrashing on the floor of a closet, rattling old brooms with my out-of-control feet. I gasp for air and clutch my throat, struggling for breath. My thoughts blend into each other, then separate into completely different paths. Azrael and her shadows chase them in vain, though, for a moment, she almost had me.

Groaning, I sit and push by back to the wall. My flashlight lies on the floor, its bright beam pointed toward the back of the cramped space. Eyes closed, head thrown back, I take deep breaths. Feeling blindly, I reach for the chocolate bar I set on top of an overturned metal bucket. The wrapper crinkles as I tear it open. I take a bite and let the chocolate and caramel melt in my mouth.

Stupid. Very stupid, my sane internal voice says. The crazy one, the one that convinced me to try medication on my own disagrees. *You're still here, aren't you?* it boasts.

"Yep, still here. You heard that, Azrael? I'm still here!" My voice cracks. I press a trembling hand to my mouth and take a deep breath. I'm drained—nothing to boast about.

The decision to do this wasn't easy. James answered my message and agreed to meet me by the Seattle Great Wheel tomorrow evening. The anticipation left me restless and full of a nagging energy that begged for something to do. I guess it didn't have to be something this dangerous, but it's not like I have choices. So I came here an hour ago, determined to grab this terrifying bull by the horns. My matador skills leave something to be desired, though, because it took me thirty minutes to simply convince myself to close my eyes and start the breathing exercises.

My t-shirt is drenched in sweat from the effort and . . . the fear, I admit. Being chased by the shadows terrifies me, and it's not an idle terror. It's jagged, sharp, determined and unrelenting. For over ten years, I've fought against it by scurrying away, filling my head with random, impossible-to-trace thoughts. Clearing my mind in meditation goes against all I know, even if an empty mind is a better punishment for the agent than one full of garbage.

The problem is that completely erasing all thoughts is difficult, and failing to do it quickly invites head-on attacks which are known to leave me twitching like a dismembered lizard's tail. The assaults are brutal, a bitch to overcome. I've always needed help. So attempting this alone wasn't only stupid, it was suicidal. But I had to. I can't trust anyone here, not even Lyra.

So was it worth the risk? Sensible Marci asks.

Only one way to find out.

After a deep breath, I stare at the metal bucket. It practically stares back, mockingly. My every tendon and muscle tenses with the effort. My eyes sting and water, but I don't blink. I go on staring, imagining laser beams shooting out of my eyes as if I'm freaking Supergirl.

Just when I'm about to admit that taking this risk deserves a Darwin Award, the bucket makes a small, rattling sound. My heart leaps with excitement. A smile curves my lips.

Well, I guess it *was* worth it.

Leaps and bounds might truly be a thing.

Guess who now has a daily date with the broom closet and the risk of eternal imprisonment?

Chapter 24

The dilapidated sight of Pike Place Market drives a stake through my heart. The iconic sign over the front is charred, its large letters barely discernible. The front stalls which used to house several well-stocked fish vendors are completely destroyed, their shelves and counters torn to pieces or entirely missing, leaving behind nothing but ghosts of what used to be.

I move closer, hands deep in pockets, boots hovering over the debris of a past I desperately ache for. My pack is strapped to my back, Dad's t-shirts stashed safely inside once more. It's ridiculous, but they feel like some sort of treasure, and you don't abandon treasure in the place where your enemies sleep.

Jagged pieces of wood, fish carcasses, torn tarps and more clutter the sidewalks. I pass Pier 63 and the aquarium, walking south until I reach the Seattle Great Wheel which is located on Pier 57. The thing is huge, stretching 175 feet into the air. I wonder if it still is the tallest Ferris wheel in the west coast. Its massive metal shape stands out against the darkening sky, looking like the wheel of a giant bicycle. It doesn't appear damaged, but, for the life of me, I can't picture it moving, making passengers exclaim in delight over the grandeur of Elliot Bay. What a waste. What a sad waste.

A cool breeze caresses my face, blows my hair into the wind. My eyes close of their own accord. I inhale and listen to the lapping water. When my head begins to buzz, I don't freak out. Though it's just come into perceivable range, I know the buzzing belongs to James. The more I pay attention, the more I can discern the subtle differences between mental signals. James's is tempered, barely there. Not weak, per se, but controlled, as if he has managed to shackle his agent—not unlikely, considering his advanced skills.

"Hello, James," I say without turning back.

"Is that your ESP talking," he asks, closing the distance between us in less than a shaved second.

"No."

He makes a sound in the back of his throat, unhappy with my clipped answer.

I sigh. "After Azrael, I can perceive differences in the buzzing." I don't like to remind him of my weakness, of what I did to his friend.

"Is that so?"

"I'm pretty sure the buzzing communicates rank."

"Interesting." James stands next to me, nodding and gazing into the distance. "Learned any other useful things?"

"Just that you don't ever want to be eclipsed. It really sucks. Even if you make it out, you might not be able to live with yourself."

"You already know I don't blame you, so it's time you stop blaming yourself."

"I know. I'm trying."

"You'll get there. It takes time." He says it as if he knows from experience. After a quiet moment, he shakes his head as if to dispel a memory. "So what's the emergency."

"How is Aydan?" It's the most pressing question in my mind.

"Aydan?" James's eyes narrow, his expression growing angry. He must think I made him come all this way just to ask him about Aydan. "I haven't heard from him in a few days," he concedes.

Damn!

"Is that why—?" James begins, but I interrupt him.

"No."

I inhale deeply and prepare myself to ask my second most pressing question. A helpless feeling washes over me. I don't want to hate this man. He and IgNiTe are the only things keeping me sane. If I lose them, what will I have left?

"I've been to Hailstone headquarters," I begin.

James looks over at me for the first time. "SeaTac?"

I nod.

"How did you find out?"

"I went back to my house. It was stupid. I should have known Luke might be waiting for that. He showed up, said he wanted to talk to me, that there was something important I ought to understand. Long story short, I followed him. Then I was stupid again and got caught." I scoff. "He . . . told me something that . . ." My voice goes hoarse. I clear my throat.

James angles his shoulders in my direction, his attention fully engaged.

I can't continue on the same train of thought, so I shift directions. "Tell me something, James, did Kristen ever noticed anything strange about my DNA?"

"Besides the Symbiot markers, you mean?" He sounds puzzled, bewildered even.

The pressure I've been carrying in my chest since the moment Luke told me we're the sole members of a new species eases a little. "Yeah, besides that."

"No, she didn't."

"If she'd found something more, would she hide it from you?"

"Absolutely not," he sounds as sure as ever. "What are you driving at, Marci?"

I finally turn and face him. His sharp, gray eyes are dark under his pinched brow. "Luke says we're not human, that the embryos we grew from were genetically modified and spliced with an agent. He says we're a new species, says we were created to . . . help Eklyptors get rid of the need for hosts." I laugh dryly. "He thinks we are the future of a brand new world." My face feels hot. Sharing this is not easy. It makes me feel oddly soiled and low.

James opens his mouth, then closes it again. He's speechless, and it's definitely a first.

Without giving him a chance to recover, I tell him everything. About Zara being my mother, about Dunn's failed attempts to create more . . . what? . . . I hate to think of the names people might come up with. As hard as it is, I tell him everything and leave nothing out. He listens without interrupting, his frown deepening with every horrible twist of the story.

When I'm done, he nods and begins to pace in front of me, hands interlaced at his back. I wait, impatience bubbling in my chest like carbonation from a canned drink. I clench and unclench my fists, try to use my powers to push a discarded bottle off the pier. I get so lost in the effort that when it finally scoots along a couple of inches, I've managed to relegate James to the back of my mind. After who knows how long, his deep voice startles me back into the moment.

"How did you escape?" he asks.

I frown, puzzled by his question. What of the genetic mumbo jumbo I just laid out in from of him? Does he not have questions about that?

"Aydan," I say simply.

"I figured that much. And he stayed behind?"

I nod. "I tried to convince him to leave with me, but . . ."

"We all make sacrifices. I'm sure you understand that better than anyone. I'll try to get in touch with him as soon as I can."

I lower my gaze to the wooden planks at my feet. I guess I do understand Aydan's sacrifice, but I'd still rather see the people I care about away from danger. At the thought, something stirs inside of me. I've never admitted to myself that I care about him. But I do. I didn't use to be able to stand him and now I would do anything to keep him safe.

"I need to you come with me," James says.

My eyes snap back up in surprise. His face is serious. I swallow, unable to believe what I'm hearing. Does he mean to take me to IgNiTe's hideout? Even though I've always felt it was my obligation to go back to Whitehouse, I've hope for this for a very long time. Night after night, I've stared up at the ceiling, wondering what the crew is doing, wishing I could be with them. And now . . .

"Where?" I ask, doubt creeping in.

"Can't tell you." He removes the bandanna he carries around his neck. "And I can't let you see either. You'll have to cover your eyes."

Chapter 25

"Give me your hand," James says.

I extend a hand toward the sound of his voice. He takes it gently and helps me off his Harley. We rode for over a half an hour to get wherever we are. He was going fast, though, his bike hugging the curves on the road while I held on to the backrest behind me.

Now we've arrived, and I have no idea where he's taken me. The bandanna pressed against my eyes is making me strangely desperate. This blindness reminds me too much of being trapped inside my own head, of Azrael controlling my body and chasing me through the endless corridors of my consciousness.

James tucks my hand under his elbow and leads me forward. "We're almost there," he reassures me.

I splay the fingers of my free hand against my side in an effort not to yank the blindfold off my face. With my sight impaired in this manner, my other senses sharpen. The wind blows, creating the rustle of many trees. I inhale and identify the fresh scent of pine trees. The sense of being away from the city, close to some sort of forest, fills me with a strange calm. My shoulders relax. My every breath seems to count more than in the middle of the city where the quest for survival makes you feel like there isn't enough oxygen in the air to keep you alive.

A metallic knock brings me back to the now. A small squeak follows.

"That you, James?" someone asks. "Who you got there?"

"A friend," he says.

"Your hand."

There's a short silence, then another small squeak as something closes.

"No password?" I ask in an half-amused tone, knowing how useless that would be since Eklyptors know everything their hosts do.

James scoff at that. "There are a few security measures in place that we check before we let anyone in. Forgive me if I can't tell you about them."

"I see. Don't worry. I get it. After . . . The Tank, it's a wonder you trust me enough to bring me here."

"As a matter of fact, only a few people know exactly where we are. Everyone else comes and goes in a blindfold. We keep our various locations as secret as possible because many worry about a mole sneaking in. They don't know some of us would be able to tell an Eklyptor from a human, though we still test everyone, just to be safe. My biggest worry is Symbiots going full-fledged."

Like me.

"But we get tested, too. They just took my blood. Anyone else who transmits a buzzing signal gets a bullet to the head."

"They didn't take *my* blood," I point out.

"Don't worry. If I pass, they know I've already tested you and you're good."

A loud *clank*—a bolt opening?—breaks our conversation.

"Walking through a door, now," James pushes me ahead.

As I walk in, there's a change in the air: a cagey smell, a closed-in resonance. Behind me, the door is secured once more.

"Let me take this off." James pulls the bandanna off.

I blink and place a hand over my brow to block the bright lights that seem to shine straight into my eyeballs. When my eyes adjust, I'm faced with a sight that sends a weakening tremor down my legs.

"Welcome to our humble . . . warehouse," James says.

The area is expansive both in width and length. As we step forward, dozens of tired faces turn up and look at us. I estimate there are over one hundred people here. A few greet James, but most just sit listlessly on the concrete floor or lie on low cots. Naked light bulbs hang from the tall ceiling, a structure of inter-crossing, rusted metal beams. Round cement columns stand every ten feet or so. They make two long files, helping support the expansive roof.

A group of children huddles in a circle, squatting low to the ground. They draw with small pieces of chalk, playing in a subdued, almost careful fashion, as if boisterous games are too much for this fragile environment.

My steps are weak, my glances furtive and full of chagrin. I don't know what I had in mind, what I thought I'd find here, but it wasn't this. I guess I'd imagined a place more like The Tank, which is absolutely stupid. This is war, not a retreat during worry-free times. This might be the end, and this is how the end looks for us.

"We have mostly civilians here," James explains. "There

are similar hideouts throughout the state, and separate places for the people who are fighting."

When the kids notice James, they leave their game and rush in our direction.

"James James James!" they all say at the same time, their young voices loud and clear. They surround him, practically trip him.

James bumps fists with them and ruffles their hair. "No goodies today, guys. Sorry."

"Oh, bummer." They drop their shoulders and walk away with exaggerated disappointment.

"I bring them candy whenever I can get my hands on it," James explains, looking a bit embarrassed about his soft spot for the kids.

For the first time since I met him, I wonder if he has kids of his own, and the thought makes me feel callous and self-centered. I know little about his family. I've always suspected he's in love with Kristen, but I could very well be wrong about that. Maybe he's married to someone else. Maybe he has kids. If he does, they must be here. I look around as if I'll spot a woman with a boy bouncing on her knee—a kid that will have James's stormy gray eyes.

When we make it to the end of the long warehouse, we walk through another door into a smaller section of the building that makes me feel as if I've crossed the threshold into a different universe. The contrast between the area I just left and this is shocking. This room is clean and bright, illuminated by strategically placed halogen lights. Far in the back, a rectangular, clear tent is set up, isolating a portion of the room.

"James!" Kristen steps out of the tent through a zippered door and walks into his arms. She clings to his neck, eyes squeezed shut, face etched in relief. He rests his cheek on her red hair and runs his hand lovingly down her back.

Well, I guess this answers my question. I look away, feeling rather awkward, and focus my attention past the clear tent walls. From the looks of it, they have managed to set up a nice lab for Kristen, not as sophisticated as what she had in The Tank, but not bad. There are state of the art microscopes, computers, centrifuges and many other machines that escape my understanding and vocabulary.

"Hello, Marci," Kristen says.

My eyes snap back and meet with her sharp, green gaze. "Kristen," I say. All the awkwardness that's ever existed between us suddenly falls upon my shoulders.

"There's been an interesting development." James drives straight to the point. "We need to talk."

"Okay." Kristen points to a group of metal chairs positioned right outside the tent.

As soon as we're seated, James jumps into a detailed, but concise explanation of everything I told him. He stops a few times when he needs me to clarify something but, for the most part, he does all the talking. Kristen, for her part, listens without interrupting. She remains quiet through the entire account, her face stoic and showing little reaction besides a curious spark in the depths of her eyes.

When James finishes, he extends both hands, palms up, to indicate everything has been laid out in the open. I regard him with pinch eyebrows, wondering why he didn't ask what I must wish to know: is my DNA human or not? As if understanding my puzzlement, he gives me a reassuring glance that seems to ask me to be patient.

He's up to something. I frown harder at him, and, after a moment, it dawns on me. He's trying to build trust between us. If he doesn't prompt Kristen, whatever she says next will have more validity.

Kristen nods to herself and ponders before speaking. Finally, she says, "This is quite a story, one I would quickly laugh at, if it came from a different source. But . . ." She shakes her head and stands, her expression a testament on the many thoughts that must be bouncing through her head.

"I've run countless tests on Marci," she says, pacing to one side.

I hold my breath, even though a wave of relief has already begun to wash over me.

She continues, "And unless they're all wrong, she *is* human."

My lungs deflate, releasing my pent up breath.

"A Symbiot, of course," she adds, "but perfectly human otherwise. Which is . . ." She paces back, her thumb caressing her lower lip as she gets lost in thought.

"Talk to us, Kristen," James says in a gentle, mildly amused tone.

She ignores him and continues to pace. James and I exchange a glance.

"I need to run more tests!" Kristen suddenly exclaims, startling us.

"What for?" I demand, going from briefly feeling human to feeling like a lab rat.

"Considering who this information comes from," she walks closer, her gaze intense and determined, "we need to take it seriously. We need to believe the embryo you came from was, in truth, comprised of a combination of human and Eklyptor DNA." Her gaze dances back and forth between James and me, a restless excitement, building, building, with every word she utters. "And if that's the case, we need to ask ourselves why your DNA is now perfectly human and how you managed to separate yourself from the agent."

"Oh," James says in a drawn out breath. He rubs his bald head, his mouth hanging open.

"What? You think that's what happened?" This is crazy talk.

Kristen squats in front of me, presses long fingers to my knee. "Do you believe what Luke told you?"

I stare at her hand, the half-moons of her cuticles. "I—I . . ."

"Do you doubt it at all?" she presses.

I shake my head. "I believe him."

"I *know* there's nothing inhuman about your DNA. Nothing. And the only way those two things are possible," she pauses and lowers her voice to a near triumphant growl, "is if you somehow extirpated the intruder from your genome."

Chapter 26

After giving Kristen a third of my blood and a sack full of tissue samples, James takes me back to the main area and introduces me to a few people. They greet me courteously, but cautiously. I know the reasons they must distrust strangers and, in that sense, I find that being here isn't much different than being at Elliot's. Over there, everyone suspects you might be a Symbiot. Here, plain humans have no way of telling who is an Eklyptor and who isn't, so they must be wary of everyone.

People around us begin to look more alert. They stand, stretch and leave their cots.

James checks his watch. "Are you hungry? We don't have much to offer, but you're welcome to whatever they're serving for dinner."

"No, I'm fine, thank you." I lower my head, feeling horrible. At Elliot's, food has never been an issue beyond the inconvenient scarcity of a few items. In fact, I've eaten very well, better than I used to before The Takeover. My diet is well-balanced, with plenty of vegetables and fruits—

none of the instant noodles or TV dinners that I used to "cook" when there was nothing else to eat around the house.

James puts a hand on my shoulder. "Your sacrifice needs not include going hungry. It goes way beyond something that small. Remember that."

I try to shape my face into a blank mask. I hate being read so easily. Besides, sacrifices can't be measured. Who is to put a price on what a person gives up?

Everyone forms a single file along the left wall, then disappears through a narrow door on the side of the warehouse.

"We connected this building with the one next door," James says. "We serve two meals a day. Breakfast and dinner. Not optimal, but no one's starving. For now. Your tips on supplies have been extremely helpful. Thank to you we have intercepted several food trucks headed for Eklyptor bases. Those provisions have made a huge difference."

I knew they needed the food. James had told me so, but I never imagined—

"Marci?"

A girl approaches me from the side, her steps tentative.

I don't recognize her at first glance but, after a couple of seconds, her name takes shape in my lips: "Hannah."

She gives me a huge smile and, as if unable to help herself, walks up to where I am and wraps me in a tight hug. I stand stiff as a rod and awkwardly pat her back.

Hannah pulls away after a moment, avoiding eye contact, the same way I do. "It's good to see you," she says. "I never thanked you for—"

"Hey, don't mention it," I rush out the words, wishing to put an end to the awkwardness.

"Hannah has turned out to be a great nurse," James says.

"She helps patch people up with some sort of magic that makes them heal pretty quickly."

Her cheeks redden, and her blue eyes light up with the compliment. James gives me a quick wink that makes me realize the Symbiot secret is still safe here, otherwise Hannah would know about our accelerated healing powers.

James is about to add something when a loud, metallic knock reverberates through the warehouse. I jump. My hand flies to my gun. James takes a step forward, his shoulders tense, his stance meaningful, threatening. His piercing gray eyes are intent on the door through which we came in. Hannah and everyone still in the room stares at the door with wide eyes, frozen on the spot.

After checking through the small window on the door and testing what I assume are blood samples, the guards call out, "All clear!"

James's shoulders lower at the exhale. Hannah takes a deep breath and allows a smile to her lips. A low murmur of relief fills the warehouse. The dread these people live in is palpable. As impossible as it seems, my hatred for Eklyptors intensifies. They have reduced us to a bunch of scared rabbits, burrowing in the depths of whatever hole we can find.

The door opens with a *clank,* two people in blindfolds step in, followed by two others. It takes me a moment to process the sense of relief that washes over me.

Aydan!

I take an involuntary step forward.

Blare and Clark are with Aydan and Rheema—she's the second blindfolded person. Blare removes the covers from around their heads. Aydan rubs his eyes and blinks. They're unfocused, at first, but as soon as they recover, they zero in

183

on me. Even from this distance, I see his relief, a mirror of mine. He smiles, his eyes narrowing in a sign of contentment.

Without hesitation, he crosses the distance between us. I think he's going to embrace me like Hannah did, but he stops abruptly, only three paces from where I stand.

James's gaze goes from Aydan to me and back again. A current passes between us. It feels like electricity, and it's so intense, I wonder if James can sense it, too.

"What are you doing here?" James asks. "You weren't due back yet." There is a slight note of humor in his voice, as if he already knows the answer.

To his credit, Aydan manages the situation with a cool demeanor. "Nothing now, I suppose. I imagine Marci has already given a full report."

"Indeed she has," James answers with a smile.

Rheema, Blare, and Clark step behind Aydan and stare at me in surprise.

My eyes lock with Clark's. I haven't seen him since the day Xave died. Laying eyes on him opens many old wounds in a single blow. He looks so much like his brother, tall and strong. And his eyes—even though they're gray and not hazel—are the same in every other way: their shape, their expressiveness, the way they change color with each emotion.

"Marci," he says my name with such longing that it breaks my heart. Apparently, my wounds aren't the only ones that have opened up, recalling the painful memories of a past that haunts us.

"If it isn't our favorite little spy," Blare says, her specialized brand of sarcasm seemingly improved with time—like a good wine. Her once jet-black hair is now half blond from the roots. There are a few extra piercings on her brow and her military-style clothes have been altered to fit her emo look. There are leather buckles wrapped around her legs, threaded through holes in the pants. She wears a hot pink belt and a matching shirt under fatigues, so not the type of clothes I would imagine an explosives expert wearing.

"Blare," James pronounces her name as a warning.

Her mouth twists in disgust. For a moment, she looks ready to tear me apart but, in the end, she spins on her heel and leaves.

"Don't mind her," Rheema says and gives me a light, welcoming hug. "She was already bitter before all of this, now she's just plain evil. It's good to see you." Rhemma was always friendly with me and that doesn't seem to have changed. Last time I saw her, she was fixing a Harley for me. I wonder what happened to it. She's IgNiTe's mechanic and keep all vehicles and equipment running in tip-top shape.

"Thank you. Same here." I return her hug, appreciating her warmth.

For a moment, we stand awkwardly, at a complete loss for words. Hannah wrings the seam of her oversized t-shirt between nervous fingers. Her big, blue eyes glance furtively at Aydan. But his gaze never leaves my face.

He looks like someone who's holding back a million words, all charged with the meaning of a million more. He makes me feel afraid that anything I say won't be enough.

Chapter 27

A while later, Clark and I are in the dining area, standing apart from everyone else. He reluctantly releases me from a tight hug. He regards me with infinite sadness, and I feel as if he sees his brother in me, the way I do in him. We each possess memories of Xave that no one else does which makes me wish I could meld my mind into his. I imagine he feels the same: a desperate need to construct a complete version of the boy we lost.

"Thanks for talking to them." Clark looks over his shoulder to where his family sits at a cheap wooden table, eating dinner.

We are in the dining area. The room is packed, with most people sitting on the floor, plates on their laps. There are few tables, all mismatched, probably salvaged from picnic areas, patios, and restaurants. In the back of the rectangular room, three folding tables serve as a food counter. A few helpers stand behind them, ladling small portions of food as people present their cardboard plates.

"No problem," I say.

It wasn't easy talking to Xave's parents and little sister, but it was the least I could do. I told them how brave he was, how hard he fought to defeat this evil. When he was killed, his family couldn't make sense out of his sudden death. It wasn't until The Takeover that Clark was able to explain how Xave had died. Knowing made it easier they said. Not right, but less wrong, somehow. I think I understand what they mean. He didn't die in vain. He died for a cause he believed in.

Talking to them helped me, too. It was good to see that, as hard as it is, they're coping and sticking together closer than ever. Their family isn't complete by any means, but they have more than people like Hannah and me have.

"He would be proud of you, you know?" Clark says.

I shake my head and open my mouth to protest, but he doesn't let me.

"You have sacrificed more than anyone here. Without you, Seattle would be in a lot worse shape. You bought the city a chance. I gotta say, I owe you big time for leading us to those Spawners. I had a heck of a time dispatching several of them."

"Man, I hate I missed that," I joke, hoping to lighten the mood a little.

"Don't worry, there's still plenty of fun to be had." He tips a smile that makes my chest feel empty. Xave used to smile like that.

Aydan walks up, holding two plates. "I got you something to eat if you're hungry."

"I'll head back." Clark gestures toward his family. "These days, I try to spend as much time as I can with them. I'll see you later." He walks backward, a hand held up in a *goodbye* gesture.

Aydan leads me to a far corner of the room, away from everyone. We sit on the floor facing each other and place the plates in the hollow of our crossed legs. Dinner consists of a small portion of canned green beans, mac & cheese from a box, and four fiber crackers. We both stare at the food for a moment.

He shakes his head. "I can't eat this."

"Me neither."

"I don't know what made me think I could. It's not fair."

I know exactly what he means. Both Whitehouse and Hailstone have much better food than this. Food I've been enjoying without a second thought for weeks while others go hungry—people holed up in their apartments, in safe houses, or out on the street, like Hannah.

Aydan takes my plate away, gets up and gives our food to a couple of preschoolers. They accept it with wide, incredulous eyes, and immediately dig in. Aydan walks back with a sad smile stretching his always-too-red lips. He sits back down, his back against the wall. I shift positions and sit beside him. The brick wall feels rough through my t-shirt.

We watch people go through the food line, then sit to share their meager meals. James, Rheema, Blare and a few other people I don't know sit at one of the few available tables. They are deep in hushed conversation. Kristen isn't with them. She must have stayed back, playing with my abundant amounts of genetic material. Seeing them all together reminds me of that time Oso cooked dinner for us, and we celebrated our small victory against Elliot. I look over with longing and find myself wondering if Rheema blames for killing Oso and is only pretending to hold no grudge against me. She's the only one I don't feel certain about.

188

Blare catches me staring and flips me the bird. For some reason, her animosity strikes me as funny. I give her a crooked smile. She looks away in disgust.

"Some people are born to add a little sour to our lives," Aydan says. "Don't pay her any mind."

"I don't."

James steals a pen from a man who sits next to him and scribbles something on a notebook. The guy steals the pen back, shaking his head at whatever James wrote and shoulder bumping him. They look very at ease with each other.

"Who's that next to James?"

"Oh, that's Sal. He and James have been buddies since high school. They've been fighting against Eklyptors since James got infected. They founded *ZeroBreach* together. You might know him as Salvador Lopez."

"Uh-uh!" I say incredulously.

"Yep."

"*The* Salvador Lopez who came up with the Tumble algorithm." A piece of programmatic gold that can process millions of business rules in a matter of seconds.

"The one and the same."

"Wow." I'm impressed. Really impressed. The man is a computer genius.

We watch in silence for a long moment.

"It's so . . . quiet. It's nice," Aydan says.

"It is."

There is the constant murmur of conversation, the shuffle of feet as people move up the food line, and the high pitched cries of children being children, but I know what Aydan is referring to. He means the buzzing. James, Rheema, Aydan and I are the only Symbiots here. Everyone else is human. I've kept my buzz-o-meter on, wondering if I would encounter any other Symbiots. I haven't. We're few and far between.

Aydan's face turns in my direction. I stare straight ahead unable to meet his gaze.

"I was worried about you," he says, undeterred by my apparent indifference.

"I was worried about *you*," I admit.

"Really?"

I don't say anything.

"What happened? What did Luke tell you?"

"I don't want to talk about it anymore. You can ask James. I'm sure he'll tell you. Are you going back? You were blindfolded when you came in. That must mean you're going back."

He shrugs. "I shouldn't have left in the first place. So I guess I'll have to. It's up to James, in the end."

"You helped me escape, didn't you?"

"I had to."

"And they didn't notice?"

"No. I sent my energy underground, through the iron bars in the concrete."

"That's some amazing control," I say, wishing I could get there with my pathetic skill.

He cracks his finger in an absentminded way. "You'll get the hang of it."

"Sooner rather than later, I hope."

"What about you?" he asks. "I bet you were also blind-folded when you came in."

I look down. My left hand worries at one of my shoelaces. My right one rests on my thigh. "I was."

"I wish we could stay. I wish we could . . ." He looks away, throws his head back against the wall and looks at the ceiling as if he will find words in the metal beams.

These times aren't made for wishing, and he knows it.

Without looking down, he tentatively lays his hand on top of mine. My immediate instinct is to pull away, but his gentle touch paralyzes me, filling me with a staggering need for human contact. Slowly—giving me a chance to pull away—Aydan turns my hand over and intertwines his fingers with mine. A shiver runs up my arm. My eyes close of their own accord.

He holds my hand tenderly and, in spite of that, I still sense the intensity and desperation in him.

"How can I keep you?" he asks in a barely audible whisper.

My heart wants to turn away, wants to reinforce the wall that locks the pain away. Caring for people isn't advisable anymore, especially when one has a track record of losing it all. Except a back door I didn't know existed cracks open, more than willing to usher him in. My heart has been dead and hollow for too long, and loneliness comes at its own pain. How can I push him away when I have so little and he offers so much?

I wish there was a way I could tell him I may not be utterly broken, after all, but words have never come easy. I hope the fact that my fingers have remained intertwined with his is proof enough because, for now, that's all I've got.

Chapter 28

After everyone has finished dinner, they file back to the adjacent warehouse to get ready for bed. Aydan and I stand from the floor and, avoiding eye contact, let go of each other's hands. We walk over to James's table where he and the others remain. He's waving us over, a stern look on his face.

James comes away from the table and puts an arm around my back. "Marci, I want you to meet everyone. Of course you know Rheema, Blare, Aydan and Clark already."

I bite my lower lip, thinking of two more people who should be here and are not, both missing because of me. Blare stares bullets at me, her expression leaving me no doubt that she's thinking the same thing. She blames me. Maybe it would mean something if I didn't blame myself already.

"This is Salvador Lopez," James says.

"Call me Sal." He shakes my hand and gives me a perfect smile. "Heard a lot about you."

"Yeah, I'm infamous." I like him immediately, his openness, his genuine smile, the familiarity of his Latin features. "I've heard a lot about you too, but that's because you're *famous*."

He throws his head back and, after a hearty laugh, leans forward and talks in a low whisper. "Only because no one knows *everything* I've done." He pulls away and winks at me.

"Marci, these here are Jori, Spencer and Margo."

They nod their heads, looking as stoic as stoic can be. From the way they carry themselves and, not to mention, their crew cuts, I guess they're military stock. Even Margo sports the same closely cropped hair. She gives me a wide smile that glows against her dark skin. She appears to be genuinely nice and friendly.

"They are the leaders of the new Seattle IgNiTe cells that formed after The Takeover. We're here tonight to discuss our unified plan. Sal is our technical consultant and a good friend of mine since high school. We were talking about the important work you and Aydan have been doing at Whitehouse and Hailstone."

Sal shakes his head vigorously. "You kids don't know how grateful we are for all you do. Your tips on shipments have been critical to our progress *and* survival. That list of Spawners you got for us," he clicks his tongue, "we wouldn't be anywhere without that. I would sure love to see you in action." He makes typing motions with his fingers, and I almost bust out laughing. Salvador Lopez, the god of rule engine heaven, wants to see *me* in action? That'll be the day.

"Let's sit." James extends a hand in invitation. Everyone takes a seat while Aydan pulls over two plastic, patio chairs from an adjacent table.

193

Blare is the only one who remains standing, a booted foot propped on her chair. She's chewing gum, making smacking sounds and popping bubbles every few minutes. She goes on staring at me, the perfect object for her discontent.

"As I'm sure you understand," James begins, "we can't discuss our plans in detail with you guys. We can't risk your detection and—"

"Your inevitable betrayal," Blare puts in, sparing one of her hateful looks toward Aydan, this time.

A muscle in James's jaw jumps in clear aggravation at Blare's comment, but he lets it go.

"But your work is very important. Critical even. Aydan has successfully infiltrated Hailstone after a few weeks of hard work to accomplish it and, already, he's provided some vital information that has greatly improved our numbers as far as armed troops is concerned. Thank you, Aydan. The weapon shipment was exactly where you said it would be."

Aydan shrugs. "It's nothing. All I had to do was follow Marci's example. She has lost and sacrificed more than *anyone* in here." He punctuates his every word, locking his gaze on Blare's.

I appreciate Aydan's solidarity, but I'd prefer it if he didn't say things like this. It doesn't help—not when half of what's happened to me is due to my own weakness. If I'd been strong enough, Oso would still be alive, and I wouldn't have to live amongst our enemies.

Blare scoffs and spits her wad of gum. It lands on the concrete floor several feet away.

Sal throws an impatient look her way. His tolerance for her seems much shorter than James's. Jori, Spencer and Margo simply listen and watch very carefully, apparently trying to make up their own minds about the situation. Rheema sits quietly, playing with the pendant at her neck. She holds it between thumb and forefinger, sliding it back and forth on a gold chain and, occasionally, taking it to her mouth. She seems distant and preoccupied. Only God knows what she's been through since last I saw her and what type of memories worry her.

James brings his hands together and presses them to his mouth as if in prayer. He sighs before continuing. "As difficult as it is to ask you to continue to put your lives at risk, it is a lot harder to give up the advantage that your presence there gives us."

So he wants us to go back. No big surprise. Though it's clear he feels bad about it.

"Maybe this time you could be a little more useful and could take care of Elliot and Luke." Blare slides a black-tipped fingernail across her neck.

"Blare," her name on James's lips is a stern reprimand. "Do I have to enumerate the ways in which you're out of line?" He keeps his gaze on the table, as if looking at Blare might cut the thin thread from which his restraint hangs.

"She killed Oso!" Blare says through twisted lips. "Has everyone forgotten that? Well, I haven't. As a matter of fact, I can't stop wondering who she'll get next."

James stands in one fluid motion. His chair scrapes against the floor and nearly topples.

"I can take care of this, James," I say, standing too.

I walk to the other end of the table and stand in front of Blare, gaze steady and unblinking.

"Not a day goes by that I don't think of Oso," I start.

"Am I supposed to be touched by that?"

I ignore her. "Not a day goes by I don't think of Xave,

195

my mother, my father. All victims of this fight as much as me, as much as any of us. If you think this is a walk in the park for me, then you're mistaken. But if it makes you feel better to tear me down, go right ahead. You can't come up with anything I haven't already thought of myself."

Blare's upper lip curls and trembles. From the corner of my eye, I notice her fists clench. All my instincts, alert me to be on guard, but I ignore them. I see her punch coming from a mile away, but I don't move. It lands on the side of my face and sends me staggering back a few steps. Everyone at the table jumps to their feet, except Rheema.

I shake my head, regain my balance and step back up to Blare. My entire body shakes with ire. I want to jump up and front-kick her right in the teeth, but sometimes it takes more strength and courage to do nothing.

My gaze issues a challenge: *Do it again, if it makes you feel better.* I have never been anyone's punching bag, and I don't really intend to be hers. But I sense this is what it will take to deflate her anger. She wants opposition, argument. She's the kind of person who craves that sort of drama. I refuse to give it to her.

Blare's shoulders shake, her fingers twitch. I wait, the side of my face throbbing. For a moment, a host of emotions war inside her dark eyes. She seems ready to punch me again but, instead, she stomps away, shoulder bumping me from her path.

When she disappears into the adjacent warehouse, there seems to be a slight exhale from those at the table. I turn, face them and evaluate their expressions, unable to discern their reaction.

"I wish she would . . ." I say apologetically, worried that I've overstepped my position.

"It's a hell of a person, the one who fights her own battles without throwing a punch," Sal says with an approving nod. "I doubt she'll bother you anymore. Thank you for defusing her. We don't need that kind of counterproductive behavior here. Don't you think?"

Everyone at the table nods in definite agreement. They sort of look glad to be rid of Blare and, for some reason, that makes me feel worse and sends my thoughts back in her direction. Reluctantly, I find myself feeling sorry for her, wondering why she's so bitter and unhappy. Not that there is any reason to be joyful, but maybe she's lost the only thing that can keep us going: hope.

God knows I've been there before.

I always thought she was in love with James, and I guess she's lost that too, now that he and Kristen are clearly a couple.

James sits back down. "She'll simmer down."

Everyone else retakes their seats, but I remain on my feet. I'm too restless for that. Maybe it would be best if I leave now. I don't want to get too used to this comforting silence and sense of belonging—even if I have to take a punch or two every once in a while.

"As I was saying," James picks up the thread of our interrupted conversation, "Marci and Aydan's help has been invaluable. They have infiltrated the strongest factions in Seattle. Their computer skills give them just the edge we need. They're irreplaceable for more than one reason. Moreover, they're brave and committed to defeating our enemy. They can correct me if I speak out of turn."

My gaze locks with Aydan's. He smiles and nods. I nod back. We're in the same boat, and apparently, we're masochistic enough to be on it voluntarily.

"I can't say very much, for obvious reasons," James goes on, "but I want you to know we are making big strides toward ridding our city of these parasites. And it's my hope that you won't have to remain with them for much longer."

My heart beats faster at the possibility. The dregs of my hope for victory rear up and begin to gather. My chest fills fuller for a moment, until I check myself, curving my expectations. With too much hope, I may lose my head. A dose of realism is always needed to temper the errant daydreams that might distract me from the everyday horrors of living among Eklyptors.

Still, it's hard to push down the elation this possibility has unleashed inside of me. "You talking about a cure?" I ask, even if the answer is obvious. A cure is all we have to hope for.

To my surprise, James throws a morsel of information my way. "A cure *and* a vaccine."

A murmur of approval goes around the table. Rheema straightens, drops the pendant she's been playing with.

"Are we finally close?" She looks so expectant, and I know, from the look in her brown eyes that she's feeling the same elation I am.

James shrugs to indicate he's already said too much.

Rheema sinks back down, disappointed. "Sucks to be a Symbiot," she says.

"Speak for yourself," Aydan puts in.

"Well, not everyone has it as easy as you do, *electric boy*. Some of us have to work harder than others." Rheema bares her neurotoxin ridden fangs at him and hisses.

Aydan examines his nails in an indifferent gesture. Tiny volts of electricity jump from one fingertip to the next, crackling gently.

Show off.

Like me, his skills just manifested. We didn't work to build them, physically changing ourselves like Rheema and James have done. At least their skills work reliably, something I can't say for myself. Though, I shouldn't complain. Kristen doesn't even have a talent—not that I know of, anyway. I guess Aydan did have it easy.

As soon as the thought forms, however, I realize it's not true. Meditation isn't easy for any Symbiot, especially in the beginning. Just because I didn't witness his struggles doesn't mean mastering his powers was a walk in the park.

"Sorry if this information remains 'needs to know' only," James says. "I'm sure I don't have to explain why."

"Yeah, yeah." Rheema waves a hand in the air. "If we're done here, I have a van that needs a new radiator. Those bullets holes just aren't helping for some reason."

Jori laughs a bit too loudly at her joke, making me think he likes her.

She pushes away from the table, then stops when there's a knock at the door from the main warehouse.

"I'll get it." Spencer gets up and opens the door.

Kristen, her eyes wide and startled, addresses James as soon as she steps in. "We need to talk."

James hops to his feet and follows her. We stay behind, our hearts in our mouths, wishing we could be flies on the wall to hear what has cool, collected Kristen looking flurried. Does it have something to do with my blood? I wouldn't be surprised.

Chapter 29

An hour later, Kristen deposits a few drops of my blood in a test tube. They break through the surface of a clear liquid and slowly sink to the bottom, dissolving to thin pink ribbons. Her eyes flash to mine, then settle back on the contents of the test tube, which she's holding close to her face. With one quick flick of her wrist, she swirls the tube. My blood and the clear liquid mix and, by some chemical reaction, the solution slowly changes color, turning a muted shade of green.

A satisfied smile spreads over Kristen's lips, and all I can do is wonder how in the world she can do any of this in an improvised lab. I don't know much about DNA tests and developing cures, but it seems to me those things are too complicated for the likes of this place.

"Did it work?" James asks, his voice vibrating with excitement.

"Did you doubt it?"

James laughs a hearty laugh, and I'm taken aback by how different his face looks. His gray eyes sparkle, his teeth flash, white and straight. I do a double take and wonder if he's much younger than I've always imagined.

He clasps a heavy hand on my back and almost knocks me off the tall stool where I'm sitting. James fetched me from the eating area a few minutes ago and dragged me in here without an explanation.

"Did *what* work?" I demand. They are using my freaking blood, the least they could do is explain why I continue to be their lab rat.

"Marci!" Kristen says my name like an exclamation. Her face is bright, making her look younger too. I don't dare guess what this is. Instead, I worry about the fact that she's being nice to me for the first time in forever. "Marci, your blood . . . your blood may have finally given me the answer."

My gaze flashes back between James and Kristen. *The answer to what?!* The question plays inside my head over and over, though I'm unable to ask it out loud.

"I've been struggling with designing a vaccine and a cure." Kristen sets the test tube in a small rack. She peels off her rubber gloves and throws them in a red, biohazard box. "But you," she takes her hands to her head, then pulls them away as if to indicate an explosion, "you have opened new paths I hadn't considered."

I lick my lips. "Wait a minute. I just talked to you like two hours ago and now you're telling me that you've figured out a cure? That's impossible . . . how?"

James chuckles. "It's her ability, Marci. She has worked for years in developing it, and it's now at its cusp. She has enhanced her senses to help her in this task. She has modified her occipital lobe to increase her spacial intelligence and see patterns more easily. She also modified her sense of smell, and it is now highly advanced. She can perceive subtle differences in substances and know exactly what's missing. She can detect diseases like cancer through her sense of smell alone."

What?! Impossible! That's my first thought, then I have to shake my head to dispel my doubt. I've heard of dogs capable of smelling cancerous cells in patients, so I know it's possible, especially for a Symbiot bent on curing the worst plague that has ever attacked the human race.

My heart begins to beat at a million miles per hour.

"No, I haven't figured out a cure, not yet," Kristen says. "But now I know exactly what I need to do. It was only a matter of time before, but now," she chuckles, "now the time is nigh." She finishes with a dramatic flair and an exuberant smile. She has been fighting this much longer than me. If I'm excited, then she's exultant.

"So . . . did you smell something in my blood?"

"No." Kristen shakes her head. "I'd examined your blood before, there's nothing unusual in it as far as scent goes. Mostly iron like everyone else's. It was the new information you brought, combined with examining your DNA under a new light plus ideas I've played with for several years."

I want more but this is all she gives me. My annoyed look must say it all because she tries to placate me.

"It's hard to explain. It has to do with antivirals, antiparasitics, vaccines, nano-trappers, and the way they all work," she says, talking as fast as my heart is beating. "It also has to do with the high levels of serotonin in your brain, and the way you separated your DNA from the agent's, in spite of the embryonic-level infection."

"The what?"

She ignores my confused question. She's too excited to hear anything besides her own thoughts. "I'd like to think

I would have stumbled upon the discovery eventually, but this will certainly speed things up." She walks to a large microscope, looks into it and tinkers with the settings, murmuring under her breath.

I give James a "some help here" look.

He shrugs. "She won't listen to anyone when she gets like this. We should let her work. C'mon." He ushers me past the tent's zippered door.

"So what do I do now? Do I go back?" I know my work at Whitehouse's is important, but the few hours I've spent here have flipped a switch inside of me that I'd left untouched for a while.

James shakes his head. "Things are changing rapidly. I have to talk to the other cell leaders. Our plans need to be fluid and, after this, it might be unwise to send you back without further discussion. The risks may outweigh the benefits at this point."

An irrational mixture of joy and relief fill my chest. I want to stay, even if there are things I could still do from Whitehouse's headquarters. I look over my shoulder. Kristen looks distorted behind the clear, plastic walls. "Can *you* explain what she was talking about?"

"Nah, she barely made any sense when she first told me. We need to let her work. This is what she's good at. Her mind works like a dynamo, especially lately." He circles a hand over his temple.

"She's tweaked something in her brain that has sent her to another level. I'm afraid she'll start thinking of me as a preschooler when all this is over. She'll be too smart for her own good." He gives an unamused chuckle.

I stop at the threshold, before stepping out into the sleeping area. "Do you think it will ever end?"

James turns to face me. There is a certain look in his eyes that reminds of my father. His storm gray eyes search me and seem to look right through my armored exterior. "It will. One way or another. And if I know Kristen, it'll be soon. Maybe it'll begin tomorrow."

I wait for a smile to indicate he's joking, but he's dead serious.

"Tomorrow?"

"Notice I said *begin*. Even with a cure and vaccine, it won't be easy. There are too many people infected. A great number of them, including you and I, have been carrying this parasite for years. There's no telling what a cure would do to us. So no, it won't be overnight. But we have plans in place to distribute a vaccine and a cure." His gaze falls to the floor, but I'm sure he's seeing a spot beyond this old warehouse. He is far away, lost in a memory, perhaps. "I have to believe that it will end, that we'll defeat them. I made a promise once, so I have no choice but to keep it."

My throat goes rigid with emotion. I can sense this is no idle promise he's talking about. It means a lot to him, too much even.

The paternal look is back in his eyes. "You remind me of her. Always have."

God.

Does he have a daughter? Did he lose her?

Please, no!

I don't dare ask.

"It's the reason I made so many mistakes with you," he continues. "I wanted to protect you. I guess I never learned my lesson. We all make our own decisions and, in the end, we can't truly protect anyone."

"W-who?" I manage to ask in a broken voice.

"My sister." James's eyes shine, even in the pale lighting on this side of the warehouse. To my surprise, he pulls out his wallet and shows me a small picture. "Her name was Farrah. She died when she was fifteen."

The girl in the photograph is beautiful, with shoulder-length brown hair, a happy smile and James's gray eyes.

"I miss her every day," he says with a sigh, then puts the wallet away.

"I'm sorry," I whisper.

"Don't be. She was brave, like you. She lived and died on her own terms."

I nod, thinking there is no better way, wishing someone will say that about me when I'm gone.

"This might seem like a strange question, but . . . " he breaks eye contact, clears his throat.

His sudden self-conscious behavior is strange, and I can't imagine what he's about to ask.

"After it's all over, I thought that maybe you would like . . . a family."

My breath catches. Tears rush to my eyes and, just like that, I'm undone. I blink rapidly to avoid crying, but my tears are too many and they spill onto my cheeks, warm and salty and ripe with incredulity and an odd sort of happiness.

I have no words. They haven't made any that match such an offer. So I do the only thing I know to do. I take a step forward and wrap my arms around his waist. He feels like a solid wall of certainty and safety. He feels just the way Dad used to feel.

He holds me, accepting my silence, and this unusual gesture that is a better answer than words could ever shape.

Chapter 30

Next morning, I wake up gradually, my senses becoming aware of my surroundings by degrees. First is the din of high-pitched laughter, then the lumpy surface beneath my back, and last the warm glow of light on my face.

My eyes spring open. I'm lying against the wall on a pile of old clothes. I sit up, blinking at the ray of light that shoots through a cracked window high up on the wall. The same children from last night are hard at play, circling the concrete columns as they run from each other in a tag game. I stretch and crack a smile. This is the best sleep I've had in weeks, in spite of the non-bed, in spite of the fact that I had a short meditation session with Aydan last night.

Once on my feet, I bend my neck from side to side and find myself aching for a workout at the dojo. There wasn't much I used to love more after a good night of sleep than an intense, early morning workout with Sensei 'Moto.

I'm feeling pretty awesome until I look down at my wrist watch.

Ten A.M.! What the hell?!

I look around for a familiar face and soon spot Aydan talking to Hannah. I stride in their direction. Aydan, as always, is dressed in all black, while Hannah wears a long, flowing skirt and a fitted white top. Her blond hair is down, draping over her well-shaped breasts. I rub my forehead to ease the frown that has formed there.

"Good Morning, Marci," Hannah says in an enthusiastic tone. Her blue eyes sparkle with the invigorating sunshine.

"'Morning," I respond a bit too coldly. I grit my teeth, puzzled by my attitude.

Aydan's gentle incline of his head is his only greeting. A shock of black hair falls over his forehead. A dot of light in his black eyes makes it look as if he's trapped the sun deep inside his soul.

"You missed breakfast, sleepy head," Hannah puts in. She seems so different from the gloomy, desperate girl I rescued. I admire her for trying to make the best of her situation.

"I saved you a granola bar." Aydan nods in a vague direction, probably toward the spot where he stashed my food.

"Thank you." For some ungodly reason, my cheeks flush. I shift my weight from one foot to another and look away.

From the corner of my eyes, I notice Hannah shifting her attention to Aydan and back again. She makes a small sound in the back of her throat, as if to acknowledge something, then excuses herself. Aydan and I stand awkwardly for a moment. When we finally decide to speak we do so in unison.

"Are you hungry?"

"What is there to do around here?"

We laugh and go back to doing the awkward, silent thing.

God, this is torture.

"Um, Jori and Margo are holding a training session next door in a few minutes."

"Training session?" I ask, curious.

"Yeah, self-defense, hand to hand combat, that sort of thing. You'd probably enjoy that. I was going to go, but if you'll be there, I guess I'll skip."

"What? Afraid of getting your butt handed to you?"

He shrugs and gives me a crooked smile. The gleam in his eyes captures my attention. It's like a firefly against a dark summer sky. He seems so different, yet so similar to the boy I first met. It's not that his eyes didn't shine this way before, I just I never looked closely enough. Maybe *I'm* the one who's different.

"No, not afraid. I just don't think I'd be able to help myself . . ." There is something suggestive in his expression, something that makes me blush again. "I'd probably be too tempted to . . ." he wiggles his fingers; they crackle with unseen energy, ". . . zap your ass, and I can't afford to give us, Symbiots, away."

I roll my eyes. "Using your skills wouldn't count."

"How do you figure? It's not like you don't have skills of your own."

I cuckle. "Hardly. Meditation's still a bitch as you well saw last night."

"I think you did much better, actually."

"Well, I did manage a short session on my own the other day," I admit.

"What?! You didn't mention that." Aydan's undisguised outrage surprises me. "You know, better than anyone, that the risk of doing that on your own is too high. You need someone to shake you awake if you don't manage to keep the agent down."

"It's not like I've forgotten that. I'm just tired of having nothing but potential. I want results." My temper rises a little, showing clearly in my voice.

Aydan takes a step closer and talks between clenched teeth. "You have to stop and think before you do stupid shit like that."

"Oh, chill out. I'm fine." I begin to turn away from him, but he takes me by the shoulders and gives me a small shake.

"If you don't care about yourself, then at least think of me."

My lungs freeze.

Think of me. Think of me. Think of me.

The words drill into me and coil themselves around my bones, settling me, grounding me, returning me to a reality where people care about me.

I lower my head. "I'm sorry." The words are nothing but a murmur, but they're a concession, nonetheless. They show him I'm willing to think of him before I risk my life.

He hooks a finger under my chin and forces my gaze to meet his. "We can practice again today, okay?"

I nod.

His eyes lower to my mouth for a split second, but he immediately looks away and takes a step back, nodding and forcing a casual smile. I swallow, surprised by the way a mere errant glance has sent my heart into a frantic pace.

"Um, they're getting started in a couple of minutes." Aydan points toward the door that leads to the dining area. He gestures with his head for me to follow as he begins a leisurely stroll in that direction. I go, glad for the distraction. These conversations with Aydan are highly informative but way too heavy.

Apparently, he still wants to kiss me. Moreover, since this assumption entered my mind, it seems it's made itself comfortable and it's now a strong theory. I press my lips together into a thin line. Would kissing Aydan means a betrayal to Xave?

Chapter 31

Inside the dining area, the available tables and chairs have been moved to the side and those in attendance have arranged themselves in a circle. Several people are here, including the young children. Rheema, Blare, Jori and Spencer are also present. Blare's dark gaze cuts across the circle directly to mine. She still looks like she has a bone to pick. Really? What's it going to take?

We join the circle. A boy of about nine stands in the middle with Margo. She's dressed in gray and black camo pants tucked into her boots and a white tank top, the spitting image of G.I. Jane, expect a lot prettier and less mean-looking. In spite of her closely cropped, black hair, she exudes femininity. There is something elegant and graceful about her, something that could make an inattentive person think that she is delicate—though they would be mistaken, because there is steel in her gaze. My first impression from last night is validated. I like her.

"So let's do it again," Margo tells the boy, wrapping her right hand around his left wrist. "Now what?"

"Lock hands," the boy says just as he interlaces the fingers of his right hand with his left. "Step back." He kicks his right foot back. "Pull to hip." With a grunt, he jerks his interlaced hand toward his right hip, effectively breaking free of Margo's clutches.

"And then?" She gives the boy a raised eyebrow.

"I run and hide."

"Great job!" She pats him on the back and gives him one of her glowing smiles.

I remember going through drills like this with Sensei 'Moto when I first started doing karate. I didn't realize then how disturbing it is to teach such things to a child, knowing that there are those who would take pleasure in injuring them. At the time, it all seemed like a game and, from the boy's eager look, I can tell he's thinking the same thing.

"All right, I need a few adults to help them practice." Margo lines up the kids on one side and adults on the other. They go through this and other self-defense moves, until the children appear comfortable with them.

After a quick lesson with the young ones, Margo dismisses them, instructing the adults to stay behind for further instruction. The kids leave, dragging their feet and protesting all the way to the door. They're too cute and make me, once more, take to heart how imperative our success is.

"Hopefully," Margo says once they've left, "they'll remember everything. Mainly to get away and hide, so we can fight without worrying about them."

"Hopefully, we won't have to," one of the remaining adults, a middle-aged man in a dirty button-up shirt, says.

"Chances are we won't, but it doesn't hurt to be prepared."

Aydan leans forward and whispers in my ear. "Last night,

I heard Rheema say that James is having the families moved to their permanent location. One of the groups that moved a few weeks back was attacked. It was . . ." He shakes his head, going paler than normal.

"Oh." I don't know what else to say.

"Why can't we stay here?" the same man demands. "Why do we have to risk our lives, the kids' lives, by leaving?"

A few in the circle nod to the question.

"James has explained already," Margo says calmly. "This is more of a holding facility. It's close enough to the city to allow us to bring those we rescue. It's not meant to be permanent. The numbers here are getting high as it is. It's not the safest place by any means." She smiles and gives the man an open invitation to contest, but he just frowns at the floor, looking unhappy.

"All right, why don't we practice some of the drills we learned yesterday? Form in pairs. I'll walk around and help those who have questions. For those who will carry a gun, we'll go over reloading, shooting and general safety instructions once more."

I look over at Aydan, wondering what we're supposed to do next. I don't know the drills, so I can't be much help on that front. I'm about to ask when I notice Blare strolling across the circle, headed straight toward me.

"Not again," I say under my breath.

When Aydan notices her, he squares his shoulders in her direction. Like me, he seems to suspect this spells trouble.

"You and I, Marci," Blare says, confirming our suspicion.

"C'mon, Blare," Aydan says. "Give it up."

"Stay out of this, geeky boy."

Aydan sighs.

Rheema joins us. "What's the matter?"

Blare rolls her shoulders like she's some sort of boxer. "I'm offering this one," she flicks a hand in my direction, "a fair fight. One where she doesn't act like the victim."

"You realize she knows karate, right?" Aydan asks with ill-concealed amusement.

"Talk is cheap," Blare says.

She has never seen me fight, so she has no idea if she's biting more than she can chew. For my part, I don't ever underestimate an opponent. It's a mistake that can get you killed. Slowly, I take off my jacket and let it fall to the floor, assessing her with narrowed eyes. I don't know her fighting skills either, so I don't take this lightly. I crack my neck and loosen my arms. Maybe this is what it'll take to finally get Blare off my back. I jump lightly on the tips of my toes, making blood rush to every corner of my body. It feels damn good. Maybe I've been missing a good sparring challenge.

Aydan and Rheema take a few steps back.

"Cat fight." Rheema laughs, attracting everyone's attention with her comment.

I take a defensive stance, one leg forward, both hands up, my weight balanced on the balls of my feet. I wait. She's the challenger, let her make the first move.

Blare doesn't waste time. She puts her fists up and immediately jumps forward and throws a quick jab. I deviate it with an outside block, then shuffle to the side. She follows up with a front kick which I stop with a low block. My forearm smarts as it connects with her heavy steel-toe boot. It'll bruise, but it's nothing I'm not used to.

Spencer and Jori jeer at her inefficient attempts. Apparently, Blare makes *non-fans* everywhere she goes. She's too heavy, true, but if there's something I've learned in the last few months, it's not to judge. No one knows what she's been through, what she's lost, she may have a perfectly good reason for her bitterness.

She attacks once more, combining kicks and punches. She's faster this time, but I'm able to either block or avoid everything she throws my way. She's not a bad fighter, just not a trained one, like me.

As she ineffectively tries to hit me, her movements get sloppy with anger, and I start noticing gaps in her defense. In one of her lapses, I sneak a hook punch to her ribs and quickly back away. She grunts, her body bending to one side in pain. Her mouth twists and, as soon as she recovers, she tackles me and drives me against the wall, growling all the way there. The crash sends the air out of my lungs with a *whoosh*.

Blare moves lightning fast and lands a couple of punches on my stomach. I lower my head and press my fists to my forehead, protecting my torso with my forearms and elbows. She continues to throw punches like some sort of blind locomotive. She's beside herself with rage—something else you don't do, if you want to win a fight.

I rotate to one side and quickly pull away from the wall. Determined to show her I'm not playing the victim or playing with her, I release a roundhouse kick to her side, followed by two jabs, the first to the stomach and the other to the side of her face. They hit the mark and leave her holding herself and blinking. She tries to hit me again and again, but fails and, instead, receives one hit after another.

After a wicked punch to the mouth, she whips her head back around to reveal a bloody lower lip. At the sight of blood, I decide it's time to end this and go for a punch that'll knock her silly. I make my move, but I'm taken aback when she suddenly twirls, pulls out a hidden knife from her waistband and, in a flash, presses its sharp tip to my neck. Several spectators cry out in warning. I step back to get away, but Blare trips me and jumps on top of me as soon as I hit the floor. The length of her blade presses against my jugular. I swallow and feel the knife bob up and down.

"Poor sportsmanship, Blare," I say in a strangled whisper.

"You think I care about that, you little shit."

"Guess not."

"Blare, let her go!" Aydan calls from the side. His fingers twitch. Static electricity crackles in the air. I give him a warning look. He needs to stay out of this one. This is *my* fight. Besides, some of the people here don't know about Symbiots and their powers.

In my peripheral vision, I see other people coming closer, but I don't take my eyes off Blare again. I'm afraid if I do, she'll slit my throat. Her gaze is certainly telling me she wants to. I just need to give her a reason to do it. Or, even better, a reason *not* to.

"What did I ever do to you?" I ask.

"You fuckin' *Symbiots* think yourselves so special," she growls between clenched teeth, low enough that only I can hear her.

What?! She has something against Symbiots? Since when?

"*So* special," she continues, "that you can kill one of us and go on with impunity."

Oh, so she doesn't have something against all Symbiots. Just me: the weak Symbiot who lost the battle against her agent and killed Oso, the gentlest bear of a man I have ever met. He was IgNiTe's driver, cook, unconditional ally.

The knife's pressure increases. A stinging sensation lets me know the blade has cut skin.

"Marci," Aydan says my name as a protest. I lift a hand

to warn him back once more.

My eyes haven't left Blare's, not for a second. "It . . . it wasn't me, Blare. I would've never hurt Oso."

"You *killed* him." The way she says "killed" sends a shiver down my spine. It feels too much like a verb she's really considering putting into practice.

"Blare, it's not Marci you're mad at," Aydan says from the side. "Let her go."

Blare's eyes tighten. Her sneer redoubles. She didn't like that comment at all. So this is about someone else? My mind reels.

Is it about Kristen? Jealousy?

"Stay out of this, Ayd—"

Blare's sentence gets cut short as someone tackles her from the side, knocking her off me. I instinctively jerk to my feet, ready for anything. Adrenaline courses uselessly through my body because Blare is already subdued. I take in the scene, blinking, willing my heart to slow down and my brain to stop seeing knives where there are none. Rheema is on top of Blare, her mouth on my attacker's neck, as if she were a hungry vampire.

The whites of Blare's eyes flash for a moment, then her head falls limply to the side. Rheema pulls away, mouth half open, fangs extended and dripping with a clear liquid. She licks her lips, runs the back of her hands across her mouth and stands. Blare stays immobile on the floor.

"She'll be out for a few hours," Rheema says, her expression oddly hungry. She walks away from Blare and comes to my side. "Are you okay?" She bends her neck to one side to better look at my neck. "A little blood." She waves a finger at her own throat.

"What the hell?" The middle-aged man says, his eyes

bouncing from Blare to Rheema and back again.

"Nothing to see here." Margo starts ushering everyone out of the room.

"But what did she just—"

"She knocked her out. That's all. C'mon, everyone out. Out!" People file out, shuffling their feet and throwing suspicious glances over their shoulders.

Jori and Spencer walk closer, their faces concerned even though they don't really know me.

"Are you okay?" Margo asks, walking back from the door.

"Yeah," I say in a hoarse voice. I straighten from my crouched, defensive position and gingerly touch my neck. My fingers come away bloody. I swallow. "Thank you, Rheema."

"Don't mention it. We need you." She winks at me, then gestures at Blare's prone shape. "Hell hath no fury like a woman scorned."

I put my hands up in question. "What does that have to do with me?"

"Nothing," she leans closer and whispers, "but it's not like she can beat up the boss's girl, the only hope we have for survival." She throws her head back and laughs.

"Lucky me. Maybe after this, she'll turn her sights on you. I mean, you just *vamped* her."

Just then, James walks in the room, his gray eyes taking in the scene. "What happened here?"

I rub my forehead, suddenly feeling very tired of this. "Just had my second welcome from Blare. Don't mind me if I just . . ." Hooking a finger toward the door, I head back into the main warehouse, aiming for that pile of clothes I slept on and wishing I would have stayed there today.

Chapter 32

I spend the rest of the day restless. There is nothing to do in the warehouse, which makes me realize why they try to entertain themselves with drills. After the morning excitement is over, there's little else but a snack of peanut butter crackers and endless card and domino games.

At some point, I find out that James left with Jori and Spencer, taking an unconscious Blare with them. Kristen said they had an errand to run, and James didn't want Blare causing any more problems when she woke up. When I asked about the errand, she just shrugged and walked away. Margo also left, taking the families away and leaving only a few, fight-capable men behind.

By dinner time, my nerves are hot-wired. All day sharp knives have been flashing across my vision, making the cut on my neck smart to attention. It's driving me nuts.

"Let that be!" Aydan smacks my hand away from my neck. We're sitting on the floor in the dining area again, bowls of canned soup steaming on our laps.

The cut is already healing, so it itches like crazy. I make

an effort to ignore it by concentrating on the fat noodles floating in the soup. "It might sound crazy, but I think I'd rather go back to Whitehouse headquarters. At least I feel useful there."

I wait for a reprimand from Aydan but, instead, he says, "I know what you mean. I feel like we're wasting our time here. I mean, if Kristen is close to finding a cure, I understand why James wants us to hang back, but is she really getting there?" He sounds like he's afraid to get his hopes high on this too-good-to-be-true prospect.

"It sounds like she is. Where is Sal?" I ask, noticing his absence for the first time.

"He comes and goes between cells, helping with communications and stuff like that, even travels back to L.A. from what I hear. He and James have singlehandedly kept the two cities alive."

"What do you think James is doing? He's been gone all day." I find that I'm worried about him, more than usual.

Aydan shrugs. "I've learned not to ask. He's still as secretive as ever, more actually."

"I guess that's my fault," I say, scooping a lonely carrot with my spoon.

"Not really. There have been several non-Symbiots who have been captured and infected. They spilled what they knew faster than you can imagine."

"That's of little consolation to me."

Aydan sets his empty bowl to the side and squares his shoulders in my direction. "You can't blame yourself for what happened."

"Everyone keeps saying that, but I think I always will." The honesty in my voice surprises me. "I was weak. I should have been able to keep the agent at bay."

"Do you think it—"

A small commotion from the entrance to the dining area interrupts our conversation. "They brought back Eklyptors!" someone shouts.

Aydan and I exchange a glance, then we're on our feet, jogging through the door toward the larger, adjoining warehouse. The few still left follow, feet shuffling as they try to funnel through the narrow door. We spill out onto the other side, craning our necks.

At first, I don't see anything, so I take a few tentative steps, peering around one of the wide, supporting columns. The buzzing in my head picks up, climbing several notches all at once. First, I spot James—who accounts for some of the noise but can hardly be responsible for such a steep spike.

As I take another step, I spot Blare, Spencer and Jori, flanking two men dressed in black military wear. They are on their knees, hands bound behind their backs.

"Shit," I say under my breath as I recognize one of them. *Gecko Man!*

His bug eyes find their way to me as if magnetized. "You?!" he exclaims in disbelief. His face disfigures into a mask of hatred. Looking ready to lynch me, he tries to stand, but Blare puts a hand on his shoulder and forces him back down.

"You're fuckin' Fender," he growls. "You'll pay for this."

Jori lightly butts him in the back of the head with the back end of his rifle. "Shut up or the next one will knock you unconscious."

I don't recognize the second Eklyptor but, judging by the black uniform, he must also be one of Elliot's. He's just a foot soldier, though. His buzzing signal is low and, considering his perfectly human appearance, I guess he hasn't been infected for very long.

"What's going on?" Aydan whispers close to my ear.

I shake my head. "I'm as clueless as you."

The *tap, tap* of heels brings our attention to the decisive figure of Kristen Albright as she approaches. Everyone watches in hushed interest as she comes to a stop in front of the two kneeling men. She's wearing a lab coat and rubber gloves.

Her sharp, green eyes take inventory of the Eklyptors for a moment, then turn to James. She nods, as if in approval. Without a word, she digs in the front pocket of her coat and pulls something out. To get a better angle, I take a step forward. A capped syringe is in her hand, held firmly.

A cure? Is she going to test a cure?!

I clutch at the first thing I find, and I'm surprised when it clutches back. Aydan's hand! Our eyes lock. The same desperate quality that I feel burrows in the depths of his black eyes. Unconsciously, we move closer to each other, looking for strength in proximity as we face this unprecedented moment.

"Him first," Kristen says, pointing the syringe at Gecko Man.

Jori and Spencer grab the reptilian Eklyptor by the arms and force him to his feet. He struggles to get free, squirming and swinging his weight from side to side.

"Damn you!" Jori curses.

They try to keep him still, but Gecko Man is strong. Pleasure shining in her eyes, Blare steps forward, aims the end of a rifle to the back of the Eklyptor's neck and releases a quick jab. The creature jerks, arms flailing, and falls back to his knees. He sways and seems about to drop flat on his face, but Jori puts him in a chokehold and manages to keep him upright. Gecko Man's bug eyes roll back and forth, his long tongue lolls.

Wasting no time, Kristen takes a knee in front of the Eklyptor and decisively wraps a wide rubber strip around his upper arm. In a matter of seconds, she finds a vein and plunges the needle into the crook of his elbow. The amber liquid in the syringe disappears.

"No, no!" the other Eklyptor says, recoiling from Kristen. "What is that? What is it?!" he demands.

The entire room goes eerily quiet. I know we're all holding our breaths because you can't hear the slightest inhale or exhale. Our entire future as individuals, as a species, seems to hang on an interminable second in which we stare at the slack face of this once-human.

My mind races as I imagine the amber solution traveling up the man's arm, making its way to his lungs, his heart, his brain—where the agent resides. Will Kristen's concoction kill the parasite? Will the long-trapped, human consciousness survive? Is that even desirable? The body's rightful owner knows nothing of what's been done to him: the enormous eyes, the flickering tongue, the utterly alien appearance, the nightmare!

God, is it right to do this? Is it fair to snatch the captive host from his mental prison to dump him into this horrid reality?

I squeeze Aydan's hand with white-knuckled strength, wondering why I never asked myself these questions, why I never realized I might have to play God in the name of my survival.

Chapter 33

Slowly, Jori sets Gecko Man on the floor and backs away. His face is pale and fixed in a fearful grimace, a strange expression for a strong man who has the upper hand.

Kristen stands next to James, her features impassive and calculated. She looks like someone who knows exactly what to expect. In contrast, James bites his lower lips, eyes unblinking, fixed on the lab specimen that now lays at our feet.

Across from us, Blare and Rheema stand side by side. The former seeming unfazed, the latter with a hand pressed to her mouth and her eyes full of something I can't quite put a finger on.

After a long hushed moment, Gecko Man stirs. His feet jerk. His hands twitch. He sits up with difficulty and looks around, rubbing the back of his neck, wincing.

"You bastards," he hisses through clenched teeth.

A thrill of disappointment runs through everyone. The other Eklyptor regains some of his color and seems to relax somewhat. I look to Kristen for a reaction. She's still looking on calmly, expectant.

Gecko Man spits on the floor, his long, fleshy tongue flicking out of his mouth like a party horn. "You can play your little games. You can hold out hope, but your efforts are pitiful. We are the dominant species now. You are . . . you are . . ." He gives a slow blink, opens and closes his mouth ineffectually.

His impossibly big eyes grow bigger still. He looks over to his Eklyptor companion, then down at the crook of his elbow. Sweat breaks on his receding hairline and slides to the protruding ridges that border the top of his eyes like bony eyelashes. His entire body begins to shake.

"What . . . w-what have you . . .?" A convulsive fit comes over him. His spine arches backward. His limbs thrash.

I press closer to Aydan as if he could spare me this horror, this cruel uncertainty. He wraps an arm around me, and we practically shake in unison.

Gecko Man collapses to the floor, quaking uncontrollably.

"Oh, no. Oh, no!" his companion cries out.

"God." Rheema pulls back and turns, unable to bear witness to whatever this is.

White foam spills from one corner of Gecko Man's mouth. His fat, pink tongue lolls out, draping across his cheek and falling all the way down to his ear.

He suddenly goes still. Very still.

I stare intently at his chest, my eyelids petrified in an unblinking, open position. I watch his breathing go from agitated to shallow to none in less than a minute.

Kristen kneels by his motionless shape, presses two fingers to his neck. Her expression remains stern, giving nothing away. Slowly, she pulls a stethoscope from her lab coat and listens for Gecko Man's heartbeat. After a drawn out minute, she puts the implement away and stands.

James searches her face. She simply shakes her head.

"What was all that?" Blare demands. "Care to explain?"

It's what we are all thinking but can hardly ask in our current state of shock.

"Cure trial," Kristen says.

"Looks like a bust," Blare puts in.

"For someone as advanced as this man, yes." Kristen pulls out a second syringe from her pocket.

"No! Not me. Stay away from me!" The more normal Eklyptor cries out, scooting backward from his kneeling position, but running into Spencer's tree-trunk legs.

"How long have you been infecting this body?" Kristen asks him.

"Stay away from me! Stay away!" he continues to cry out, his eyes wide and staring fixedly at the syringe in Kristen's hand.

"How long have you been infecting this body?" Kristen asks again, raising her voice.

But the Eklyptor is beside himself, gone into full hysterics, begging over and over to be left alone.

Kristen shrugs and gestures to Jori and Spencer to subdue him. She's about to plunge the syringe into his arm when Rheema's voice resonates hollowly through the warehouse.

"Is no one concerned with the ethical aspects of this *trial*?"

Kristen caps the syringe and puts it back in her pocket. The Eklyptor whimpers and curls into a ball.

Rheema's eyes move over the crowd, searching for—what?—a sounding board? A challenger? An ally?

"Ethics were forgone the moment they started stealing bodies," Kristen says calmly.

"Are you saying we aren't any better than they are?"

"It's not about *better*, at this point. It's about smarter and stronger. If you want to survive, that is."

"I do," Rheema says, her eyes flickering down.

"At what cost?" Kristen challenges.

Rheema doesn't answer.

"At what cost?" Kristen insists.

"At any cost," Rheema admits, lowering her chin in embarrassment.

Kristen's intense gaze goes around in a circle, making eye contact with everyone.

My mind reels with more questions than before. When Kristen's gaze locks with mine, my thoughts freeze. She searches, reaches deep inside of me for doubt, disapproval, defiance, anything. I'm unable to offer her any of those. Her eyes are clear, offering no judgment, no recrimination. She wants a consensus, an honest one. We either agree and go on with this, or we don't.

But if we don't, then what?

We know that without a cure our chances are none to zero. So yeah, as unethical as this might be, it seems I'm on board.

At any cost.

"At any cost," Aydan whispers next to me.

"At any cost. At any cost. At any cost." Kristen's words are repeated quietly, but confidently by everyone.

Rheema shakes her head, turns away and walks to the back of the room. No one judges her for the challenge, for her humanity. I know I don't. We're all thinking the same things. It's just some of us are less emotional than others, more logical than others, more battered than others.

Whatever the reason, it all boils down to one thing . . .

227

We are selfishly human.

With everyone's consensus, Kristen wastes no time and plunges the contents of her second syringe into a struggling, but easily subdued Eklyptor.

We wait in suspense for the seizure, the foaming at the mouth, the stillness, but only the latter comes.

The Eklyptor passes out at Jori and Spencer's feet. He lays immobile, breathing heavily for a long moment. We inch closer, focused on his chest and twitching face.

Kristen checks his vitals, then orders him moved to a cot. She runs back toward the lab and returns with a blood pressure cuff. She sits at the edge of the cot, pumps air into the cuff and listens with her stethoscope, her face less indifferent by the moment.

Aydan and I exchange many charged glances, standing at a short distance like faithful sentinels.

"How are his vitals?" James inquires five minutes later.

"Normal, now," Kristen says.

"Why isn't he . . . coming to?"

"I don't know. If it worked, it could take time for his consciousness to find its way out."

We watch on, barely breathing. After another five long minutes, the surge of hope that rippled through the group seems to have deflated. Blare makes a disgusted sound in the back of her throat and walks away.

The man groans and stirs.

Blare turns on her heel and returns.

His eyes open one millimeter at a time. He grimaces and puts a hand to his brow as if the light is too much for him to bear.

He groans again, shaking his head from side to side, heaving as if he's been running. He swallows with difficulty and croaks out a word.

Kristen leans in closer. "What is it?" she asks.

"Water," he says a little louder.

"God, his buzzing is gone," Aydan murmurs at my side, touching a hand to his head. I blink, noticing this for the first time. My heart stops.

It worked. It worked!

Jori hurries off to the side and returns with a metal canteen. He hands it to Kristen who lets the man take a few swigs. He licks his lips and looks around. At the sight of those around him, he seems to want to melt into the cot. His eyes are wide and full of fear.

"W-where am I?"

"You're safe," Kristen says in a sweet reassuring tone. "You're safe now."

Chapter 34

"From my conversation with him, I ascertain he was infected no more than three months ago," Kristen says.

We're back in the dining area, sitting around the largest available table. Speculations have been running high since Simon Whitebear—the first human to receive the cure—rejoined the human ranks.

The event begs several questions.

Does the cure only work on people who were infected recently? If so, what is the magic number? Three months? Six? A year? Does the cure only work on hosts without mutations? Would it work on Symbiots? How do we keep testing? How long do we test? What is the most effective way to distribute this cure? Can it be refined to save long-infected humans from a death like Gecko Man's?

On and on. The questions are endless, and none of them have straight answers. Not this early. Not without more data. Not without more time. Something we don't have.

James has been pacing alongside the table, deep in thought. His brow is etched with worry lines, his mouth set in a tight line. I don't think I've ever seen him this conflicted, not even the time IgNiTe openly declared war against Eklyptors, and he gave all IgNiTe members carte blanche to leave the team.

"I hope that during all your *secret* planning you came up with a way to massively distribute this cure," Blare says. "Water system? Airborne? What's it gonna be? We can hardly run around the city interviewing Eklyptors, asking when they were infected before we shoot them up. Not that *I* would ask."

"Shit, Blare!" Aydan exclaims, losing his cool. "For once, I'd like to hear something helpful come out of your fucking mouth. You're always full of sarcastic opinions, but ZERO solutions. Next time you wag your tongue, why don't you make it something we'd actually want to hear?"

Several heads bob up and down in agreement. To my surprise, Blare tips a smile at Aydan and simply flips him the bird. If I'd been the one to say that, she'd have jumped my ass. It seems she and Aydan have built more than a decent rapport while I've been gone.

Before we came in here, James asked me if I was okay with Blare coming in. He told me he'd talked to her, and she had promised not to bother me anymore. I told him it was fine. I'm no one to decide she should stay out of the crew—not when she's been at it longer than I have.

James stops his pacing and stands at the foot of the table. All eyes turn in his direction.

"Everyone knows why secrecy has been and *is* necessary. Cell members who are captured and infected immediately divulge everything they know. So *secret plans* are and will continue to be crucial to our success. Rest assured, however," he looks over at Blare who seems barely able to hold his gaze, "the dissemination of a cure as well as many others topics have been thoroughly discussed, whether or not you are aware of it.

"Much work is already underway. Additional tests will be necessary, of course. We need to make sure a massively distributed cure won't have any adverse effects on the uninfected human population.

"What I'd like for us to discuss, at the moment, is more immediate than that, however. I know some of you are concerned with ethical questions." He looks around for Rheema, but it seems this conversation is one she decided to pass.

"We're beyond ethics at this point," Jori says. "The majority agrees already, even before Kristen administered the second shot. After seeing Simon reclaim his body, whatever qualms I had to begin with are gone."

"Yes."

"I agree."

"Couldn't have said it better myself."

There's general accord among everyone present. It's hard to argue with words like *reclaim*. Simon was only given back what was taken from him. Nothing more. Nothing less. Every hijacked human who still has hope to regain what was stolen from them deserves a chance.

"Okay," James says, his unwavering command back in place in light of his team's unequivocal support. "As plans for refinement and widespread distribution of a cure continue, I would like to discuss more pressing matters." His gaze drifts in my direction then moves over to Aydan.

I don't need to hear more. I can put names and faces to these pressing matters James is talking about: Whitehouse and Hailstone.

I guess my stay here has come to an end. It was good while it lasted.

Chapter 35

After a detailed conversation with James, the *pressing matters* he referred to earlier are now floating inside my head like rogue balloons impossible to gather in one place. They flow in and out of my field of vision, while I struggle to grasp them and look at them closer. But it's hopeless. What I need is time to get my head around what I must do. There's just never enough of that. All I know is that what James laid out in front of us is not some hastily arranged plan, but something that must have been in the works for a while, anticipating the final creation of a cure.

Aydan and I sit at the table, staring at our hands, still digesting everything. Everyone else has moved along, back to the main warehouse to make their own preparations. Kristen is moving out, permanently relocating to a larger, well-equipped facility that, apparently, she uses on and off. James left to get in touch with other IgNiTe cell leaders and unify our attack plan. Jori, Spencer and Margo are returning to their respective cells, eager to share what they have seen, eager to return to the fight with renewed hope.

We'll have to stop staring at our hands soon. We'll have to pack and head back where we're needed most. Maybe we were hoping to stay and be able to fight together, rather than alone, but that would have been too good to be true.

"It's stupid," I say. "But I keep wishing he'll come back and tell us we don't have to go. I know I said I'd rather go back to Whitehouse, but now . . ."

Aydan chuckles. "Me, too."

His black eyes lock with mine. After a beat, they move slowly across my face, searching my features with such intensity that I become self-conscious. Heat rises to my cheeks. I fidget on the spot, unsure of what to do or say. He scrutinizes me unapologetically, as if he's trying to memorize me before we leave, before we go back and risk our lives and maybe never see each other again.

"I wish things were different," he says." I wish I could allow myself to hope, but I can't. It hurts too much. I look at the future and, in spite of this cure, I don't see anything. I try, but everything seems so dark, so uncertain. I fear what we'll become in the end. Only God knows how many will die. I don't see how anything will ever be the same in the end. Hope and dreams just seem a thing of the past."

Aydan's words resonate inside my head. They hit home and stick there because he's describing the exact way I feel. Reality and hope don't mix. Not anymore.

He stands abruptly, takes my hands and pulls me to my feet. His eyes are brimming with a desperate quality I've never seen in them before.

"What if I don't see you again?" He takes a step closer. He's barely a couple of inches away from me. "I know you've figured it out, but I have to . . . I have to tell you."

My hand moves up, ready to land across his lips to silence

him. It's typical Marci, unable to give, unable to even take. But I've done this before. I silenced Xave when it most mattered. So, this time, I make a fist and press it to my side.

Opening up is hard, no matter what, but it's a lot easier to do when it's the right time. And this *is* the right time, if only because we're alive.

"From the moment I met you at Howls," Aydan says, "that day James brought you in to meet the team, you made an impression."

I frown. He acted like he hated me. Now he says I made an impression?

"I know. I know." He nods, noticing my skepticism. "From the way I acted, no one could have been able to tell, but it's true. I just . . . well . . . you were with Xave, and I've never been good at these kinds of things. It didn't help that you unsettled me. Your confidence, your attitude, your strength, and the fact that you were like me, a Symbiot. Don't even mention your computer skills. They're enough to intimidate any self-respecting hacker." He gives me a wry smile. "You're smart and witty and . . ."

He brushes my cheek with the back of his hand. A warm thrill washes over me. I want to pull away and I want to stay. Emotions crash inside of me like worlds colliding. This is betrayal when I think of Xave. But, when I'm selfish, it feels right and fair and deserved. There's no one left who truly loves me. Is it wrong to hope for one person to think I'm all the things Aydan says I am?

"And, on top of that, you're beautiful." He pauses. His eyes waver. "Marci, I'm in love with you. I know it's the wrong time. It's too soon, but I wanted to tell you in case we . . ." His voice breaks. He looks down and takes a deep, shuddering breath.

I lean forward slowly, as if he's some sort of magnet I can't resist. Gently, I rest my cheek on his chest. He lets out a small, startled sound at my unexpected closeness and wraps his arms around me in a tender, almost shy hug. His lips brush my forehead and stay there as we dare to relish this quiet, intimate moment.

I marvel that, in spite of my aloofness and all we've been through, he's managed to build these feelings for me. I'm nothing like the way he sees me, not when I look in the mirror or think of the things I've done, and it makes me wonder about his sanity, but especially about the depth of his loneliness. But even though I might be the only option in his solitary life, I'm grateful he chose me, grateful his heart is big enough to love someone like me.

"Thank you." It's all I manage, even though I'd like to be able to offer more. There's something new stirring inside of me, but how can I allow myself to explore it, to find a name for it? Hoping is so hard, especially when life has already taught me to fear instead.

Chapter 36

"Where the hell have you been?" Lamia comes out of nowhere, grabs me by the shoulders and pushes me against the wall as soon as I come out of the elevator on my floor at Whitehouse's building. Her voice is an angry, rumbling whisper. A puff of air escapes past my lips as my back slams against the wall. She presses her muscular forearm along the length of my clavicle and leans into me. I wince. She feels like five hundred pounds of brick, ready to crush me.

Lamia sticks her nose right up to mine, her breath smelling of garlic. Has she been waiting for me here? Ready to pounce as if I were a helpless mouse? That seems hard to believe, considering that I've been gone for over a day. Except it's late, and she should be sleeping—not harassing me. I try to shrug out of her grasp, but she's got me pinned like a bug.

I'm about to demand that she let me go when I remember who I'm supposed to be. In a snap, I change my challenging expression into one of submission.

"I was just repurposing, repurposing. Have to find just the ride, the perfect ride." I lay my Azrael-crazy really thick and stick to my previous story, the one I gave Lyra and Onyx. I despise the sniveling act, but it's necessary. Lamia is a mean beast. Antagonizing her could get me killed in a snap. There's no need to be reckless—especially now that someone cares about what happens to me.

"Bullshit! You're up to something. I don't trust you."

Lamia's reptilian gaze pierces mine unrelentingly. Her eyes used to be normal, but she's been busy making them match her tail. A wicked smile spreads over her lips and her long, barbed tail swings from side to side as if in pleasure.

"You don't fool me," she says. "I'll find out what you're up to, and then Elliot won't be so grateful to you for *saving* his life. I bet you'd love to visit Dr. Sting again, 'cause that's where you're headed. Count on that."

An icy shiver climbs up my spine as an image of Dr. Sting's torture chair rises inside my mind. In an effort not to give away my fear, I say, "Repurpose. Need to repurpose. Came back just to sleep, rest for a while. Need energy to repurpose. Have to find the perfect ride, just for me. Unique," I ramble on, not trying to deny the fact that I've been gone, but owning it instead.

"Shut the fuck up!" Lamia's tail rises straight up in the air, stiff as her tone of voice. Her eyes flash with anger, and I'm sure she's about to tear into me when a sound from the barracks startles us. Our heads snap in that direction. She snarls in displeasure.

Reluctantly, she pulls away, releasing me. I take a hand to my chest, dare to think I've gotten away with little more than a sore pride, when, suddenly, Lamia's tail coils, snaps, and lands a stinging lash across my left cheek. I yelp, both in surprise and pain. My hand flies to my face. Warm blood seeps from the wound and wets my fingers.

It takes every ounce of restraint I possess to hold back and simply hunch over, holding my cheek. This is the second time I've been smacked only to find that grinning and bearing it is my best option. Blare and Lamia owe me big time.

Lyra comes around the corner and finds Lamia glowering at me and enjoying my cowardly stance.

"What is going on here?" Lyra asks.

"The little bitch's been gone again," Lamia says. "She says she's been repurposing, but I don't buy it."

Lyra lets out a tired sigh. "Don't you have better things to do than worry about this useless piece of crap?" She gestures in my direction with a furry hand.

Useless piece of crap? Gee, thanks!

"I have many things to worry about," Lamia says, "and I worry about *all of them,* thoroughly."

"Oui. Oui." Lyra waves a hand in the air and continues her trek toward the bathroom, which is where she was headed in the first place, I suppose.

"Pit stop. Also need a pit stop," I say, following Lyra and throwing Lamia a dirty look over my shoulder. She snaps her tail against the floor as a reminder that has the desired effect. I put a hand to my face and wince at the sting.

Lyra pushes the bathroom door open and walks in. I follow, glad to get away from Lizard Witch, but soon find myself in the clutches of Perverse Kitty.

"Putain!" Lyra curses and whirls to face me. "Didn't I say you couldn't keep disappearing like this?" "This" comes out like *dzees*. Her French accent is thick when she loses her temper. She's definitely lost it now. Too bad.

"There's shit going down, Lyra. I suggest you check with your IgNiTe contacts if you haven't heard from them yet."

Her round eyes narrow. "Regardless, you can't keep screwing up like this." She leans closer and puts a hand on my shoulder. "If you blow my cover, I will kill you," she purrs, her claws digging into my skin.

"Ow!"

She pulls away and locks herself in a stall. I rub my shoulder as I walk to the mirror. There's a two-inch slash across my cheek and blood still pouring out of it.

"Just great." I shake my head and run the warm water in the sink. It takes a handful of paper towels to clean the wound. When I'm done, I keep pressure on it to stop the bleeding.

Lyra comes out of the stall. "What are you talking about *shit going down.*" She walks to the sink to wash her hands.

"Need to know basis," I say with a smile. "Like I said, you'd better get in touch with your people. See if they have any news for you. Any order coming down from James."

She whirls, looking ready to jump me. We get into a staring match. I don't blink. I have no reason to be afraid of Lyra and nothing to hide. If she thinks being a higher-up in Whitehouse's organization gives her authority over me, she's sorely mistaken.

"I'll make sure to check with my cell leaders," she says when she realizes I won't let her intimidate me.

"Good." I nod and turn to leave.

Before I get to the door, Lyra decides to have the last word. "You'd better watch your back. Lamia is on to you and, for my part, I'm starting to think you're more trouble than it's worth."

I could sit here and argue with her, but that'd be a waste of time. She'll get her panties on straight once orders trickle down from James to the other IgNiTe cells.

For now, I'll try a quick meditation session, then I'll worry about the important things I must set in motion.

Chapter 37

When I get back to my bed in the barracks, I lay back and pretend to go to sleep. Lamia watched me come in from her own bed, where she's sitting reclined against the headboard, still as a stone figure. Only her creepy eyes move, following my every step. Hopping on the computer right now would be a big mistake, no matter how desperate I am to get James's crazy scheme rolling.

Lyra comes back to bed a few minutes later, lays down and stares at the ceiling. I watch her dark silhouette from the corner of my eye. I don't see how she'll be able to go back to sleep now. For my part, I know there'll be no rest—not with all the things whirling inside my head and the fact that I'm back here, sleeping under the same roof as Lizard Witch. I wish her hideous tail would quit flashing in front of my eyes everytime I close them. I keep imagining the grotesque appendage wrapping around my neck and squeezing.

I toss and turn even after Lamia lays down and Lyra's breaths grow regular. I remind myself that no one is expecting immediate action. James and Aydan will both wait for me to do my part first, and the plan is to wait for a couple of days, anyway. So I shouldn't be itching this badly to get started with my hack?

Take it easy, Marci. You have time.

Lamia may have laid down, but she might be wide awake, watching, waiting for me to screw up. I need to do this when no one's around. Keeping my ass in bed is the best course of action. I take several deep breaths, but I'm still restless. The decision makes sense, but that doesn't mean I'm happy about it.

Three miserable hours and one harrowing meditation later, I'm still awake in bed. It's 6 A.M. and I feel like shit. I wait for Lamia to leave the barracks before even stirring. Bleary-eyed, I jumped out of bed and go to the lower level for a quick shower. It's the only area set up for that purpose. This was an office building, so the other floors have only restrooms. The showers in the basement were probably in place for the maintenance crews and guards who, before The Takeover, must have worked here around the clock. They aren't communal, which is a blessing, though new curtains and a deep-grout cleanse couldn't hurt. There aren't many stalls, twenty at most, so it gets crowded down there. But most people shower much earlier, so by the time I show up, there are only a few people still using the rundown facilities. Everyone else is already in the mess hall eating breakfast.

When I'm done, I head back upstairs, a towel wrapped around my head. I'm hungry and would love to get a warm breakfast, but this is a perfect opportunity to get to work.

I'm wearing a clean pair of black army pants and a tight, wife-beater top, standard issue for everyone here. Hesitantly,

I dig in my backpack and pull out the zipper bags that contain Dad's old t-shirts. I would love to wear one of them, but I'm not sure it's a good idea. I should probably keep them in the bags, safe, preserved. It's not like I have a lot of things that used to belong to him. What little is left, I should save as a memento. Except mementos are for people who expect to have long, prudent lives in homes with shelves and attics and places where to store their memories, safe from dust and decay. I'm clearly not one of those people. Not sure anyone is anymore.

What life I still have to live is right here, right now. Tomorrow is nothing but an illusion, a place I might never get to visit, a mirage that might disappear when I blink out of today.

Fingers trembling, I open one of the bags, pull the t-shirt out and shake it loose. It's charcoal gray with a band logo on the front: Def Leppard. I grin. Dad liked Def Leppard? Judging from the size, he owned this t-shirt before joining the army. There's no way he would have been able to fit in it afterward. I remember him sturdy, able to pick me up with one muscular arm.

I shake my hair loose from the towel, then slip the t-shirt over my head. For a moment, I think I catch Dad's clean scent on the fabric, a scent that must be embedded in my memories like no other scent will ever be. But the t-shirt is old and has been in storage for too long to hold onto any traces of Dad.

I tuck the t-shirt into my pants, finger-comb my hair and take a deep inhale.

Time to kick some cyber ass.

Chapter 38

I'm glad I didn't underestimate the task and started as soon as I could because it takes me the whole two days to plant all the pieces of information needed to create the biggest distraction in the history of distractions.

Elliot may not be keeping much about his whereabouts and personal plans on the network, but some of his captains are still making use of it, and that certainly made my job a lot easier to accomplish.

Surreptitiously, I sneak out of the corner office from which I've performed most of my hacking tasks. I worked from the terminal by my bed a few times, but I kept that to a minimum for fear of raising more suspicions in an already-suspicious Lamia. For the most part, I played Space Invaders, making crazy shooting sounds, cursing at the screen and threatening to blow it up. She watched me from a distance, her eyes full of hate and ill intent, but mostly frustration.

I take the elevator down to the mess hall, thinking it's just a matter of time before one of Elliot's captains puts two and two together. And once they do, they'll be so eager to please their leader that they won't hesitate to jump into action.

Things in the mess hall are already in full swing by the time I get there. I get a small lunch, trying not to feel guilty I get to eat this way. As I chew, I think of chicken Parmesan as the fuel I need to do a job no one else can do, a job that may, if everything goes as planned, be the snowflake that will cause the avalanche.

I'm halfway through my meal when Lyra, accompanied by two of Elliot's higher ups, comes in the mess hall and starts calling names. This is nothing new. When there are impromptu raids that less-elite Whitehouse soldiers can't handle, teams are assembled in this fashion to go lend a hand. But—when I notice they're calling the best fighters they've got—my ears really perk up.

It's happening. It must be happening.

When she's done calling names, there is a group of about thirty of their meanest, best-trained soldiers, Lamia included. Hunched over my plate, I watch the proceedings from under my eyebrows, willing Lyra to look my way. She doesn't.

C'mon, c'mon, Lyra! She's in now, aware of our plan, and she's supposed to raise a flag. The group starts filing out the double doors. Lyra turns her back on me. I bite my knuckles to hold back a string of curses. Lyra is the last one to leave. She holds the door open and takes a step out of the room.

I exhale in frustration. I really thought this was it. I send one last, frustrated look at Lyra's retreating figure. The door begins to swing close behind her and, just as I've become convinced it's not time yet, she looks over her shoulder, her round green eyes flashing with such intensity that she leaves me no doubt the first stage of our plan is in motion.

Knees bouncing out of control, I force myself to remain in my seat until I finish the food on my plate. When I'm done, I dispose of my tray and leave the mess hall at a leisurely pace. With Lamia gone, no one really cares about me, but I keep up the act. In my mind, I'm running toward my computer terminal, flying down the corridors, my loose hair flying behind me. In reality, every slow step hurts and feels like a wasted lifetime. I must warn Aydan, and this play-pretend calmness seems reckless in the face of his safety. But when I step out of the elevator into my floor, all caution dies, and I run. I run so fast my heart hammers out of control, and I arrive at my desk in a matter of seconds.

I sit, pull out the keyboard and can hardly type. Aydan knows everything is in place on my end. I let him known as soon as I finished. Now, he's just waiting for my signal that it has begun.

I'm supposed to send him an encoded message, one he can check whenever he has a chance to log in, so I do that first. We've been messaging this way for the last couple of days, using a custom tool I developed. Me from here. Aydan from SeaTac where, to my surprise, Luke remains. The tokens Aydan and I send back and forth are ultra-secure and authenticated to a private key that only we know. Our communications are, therefore, safer than text messages, emails, or phone calls, especially when all of those means of communication are now controlled by Eklyptors.

After sending the message, I crack my fingers. Uncertainty fills me. There's no reason for it. He'll get my message. Still, I'd like confirmation. I'd like to know he's okay.

I fire up our custom chatting tool in the hopes that he's logged in.

$Dr.V> You did it

I breathe a sigh of relief. He got my message.

$Warrior> They'll be on their way soon

Whitehouse is deploying his elite forces to attack Hailstone. This was step one of my mission: inserting a few clever reports into Elliot's military intelligence machine to help his captains figure out Hailstone's location. I carefully altered several documents to contain suggestive hints about their enemy faction, inserting information on supply runs, attack patterns, electricity usage and anything that would cause those who review the documents to look more closely at SeaTac. But more importantly, I planted enough information that makes it look as if Hailstone is planning an attack on Whitehouse.

Now, it's Aydan's turn to put his hacker skills to the test. His job is to deactivate Hailstone's security and leave them exposed to the attack. Intentionally letting Whitehouse grow his faction is risky, but we need them distracted. Besides, we plan to hit them hard before they have a chance to reorganize.

Again, my thoughts turn in Luke's direction of their own accord. They've been doing that ever since we got our orders from James. I shake my head. I don't want to think about Luke. Lyra has been instructed to take care of him, and there's nothing I can do about that. I'm not the leader of this rebellion, and even if I was, making decisions about Luke's fate could hardly be left up to me. *This is for the best*, I tell myself. Lyra is in the dark about my real relationship with Luke. James thought it would be better that way, for my safety, and I agree with him.

I refocus on the words flashing on the screen.

$Dr. V> Everything's ready on my end
$Warrior> Really?! That's great!
$Dr. V> Just need to hit a button when they get close
$Warrior> Get out of there as soon as you can, k?
$Dr. V> I will
$Warrior> Don't play the hero. Just get out
$Dr. V> Already said I would. What? Worried about me?
$Warrior> Of course, I'm worried. Duh!
$Dr. V> Why?
$Warrior> Why?! What do you mean why?
$Dr. V> Why are you worried about me?
$Warrior> Because Whitehouse's sending his best and they'll be armed to the teeth. That's why
$Dr. V> Is that all?

I'm about to curse him for being dense when I realize *I'm* the one who's not getting it.

Why are you worried about me? This is what he wants to know.

I stare at my fingers, frozen over the keyboard. The cursor blinks and blinks.

There is a right time for everything, and this is the right time for this question, isn't it? Maybe it's also the right time for an answer, even an honest one.

$Warrior> Because I

I don't type for a long time. Words tumble inside my

mind, trying to align themselves into the correct sentence. I don't want to say too much. I don't want to say too little. I just want to . . .

Oh, the hell with it!

$Warrior> Because I care about you and I don't want to lose you

It's not "I love you" by any means because I don't know if I'm capable of ever allowing myself to fall in love again, but it's the truth. I care about him. He's my friend, and it's not hard to imagine him becoming more than that—not now that I know him, that I understand him. I just don't know if I'll ever get there. If it'll ever feel right to push Xave aside to fill the space he occupies with someone else.

$Warrior> So just be safe, k?
$Dr. V> I promise I'll be fine.
$Warrior> Don't make promises!

Xave promised he would be fine right before he went into that nightclub.

$Dr. V> I promise I'll see you again
$Warrior> !! DON'T MAKE PROMISES !!
$Dr. V> I'll be fine. I'll see you again

I shake my head.

$Warrior> That still sounded like a promise
$Dr. V> That's because it is, whether you like it or not

I scoff, clenching my teeth, a simmering anger rising to the surface.

Whether I like it or not.

Aydan knows hope isn't fit for this reality anymore, so why doesn't he see promises aren't either? I've been mad at Xave for *his* promise, for saying he would be fine, then leaving me behind. And it's stupid to hold that against him when the only thing his promise represented was his *desire* to be fine, to come back and be with me once more, the way we were that night. He didn't betray me or break a real promise. He simply used the wrong words, and it was my job to realize that.

I type a quick response.

$Warrior> I want you to be fine AND I want to see you again

This is what Aydan is really saying and I agree with him. No promises needed.

$Dr. V> I see what you're doing, Ms. Stickler
$Warrior> Do you?
$Dr. V> Yep. So, how about you argue with this: I *promise* I will be thinking of you

A sad smile stretches my lips this time.

$Warrior> I *promise* not to argue about that
$Dr. V> I think I'd better go
$Warrior> Okay. Send me a message as soon as you can
$Dr. V> I will (no promises)

DISCONNECTED.

I stare at the word for what feels like hours. Time stands still, so still I feel I've turned to stone. At some point, I lock my computer and turn away from it. My eyes dart around the room, stopping at each perfectly made bed. I'm the only one here.

The fluorescent lights hum overhead. The air conditioning blows its constantly frigid air. I shiver, hug myself, realizing I don't want to be here. I want to be headed to that battle with Lyra and the others—not because my presence there would make any difference, but because I wouldn't have to sit here wondering if Aydan is all right.

* * *

Someone is back.

I see them on the feed from the security cameras which I pulled up on my computer and have been watching for eight hours, nonstop.

The black and white images show me only one van pulling up to the delivery area in the back of the building. Where is everyone else? Did Luke beat them? Is this all that's left of them?

The van's back doors open and a couple of Whitehouse's soldiers jump out. Even in the grainy footage, I sense their self-satisfaction, their smugness. It's in the way they step so lightly, the way they hold their heads high.

They succeeded.

It's what we wanted but, still, it makes me sick.

I push to the edge of my desk chair, my thoughts flying

to Luke once more, wondering about his fate. Did Lyra kill him as she was supposed to? I don't have to wonder for long because she soon steps out of the van, pushing someone ahead of her. The prisoner's hands are tied at the back. His head is low, blond hair obscuring his eyes.

Luke. He's alive!

An odd wave of relief passes over me, surprising me and angering me at the same time. I shouldn't care what happens to him. I shouldn't.

I watch Lyra's lithe figure as she pushes Luke along. *What are you up to, Lyra? Why didn't you follow James's orders?*

Tauro gets out next, manhandled by one of the twin dwarfs who usually guards Elliot's floor. I shake my head at the odd sight. I'm about to walk away from the computer to go downstairs when someone flies out of the van, lands on the ground, and flops helplessly like a fish. Something is wrapped all around his torso, pinning his arms to the sides.

My heart freezes and drops to my stomach. The crumpled shape struggles to his feet. He has the darkest mass of hair out of anyone out there.

You fucking idiot. What happened to all your promises?!

They've captured Aydan.

Chapter 39

I'm pacing like a caged beast alongside my bed. My fists tremble at my sides as my thoughts hit me like ramrods, one after another. They slam against me, then skitter away to hide from the shadows that have suddenly decided to revisit me.

Damn you, Azrael!

I press the palms of my hands into my eyes and push as if to put a plug to the mental flood.

My thoughts mix, compound, then boil down to one crucial question.

Do they know?

Did they capture Aydan as an Eklyptor? Or did they capture him as a Symbiot?

The logical answer rears its head, but I shut it away.

Neither option is good, but the last one could mean his death.

What do I do? What do I do?!

More than once I begin to walk out of the barracks just to turn back around. If they know he's a Symbiot and my own experience is any indication, they will take him to Elliot's office. The bastard will want to talk to him, not to mention Luke and Tauro. He'll want to state his superiority. He'll want to gloat in their faces.

But I can't go there. I don't have access to his floor—not through regular means, not through any means, really. Before, I would have used the air ducts to reach them, but after I popped out of one of them and nearly blew Elliot's head off, he had them secured, reinforced with steel grates that would take a giant to pry off.

Okay, okay . . . think, think!

Where would they take them after Elliot's office? Dr. Sting's basement? That's where they took me, to a near-fatal date with pain. I try to convince myself that there is no reason to have them tortured, but my damn logic tells me otherwise.

I keep trying to shut away my most terrifying, rational thought, but it's no use. It has made itself comfortable, mocking my optimistic emotions.

They know Aydan is a Symbiot.

They have to. Otherwise, he wouldn't be here. They brought Luke and his second in command. And then, they also brought Aydan, someone supposed to be of no consequence.

I sit at the edge of my bed, facing the wall. I bite the collar of my jacket, trying to control my ragged breaths.

Lyra! She has to help me get him out of here! James should know, too.

I hop on the computer and quickly type up a message. After I hit send, I sit there, feeling as useful and abstract as a handful of zeroes and ones traveling down a wire. I hope someone is listening.

What now?

My only sensible alternative it to sit here and wait for Lyra to get back. If I try to do something without knowing exactly what's going on, I might make things worse for Aydan. So I wait, chewing my nails until my fingertips hurt. I'm near a nervous breakdown when Lamia marches into the barracks, snarling my name before she even walks through the door.

"So you *are* here!" she says with a mixture of annoyance and relief. "I was sort of hoping you'd be gone, and I'd be given the chance to hunt you down."

I stand, pushing my desk chair out of the way. My chest fills with defiance. I'm not in the mood for submissiveness. Lamia does a double-take. Her steps get shorter and slower, and it's this caution of her that makes me realize my act is more important than ever. Too many things depend on it, and Aydan has just been added to the list.

"No need. No need. I'm right here." My stomach churns with disgust, but I tell myself her day is coming.

Lamia looks as disgusted as I feel. Who knew I could act so slimy? "You are *summoned*," she says, her earlier hesitation forgotten.

"Who needs me? Why? Why?"

"Elliot. The hell if I know why, but I have a feeling it ain't good." Her snake eyes glint. "I think you're about to get what you deserve."

I try to look scared which is not hard to do—not when ending up in Dr. Sting's chair again suddenly seems like a possibility.

Lamia stops at the foot of Lyra's bed and puts and hand on her holstered automatic. "Move it!" she says, gesturing with her head for me to walk ahead.

For a moment, I consider fighting her, but I'm unarmed and in the depths of Elliot's lair, I have a feeling I wouldn't get very far, even if I manage to be faster than Lamia's whiplash tail.

I move away from the desk, step into the middle aisle and walk toward the door. Lamia shoves me unnecessarily, making me stagger. I swallow my rage and lace my finger over my stomach. I want to swing at her so bad that this restricting action is the only thing keeping me from throwing caution to the wind.

A moment later, we're on the tenth floor in front of Elliot's office. Lamia knocks. Lyra opens the door. Her green eyes lock with mine, and I don't like what I see in them. Not at all. I shiver. Lyra steps aside to let me through.

"Not you," she tells Lamia and closes the door in her face.

The scene inside the office sends my heart into a wild pounding.

I shouldn't be here. I shouldn't be here.

There can be no good reason for being asked to join this group.

The first thing I register is Aydan kneeling in the middle of the office, his feet bare, his body tightly wound with what looks like several lengths of insulated wire. There's a red streak of blood smeared across his cheek. His head remains down, his gaze on the floor. I want to run to him, wipe the blood off his face, but I can't. Not if I'm to hold on to the slim possibility of protecting him.

I tear my gaze away from him and let it fall on Luke. He's standing behind Aydan, his blue eyes intent on mine, their inhuman iridescence doing nothing to hide his distress. His lips tremble, and I think there's a warning he wants to offer. But he remains silent.

Tauro stands next to him, tall and proud. His flat, black eyes give no indications as to where his focus is. But his expression is unmistakable. He is not happy.

Casually reclining on his desk, Elliot stands, arms crossed over his chest. An extremely amused expression has replaced his stick-up-the-ass normal one.

The twin dwarfs stand to his side, facing Aydan, their squat, muscular bodies resembling huge wine barrels. Their matching beards curl down to their stomachs, almost draping over the rifles they hold at the ready. Lyra joins them and stands at attention like a good little soldier. God, sometimes I hate her, and this is one of those times.

"My dear Azrael," Elliot drolls, pushing away from the desk. He pulls on the cuffs of his shirt and straightens his jacket, an affectation that I've come to despise. He wears the most expensive clothes money can buy, but his stuck-up ass never seems comfortable in them.

I imagine a syringe with his name on it.

Damn it, pay attention! He called you Azrael. Not Marci.

I repeat that several times until it sinks in and my heart marginally slows its frantic beating. This is *fubar*, but less so if he still thinks I'm an Eklyptor.

"Come in, come in." He gestures for me to step away from the closed door.

I take three steps forward, then stop.

"I'm starting to get the impression you will never cease to amaze me."

My teeth clench. My gaze darts to Aydan, then to Luke. Which one told Elliot to call me here? I don't guess I really need to ask. Only one of them is a coward. Hatred toward Luke churns in my gut. And to think I actually worried about him. *Idiot!*

Elliot cocks his head to the side, probably expecting my usual chattiness. I give him nothing.

"How come you never mentioned you knew Luke Hailstone?" Elliot asks, his unnatural golden eyes shining with malice as he points a finger at the blond boy with the face of an angel.

"Uh . . ."

Think fast, Marci. Think!

"Hailstone?!" I exclaim. " Hailstone?! Did you say Luke Hailstone?! He ain't no Hailstone. He's trying to fool ya. He's Luke Smith."

Elliot's eyebrows go up. He looks over at Luke in question.

"Her . . . host always thought my last name was Smith," Luke says, giving me a strange look since he doesn't know about my crazy act.

"I see." Elliot nods, satisfied with the explanation.

Azrael would have had no reason to tell Elliot about any of my family members or friends, so this is quite acceptable. My thoughts race, thinking of more excuses, trying to stay ahead. I've dodged not only a bullet but a missile. This is far from over, though.

I sneer at the coward, fear writhing in my gut. Why is he being so helpful? What has he told them? My knees feel so weak I have to shuffle restlessly not to give myself away.

"I have to admit this is the most convoluted story I've ever heard."

Convoluted story? My heart goes back to sledgehammer intensity. My hatred for Luke redoubles, and I want to march toward him, wrap my hands around his neck and strangle him. He's told Elliot about our origin. How could he?! To think I was glad Lyra didn't kill him.

Elliot walks to the terrarium where he keeps his huge scorpion. He bends at the waist to look at his hideous pet through the glass. A warm light glows on the arachnid's ebony exoskeleton. Noticing the presence of his master, it does a skittering, sideways dance, its huge pincers opening and closing, its stinger curled above its body.

"Tom Hailstone was a very ingenious chap but, with this, he truly outdid himself." Elliot drops a few live crickets into the terrarium. The scorpion lunges forward, its stinger striking without mercy. The cricket jumps, trying to get away, but it's caught in mid-air by one of the large pincers.

Everyone stares at the spectacle in morbid fascination. Elliot smiles fondly, his golden eyes creasing with contentment. I feel cold inside, no more than one of those crickets in the hands of a monster. My gaze flashes to Aydan. He's looking at me for the first time. Dry blood is crusted over his right cheek. Worry lines mark his forehead. Yet, something in his eyes gives me strength.

I'm here with you, his gaze seems to say.

It should be little relief—considering he's tied up and doesn't seem able to use his powers—but his presence does comfort me. At least I'm not alone, and he isn't either. We have each other.

Elliot pulls a sanitary wipe from a canister and carefully cleans his fingers. He throws the used wipe in a garbage can to the side, then absently rubs his hands together. "A new species," he says, slowly, rolling the words in his mouth.

My throat closes up and I'm glad for it, because I'd be screaming at the top of my lungs otherwise. It feels as if my voice would be so loud and shrill that Luke's head would explode, dispersing bits of his beautiful face all over the office—exactly what he deserves.

He's betrayed me. Yet again.

Yes, I gave away his location, but at least I gave him a fighting chance. He could have escaped Whitehouse's attack, if not for the fact that he's a useless coward. That's also why he's sold me out now. He couldn't stand to suffer this alone. He had to pull me down with him. Misery loves company. If this is how he treats those he cares about, I'd hate to see what he does to the rest.

I don't want to imagine what Elliot will make out of this information, and how he'd want to exploit it. It can't be anything good.

He walks back to his desk, looks down at Aydan. Elliot's face twists in surprised disgust, as if he'd forgotten Aydan was there and he's just rediscovered the helplessly bound boy.

"You," Elliot points at one of the twin dwarfs, "take this Fender down to Dr. Sting. I don't want to see him anymore. Hopefully, he'll turn out to be as useful as our dear Azrael after a visit to our *skillful* doctor."

No! I take a step forward. I can't let him take Aydan to that cruel monster. The torture will be too much for him. The pain will weaken him and then . . . *I can't lose him. I can't.* If Aydan succumbs to his agent, he may be lost forever; he may not be able to come back the way I did. I can't let that happen.

Both Lyra and Aydan cast warning glances in my direction. I freeze, eyes pleading. *We have to do something.* Aydan's gaze remains stern. I swallow and force myself to unclench my fists.

The twin hoists Aydan to his feet.

"Oh, one more thing," Elliot adds, "send Lamia in to

take your place."

The dwarf nods as he pushes Aydan toward the door. Aydan staggers and, without thinking, I reach out and help him regain his balance. His dark eyes give me a pointed look. He shrugs out of my grasp. I let my stupid hands fall to the side and avoid eye contact with Elliot and the dwarf. If I don't, they'll see my worry, my desperation and fear for Aydan.

Just get out of here in one piece, Marci. Then you can help him.

The door opens and closes. A moment later it opens again and Lamia strolls in, throwing Lyra a contemptuous look. She takes a guarding post next to Elliot.

The room seems to shrink around me, the walls moving closer together, pushing us into a tighter circle.

Aydan is gone, and every face in the room seems to leer in my direction. Even the scorpion appears nearer, its jaws snapping hungrily. Lyra is still here, but why doesn't her presence seem to matter anymore?

Aydan.

He's the only one who matters.

My eyes wander toward the door as if they could transmit a message. *Hang on. I'll get out of here in one piece, then I'll come for you. Promise.*

Chapter 40

"Well, Mr. Hailstone," Elliot stands in front of Luke. He's a few inches shorter but manages to appear the same height, somehow. "It seems your colleague," he inclines his head toward Tauro, "has managed to save your life. This *new species* claim warrants a careful look. If what he says is true, it would be remarkable. No need for hosts! What a dream!" He clasps his hands together.

Luke's lips are pale, pressed together in a thin line. His blue gaze meets mine, carrying an apology.

So it was Tauro. He was the one who sold me out in order to protect Luke's life, and he used the only card Elliot would never be able to resist. All his reproductively viable Eklyptors are dead, of course this seems like a dream to him.

"There will have to be tests to corroborate this, of course." Elliot rubs his chin, his eyes sparkling with a million ideas. "And I'll require Dr. Dunn's research—that was his name, right? I cannot believe nobody has continued his work!"

"Well, sir," Tauro says in a tone almost as refined as

Elliot's, "he did continue his research for many years, unfortunately without success. Then he was killed a few months back."

I exchange a quick glance with Lyra. It was her IgNiTe faction that killed Dunn. Now she just stands there, letting this happen. If she'd killed Luke like she was supposed to, we wouldn't be in this situation. We can't become Elliot's lab rats. He can't be allowed to learn the secrets hidden in our DNA. If that information falls into his hands, it could end humanity.

More than ever, I wish I was capable of giving this monster a heart attack, but my skills seem frozen.

"IgNiTe is responsible for the good doctor's death," Tauro continues. "Since then we've been too busy with The Takeover and attempting to contain the human rebellion. But it's our plan to continue his work."

Luke throws a hateful look over his shoulder. "Go right ahead, tell him everything. Lick his shoes while you're at it, why don't you?" His words drip with disgust.

Tauro regards Luke as if he's nothing but a child who doesn't understand what makes the world turn. "The alternative is simply unacceptable, Luke. I will not let you die and waste years of work. I promised your parents I would take care of you. One way or another, you have a destiny to fulfill. If this is the only way, so be it."

"Listen to your adviser, Mr. Hailstone," Elliot says. "He sounds like a very smart man." He walks to the other side of his desk and lays a hand on the phone. "If you'll excuse me now, a few important phone calls are in order. There are several geneticists in my staff who will be highly interested in this." He straightens his silk cravat and turns his attention to the remaining dwarf. "Take him to Donaldson," he points at Tauro. "He will lead him to Dunn's research materials."

Geneticists? That can't be good. It would take them no time to find out I'm a Symbiot. But they won't get that far. I would die before I let them take one single hair from my head.

Tauro takes a step forward, a model of contrition *and* obedience. "I shall do so, as long as you can guarantee Luke's safety."

Elliot takes a seat on his high back, leather chair. "But of course," he says in a syrupy sweet tone. He addressed Lyra, "I want Mr. Hailstone and Azrael to be kept safe. Bring them to a comfortable and secure room. Place guards outside. And don't let them out until I say so. Understood?"

No! I can't be locked up. I have to help Aydan, and I have to work on the next part of our plan. James is counting on me.

"Sir." Lyra assents in her best military voice. She takes a step toward Luke, a catlike smile making her whiskers twitch.

I stare at her, eyes burning. She swore to kill Luke, to kill *me*. Ridding the world of the Hailstone faction and its plans has always been her goal, and now she has the perfect opportunity to destroy the last two pieces of the puzzle. This is why she didn't kill Luke as James ordered. She wanted to know and understand the plan for herself, so she could tie all the loose ends.

"Lock me up? Lock me up?!" I whine. "But why? I wouldn't go anywhere."

"Ha!" Lamia exclaims. "She disappears for hours on end. Definitely needs to be locked up."

"Just do as I say." Elliot's eyes are on the phone. He's

dialing a number and, in his mind, we've already been dismissed. "I have more pressing matters at the moment. Apparently, the airport has become *the* destination—lots of wonders to be acquired there all of a sudden." He throws a satisfied glance in Luke's direction.

Luke and Tauro frown, then regard me with questioning expressions. I lower my eyes, praying they don't say anything that could ruin our plans. Because Elliot has just been informed by Lyra that there are Spawners at SeaTac—a treasure he plans to keep all to himself and has to personally oversee, just as we suspected. Elliot's eyes rest on me for a moment, an odd glint in their depths.

I frown at him, but Lyra steps in front of me and obstructs the view. She pulls out her gun and flicks it toward the door, showing Luke the way. He doesn't wait to be told twice. He's as eager as I am to get out of here.

"You too, *princess*." Lamia grabs my shoulder and forces me to face the door. I follow behind Luke and Lyra. They take us to the ninth floor and push us into one of the private rooms. I think it's the same place where I woke up after I killed Tusks and Lyra had knocked me out.

There's a queen-size bed, a sofa, a small desk, an armoire. Mass-produced prints hang on the walls. The place looks as cheap as a nondescript hotel room.

"Guard the door," Lyra orders Lamia.

"Screw that!" Lamia exclaims. "I don't want to stay here babysitting these worthless brats."

"Don't worry. I will send someone to replace you and will set a schedule around the clock."

They step out of the room and close the door. Lyra wouldn't dare hurt us in front of Lamia, but what after the Lizard Witch has been replaced? All bets will be off then.

Whatever Lyra is planning, I have to be prepared.

With a pointed look, I gesture toward the back of the room. Luke joins me in the corner furthest from the door.

"Lyra, that cat woman," I whisper, "she was the one who killed Dunn and your mother," I say this ruthlessly, not stopping to think about his feelings.

"I know. I would never forget that. I swore to take revenge if I ever saw her again." His blue eyes are dark with hatred.

"Well, you'd better start thinking of how because she's gonna kill you, first chance she gets."

I fail to mention she will kill me too. His selfish ass is used to being the center of attention anyway.

Luke frowns. "Why would she do that? Whitehouse would . . ." He thinks for a moment. "You said she also killed Dunn?"

I nod.

His eyes dart around the room, then stop and widen in realization. "She's with IgNiTe then."

Luke is smart, has always been.

"She is. Her goal has forever been to destroy Hailstone and your big plan. And now she's only *one* step away from accomplishing that."

I pause, let my gaze drill into his to make sure the message gets across.

Luke searches my face. "And you care because . . . ?"

I begin to answer, but he interrupts.

"No, don't bother. That was a stupid question." He turns away, sits on the bed. "You don't really care. This is about saving your own skin. Because if her goal is to destroy our plan, that means she'll have to kill you, too."

Why does he always have to up my *check* with a *checkmate*?

"Either way, it doesn't matter." I shrug as if I really don't care, but the odd thing is, maybe I'm not as oblivious as he thinks. I don't know exactly how I feel about Luke anymore, but the fact that he didn't sell me out . . . well . . . that is something.

"You betrayed me." His words are but a breath.

"You honestly expected me to . . . ?" I don't finish.

His gaze meets mine, and I can barely hold it. He looks truly injured.

I shake my head. "You can't be that naive! You destroyed my life."

"Did I?"

A muscle jumps in my jaw as I clench my teeth, pondering his question.

"Forgive me if I didn't realize Karen meant that much to you," he says. "It never seemed that way to me. Because, mind you, that's been my only . . . mistake when it comes to you."

"You keep telling yourself that."

With an easiness I can barely fake, I walk to the sofa and sit. "Now, quit all the bullshit and try to think of a way to get out of here." I cross my legs and close my eyes.

This might be the worst time for meditation but . . . leaps and bound.

Quicker than ever before, I clear my mind of all thoughts. Nothing like motivation. My breaths become deep and focused and, gradually, a vast whiteness spreads before me.

First, there was a brooding, blond boy sitting in front of me.

Now there is nothing.

Chapter 41

"Marci! Marci!"

My eyes spring open. I'm still sitting, not floundering on the floor. I didn't flop and drool back into consciousness? Really?! I'm almost ecstatic.

"Hey!" Luke snaps his fingers in front of my face. He's leaning forward, his face a few inches from mine.

"What the hell are you doing?" he demands. "You were like paralyzed for a few minutes."

I shake myself, pop my neck. "Azrael, call me Azrael."

He steps back, looking irritated.

"Don't let anyone hear you call me Marci, okay?"

I stand, look around the room.

Leaps and bounds, Marci. Leaps and bounds. I've had a few extra meditations since Aydan told me that. And this still feels slower than baby steps. Well, I'm too impatient for that.

My gaze stops on the largest of the pictures on the wall. It's an oak tree in the middle of a sunny field. The wooden frame is dark and heavy-looking, probably five by three feet.

I focus, immediately sense its rectangular shape and less-than-precise dimensions. There's a nail on the wall, holding me in place. I shake, unhappy with what I am. The picture sways on its nail, making a slight *whoosh, whoosh* sound.

I snap out of it. Luke startles, whirls in the direction of the sound. He stares at the moving picture as if he's seen a ghost. "What the hell?!" he exclaims.

My heart beats faster. With effort, I reach out once more. I sense the picture frame but don't manage to experience the same feeling of *oneness*. This time I'm separate, an outside entity with no business being an inanimate object.

Anger settles heavily in my stomach. *Why is this so freakin' hard? I need to get out of here. I need to help Aydan!* I lash out at the picture, my power unfurling like a whip. There's a crack, then the scraping of the frame against the wall as it comes unhooked and crashes to the floor. Luke jumps back. The picture hovers for a moment then face-plants on the carpeted floor.

"Crap!" Luke turns pale, as if he's seen a ghost.

I bite my lower lip to stop from busting out laughing. I'm not sure why I think this is so hilarious. It isn't. This is pathetic. I still have no control. Imminent danger or frustration can't continue to be the only things to truly activate my powers. That'll get me killed, sooner or later.

"Hey!" A loud knock at the door. "What are you two doing in there?" Lamia sounds furious. She's still out there, alone. No replacements. One guard, against two of us.

"Um, nothing," I say, making it sound like *something*. I wait, exchange a glance with Luke.

"Don't fuck with me," she calls out from the other side. I stare at the door knob, move closer. My hands are up, ready to grab her if she comes in. A quiet moment passes.

"She's not coming in," Luke says.

I exhale, deflated. My hands fall to my sides.

"What were you doing?" he points toward the sofa.

"Trying to sleep," I say.

Luke doesn't buy it. I'm sure he knows about "Fenders," but the fact that meditation helps us hone our skills is something only Symbiots know, and I'm not about to inform him about it.

"Sleep? At a time like this?" He looks me up and down, scowling. "To me, it looked like you were . . . meditating or something."

"And what if I was? I'm stuck in here with you, aren't I? That surely entitles me to some peace and quiet."

"Fine. Whatever!" He throws up his hands and paces toward the door.

I sit back down, place elbows on knees and rest my chin in my hands, thinking, thinking. Luke watches me, chewing on his lower lip. I ignore him.

An hour seems to pass before we hear activity outside the door. The voices are muffled, but it seems Lamia's replacements have finally arrived. Luke and I glare at the door. He looks as tense as I feel. I know this isn't good and, for once, I prefer Lamia over anybody else. With her gone, Lyra could dismiss the new guards without raising suspicion, then she'd be free to waltz in here and shoot us.

Convinced that this is what Lyra will do, I jump to my feet and pick up the fallen picture frame. After inspecting it, I set it back down and rest it against the wall, angling it just so.

"What now?" Luke asks.

"Nothing."

"Marci—"

"I already told you not to call me that!"

"Sorry," he mumbles.

I rub sweaty hands against my thighs, eyes roving around the room, hoping for the spark of a better idea to come to life.

"Elliot Whitehouse is a twisted man," Luke says out of nowhere.

"No shit," I respond absentmindedly.

"I didn't want things to be this way. I wanted us to start over, to really get to know each other. I wanted to help you see things the way I do."

My eyes stop wandering and lock with his. "Again with that. I already told you that would never happen, and you well know it."

He sighs. "Once you understood what we are, once you came to terms with—"

"I'm human, Luke," I interrupt.

"Of course you feel that way. You grew up thinking—"

"No! I am human. My DNA is human. And Elliot isn't going to be happy when he finds that out."

Luke shakes his head and looks at me sadly, as if I'm a deluded child who thinks her plain vanilla ice cream is better than cookies and creams. But he's the one who's deluded.

"Think what you want," I say in disgust. "Either way, that's not going to stop the bastard from turning us into lab rats. You've got your trusty Tauro to thank for that."

"He's just trying to keep me alive. Elliot was going to kill me, and Tauro has worked too hard to see it all go up in smoke."

I scoff. "Of course you'd think he's justified. For my part, I think he's a jerk."

Luke rubs a hand over his face, then lies down on the

bed, his feet touching the floor. Suddenly, I'm reminded of the easy-going boy I've known for over ten years, the one I found intriguing and challenging, the one I once considered a friend, a brother. For a moment, I wonder if, deep down inside, he's still the same. But when he turns to face me and his unreal eyes connect with mine, I curse my stupidity.

Of course, he's not the same.

The person I used to know never existed. He was just a facade to hide an otherworldly creature that was created to exterminate an obsolete species and personally replace it with a new and improved one. He's the *Adam* to a couple of Eklyptors who dared play God. He even thinks I'm his damn Eve. What a load!

Luke sits up with a jolt, pulling me out of my thoughts. He cocks an ear toward the door.

"What is it?" I ask.

He presses a finger to his mouth and closes his eyes, listening. "She's here," he whispers.

"Who?" I whisper back, my eyes flicking to the picture frame resting against the wall.

"Lyra."

Adrenaline bursts into my system. My heart begins to drum.

Luke gets to his feet. "She's ordering the guards to leave."

"What?! How do you know that?"

He taps his ear.

My eyebrows go up. So he also enhanced his senses, not only his appearance. I should have guessed. I wonder how long he's been this way. When I was hiding in the vent ready to shoot Elliot, he seemed to hear me cock the gun. I guess he did. Bastard!

I shake my head and focus on the now. My attention flies

back to the door. I take a few steps closer to the picture frame, fingers twitching at my sides. Luke steps next to me. I cast a glance in his direction.

"Don't do anything stupid, Marci," he warns.

"I told you she wants to kill us."

"Maybe we—"

The lock on the door clicks open. The knob turns. My heart is a pounding hammer in my chest. I don't want to fight Lyra. She's fast. Way too fast. I'm not confident about my chances with her. But what other choice do I have? God, I hope I'm wrong about her.

The door opens slowly. Lyra's dark shape comes into focus. She's standing in a slight crouch, her round eyes all pupils with thin slivers of green around them. She looks feral.

"Lyra," I greet her.

She says nothing.

"Are you letting us out?" I ask, still holding on to a little bit of hope.

She doesn't even look at me. Her eyes have gotten stuck on Luke.

So she's here for him.

Good.

Good.

Good.

I repeat it several times, but the idea doesn't sink in—not the way I want it to. Instead, I find that my head is shaking from side to side, and I'm stepping protectively in front of Luke.

"Why are you here?" I need her to say it. I need to be 100% sure before I do something I might regret.

Lyra steps into the room, shuts the door behind her. Her

furry breasts move up and down with each deep breath she takes. She looks like someone getting ready for something. I stare at the twitching fingers at her side, the gun mere inches away from them. If she shoots, will I be able to stop that bullet? I did it once, after only a few meditation sessions. In theory, I should be able to do it again—except theories are worth jack when a life is on the line.

My right eyelid jumps with a nervous tick as I feel an imaginary bullet strike the middle of my forehead. *Great confidence booster, Marci.*

"You know my orders, Cher," Lyra says.

Her orders from James are to kill Luke. Her orders from her French IgNiTe leader have always been to finish the Hailstone faction and its grand plan. It's not hard to guess which ones she'll follow.

"Lyra," I say in a pleading tone as I take a step forward.

She stiffens, leans back and rests her hand on her gun.

At least she hasn't drawn. Maybe there *is* hope.

"Killing him right now is a bad idea," I say, my thoughts speeding their way through words, sentences, paragraphs that can offer an argument she will understand.

"Um, you . . . *we* need to look at the bigger picture. It's not just Hailstone. There's Whitehouse to consider, too. There's the rest of the world and who knows how many other Eklyptor factions out there. We have to think of James, of his plan."

Lyra's gaze drifts away from mine and focuses somewhere over my shoulder. Hatred burns in the depths of her huge pupils—a smoldering flame against depthless black.

"That's a twisted, twisted thing you've done, connard." She talks to Luke as if I've suddenly gone up in smoke.

Stupidly, I want to argue it's not his fault. He didn't come

276

up with this plan. He's just another pawn on the game board. But showing any sympathy for Luke would be a mistake, so I don't.

"It's fucked up, yeah," I put in. "But if you kill him now, we'd have to leave this place, and we can't do that. We have to help Aydan. We have to set things up for the rest of James's plan. Bigger picture, Lyra."

Her eyes return to mine. "We?" Her whisker-like eyebrows move up. "Non, Cher. I have only one set of plans that matter."

I'm opening my mouth to protest when she jerks out her gun and aims.

"No!" I put out a hand and desperately call on my power. Energy pulses in my chest, filling me to the brim. My eyes go wide with shock at the quick, obedient response. Something like an electric impulse darts through my arm. My wrist flicks as if swatting at a bug, and Lyra's gun flies from her hand and crashes against the wall.

She hisses and, in spite of her surprise, whirls into action, going after the gun. I jump sideways and crash my boot against the picture frame. It cracks and splinters. I pick up a jagged slat and wield it like a sword, twirling it over my head, then smash it against the base of Lyra's neck. She staggers forward, hits the wall and falls.

I jump on her back, force her flat against the floor, and press the splintered side of the wood to the side of her neck.

"Lyra, please," I say. "I don't want to—"

She bucks with incredible force. I'm thrown off balance. Rolling on top of me, she grabs my arm. We struggle for control of the jagged board. I press my free hand to her chest. She feels like a solid wall of muscle. I seize a handful of black, orange-stripped fur. She growls and angles her mouth to my neck, baring sharp canine teeth.

"Stop!" Luke commands. There's a click, the unmistakable sound of a gun cocking.

Lyra freezes. There's a rumble deep in her chest. *"This is your fault,"* her eyes say to me. Her face turns away from mine, toward Luke. The gun is held firmly between his large hands, pointed straight at Lyra's head.

"Get up." He flicks the weapon upward.

Lyra stands. I follow suit, the broken piece of wood still in my hand.

"Drop that," Luke orders me.

What?! Wait, what is he doing?

"DROP IT!"

My fingers go limp. The board falls to the floor.

I call on my energy again, trying to yank the gun from his grasp. The surge comes, but it's weaker than before. Luke's arm jerks a bit to the side, but his grip holds fast.

He shakes his head at me and holds the gun with both hands. "Nice trick," he says. "You never mentioned you had such skills." His tone is conceited, nothing like the repentant one he was using just minutes ago.

What a fool I am. I thought he . . . I don't know what the hell I thought.

"Now you're going to take me out of here," he says, "and you're going to come with me. I tried to do this the nice way, Marci."

Lyra's gaze dances between us.

"But I suppose this is the way it was always meant to be." He points the gun at Lyra. "Turn around and walk to the wall!"

Lyra gives me a hateful glance before doing as she's told. When she stops, Luke steps forward and smashes the butt of the gun against the base of her neck. She goes limp and crumbles, unconscious.

He turns to face me. "Let's go get your friend," he says, offering me the gun.

Chapter 42

I dumbly stare at the gun in Luke's hand, disbelieving my eyes.

He gives me a sad smile. "Take it."

Fearing he might change his mind, I snatch it away and grip it so tightly that the rough surface of the handle molds into my sweaty palm. His gaze falls to the floor. He looks exhausted like he's been through hell and back, when all he did was threaten us with a gun.

"So, are we going or not?" he asks when I just stand there looking at him as if he were a mind-bending puzzle.

"I thought you . . ."

. . . were going to blow my brains out?

. . . were going to kidnap me and force me to bear your babies?

Those were definitely my top guesses just a minute ago. Now I learn he wants to help me save Aydan.

"Without you, I'm just one person," he says, the sadness in his voice so thick, so heavy, it seems to compress the room to half its size. "I once believed I could change the world, make it a better place. Now I know it was absurd to wish for that."

"What's absurd is trying to wipe out an entire race in the process."

"I never set out to do that," he says angrily. "That was not *my* plan. Although sometimes I don't think it's so wrong. Humans are doing the same to us."

"Well, you started it."

"Do you really think that matters? If humans had learned about us beforehand, they would've tried to exterminate us, although I'm sure they would've also kept a few specimens for research purposes, just to see what they could gain from us."

"You've watched too many movies," I say half-heartedly. I can very well imagine the governments of the world doing exactly what he's describing.

"I had so many dreams for us. Now I don't care if I die." He sounds as if he's truly been sentenced to death and today is his execution day.

If he thinks that making me feel sorry for him is going to change my mind about his crazy scheme, he's high. Not that his scheme would work anyway. I'm perfectly human, even if he doesn't want to believe it.

I turn and face the door, trying to figure out what to do. "Elliot sent Aydan to Dr. Sting," I say with a shiver. "That means he's in the service level. Our best bet it to take the stairwell." I look at the gun in my hand, then at Lyra's immobile shape on the floor.

"Search her," I say. "She might have another gun."

Luke hesitates only for a moment, then squats by her side and pats her down. When he straightens, he shows me a small pistol. "Had this on her ankle."

I nod and head to the door. After a deep breath, I ease it open. There are no guards outside. I take half a step into the hall and look both ways. "We're clear," I whisper and gesture for Luke to follow.

We close the door behind us and hurry toward the emergency exit. When we enter the stairwell, I breathe a little easier since most people take the elevator. I hurry downstairs, taking two and three steps at a time. We reach the service level a minute later. Our chests pump in unison. We stop for a beat to catch our breath.

The door has a card reader. I take mine out of my pocket, glad no one thought of taking it away. I wave it in front of the small scanner. Its red light flashes green. I yank the door open. Most of the time only Dr. Sting roams this level, so I charge in.

I head down the long, bare corridor at a run. I know exactly where the Doctor's favorite room is, so I waste no time—not even to make sure Luke is following. Exposed pipes and ducts run overhead. The walls are rough and the floor is slick, red-painted concrete. We pass several closed metal doors before we reach the one I remember all-too-well.

Without pause, I turn the knob and shoulder my way in.

* * *

My heart booms in my ears as I raise step into the room. Immediately, my gaze zeroes in on the far corner where the torture chair is bolted to the floor. Dr. Sting stands next to it, his shape stooped over, his back to us. All I can see past him are Aydan's jean-clad legs and bare feet.

The evil doctor turns slowly to look over his shoulder. I put my gun away before he's made a full circle. Luke does the same. Maybe I can do this without risking too much.

Dr. Sting's goat-like eyes take us in without surprise. I see his face in my nightmares more than I'd like to, the multi-color fur, the block teeth, the horizontal pupils. A chill spreads across my back. I clench my teeth and gather my courage. He moves away from his victim, holding something gingerly between his long fingers.

"What is it?" he asks in an aggravated, high-pitched voice that once made me wonder if he was female.

Trying to keep my agitated breaths under control and my gaze away from Aydan, I stroll toward him, gesturing to Luke to wait. "The boss wants him." I point at Aydan. "Has some questions for the fucking Fender. Yep, he does. Gonna find out everything about those Igniters, and then we'll show'em."

I stop a mere two paces away from Dr. Sting. His furry forehead makes him look like one of those Mastiff dogs as he frowns. My eyes involuntarily drift toward Aydan's prone shape. At the sight of it, a silent cry goes through me.

Blood. So much blood.

I bite my tongue to keep the cry from escaping, but it's no good. It comes loose, turning into a squeak. At once, Dr. Sting's vertical pupils flatten to thin lines. He steps back and raises the weird tool in his hand, taking a threatening stance.

"I only take orders from Whitehouse," he says.

The metal tool is caked with blood and bits of tissue. It's a contraption unlike any I have ever seen, a rod with something like a trigger and a sharp, jagged cookie-cutter-looking head.

The heck with the risk. You owe me!

I jump him. He's slow to react, and I manage to snatch

his wrist and twist it.

"No," he cries out. "Not my hand. Don't you dare hurt my hand."

"Drop it, then!"

He does as I say, but just as the tool clatters to the floor. He produces a knife out of nowhere.

"Watch out!" Luke calls.

I sidestep the knife's path as he stabs down.

"You asked for it," I say, bending his wrist past the breaking point.

There is a sickening crunch that makes my stomach flip. Dr. Sting screams and folds on bent knees, tucking the injured wrist between his thighs. He's still mid-scream when I release a powerful roundhouse kick and strike him on the side of the head. His eyes roll back, and he falls to the side, unconscious.

I stare at his immobile shape. His freaky fingers twitch. I step on them and put all my weight down until I hear them crack. I feel vicious, as evil as he is, but he hurt me, stuck hot pokers under my fingernails. Worst of all, he hurt Aydan. He deserves worse.

Shaking, I turn and slowly turn my attention to the bloody, unconscious figure that lies on top of the awful torture contraption.

"Aydan!" I start toward him but immediately stop. He's still, so still. "No, please."

Not this. Not again.

My throat closes. My vision swims, and I feel I might pass out. I press a hand to the edge of the torture chair, my fingers inches from his pale hand. His bare chest is dotted with perfectly round wounds, oozing with blood. The skin around each quarter-size laceration is bright red and swollen.

A trail of marks runs from his collarbone all the way to the edge of his jeans, a red sea of blood splitting him into two hemispheres right down the middle.

I stare at his chest, my lungs paralyzed as if I could give him my air, my breaths.

"Aydan," I whisper. A tear spills down my cheek and splatters on his hand.

He makes a small sound in the back of his throat.

My chest jumps starts. "Aydan!" I lean closer.

He groans, turns his head my way. His eyelids flutter open, black lashes trembling. His normally red lips are white, almost blue.

"Aydan, it's me, Marci. I'm gonna get you outta here, okay?"

He tries to say something but coughs instead.

"Help me unstrap him." I point at Aydan's feet. Luke gets to work on the wide, leather straps. I undo the ones at the wrists. "C'mon. I know it's hard, but you have to move."

I try to pull him up, but he's too heavy. Luke helps me get him to a sitting position. I don't even have to ask.

"Okay, hold him right there. I have to do something," I say.

"What? Now?"

"It's important. It'll only take a moment."

I rush to the corner of the room where a PC sits on a dusty desk. I know where all the computers reside in this building. I made it my business to learn that. This one was installed a couple of weeks ago at Elliot's request, along with a phone. Dr. Sting spends a considerable amount of time in his dungeon, and his boss wants to be able to reach him whenever his torturous services are required.

My hands are shaking as I set them over the keyboard and connect to my PC to access the communication program I wrote. In spite of my unsteady fingers, I type quickly, connect and fire off a message.

$Warrior> Target is go

I wait for an answer, holding my breath. It comes immediately, practically deflating me with relief.

$Sal> Ten-Four

This is all we agreed on, two quick messages. And it's a tremendous load off my shoulders to see Sal's response. He was supposed to keep tabs on any communications from me. From the looks of it, he wasn't even taking a break to blink.

$Sal> Dr. V?

I guess Sal got my last desperate message about Aydan's capture.

$Warrior> Disregard

I close my connection, send the computer into sleep mode and rush back to Aydan. I'll take care of Dr. Volt. I'm getting him the hell out of here.

Luke gives me an inquiring glance which I ignore. Instead, I help him set Aydan's bare feet on the floor. Ready to abandon this place for good, I drape one of his arms over my neck. Luke does the same on the other side. As we head to the door, Aydan tries to walk, but his legs mostly drag behind.

"We'll have to use the elevator," I say, repositioning Aydan's arm. He's way heavier than he looks.

"I'll carry him. You clear the way." Luke hands me his gun, slips an arm behind Aydan's legs and picks him up.

Luke groans, his face going red with the effort. I give myself no time to gawk at the unexpected sight: Luke Hailstone—an Eklyptor, or whatever he is—helping an IgNiTe member. Instead, I rush toward the elevator and punch the "up" arrow.

Sweat slides down my temple. I plant my feet on the ground and point both guns at the elevator doors. If anyone is inside when they slide open, they'll face the end of these barrels and get acquainted with the tip of these bullets.

Chapter 43

The numbers above the elevator door count down like seconds on a ticking bomb. Luke stands next to me, breathing heavily, struggling with Aydan's weight. The doors slide open. My tension deflates like a popped balloon. The cabin is empty. We hurry inside, press the button to the ground floor.

Suddenly, Aydan's eyes spring open. They swivel around from Luke to me. "W-what—" he sputters, coughs. Face twisted in pain, disgust or both, he pushes away from Luke. He sets Aydan down and tries to steady him. Aydan swats him away.

Luke takes a step back, holds his hands up in a pacifying gesture. "All right. All right."

Aydan sways on his feet, presses his back to the back of the cabin to avoid a fall. In spite of his shaky stance, he manages to stay upright.

He looks down at his chest. "Shit. Oh, shit."

I want to tell him he'll be fine, but the elevator is almost there. I stand at the ready. There's a *ding*. The doors open onto the marble-floored lobby. We step out cautiously. No one's around, and I can't believe our luck.

"This way." I point toward one of the side exits. The front doors are always guarded by several Eklyptors. Each side door has at most one guard, none when they get over-confident.

I slink to the side, already imagining stepping out of the building and breathing the clean air. We can make it. We *will* make it.

"Damn it, let me help you!" Luke says in an aggravated whisper.

I glance back and realize they didn't follow me out of the elevator. I rush back. Aydan is standing in a corner of the cabin, shying away from Luke.

"C'mon, we're getting you out of here," Luke insists.

"W-where?" Aydan looks as terrified as a child. "You . . . you're Hailstone."

"Aydan!" I mock whisper. "He's helping us. It's okay. C'mon, before someone comes."

He looks at me. His upper lip curls up as he shakes his head. "No," he says in a loud but raspy voice.

I look over my shoulder. Someone will hear us. For a moment, I stand frozen, a cold, sharp sensation sliding down my back. I blink slowly. My gaze flashes back to Aydan, his bare feet, his torn chest, his dark, inexpressive eyes.

"Aydan." His name becomes nothing but a wisp of air brushing past my lips. The cold sensation seeps into my bones and makes itself comfortable.

He begins to scream.

His hoarse voice is weak at first but quickly rises to an angry, desperate cry. "He-here! Somebody! Q-quick!"

Luke's blue eyes open wide as he stares at Aydan in

bewilderment. "What the . . . ?"

I growl in anger, impotence, pain.

Not Aydan. Not him!

"Luke, run!" I shout, then turn away from this nightmare and run myself.

Tears spill down my face, blurring my vision. Luke is suddenly at my side, running, throwing confused glances over his shoulder.

"What the hell just happened?" he asks.

My throat is closing. My lungs screaming for oxygen.

"Somebody! They're getting a-away!" Aydan screams behind us.

It's not Aydan. It's not him, I tell myself, because the betrayal feels too real, though it's no betrayal at all. It isn't him trying to give us away. It's the thief, the creature that's been living inside him, waiting for just this opportunity.

Our boots *thump* against the floor as we run toward a metal door marked with an exit sign. The door seems to stretch away as the sound of other steps and voices fill the hall.

I cast a backward glance and see a swarm of black-uniformed Eklyptors headed in our direction. The buzzing in my head picks up and rages out of control. I try to turn it off, but I can't seem to remember how. I'm breaking from the inside, splitting in two, and the fractures that have started in my core are spreading outward like an earthquake from its epicenter. Soon, my skin will crack open and all the hope I didn't know I'd been harboring will spill out.

Aydan. Aydan. Aydan, his name is a beating force inside my head, two syllables full of denial. *He can't be gone. He can't.*

A barrage of shots spray over my head. I crouch and

keep running. The bullets strike the wall in front of us.
Plaster and wooden splinters rain on us. I fire two shots
backward, without looking.

Luke wraps his arms around his head and stops. He
shrinks, making himself as small as possible. I keep on
moving, Aydan's face flashing before my eyes: his black eyes,
his red lips tipped into a rare smile.

He isn't gone!

Bullets ping at my feet. They ricochet and hit the walls
at my sides.

He's still there. Still there.

"Marci, stop! There's no point." Luke pleads.

Something hot hits my ear, hissing, stinging. My hand
flies to the side of my head. Warm, wet blood stains my
fingers, Dad's t-shirt. I stop and fall to my knees, dropping
my guns. If I die, I won't be able to help Aydan. He would
be lost forever, and I can't let that happen. I am not losing
him, too. I've lost enough already. I won't allow Eklyptors
to take anything else from me.

Chapter 44

"Put your hands behind your head!" someone screams from behind.

I do as I'm told, looking over my shoulder. Luke interlaces his fingers, presses them to the top of his head, elbows sticking out. We look at each other. Regret shapes his expression, and—today, in this emotion—we could actually be twins.

At least I got the message out to James. At least I didn't completely fail.

Elliot's soldiers jerk us to our feet and push our backs against the wall. They are all dressed in black. One of them wears only pants. His arms and torso are covered in brown and tan scales, forming a snake-like pattern. He forces Luke's legs apart and pats him down, a forked tongue tasting his cheek. Luke recoils. The creature hisses in delight.

"He's clean," the Eklyptor says, then checks me, though not with as much delight as he did Luke.

"Let me through." Lamia pushes her way between the ten or twelve guards who chased us down the corridor, her tail nudging spectators out of the way. "What do we have here?" she says, satisfaction dripping like honey from her mouth. Her disturbing eyes glint, her mouth cocks to one side.

She looks at us, then Aydan who's limping his way through the crowd. Lamia uses the tip of her long tail to scratch her head. The motion would be comical if it wasn't so creepy, so impossibly inhuman.

"What just happened here?" she asks, truly confused. "Where's Lyra?"

"I'll te-tell you w-what happened." Aydan has made it to the front.

Lamia's tail whips up in flash and wraps around Aydan's neck. "Shut your mouth, little Fender." She pushes him against the wall with us, her tail whipping back, recoiling to hover over her head.

Aydan clears his throat. He swallows with difficulty. "I'm no Fender. I'm fi-finally free of him."

Lamia narrows her lizard eyes at him, judging.

"She," Aydan points a trembling finger at me, "she's the Fe-fender."

Lamia ponders for a moment, then unexpectedly burst out laughing. The guards look at each other, confused, then laugh just to be in on the joke.

"I love it when I'm right," Lamia says, turning to me. "You *are* still a Fender and always have been." She spits on my face.

I wipe the spit off with the back of my hand.

Lamia laughs again, louder this time. "And you were trying to save *him*," she points at Aydan, "after he went full-fledged on Dr. Sting's table? Oh, this is just too good, too good!" She slaps her thigh, laughing like a maniac, then stops abruptly. "Wait! That must mean that Lyra . . . ?" A wicked grin tips her lips. She's probably imagining herself as Elliot's second now. "You and you, go find Lyra, cuff her and bring her to me."

The two guards she singled out look confused.

"She's a traitor, you idiots. Do as I say. It's an order!"

They nod nervously and back out of the circle, their scared eyes on Lamia. Once they are far enough, they turn and set out to find Lyra. She wanted to kill me before. After this, she'll want to include torture as a preamble.

My attention returns to Aydan who's looking at me with the most intense hatred I've ever seen in his eyes. My heart tightens, pain wrapping itself around it as I remember the tenderness and warmth his gaze used to hold for me.

"Aydan, you can fight it!" I tell him, hoping he can still hear me, hoping he hasn't been completely shrouded by his agent.

"My name is n-not Aydan." He limps closer, a hand extended in my direction. "My name is Charger." His fingers shake. His face twists with effort.

I press my back closer to the wall, expecting electricity to burst from his fingertips, but nothing happens. He shakes his arm, slaps it against his side, then tries again. Nothing. He stares at his ineffectual hand, then at his bare feet. He's grounded, but there was no crackle of energy in him, so I don't think that's the problem. It seems that skill belonged to Aydan, and this impostor can't wield it.

"Looks like you're gonna need to find a new name," I mock. "On the other hand, don't bother. He'll find a way to crush you. He'll find his way—"

My words get cut off. I choke. My hands fly to Lamia's tail as it tightens around my neck.

"Ooh, you sound so different. What happened to your whiny, sniveling talk, huh?"

She squeezes so hard a strangled sound escapes me, and I lose control of my legs.

Luke forgets he's supposed to keep his hands up and pulls on Lamia's tail. "Let her go, you hideous bitch."

Lamia's eyes startle at the forceful order. Still, she doesn't release me and, instead, squeezes harder. I sputter. My windpipe feels ready to snap. A guard tries to tear Luke away but fails. It takes two huge, gorilla-looking freaks to finally restrain him.

"You'll have to explain yourself to Whitehouse if something happens to her," Luke growls, still kicking.

Through the haze of my pain, I see Lamia's face twist with displeasure. As much as she'd like to snap me in two, she knows Luke is right. If she hurts me, Elliot will have her scaly hide. Reluctantly, she lets me go. I collapse to my knees, gasping for air.

Charger growls with disappointment. "Somebody n-needs to . . . to kill the bitch."

"Couldn't agree more." Lamia turns her back on us, her tail slamming against the floor in aggravation. "Cuff them and follow me. We'll take them to Elliot."

What? Why is Elliot still here?! He's supposed to be on his way to SeaTac.

Luke and I exchange a glance.

When I look away I find that Lamia is staring at us over her shoulder. There's suspicion in her expression. For a moment, she seems ready to lash out, but for some reason, she restrains herself and marches down the hall.

The guards yank me to my feet and cuff my hands behind my back. I try to think of a way I could use my powers to fight them off, but it's twelve against two, and my skills as reliable as a weather forecast. We wouldn't stand a chance. So I lower my head and stumble forward as one of the guards pushes me along.

What little hope I had left disintegrates as I think of James chasing a false lead while Elliot sits safely in his office.

Chapter 45

I roll my neck and shoulders. The cuffs are on too tightly, pulling me taut.

Surrounded by guards, Luke and I wait for the elevator as it slowly makes its way down from the higher floors. When it arrives, the doors slide with a *ding* and a *whoosh*.

Lamia takes a step forward but freezes when Elliot and his twin dwarfs step out.

My senses go on high alert. I take a step back and run into a guard. He pushes me away. Elliot stops and surveys us with calm, golden eyes. There's no surprise, anger or any type of emotion in his expression.

He brings his hands together and rubs them up and down. "Not a dull moment."

Lamia jumps in front of him, making herself look taller. "I caught them trying to get away. She's a traitor. And Lyra, too. I'm pretty sure. This one's a Fender. She never—"

Elliot puts a hand up. "I know. I know," he says. "Do you think me an idiot? Think I would have a snake in my own lair and not be aware of it?"

My blood freezes in my veins. *He knows?! Oh God. How long? How much?*

"Lyra's been taken care of and won't be a problem anymore."

Lyra! She's dead. How did Elliot know? How?!

The answer steps out of the elevator, turning my heart into a cold, hard piece of rock.

Rheema.

"How is our dear James?" Elliot leans his face close to mine, then flicks a triumphant grin in Rheema's direction.

My mouth goes dry. I can't swallow the lump in my throat.

God, she's an Eklyptor. But how did she fool Kristen's test?

"You saw James recently, didn't you?" Elliot asks me.

I struggle to pull my eyes away from Rheema and the odd expression on her face.

"In a cemetery, if I'm not mistaken," he continues, a faraway buzz in my ears. "Quite appropriate, I think. At least for him. You, on the other hand, I'll have to keep around, at least until you cease being useful." He gives Luke a sly smile.

"How?" I ask Rheema in a trembling voice. "How did you—?"

"Proved negative to those stupid blood tests? I know that's what you're gonna ask," she says, her brown eyes hard and hollow.

I give her a weak nod.

"Because . . ." She puts her hands out in a demonstrative fashion without giving me an answer. She doesn't have to. It comes to me of its own horrifying accord.

"Because you're human," I say, indignation coating me

in a three-inch thick layer. "You fucking bitch," I snarl, throwing myself in her direction. Someone grabs me from the back keeping me from biting her to death. I growl with impotence, baring my teeth at her.

"I'm not going to be on the losing end of this battle," she says from under her nose. "I'm not going to end up like Oso, Xave and so many others. I get a pass."

"You'll pay for this."

Elliot steps between us, barring her from my view. "Isn't this fantastic?" he asks in his most sarcastic tone. "And the best part of everything," he puts his hands out, palms up, then brings them back together again, "is that you have helped deliver James on a silver platter. I know all about your little hacking efforts, *Marci*." He bares his teeth as he struggles to contain his anger. "My Spawners were . . ." He can't finish. His eyes waver as if the dead creatures were his children. He takes a step forward, grabs my face and squeezes it, his fingers digging into my cheeks. A shiver runs through my body at the icy quality of his touch. "You have cost me too much, *little crass girl*." He pushes me, lets go and wipes his hand on the front of his suit.

"But, in the end, it's all working out in my favor. It will be sweet making you pay, you know. You owe me in blood, and blood I shall have. It makes no difference to me if it's in a test tube—not when you have given me James and his pathetic IgNiTe rebels. You've led them astray, my dear. They will be highly disappointed when they don't find me there and, instead, encounter the best members of my army. Quite a failure you'll have to live with from now on. Clever plan. Clever lies. I know there are no Spawners at SeaTac. And that's just the tip of the iceberg. I know much more." He looks almost lovingly in Rheema's direction. "Your *cure* will never go anywhere."

For the first time, I'm happy about James's secrecy. Rheema only knows there is a cure, not where it came from.

Elliot scoffs and takes a step back, his face heavy with disgust. "Lock them up!" He orders abruptly, pointing at Lamia. "I make you personally responsible for them. They are to be kept contained *and* unharmed. Understood?"

"Yes, sir." She responds between clenched teeth.

"Now, everyone else, I have a mission for you. A mission you cannot fail."

With that, he walks off, spewing orders. He wants everyone to go to SeaTac and join his other forces, the soldiers who stayed behind after capturing Luke. There, they will ambush IgNiTe, killing every single one of them. When they're done, they will chop James's head off and bring it to Elliot. It's what he wants and makes sure I hear it all.

He glances over his shoulder, a glint of pleasure in his eyes.

"There's someone who needs to see their defeated leader personally."

Like a thin sheet of ice, my hope shatters, revealing what lays beyond: the darkness I've always known, the shadows that have haunted me for over ten years.

They never left, and they will never leave.

They will forever obscure any dreams of happiness.

Chapter 46

Lamia paces in front of us, her tail swinging from side to side with every slap of her boot against the floor.

She brought us to a small conference room in the main floor, probably trying to stay close to her leader. Ironic how, now, she's stuck with what she called babysitting duty while Elliot headed toward the auditorium with Rheema, his twin dwarfs, and Charger, leaving Lamia looking pissed. I've never been in there—it's off limits to most, except Elliot's closest captains. Lyra calls it his war room. *Called it*, I remind myself, regret for her wasted life filling my chest in spite of everything.

Luke and I sit in conference chairs side by side, hands cuffed to the armrests.

I close my eyes and lower my head. I can't stand to look at her face, which has slowly changed from a gloating mask to a pissed off grimace.

At the verge of tears, I think of James and the assault he'd planned on Whitehouse. He and the best from his crew were supposed to ambush Elliot, supposed to capture him, supposed to administer an improved cure, one that may not kill him, though if it did, the world would be better off.

Now, instead, James and his crew will be the ones ambushed, greatly outnumbered by Elliot's personal army, the best Eklyptors the Whitehouse faction has to offer. Monsters and soldiers alike, all with express orders to behead James.

He'll get away. He'll get away.

The chant rings inside my head over and over. There's no IgNiTe without James. No home without James. I chide myself for this selfish thought. There are far more important people than me and my daddy issues in this fight.

If there was a way I could warn him. . . My eyes drift to the conference room computer. It is hooked to the projector overhead, meant for presentations during meetings. It's just a basic machine, but one I could use to connect to mine in the barracks.

But there is no time for a warning. I look at the round clock on the wall. It reads 4:02 P.M. James is surely on his way to SeaTac, and I'm bound to this chair with no way of reaching a computer.

Unless . . .

I stare at the cuffs on my left wrist and focus. The metal is tight against my skin, biting into it. It was cold when Lamia first fastened it, now it's warm, though not the least bit more comforting for it.

A handcuff is simple compared to cylinder locks like those I opened at Elliot's fertility clinic. So I concentrate, imagining myself becoming one with the metal. At once, my body becomes rigid, dense. Nearby, I perceive a hollow space, a small chamber that holds a simple lock. I clench my teeth, sharpening in my focus. The mechanism materializes before my eyes. I almost gasp at its simplicity. All I have to do is push a metal bar out of the way. With more ease than I could have imagined, I drive the obstruction out of the way.

Click.

My eyes spring open.

"What the hell?" Lamia covers the short distance between us, her keen eyes immediately on my wrists. She tests the cuffs, squeezes them even tighter, activating the lock once more.

"No!" I exclaim, anger exploding from my mouth in this one word of frustration.

Lamia stares at my face, confused. "I know I secured those. How'd you do that?"

"Don't be stupid. I didn't do anything."

In one swift motion, she grabs the back of my hair and pulls, throwing my head back. "Are you like that electric Fender?" Her breath blows over my nose.

I wrinkle my face and turn away. "Are dead mice your favorite snack or something?"

For a moment, she looks ready to slap me but—by some miracle, or Elliot's warning to make sure we're unharmed—she jerks away with a frustrated growl and begins to pace again.

Determined to make something happen, I do one of my best Azrael impersonations. "Why don't you fuckin' sit, huh? Huh? Just fuckin' sit, will ya?"

Lamia comes to an abrupt stop and whirls to face me.

"Shut your mouth, bitch. Or . . ."

"Or what?" I challenge.

"Marci." Luke shakes his head at me, letting me know it's not smart to piss this creature off.

"Listen to your baby daddy," she says with a laugh.

The comment sends my hackles up, but I hide my reaction and keep poking. "How do you like missing all the action while you *babysit*?"

Her mouth twists, looking as if she'll say something. Instead, she presses her lips together and resumes her pacing.

My fists clench as I try to think of something that will make her lose it. Words might work eventually, but time is running out. An idea occurs to me. I straighten and do something sure to throw her for a loop.

I turn off my buzzing so she can't sense me. No need to pretend I'm one of them anymore. Just as I expected, she reacts. Immediately. Her spine shoots up straight. Her tail uncurls to its full length. Very slowly, her eyes swivel in my direction. When they lock with mine, her face turns red with fury.

I don't miss my chance to taunt her. "How do you like that trick? I've been using it all the time to sneak around this place with no one the wiser. You Eklyptors are such idiots."

"Marci, you're gonna get yourself killed," Luke says in a near growl.

"Shut up!" I snap back, then refocus my attention on Lamia. "I can flip it both ways, you know? I bet you'd love to learn how to do that. It would be nice not to have to feel inferior to the likes of Lyra and Elliot all the time, wouldn't it?"

I know I've done it when her face goes from red to incandescent. Temper clearly out of control, she stomps back in my direction. Faster than the eye can see, her tail slices through the air and lashes across my face. My neck whips back. Pain erupts down my spine. White lights flash before my eyes and, for a moment, I think I'll pass out. I inhale in short spasms, willing myself not to lose consciousness.

It takes me a moment to recover and another to gather back my courage. I can't break now, not when lives depend on me.

Ignoring the pain, I peer up at Lamia. She's breathing heavily, her chest rising and falling, her fists clenched at her sides. I taste blood in my mouth. One of my teeth feels loose. *Dammit!* If she's messed up my teeth, I'm going to make her pay.

"You're a coward," I say. "You couldn't even touch me if I wasn't tied up." I struggle with the cuffs, making them rattle against the chair. "Just wait 'till I get loose. You'll get the ass whipping of your life."

Lamia bares her teeth in a parody of laughter. "I see what you're trying to do, bitch. You think I'm gonna take off the cuffs and give you a *fair* fight. Ha! I guess you haven't learned nothing in your time here. Only humans care about stupid things like fairness and honor." And with that, she raises her tail and clobbers my face again.

"Stop!" Luke screams. I hear him as if from far away, his voice barely filtering through the ringing in my ears. My head swims. Lamia could kill me in her rage and no one would know. These conference rooms are nearly soundproof.

Impotence settles in the pit of stomach, pain fueling it, stoking it, like coal into a fire. It trembles inside of me, fuses with my anger and hatred for this woman, for her kind. Like lava inside a volcano, the mixture of emotions rise, rise, rise until they have nowhere to go but out.

The chair trembles under me. A whining metallic sound fills the air. Suddenly, the armrests twist as if made from play dough. Screws drop to the floor with a *ding*.

For an instant, I sit, dumbfounded, not realizing what

has happened, then it hits me.

The armrests aren't attached to the chair anymore.

I don't wait for an invitation.

I shoot to my feet and swing my arms upward. Pieces of chair fly into the air. The armrests slip out of the handcuffs and hit the carpeted floor while the cuffs dangle uselessly from my wrists.

I'm free.

Chapter 47

It takes Lamia an instant to get over her shock, but that instant is all I need. She's too slow pulling out her gun which gives me enough time to throw a roundhouse kick and knock the automatic out of her grasp. The weapon flies out of sight under the conference room desk. Luke struggles uselessly with his handcuffs, his eyes flicking to the gun.

I follow my kick with an elbow to the side of Lamia's head. She staggers, blinking and shaking her head. I go forward in a jump kick aimed at her face, but her long, easily-forgotten appendage comes out of nowhere and blocks me. One of the barbs in her tail catches on Dad's t-shirt, almost ripping it.

"Damn it!" Stepping out of reach from Lamia's swinging extremity, I pick up my wrecked chair and throw it at her. She bats it down with her tail as if it were a fluffy pillow and sends it crashing on top of the desk, smashing the conference speaker to bits.

Pupils reduced to thin, vertical slits, she charges forward. Like the prankster he was in kindergarten, Luke sticks out a foot and trips her. Lamia braces her fall with her hands but, at the same time, raises her tail and smacks it against the side of Luke's face. His head lashes to one side, making his neck look as if it were made of rubber. His face disfigures in pain.

My first instinct is to jump on her back to put her in a strangling chokehold but, this time, I'm more aware of her damn tail. Not to let Luke's efforts go in vain, I unleash a kick at her face. I imagine the sound on her nose crunching to bits, but she's fast and throws her arms up protectively. My boot connects with her forearm.

Looking around for a weapon, I spot one of the detached armrests, a metal tube with a rectangular piece of wood attached to it. I pick it up and whirl, ready to smack Lamia unconscious. Instead, I'm shocked into stillness. She's now standing behind Luke, her long tail entwined around his neck, the bony barbs digging into his neck.

"Stand down or he dies," she says.

Luke's face is red, and his blue eyes wide and ready to pop out of their sockets.

"Be my guest," I say. "One less creep to worry about."

My tone is steady, even though I thought for a second it might betray me. I shouldn't care if Luke dies but, as much as I'd like to deny it, we are connected. He was always there, sitting at the next desk over, standing by the locker across from mine, walking down the hall looking back at me, in chess club beating my pants off, in the cafeteria line offering me his dessert—more than that, in the very beginning when we were nothing but a couple of cells.

She squeezes harder. "I agree."

I want to remind her that Elliot wants us unharmed, but that would give me away. So I say nothing and, instead, let coldness and indifference seep into my gaze.

The front legs of Luke's chair lift off the floor as she increases the pressure on his neck. My heart wavers with dread. Luke's eyes are bloodshot and locked on mine. There's no plea in his gaze, only resignation. He truly wouldn't mind dying. The world he imagined for himself has slipped away from his grasp, and he can't see past the empty space left behind. He's lost as much as I have, and it's hard to believe I can actually relate.

Luke makes a wheezing sound. Lamia's mouth stretches in a satisfied grin. Her eyes glint, making her look like viciousness itself. She's a monster who loves imparting pain and death and, apparently, her desire to do so goes beyond logic.

She's going to kill Luke, damn the consequences.

"Stop," I say, putting my right hand up.

My fingers tremble, reaching, reaching. Lamia eases her hold on Luke, but just barely. A breath hisses into his lung. He blinks, letting me know the pressure isn't the killing kind, not at the moment.

"I don't bluff," Lamia says. "Cuff yourself to that chair." She gestures at one of the other chairs. There are twelve available, after all.

I don't move. I stand still with my hand held in midair. There's no way in hell I'll willingly cuff myself, just like there's no way in hell I'll let her kill Luke. She must see this in my eyes, because her tail twitches and squeezes harder than before.

"Stop I said." Determination courses through my veins. It's a calm, self-assured tenacity like I've never felt before. I don't know where it's coming from, but I know, for the first time since my powers manifested, that as I reach for

Lamia with murderous intent, my abilities will do exactly as I command them.

The sinew of her beating heart suddenly throbs in my fingers. The muscle is strong and steady, not wild like the one that knocks inside my own chest. I'm ready to kill just as she is, but it's clear that, for me, it's not a remorseless, everyday task.

"Make. Me. Stop," she says with relish.

"As you wish."

Slowly, I curl my fingers inwardly.

At first, Lamia looks perplexed, even a bit amused. But as my reaching, invisible fingers close around the soft flesh of her heart, her eyes spring wide open screaming: *"Something's wrong. Something's terribly wrong!"*

I squeeze harder still. Lamia's hands fly to her chest. She gasps for air. Her chokehold on Luke eases off as her tail visibly slackens, suddenly forgetting its job.

"W-what are you . . . doing?" she stammers. Her left arm curls toward her chest. She cradles it with her other hand, groaning in pain.

Staggering backward, she beats on her chest as if that will make the pain go away. It won't. I won't let go, not until her heart is stillness and silence, until she ceases to be a problem. She moans. Her tail falls away from Luke and hits the floor with a heavy smack, twitching as she fights for breath.

I squeeze my finger further, my fingernails digging into the now slow, dying heart. With a jerk, her back hits the wall. She fights—her will strong—but, in time, her legs give out and she slides down to the floor. She sits for a moment, her eyelids fluttering, then tips to one side and falls on her shoulder. She rests her face on the carpet, small puffs of air brushing past her parted lips.

Her heart gives two last, barely noticeable beats, then stops.

I stare at my hand, at the claw-like shape in which it has twisted itself. Trembling, I stretch out my fingers and, even though they are clean, I feel blood staining them, dripping down to the floor.

I've killed, yet again.

Chapter 48

Luke's head slumps forward. I inch toward him, my steps slow and mechanical. When I'm but a foot away from him, he looks up with effort. His face has regained some of its normal color, but the whites of his eyes swim with blood.

"Are you okay?" I ask.

He moves his head, and I don't know if it's a yes or a no. Knowing I have no time to lose, I search in Lamia's pockets and find the key for the handcuffs, never looking at her face. I free one of Luke's hands, then press the key into it. "Get the other one, I have to . . ." I don't finish and hurry to the computer in the corner of the room.

It feels like forever before it comes on. My hands twist together as I wait. As soon as the cursor becomes responsive, I try to remotely connect to my machine in the barracks.

The request isn't accepted.

What?

I always leave that computer on. It should allow me to connect, unless . . . unless they took it down. Elliot must have ordered someone to unplug it from the network.

Good try, Elliot, but it won't be that easy.

A good hacker is always prepared for stuff like this, and I'm not only a good hacker, I'm the best. A painful pang hits me in the middle of the chest as I think of Aydan. *He* is the best hacker there is. I'm a script kiddie compared to him.

I crack my neck and set to work. It will take a little longer to pull all the code off the network from all the secret places where I stashed it, right in front of Elliot's nose.

My fingers fly over the keyboard. The handcuffs dangle from my wrists, hitting the edge of the cabinet where the computer sits. I'm dimly aware of Luke, moving, coughing, freeing his other hand.

In a few minutes, I've got the bare minimum of what I need. Wasting no time, I send an urgent ping. I hope Sal is still listening. His response is almost immediate.

$Sal> ?
$Warrior> It's a trap. Stand back. NOW!
$Sal> What?
$Warrior> Stand back!
$Sal> I'd just established a remote connection with James. Switching you over to him.

A new handle appears. Dalí?

$Dalí> What the hell is wrong, Marci?
$Warrior> It's a TRAP

He asks no more questions, types nothing else. The cursor just sits there, blinking, waiting for his input on the other side. After a long moment, he replies.

$Dalí> Okay. Standing down

I exhale a shuddering breath of relief.

$Dalí> I hope that's really you, Marci. I don't like this.
What's going on there?
$Warrior> Nothing, just that Rheema is a damn
HUMAN traitor. She's here. Sold us out to Elliot
$Dalí> WTF?
$Warrior> I have to get out of here
$Dalí> What about Elliot?
$Warrior> He's here, but we'll have to get him another
time. Elliot sent

Shit!
I'm an idiot.

$Dalí> U still there?

I was going to say that Elliot sent everyone away. Everyone
but a few of his personal guards and, of course, those who
protect the building.

$Warrior> Yeah, still here. Just realized something
$Dalí> What?
$Warrior> Elliot sent everyone to ambush YOU. He's
practically unprotected here
$Dalí> What are you thinking?
$Warrior> We can still get him. He has even fewer
guards than he would have had at SeaTac
$Dalí> I'm having a hard time trusting you right now
$Warrior> We talked about this. You have to

We discussed this at length and decided that not trusting each other under the circumstances was a luxury and a waste of time.

$Dalí> I know, but
$Warrior> I'm me. I can meet you and prove it, but we have to be quick before they realize you're a no show

Again, the line goes silent. My lungs stop working. My heart picks up the slack. I'm startled when Luke appears at my side, key in hand. He attacks one of my dangling hand-cuffs with it. The thing falls uselessly to the floor. Just as he moves to my other wrist, James responds.

$Dalí> Let's do it
$Warrior> James
$Dalí> What?
$Warrior> They broke Aydan. He's one of them

Tears threaten to fall. My throat aches with the effort of keeping them in. James is slow to respond. I know just the emotions that must be surging within him and the effort it'd take to get them under control.

$Dalí> We'll get him back

I don't know if we can get him back and have no way of telling how much conviction is behind James's message, but I believe the words on the screen. I have to.

James and Kristen will do what it takes to free Aydan. Giving up on him is not an alternative for me, James or anyone in the crew.

Chapter 49

With so many of Whitehouse's soldiers gone, leaving the building unnoticed is almost too easy. Luke and I hurry down Pacific Place, moving north. I am to meet James in the same spot where I stash my bike—used to stash my bike, I remind myself with a pang of regret.

Luke is having a hard time keeping up. He's still coughing and keeping a hand on his throat to ease the pain. I don't wait for him, though. James might be there already. He needs to know I'm still me, needs to know he can trust me. If I'm late, they might get suspicious.

Every few steps, I peer up at the darkening sky, expecting the shimmer of scouts' wings to reflect the dwindling light. To my relief, the skies are clear, normal, and I can almost imagine a previous life in which Xave and I sped down the streets on our bikes, headed to the arcade for a game of pool and a Cajun dinner.

When I arrive at the parking lot, James isn't there. For a moment, I freak out and think I've missed him, but my worries are in vain since he pulls up in an armored van within minutes.

James, Blare, Clark, and Jori jump out of the van guns in hand. They all wear their IgNiTe jackets, black with the triangular insignia over the breast of flames devouring shadows. IgNiTe and FiGhT.

I rush in their direction but freeze mid-step. James blurs out of sight. My eyes flash back and forth, looking for him.

"What is he doing here?" he asks.

I look back. He's standing behind Luke who has a stiff back and a not-this-again look on his face. But hey, we're all having a rough day. If James has a gun pressed to his back, he needs to suck it up.

"He helped me escape," I say.

One of James's eyebrows goes up.

"We don't have time for this. Tie him up and throw him into that van, if you want."

"Hey," Luke protests.

"Do it," James orders.

Jori sets to the task right away.

Blare and Clark keep their guns on me the entire time. I put my hands up. It can only speed things up.

"Hey, little girl," Clark greets me the way Oso used to. A pang of regret hits me. So much loss. I shake my head and order myself to keep these thoughts away.

With Luke out of the way, James comes to me, takes one of my hands and, without preamble, cuts my finger tip with a sharp pocket knife. I yelp in surprise more than pain. He pulls out a small tube from his jacket's inner pocket, presses my finger into it and squeezes. My blood *drips, drips, drips,* and mixes with the substance inside the bottle. James caps the container and shakes it. I suck on my finger and wait.

A few seconds later the liquid turns murky green. James

nods.

"Let's go."

"What do I do with this one?" Jori asks.

James looks surprised for a moment like he'd completely forgotten about Luke.

"I'm sorry, Marci, but we can't trust him, even if he helped you escaped."

"I know."

"We can't leave him here unattended, though. Not considering who he is." James turns to Jori. "We'll take him with us. Jori cuff him to the seat. You'll have to keep an eye on him."

Once everyone is inside the armored vehicle, James talks into a handheld radio. "IgNiTe leader to all units. It's a go. Confirm. Ten-four."

All units? How many people does James have with him? I thought only our small cell was going to ambush Elliot. I guess I wasn't trusted with the full plan, after all.

I sit in the second row of bench seats. James is in the passenger seat, Clark at the wheel, and Blare in the first row. Oso should be the one driving. The thought hits me in spite of my efforts to push it away. It leaves me raw inside. Pushing is too much effort. Maybe I just need to embrace the pain, but that's a decision for a different time. Now, I need to focus.

Voices crackle through James's radio, helping my senses sharpen. One after another IgNiTe forces confirm they've received the message. When the line goes silent. James and Clark exchange a nod. Clark shifts into gear and speeds toward Whitehouse's headquarters.

I look over my shoulder to check on Luke. He's at the very back of the van, sandwiched between Jori and the windowless side. His hands are cuffed to a metal bar over his head. Jori sits alert, focused entirely on his prisoner.

"James said Rheema betrayed us, is that true?" Blare asks, glancing back at me.

"Yes."

She shakes her head, her lips trembling in anger. "I wonder how long she's been . . . I never suspected her."

"It could have been much worse," James says. "Be glad for our secrecy. It paid off, don't you think?" He gives Blare a sideways glance.

She flips him the bird, but then says, "I guess it did." She laughs a dry laugh and runs her fingers through her hair. She adjusts her backpack and cracks her neck. "Leave the bitch to me," she says. "I'll take care of her."

James turns his attention to me. "Here." He offers me a weird looking gun. I take it. "How about you take care of Aydan. Elliot is mine, of course. It'll be a pleasure."

I look down at the gun and frown.

"Tranquilizers," James explains. "We won't risk giving Aydan the cure, even if it's been reformulated. We'll bring him to Kristen and let her run a few tests before we use any version of *this* on our friends." He lifts his own gun which must be loaded with the real thing, a cure shot reserved for Elliot. For my part, I would kill him, but James wants to use him as an example to show the world Eklyptors aren't indestructible. He says most people need that kind of demonstration. Elliot has been a pretty public figure during their short reign.

"Here's a real gun, too." Blare hands me an automatic and a pouch full of clips. "These are tranquilizer refills." She hands me a second pouch. I frown at her, surprised by the fact that she's not barking at me. She shrugs one shoulder, and it's like she's saying *"I'm sorry."* It's lame, but I think that's the best I'm going to get. For Blare, this almost counts as a full speech. I wonder what made her decide to let the grudge go. Maybe she just found someone better to hate. I almost feel sorry for Rheema.

I quickly stuff the contents of the pouches into the pockets of my cargo pants.

"All in position." James's radio crackles with messages.

The armored van lurches. Clark drives it over the sidewalk, right to the front of Elliot's building. Two more vans come to a screeching halt next to ours. Men and women dressed in green camo spill out and storm the building like locusts.

"We have the place surrounded," he says. "It's now or never."

We jump out of the van, only Luke stays back, cuffed to the seat. He'll be safe in there. At least that's what I think until the shooting begins and bullets zip by and *ding* against the van's side panel. That's when I forget all about him and start worrying about my own hide.

Bullets hit the sidewalk in front of us. I fire two shots and begin to roll toward a tall planter, desperate for cover, but I never manage. Instead, my feet leave the ground and everything blurs.

At first, I think I've been shot in the head, and this is it. This is how death feels, the whole world speeds by, your life flashes before your eyes in a matter of seconds and into the big white light you go. I've almost come to terms with the idea when everything comes to an abrupt stop.

I blink, head spinning.

"Which way, Marci?" James asks.

My stomach flips, and I think I might throw up. My

surroundings come into focus in stages. I'm not outside anymore. I'm in the lobby in front of the elevators, while the shooting goes on behind us.

I look over at James, then notice Blare on his other side. I open my mouth, but nothing comes out.

"Which way?!" he asks again, his tone urgent and commanding.

God, James must be growing stronger. I've never known him to do anything like this before. I swallow and look around. "Um . . ." I breathe rapidly, trying to get oxygen into my confused brain. Two beats later, I have my bearings back. "This way!" I take off down the hall to the right, hoping Elliot is still there. If he's not, I'll find him.

He can't hide from us. Not this time.

Chapter 50

We burst into the auditorium guns at the ready. James goes down the middle of the row seats with Blare and I flanking him. We walk slowly, our weapons sweeping from side to side.

No one's here, only junk. Boxes, papers strewn over an improvised work area, maps pinned to the wall. Some war room. But I guess this is how such a place is bound to look when you repudiate technology.

James throws a questioning look in my direction. I shake my head and shrug, then notice a half-open door at the back of the room. I flick my gun in that direction.

In a flash, he disappears and reappears by the door. Blare heaves an aggravated sigh and takes off after him. I'm fast on her heels. James peeks past the door, then gives us a thumbs up without even turning to look at us, and again disappears in the blink of an eye.

Blare curses and runs faster. She pushes past the door without a pause. I try to keep up, but she's fast. My heart pounds in my ears. I breathe through my nose and out my mouth in ragged exhales. I enter the next room, looking around desperately. The area is set up with gray cubicles that once must have been someone's eight-to-five ball and chain.

I spot Blare's back end and make a sharp turn in her direction. I wish James had just hauled me with him. I'm not *that* heavy. I give it all I've got and shorten the distance between Blare and me. Past a narrow threshold ahead, there's a larger space. It's also full of cubicles, tons and tons of them.

I'm starting to think this corporate hell will never end when I spot a few figures at the end of the large area. I can't tell if Elliot is among them. It's hard to see with Blare in front of me and my vision bouncing with every step I take.

Suddenly, a sinking feeling settles in the bottom of my stomach. I haven't had any premonitions in a while, but this definitely feels like one. I shake my head and keep running.

Don't be stupid. Of course it feels like it's all going to the shitter. That's all there's been for months.

Blare slows then ducks inside a cubicle for cover when a bullet whizzes by. She points her gun over the short wall, breathing heavily and looking paler than ever. Following her lead, I run into the cubicle opposite hers and take aim. Like Blare, I'm using the gun with real bullets, the other one is holstered at my hip. The darts are for friends. Enemies get the real thing.

The scene unfolds before me like a letter full of bad news. James stands firmly, back to us, in the middle of the hall that separates two rows of cubicles. His hands are at his sides, tranquilizer gun pointed to the floor. For the life of me, I can't understand why he wants to try the cure on Elliot. For my part, I'd just use a bullet straight through the temple.

Beyond James, the news gets worse than bad. Elliot stands opposite us, flanked by his twin dwarfs and the person we once thought was our friend: Rheema.

Elliot wears a smile on his face that has no place being there. He would be less smug if one of his barrel-chested freaks didn't have Aydan in a chokehold, a gun pressed to the side of his head. Rheema must have told him to do this. I would also suspect Charger's self-sacrifice if it wasn't for the injured look in his eyes.

"Hello, James," Elliot says with a sarcastic smile.

James says nothing.

"This boy . . . he's one of yours, is he not?" He flicks a hand in Aydan's direction.

"Your building is surrounded," James says in a calm voice. "We outnumber your men since you so graciously sent most of them away to kill me."

The Eklyptor leader looks in my direction, fully aware of my presence and Lamia's failure to stop me. Hatred simmers in his golden eyes. I give him the peace sign. He snarls and looks away.

"Let him go." James uses a businessman's tone, negotiating. "Let him go and we can talk, decide what we do from here."

Elliot scoffs. "I know about your *cure*, James." He gestures toward Rheema. "I know that's why you're here. You want to show the world a *recovered* faction leader. You think that will give your weak humans hope and trust in your injection. But will you tell them it's more likely to kill us than actually *cure* us? Will you be honest?"

"The cure will be perfect. We already have a different version. We also have a vaccine. You won't be able to infect anyone else. It's just a matter of time before we regain control. But that's not the matter at hand, is it? That's in the future, and you should worry about *now*."

"Now," Elliot says as if reflecting on the philosophical implications of the word. He loosens his cravat, pulls it off and dries his forehead with it, then throws it to the floor. The silk piece of fabric flutters down gently, gentler than anything "now" is likely to bring.

Blare looks pointedly in my direction. Our gazes meet. She nods, turns her shark, dark eyes on the dwarf holding Aydan. Her gaze returns to me, then flashes quickly to the second dwarf. I get her message as loudly as if she had screamed it in my ear.

I adjust my aim, point my gun directly at my target. He has a big enough chest that even a child with a toy gun should be able to hit him. I'm worried about Blare, though. Is her aim good enough to hit *her* target? Or will she think of Aydan as collateral damage, if it gets down to that? I shake my head and take a deep breath, deciding to trust her. She can't be that heartless. She can't. Aydan is our friend, our family.

"Now," Elliot repeats while slowly removing his jacket. He also drops it to the floor. I frown at his now-casual look. I don't think I've ever seen him without his jacket and cravat. He looks odd, like a peacock without its plumage. It's as cold as usual in the building, but he seems to be sweating bullets. Good, that means he understands we mean business.

"Now," he repeats yet again, "right this second, *we* outnumber you."

He smiles with self-confident pleasure, making me doubt

he understands anything at all. My heart beats faster. The gun shakes in my hand. *Shit*. The heavy feeling in the pit of my stomach redoubles, making me wonder if Elliot has an ace up his sleeve.

The freak fiddles with his diamond-studded cufflinks, the way he always does. The action is so casual, he almost looks at ease. Besides the heavy sweat pouring down his forehead, he looks almost relaxed. I don't like this at all.

Slowly, Elliot sticks his hand in his pants pocket. I tense. My finger hugs the trigger a little tighter, my vision blurs for a beat as I sharpen my aim. I can sense James and Blare tensing, too. A moment later, Elliot's hand comes out, empty, and fall to his sides.

"So what's it gonna be, Elliot?" James asks.

"It's simple, you let us go, or we kill him."

Aydan's supplanter squirms and lets out a frustrated growl. All that time waiting to come out, and this is what he gets. *Serves him right.*

"You are not in a position to set conditions."

I'm starting to wonder how long this standoff will last when James disappears all of sudden, turning into nothing but a blur. I reel, uncertain of what to do when Blare gives the order.

"Shoot!"

I don't think twice and pull the trigger. My bullet hits its target before I'm done wondering whether it might hit James by accident. My dwarf gives a low grunt, takes a hand to his chest and looks at his own bloody fingers. I shoot again and again. He jerks on the spot and it takes two more shots to bring him down.

It's only until he falls flat that I give myself time to assess the situation.

Aydan!

He's the first one I look for. I find him on the floor, the other dwarf crumpled on top of him. He seems to be unconscious.

Oh, God!

I want to run to him, make sure he's alright, but bullets are whizzing out of Rheema's guns; she's always been good at the two-handed shooting. I take cover. Blare is already low to the floor. Our gazes lock for a moment, then she runs out of her cubicle—head low, knees bent—and backtracks the way we came. Maybe she's planning to go around?

Thoughts jumping in a stress-induced habit that will never leave me, I try to figure out what to do, where to go. But before I can decide, the shooting ceases and a dead silence falls over the place like fog. I hold my breath and listen intently. Slowly, I peek over the edge of the cubicle. What I see freezes my bones down to the marrow, even though logic tells me I shouldn't worry.

Rheema's guns are trained on James as he stands between her and Elliot, staring into the barrels of her double weapons.

"Are you faster than a bullet, James?" Elliot asks in his cool British accent.

"Much faster," James says, and with that, he blurs into nothingness, knocking away Rheema's guns in the process. An instant later, he's behind her, the tranquilizer gun pressed to her side. There is a zip sound. Rheema jerks, her eyes going wide. A moment later her knees go weak, and she falls to the ground, James eases her fall, depositing her gently on the floor. Why James has decided to keep that traitor alive is beyond me, but I breathe a sigh of relief, anyway.

He never takes his eyes off Elliot and watches him warily, even though he doesn't hold a gun. Elliot has always under-

327

estimated James. He had no real idea of his speed, and it seems Rheema didn't either. James could dodge bullets all day long. Almost. Rheema is just too cocky with her double guns to accept that.

"Who is outnumbered know?" James asks, switching guns in a barely perceptible movement, forsaking the tranquilizers for the cure. "It's time to surrender, Elliot. Your power struggle has come to an end. It's time you accept that."

Elliot trembles, but it's not fear. It's anger. He can't believe it has come down to this. Just moments ago, he was so sure James's head would be delivered on a platter. He probably even looked forward to torturing me with the sight of it. Now, the tables have more than turned, and it's his head that will be on the platter soon.

"In all those years that you stood by me, lying, didn't you learn I'm not the surrendering kind?" Elliot asks between clenched teeth. He stands so firmly, the angles of his body so precise that it sends a shiver down my spine.

He's not scared. Not in the least. I guess I've underestimated him, too. James doesn't, though. His gray eyes are dark and full of caution.

"It's polite to ask," he says.

"So your plan is to shoot me with that," he points at the gun in James's hand, "and then what? You think one Eklyptor leader will be enough to undo our confidence?"

"No. I'm familiar enough with your kind, and its arrogant boldness. I'm more concerned with giving hope to the many humans who are still fighting. It will let them know they can bide their time. Hide for a while if they have to, just until we're ready. It won't be long, though." James tweaks his wrist to call attention to his dart gun. "This works well enough. I can show you." He takes a step forward.

Elliot doesn't even flinch. He seems almost happy to let him approach.

A strange feeling washes over me. I take a step out of the cubicle into the middle passage. My eyes dart from James to Elliot and back again. The strange feeling grows inside me, building, building. My stomach feels as if it's been weighted down by rocks.

"James," I say in a whisper no one but I can hear.

He takes another step closer, gun at the ready.

I shake my head. "Don't get close to him," I say, finally finding my voice.

He stops and nods in my direction.

I exhale through my open mouth and aim my gun at Elliot.

"Always in the middle of things, spoiling everything." Elliot looks at me, his face disfiguring with the purest of hatreds. "You have ruined so much. You, a snotty, American girl with no manners."

"It's time *you* learn some manners of your own." And with that, James shoots his dart and hits the Eklyptor leader right in the middle of the chest.

Elliot Whitehouse looks down at his chest, his hand jerking to the spot. He pulls the dart out and lets it fall to the floor on top of his discarded jacket. His cuffs dangle open. I frown, realizing his diamond links are missing. My eyes search around the jacket. They're not there. Why would he take off his cufflinks? My minds races. He put them in his pants pocket, I suddenly realize.

Elliot coughs, gasps for breaths. He eases himself to the floor, taking one knee, then another. He throws his head back and wheezes in a long breath.

James takes a knee next to him, watching him warily.

"No, James," I remind him.

Elliot staggers forward, falling into James. I rush toward them, seized by an urgent desire to pull them apart. James holds him by the shoulders and lays him on the floor.

"It's fine, Marci," James says.

But my chest is too tight, too full of a desperation. I'm almost there when Elliot suddenly pulls up the sleeve of his right arm, revealing an extremity that looks anything but human. With a quick burst of power, something unfolds from his forearm and shoots straight into James's jugular. It hits, faster than the eye can see, faster than James, then recoils.

A large stinger like a scorpion's.

"No!" I scream, still running, running, running.

Blare screams as she runs over from one side, but her presence barely registers.

"James!" I cry.

Elliot laughs on the floor, his eyes full of delight as they stare at the ceiling.

"You bastard."

I aim and shoot at his prone shape over and over again. I'm running and shooting and watching his body jerk as bullets hit his chest, making it bloodier with each impact. The gun clicks empty before I get there. Elliot is deader than dead, but if I had more bullets, I'd empty them all into him, until there was nothing left but a flowing river of blood.

I crash to my knees and slide right behind James just as he begins to fall.

He drops into my arms, his eyes opening and closing at an alarming speed.

"I—I should have listened," he says, then goes utterly still.

* * *

"James James James," his name a desperate plea from my lips.

I shake him, slap him on the face. His limbs thrash for a moment then go still. Blare falls to her knees on the other side of him. She's saying something, but I don't know what. Her lips move in a fast litany of words with no sounds. Her fingers check the pulse at his throat. Her face disfigures after a few seconds. She recoils, turns her face away to hide the pain.

"Not James. Not James. No no no."

All I hear is my own voice.

All I see is the swollen, red spot at his throat, the wound through which the venom entered his body.

All I feel is impotence and crippling sorrow.

I was going to move in with him. We were going to be a family.

"James."

I put a hand on his chest, next to the "IgNiTe and FiGhT" emblem on his jacket. Warmth seeps through his jacket and into my hand. He was just here, just here. He can't have gone far. He can't be dead. He can't be! If I could just . . .

My mind races then comes to a screeching halt as a desperate idea takes hold of me. But what I'm thinking is impossible, it's—

No! This is James. I can't hesitate.

Giving myself no more time for uncertainty, no chance to doubt, I close my eyes and reach for my skill.

Inside. Inside, I chant inside my head.

"What are you doing?" Blare asks, her voice is but a whisper in my head, a bothersome noise I must ignore.

Inside! I want to be in his blood. I want to *be* his blood.

Suddenly, I'm indefinite and flowing, slowly, but flowing. He's still here, warm and malleable. Death and its cold hand have not reached him yet. I search frantically, acting fast, becoming one with James's body, with his blood.

If I transform into his blood, I won't be the venom and that's how I'll know . . .

I'll know what doesn't belong.

I'll know what must be gone.

The first traces of the poison are by the wound. I become acquainted with it, become it for just an instant. Know thy enemy. It takes but a moment to understand the structure of the evil substance. I see how its molecules bind, what makes them deadly. I see how they differ from all the life-giving, life-carrying particles that make up James's blood.

Disgusted, I push away and become one with James's blood once more. I'm nothing else, not even Marci. Methodically, I look for what doesn't belong. I'm complex, made out of a million different particles. I sift through what seems like chaos but is a perfectly orchestrated miracle. Slowly, the venom stands out like splinters that must be removed, foreign objects that have no business being part of me.

I pull them out, examine them. They're strange and vile. *You don't belong here.* I recoil and push away.

Lost inside of James, my body feels far away, a mirage that was never real. Still, I sense my left hand on James's neck, close to his wound, while my right one moves over his prone figure, directing my energy into the right places, all the quiet corners that need to roar back to life.

I seep out of the puncture at his neck, slide down the side of his neck, flowing thickly, staining the carpet, seeping into its fibers and spreading.

The poison is everywhere, so much of it. It went into his heart and from there it spread to all his organs in just a few beats of his fierce, strong heart.

I do my best, force what I can out, but soon realize I can't get to it fast enough. It's too much, tiny particles, everywhere. Everywhere!

My eyes spring open. Blare is staring at me in horror. My left hand is covered in James's blood. I'm panting, sweating. I can't even fathom how I look.

"CPR," I burst out. "He needs CPR." I begin pumping his chest.

One-one-thousand.

Two-one-thousand.

Three-one-thousand.

I stop, wait for Blare to help. She just stares with wide, disbelieving eyes. With a growl of frustration, I tip James's head back and blow air into his mouth. I do this a few times before Blare decides it might do some good. Soon, she's helping, keeping rhythm with me.

For a moment, there's a spark of hope in her eyes, but every passing second James fails to breathe, it dies, dimming, turning to darkness.

"C'mon, James." I count while my hands, one on top of the other, press against his sternum, willing his heart to remember what to do, to give me back the man I love like a father. "Please, James."

Abruptly, Blares turns away, sobs into the wall of the cubicle behind her. She's giving up on him. She can't do that. We can't do that.

I take up for her, blow air into James's mouth then compress his chest.

I won't stop. I won't stop.

I won't.

James's spring eyes open.

I stop.

"James!"

He sputters, then gasps for air. Blare whirls, tears frozen on her face, mouth agape. I sit back on the floor, trembling. I laugh and cry at the same time, chest shaking out of control.

Blare helps James as I fall apart into a pile of raw emotions I'm unable to reign in.

Elliot is dead.

James is alive.

Aydan is alive.

And this is over. Over. Over.

Chapter 51

Clarck turns corners barely stepping on the brakes, making us all lurch to the side and pray over the armored van stays upright. Buildings blur by, a part of town I don't recognize.

I thought it was over. I thought too soon.

James is alive. I brought him back to life, but his vitals are weak. His face is pale, his lips so white they make me fear I didn't do enough.

After he opened his eyes, Blare ran out and got help. By then, IgNiTe had secured the building, the few remaining Eklyptors no match for our numbers. A few minutes later, Clark, Jori and others rushed in following Blare. We loaded Rheema, Aydan and James into the van and took off. Jori got hold of Kristen on the radio and explained the situation. She's now waiting for us, ready to do whatever it takes to save James. I don't even want to think about what she must be feeling. Will she blame me? Do I blame myself for never being strong enough, fast enough, brave enough?

James lays in the front row with Blare and I kneeling by his side, holding him in place, preventing him from sliding off the seat with every turn we take.

Jori is in the back, keeping an eye on Luke, Rheema and Aydan.

It feels like forever before we arrive at a large, modern building. A sign that reads United Private Laboratories sits by the entrance to the parking area.

Clark follows the instructions from someone on the crackling radio and pulls right up to the front door. When he screeches to a halt, there's a host of people already waiting. They have stretchers and medical bags with them and rush to retrieve James from the van. In a matter of seconds, they're rushing him in, barking out instructions and forcing us to stay back.

Jori pulls Luke from the van, hands cuffed at his back. He stares at the ground, riddled with shame. He doesn't even make eye contact with me. Others tend to Rheema and Aydan. They settle their unconscious shapes on stretchers, too. But there's a difference. These stretchers have straps for their ankles and wrists.

I stand with the others on the sidewalk as they roll them inside. Then, like a zombie, I follow them inside and watch as they are pushed past a set of double doors where I'm not allowed to follow. Luke is taken through a different door, and I don't care enough to ask where they're taking him. James and Aydan are the only ones that matter.

As they roll Aydan away, his pale face looks calm, as if he's just sleeping after a long night of hacking. He doesn't look like a man possessed by an evil creature. Yet something dark slips into my mind, something I refuse to look at straight on.

"Where are they taking them?" I ask, not really expecting a response.

"To a secure area," Clark answers behind me. "They'll be fine." He puts a hand on my shoulder and I nearly crumble. "Are you okay?"

I turn into him, bury my face in his chest and cry.

* * *

"Drink this. You'll feel better." Clark hands me a tall cup of coffee. "Ten sugars. Just how you like it."

I take the cup and cradle it between my hands, enjoying its warmth. A smile stretches my lips. The gesture feels foreign. My face is too stiff for such a lighthearted response. But it's nice to know there is someone who still knows me. Clark witnessed Xave and I bicker over who should get the most sugar packets every time we bought coffee—moments from a past that, although inconsequential, make up the bulk of my simple, past life.

He sits next to me, nursing his own cup. We've been waiting for news for over an hour now, but no one has come to tell us anything. It's like we don't exist.

I look to the secured door. My heart does a weird flip again. God, I need to stop staring in that direction, especially since Blare is sitting on the floor right next to the door, her back to the wall, knees drawn to her chest, eyes closed as if in prayer. She almost looks like someone who believes in a higher power.

Jori, Spencer, Margo and others are here too, pacing, talking in their radios, waiting for some good news.

"I'm so glad Kristen was here and not at one of the safe houses," Clark says. "This place is as good as any hospital. It's got everything." He doesn't seem to be talking to me. It's like he's just trying to reassure himself, which is fine by me, because I'm all for reassuring rants right now.

Clark says this is one of the places where Kristen has been working on the cure. Apparently, she's been conducting her work in several different locations, with different sets of scientists to help. It was naive of me to think she was doing all her work in an improvised lab. They've kept this a secret, making sure not to put all their efforts in a single place. This is the lesson they learned after they lost The Tank thanks to a stupid girl who was too weak to guard the beans and, instead, spilled them in the worst manner possible.

I drink the sweet coffee and close my eyes. Questions, so many questions, swim inside my head. I reach for the answers, but they don't come. Mostly, what I find are doubt and fear.

Suddenly, Blare jumps to her feet. A second later the doors open and Kristen walks out. Her red hair stands on end. Her face is sallow, without makeup. She rubs the back of her neck, looking as if she hasn't slept in decades.

Clark and I rush to her and come to a halt next to Blare. I stare at Kristen's red-rimmed eyes, searching for some of the answers I've been desperately waiting for. For a moment, I think she'll break down into tears and tell me all the things I don't want to hear, but then she smiles, and the small gesture is enough to kill the worst of my fears, enough to make me forget all those times I thought she was a witch.

Clark slaps his thigh and laughs. "He's fine then?" he says in a loud, rambunctious voice that causes the rest of the IgNiTe soldiers to come nearer, eager to find out if their leader will be all right.

"He'll be fine. Sooner than most," Kristen says, her smile deepening.

She patched him up and now James's Symbiot healing abilities will do the rest.

Tears prickle at the corner of my eyes, the joyous kind. I've cried plenty in the last few months, but it's always been about pain, not joy, not happiness. Emotions swirl inside of me. They surge at a dizzying speed. They're all good, but feel completely foreign. Grief, pain, fear, those emotions I'm used to. But relief and contentment haven't visited me in a long time.

"Hey, you all right there, Marci?" Clark mock punches me in the arm and gives me the biggest smile he has to offer.

"I'm fine," I manage to say, then have to turn to hide my face and the tears that inevitably spill onto my cheeks.

"She saved him," Blare says. "He was dead, by all rights. But Marci didn't give up on him. She saved him."

In a tone I barely recognize coming from her, Blare jumps into a detailed retelling of Elliot's attack. She tells them about his secret mutation and his lightning-fast assault on James. She tells them how the poison stopped his heart in a matter of seconds and how she thought him lost forever.

In the same breath, she shares all the rest: my refusal to let him go, the unexpected use of my skills to draw out the poison, my desperate efforts to restart his heart.

Everyone cheers. Hands pat me on the back while I struggle to hide my tears. I cover my face, confused by all the emotions crashing into me. I want to hide and get a chance to compose myself, to understand what I'm feeling, but they don't let me.

Instead, they pull me off my feet and lift me up in the air. They're cheering, chanting and, some, like me, crying. They make my name into a song.

Most of these people don't even know me, but they have

a reason to celebrate. They have their leader and a new hope.

They pass me over the crowd, their hands supporting me, making me feel weightless. I throw my head back. Warm tears spill into my ears, my hair. They flow without regard now, as I finally let my emotions free.

I'm floating on my back, crying, laughing, daring to hope.

Seattle is free of its strongest factions.

Is the world next?

I embrace the thought, believe in it.

We can do this. We have each other.

Hands press against the back of my arms, my legs, my head. They got me and will never let me go. I'm not alone anymore and won't ever have to be.

Chapter 52

Several hours later, James sits up in the bed, a huge smile on his face. Most of the soldiers have left and only the members of our original cell are still here. I press through the door timidly, afraid to start crying again. He shakes his head and opens his arms invitingly.

"Come here," he says.

Kristen gives me a little shove toward the bed. James seizes me and wraps me in a tight hug. I bite my trembling lower lip, turning into nothing but a little girl in the embrace of a steadfast man. An IV line still runs from his arm. He's getting medication to control the high blood pressure and muscle spasms the venom cause.

"I heard you saved my life," he says in a thick, low murmur. "Again."

"You offered me something I sorely need." *A family.* "I intend to make that a reality."

"Damn right." He holds me at arm's length. There are tears in his eyes that he doesn't bother to hide. He puts a hand on my cheek and looks at me with pride. My cheeks turn hot.

For the first time, I wonder how Kristen feels about this whole family thing. My eyes cut to her, then to the floor.

"You have nothing to worry about, kiddo," James says as if reading my mind.

Kristen smiles reassuringly as if all our differences never existed.

My cheeks are now on fire. I clear my throat. "Kristen said you wanted to talk to me." I continue to stare at the floor. "Um, shouldn't you be resting?"

"Nah, I feel ready to get back out there. We have so much to do."

Kristen shakes her head disapprovingly. "You're not invincible. No matter how many times you manage to come back from the dead."

"I don't know, with my team by my side, it seems I may be." He laughs, but in a lighthearted way, making it clear he will be following doctor's directions.

"Actually," James says, "both Kristen and I wanted to talk to you."

There is an ominous ring to his tone that I don't like at all.

"Why don't you sit?"

I shake my head and hug myself. This is about Aydan and they want me to sit. I won't sit. I will face this standing, even as I fight the urge to plug my ears and chant *la la la* like a child.

"We know you and Aydan have grown close to each other." James gives me a knowing smile. "We've known for a while that he loves you."

I inhale, look at a spot in the ceiling.

"And I think maybe this is a reciprocal feeling?" James

cocks his head to one side, as if trying to get a better angle, one that will let him see me more clearly.

Maybe Aydan was easy for them to read. Me? Not so much. *I* don't even know what I feel. I've been too busy deciding whether loving people is a blessing or a curse.

"Am I right?" he prods when I don't answer.

Hiding, concealing who I am and how I feel has been a necessity my entire life, not to mention lately. But here and now, there's no reason for me to disguise who I am or how I feel. And even if an obstacle arose, I have to make a choice to come out of the darkness and the shadows that have haunted me for so long.

It's time for me to shine. It's time to be whole, to feel fully, to live without fear.

So I answer, my voice strong and clear. "Yes, you're right. I care about him. A lot."

As the words leave my lips, a warm feeling slowly fills my chest. It's the best thing I've felt in a very long time.

James nods with a smile that's sweet and mellow at first, but then turns sad.

"He's gonna be okay," I say. It should be a question. It almost sounds like one, but I refuse to think he won't be.

On the other side of the bed, Kristen takes a step closer to James's bed and reaches for his hand. "He's in there, as we well know. But . . ."

I shake my head, take a step back. "But" is the type of word I don't want to hear.

"Marci," Kristen inhales as if to gather courage from the air, "if we give him the cure—"

"He'll be gone," I finish for her. I knew this. The knowledge has been there, nagging me, wanting to get noticed, but I've ignored it.

"We think he would still be Aydan. Human, but different," James says. "He wouldn't be a Symbiot. He . . . would be whoever he was before he was infected, before his mind learned to take advantage of the agent."

In other words, he *wouldn't* be the Aydan I admire and fell in love with. He would be average, unremarkable. And it sounds terrible to think I couldn't love an Aydan who is less bright, less strong. It makes me seem shallow, but it isn't, because love is strange and set in its ways, because we can't tell our hearts who to love when its mind is already made up.

"We thought we should tell you before we tried to . . ." Kristen can't finish.

James continues, "You came back from it. Maybe he can too." There's a spark in his eye and I seize it like a lifeline.

"Yeah, yeah," I say, nodding my head over and over. "He can fight his way out and maybe . . ." I take a deep breath and let the realization sink in. "Maybe I can help him."

Chapter 53

I enter the room with my heart pounding in my throat. It is a windowless space with sterile walls and little furniture: a tall, medical table, a chair and a built in cabinet with a small sink. Clark enters behind me and closes the door. He stands next to it, hanging back. He's here to "protect" me. James wouldn't let me come in by myself.

Charger sits on the medical table, his back against the corner where the two far walls meet. His knees are drawn up to his chest, his head thrown back and his eyes closed.

"Hello, Aydan," I say after clearing my throat.

His eyes don't open, but his mouth twitches, which is enough to let me know he's awake and listening.

"We did it," I say. "We took down Whitehouse and Hailstone."

"I'm n-not Aydan," he growls, still refusing to look at me.

I ignore his comment and continue, "We don't know if the cure would've worked on Elliot, and that's my fault, I guess. I had to shoot him." It's not easy to say it in a cold tone, but I manage. Killing, even killing monsters, will never be easy or something I can casually talk about.

"Either way, the hope is real. IgNiTe cells are already out there, using darts instead of bullets. It's slow going, but it really is working, especially on the newer Eklyptors which is the majority, anyway. Now it's just a matter of time. Kristen and the others are still trying to create new formulations, and I have no doubt they'll get something that works on everyone—not to mention a better way to mass distribute it." This is wishful thinking on my part, the only hope I have if I can't help Aydan.

Charger clenches his fists and presses them to his eyes, trembling. "Did y-you come to give me my sh-shot? Or just torture me with your incessant t-talk, bitch?"

"Hey, watch it, asshole," Clark says.

I put a hand up and mouthed "it's okay" over my shoulder.

"I'm not talking to you," I say. "I don't give a crap about you, as a matter of fact. I'm talking to my friend."

"He c-can't hear you. He's deaf and blind like a mo-mole. You're wasting your time." Charger finally opens his eyes and looks at me.

A chill runs down my back as his black eyes connect with mine. They're Aydan's eyes, but the essence that flickers behind them is clearly someone else's.

"Maybe," I say, "but I know he's in there and you know it too. And I bet you're afraid, very afraid. You know it's possible to come back after being eclipsed. I did it and Aydan will do it too. That's why I'm here, to welcome him back."

With one quick jolt, Charger jumps off the table, his bare feet slapping against the linoleum floor. "H-he won't!" He's trembling with fury. His lips are pulled back, giving his face a murderous expression. This creature would gladly kill me.

The way Azrael killed Oso.

An idea goes off like a light bulb in my head.

If Aydan is aware the way I was when Azrael took over me, he would never let Charger hurt me. I take a step forward. Clark puts a hand on my shoulder to stop me.

I turn back. "Maybe it'd be better if you wait outside."

"No way. He's crazy," Clark says.

"He's Aydan."

Clark looks down and shakes his head.

I lean forward and talk into his ear. "I can help him. I have an idea, but it would work better if it's just me."

"Marci, that's not smart."

"Please. You know I can take care of myself."

He purses his lips and lifts an eyebrow in agreement. "Okay, but I'll be right outside the door."

"Don't come in no matter what you hear. I'll call you if I need you. All right?"

"You got it." He leaves, but not without giving me a disapproving glance.

I turn around and face Charger again. He's standing, feet shoulder-width apart. His chest pumps up and down, breaths as loud as an angry bull's, ready to attack.

"Yep, it's clear you're afraid," I say, extending a hand in his direction to demonstrate. "Crapping your pants from the looks of it. You're going back and this, in here," I look around the room, "will be all the life you'll get to live."

"NO! N-NO!" he shouts. "Not going back. Never. I'd rather die." He looks around the room as if trying to find something he could use to harm himself. It makes me glad the room is bare.

I take a step closer, questing forward with my skill,

wondering if I'd be able to feel Aydan's consciousness, the way I felt the poison in James's veins.

"We care about him and we won't let you hurt him," I say, making my tone as conceited as possible, going for what I think will make Charger angrier.

I push further with my skill, searching, sifting through a host of confusing things: a rapid heartbeat, the loud *whooshing* of blood through veins and arteries, the frantic pumping of lungs. I feel it all, except what I'm looking for.

For a moment, I almost despair thinking he's not there. Then I realize I don't even know what to look for. What is a consciousness? It's not something physical that we can grasp. It's not a chemical we can observe under a microscope to then decompose into its different elements.

I pull my power away and focus on Charger's shape. He's furious, shaking like some sort of machinery ready to implode.

"But maybe you don't understand that we would go to any lengths to save him." I step closer still. "No one has ever cared for you, after all. And no one ever will."

"S-shut up. Shut up!"

"Aydan," I look straight into his eyes, "keep fighting. You can beat him. He's always been weaker than you. Come back. We miss you."

"Shut up, I said."

When his hand abruptly comes up, I have to force myself to stay put and take it. The slap lands across my cheek, causing my head to snap to one side. Blood pools inside my mouth. I swallow, straighten my shoulders and press forward.

"I know you're not giving up until you—"

Charger jumps me. He crashes into me, tackles me to the

floor and straddles me. "You don't k-know how to keep y-your trap shut, but I will tea-teach you."

He wraps his hands around my throat and leans forward, bearing down on me. I buck and pull on his wrists, fighting my panic.

Aydan won't let him kill me.

Aydan won't let him kill me.

My lungs begin to burn. "Aydan, help me," I mouth, my gaze locked with Charger's own crazed gaze.

"He's not co-coming. I won't let him." Charger squeezes harder.

Aydan won't let him kill me. He won't.

I plead with my eyes as I fight for my next breath.

Please, Aydan. Fight. Stop him.

My body tingles, going cold. Images swim in front of me as my vision blurs.

Oh God, I have to fight. Aydan isn't coming.

He's not . . . coming.

With the last of my strength, I pull on Charger's wrists, trying to pry him away. A bit of air seeps into my lungs, giving me what I need to call for help.

Clark is one plea away, but so is Aydan.

Maybe this one breath is the last chance I'll get to make it out of this room alive. Maybe it is the last break I'll ever get. But the truth is that it doesn't matter. I can't give up on Aydan. I can't put myself ahead of him. He's part of me. So this last breath is for him.

"I love you, Aydan." The words are but a choked whisper.

Charger's ferocious expression deepens. He has no regard for my feelings. The grip around my neck grows fiercer, sending a shock through my limbs. My hands fall limp at my sides.

He shakes his head violently as he tries to squeeze the last bit of life out of me.

My eyes roll into the back of my head. The world goes dark around me and everything is suddenly curiously still and numb. I feel nothing, not even the choking pressure around my neck.

Then I'm coughing and gasping for air. My hands fly to my neck. Breaths rasp in and out through my slack mouth. *I'm not dead.*

My eyes spring open at the realization. I'm still breathing, and Charger isn't choking me anymore. Through blurry eyes, I see him, hovering on top of me.

He blinks, looks down at his hands, then at me. His face is twisted in confusion and something like pain.

"Marci," he says, hands shaking in front of him. "What have I—?"

"Aydan?!"

His black eyes are soft and deep, not sharp and flat as they were just a moment ago.

"Aydan is that you?"

Tears slide down his cheeks. "Oh, God. I'm sorry. I'm so sorry," he says, his voice so full of pain and guilt that it touches something deep inside of me. Emotions rise from that hidden place and rush through me with merciless violence.

I know just how he feels. His pain was mine the day Azrael spilled Oso's blood and left it on my hands.

My own tears find their way out. "Aydan, you did it." I struggle upright, wrap my arms around him and press my face to his chest.

His heart is loud and fast. I feel it like a pounding fist through his shirt. Slowly, his arms find their way around my back. He pulls me close and we both cry.

We cry for each other, for those we've loved who are now gone, for a life lost and recovered, for all those who will never be as miserable or as lucky as we are.

We cry because it's finally over.

Epilogue

Today, Seattle is the first city in the world to officially be back under human control. It wasn't easy to get here, but the worst of it has passed, even if there's still much work to do. Other cities are on their way to regaining their human sovereignty. They will need help and many—like the members of our IgNiTe cell, Clark, Blare, Aydan and I—are willing to provide it. Los Angeles, James's childhood home, will be our first stop.

With the Seattle Wheel behind me, I stand facing the water. My bike sits within arm's reach. I barely leave it out my sight unless it's stored safely. When everything was said and done and it was reasonably safe to do so, I went to SeaTac to find it. I almost cried when I spotted it parked next to the bike racks outside of the baggage claim area. Like my father's house or the Def Leppard t-shirt I'm wearing, I feel as if the bike is part of me, a link to Xave and what he means in my life.

The sun shines in the distance, dipping slowly into the Pacific Ocean. My gaze drifts over the sun-kissed surface of

Puget Sound. It's a beautiful summer day, the kind that used to drive city residents outdoors with half their clothes missing.

These days, there are few brave souls out, though. Fear still reigns in people's hearts, so they stick to their homes or shelters. For the most part, those out and about enjoying the day are emergency workers: police, firefighters, military, cleaning crews. And they *are* enjoying the day. I don't think I've ever seen people work with such pleasure and energy. We have our world and lives back, and everything seems twice as bright after being in the shadows for so long. So much to be thankful for.

"Think fast," Aydan says behind me.

I turn and realize a bottle of water is sailing through the air, headed straight for my face. Reflexively, energy flows from my core and travels outward. The bottle stops just inches from my nose and hovers in midair.

"Impressive. You're getting really good," he says.

Meditation is nothing for me these days. I do it for about thirty minutes every morning with no ill effects or help from anyone. I enjoy it immensely, especially when I think of Azrael suffering the torture through each session.

I let the bottle glide gently to my hand, unscrew it and take a sip.

"All the workers checked out." Aydan closes the distance between us and stops at my side.

For weeks, this has been our job: mingling with the emergency crews, trying to spot Eklyptors among them. We have found many attempting to pass themselves as human. Sometimes everyone feels like a threat, and it makes me wonder if we'll ever stop looking. An ingestible version of the cure is in the water system now, but we can't be sure everyone's got a taste. The airborne version has proven more difficult to develop, though Kristen and her lab soldiers work restlessly on it day and night. She's confident they'll manage, though, and I trust her.

Our relationship has grown leaps and bounds just like my meditation skills. We moved into James's condo. It's in the same building where The Tank used to be. It's still awkward living with them, but it gets easier every day. They are making a big effort to be parents. I have a curfew, chores and even an allowance. It's weird and great all at the same time. The weirdest thing is living in a different house than my own, than Dad's, but James says it's temporary, at least until I turn eighteen and can live on my own. For now, he's helped me get the deed under my name and put it under the care of a real estate management company.

"I'm glad we didn't have to use these today." Aydan points at the pouch of cure cartridges at his belt.

We both carry them along with authorization to administer them. James made it all happen through his friends in high places. We can sense Eklyptors through their buzzing and are uniquely equipped to detect them. James and Kristen control the cure, its production, distribution, administration channels and tracking. As it's to be expected, there has been much controversy around this: people questioning the wisdom of a private company wielding such power. Congress was in session until their faces turned blue, arguing that this responsibility should belong solely to the government. But there's no way in hell James and Kristen would ever trust bureaucrats with such a crucial task. And what can the government do? Jail the only man and woman who know what's what? The literal saviors of the human race? Instead, President Helms, someone who has received the cure and lived, put them in charge, and everyone else follows their orders. Smart man.

Aydan's black eyes take in the view of the sound and Bainbridge Island in the far distance. "What a magnificent day." He inhales and closes his eyes, relishing the fresh air.

I don't think this area of town has ever smelled so clean. Months of reduced traffic on land and water have really made a difference in air quality.

I look up at Aydan as he throws his head back and lets the sun shine on his face. His longish, black hair tickles his brow as a briny breeze blows from the north, carrying a small, winter bite in its midst. He shivers slightly, his eyes still closed. I smile at the sight of his sharp profile, feeling so grateful for his company. Since he resurfaced and regained control of his body, he's been with me as much as possible. It seems we can't stand to be apart from each other. Our similar experiences have linked us more than ever. To our knowledge, we're the only ones who have come back after being eclipsed which has given us a unique understanding of one another.

We are both recovering, getting our lives and our minds back in order. Sometimes we have nightmares. They normally involve losing control and being lost in the dark. We talk about them, and it helps process the fear. But, for the most part, we are okay, adapting, getting back to normal.

I wish I could say the same about everyone else, but some of us will never get back to anything resembling normalcy. Rheema is under arrest. She will go to prison for a very long time, if not for life. Lyra is dead, sacrificed by Elliot. Our IgNiTe cell retrieved her body from Whitehouse head-quarters and took care of the arrangements to send her back to France. James says she had no family to mourn her, and

I don't know if that's better or sadder than the alternative.

Then there is Luke. Poor, deluded Luke Hailstone who dreamed a twisted, impossible dream. I've seen him once in the last couple of months. It wasn't easy and hardly an experience I want to repeat. That makes me feel guilty, like I owe him something, like I've abandoned a part of myself. But I would rather deny there's a connection between us, even if that makes me callous or the most despicable human being on the planet. I just don't think I could ever truly forgive him for trying to make me part of his delusional plan, for thinking I would become some kind of freak factory. So, again and again, I have resolved not to feel sorry for him. At least, he's better off than all the people his faction killed. He has three square meals a day and a nice view from his cell's window—never mind that his DNA-changing body is now a wonder of science. It's nothing worse than what he planned to do to us. I'm glad he is alive because the thought of his death is still repulsive to me. I'm not sure he feels the same way.

"We'll need to be back in a couple of hours." Aydan opens his eyes and catches me watching. He blushes and smiles wryly. "What?"

"Nothing, just looking at you."

He turns and stands in front of me, his arms finding their way around my waist. "I'm the one who needs to be looking at you." He tucks a strand of hair behind my ear and presses a warm, tender kiss to my forehead.

The way he kisses me and touches me makes me feel delicate. It's as if he's afraid I will break, even though he knows well, better than anyone, I won't. His love is gentle, patient, imbued with an even mixture of passion and rationality. He says he loves me because it makes total sense and because it doesn't. We're so different and yet so similar.

He calls it perfection.

In his arms, I feel safe and whole. Most of the time, anyway. Some days, dread finds its way into my heart and, no matter how hard I try, I can't push away the fear of losing him. I guess he feels the same way. We carry a constant threat inside our brains, and the possibility of losing control is always there, no matter how small. I wish we could take the cure, but it would destroy us. We are so intertwined with our agents that the person left behind would be nothing like us.

I pull Aydan to me, bury my face into his chest.

I will not lose you.

He brushes the length of my hair, his hands traveling gently down my back. With his nose pressed to my forehead, he inhales deeply and makes a sound in the back of his throat. "You smell so pretty, like the wind and sunshine have found their way into your hair, like a beautiful day."

I chuckle. He manages to do and say the goofiest things—like that day he made fireworks over the surface of Lake Union for me. All for me. And I'm such an insipid, unromantic girlfriend, but I guess that's just another way in which we're fundamentally different—not that I'm not capable of being goofy myself.

Suddenly, an idea occurs to me. I pull away and look up at the Ferris wheel. "Is there any power in that thing?"

"Hmm." Aydan closes his eyes as if listening. "Yeah, there is," he says after a moment. He's so attuned to his skill that he can sense electricity, or the lack of it, all around him.

"How about you close your eyes," I say.

He looks down at me, a question twinkling in the depths

of his eyes. But he doesn't ask anything. He just does as I say and closes his eyes.

I guide him toward the wheel and the gondola area. "Don't peek!"

"I won't."

The gondolas are all closed, but their sliding, glass doors pose no obstacle when I reach forward with my power and ease them open. We step inside. I help Aydan sit opposite me. As I push the doors closed with my mind, a knowing smile plays over Aydan's lips. He knows just where we are, but he doesn't know I plan to keep him here until the sun kisses the horizon.

I close my eyes and become one with the giant wheel. My power spreads tall and wide. It's dizzying at first. I've never tried to control anything this big. I narrow my focus. It's the motor that matters, what makes the wheel turn. I relax, searching my core, the wheel's core, until I find it and understand its inner-workings, the source of its power. This leads me straight to the controls, the right combination of switches and settings.

Once I know just what I need to do, my eyes spring open. Aydan's chest is moving up and down faster than normal. Even though he knows what I plan to do, he's still nervous.

With a small push of my power, the Ferris wheel comes to life. Aydan rolls his shoulders. I'm sure he feels the surge of electricity like fingers dancing over his skin. The gondola swings slightly as the wheel turns. I never had a chance to ride it before and, if I'm honest, I must admit I'm feeling excited to be here with Aydan.

We begin to rise into the vast blueness of the sky.

"You can look now," I say.

His eyes open slowly and lock with mine before they

wander outside of the gondola's glass walls. Downtown is to the right and Puget Sound to the left. Bits of afternoon sun still sparkle on the water, like tiny, fallen stars. When the gondola reaches the very top, I switch the power off, and we come to a stop. Our gondola dangles one hundred and seventy-five feet off the ground.

Blue-gray mountains outline the horizon in the distance. Gulls float lazily around, riding the currents. The Space Needle seems small and close, as if we could reach out and grab it.

"Wow! I never rode it before," Aydan says.

"Me neither!" I switch places and sit next to him, leaning my back against his chest. He wraps his arms around my waist and silently enjoys the view, the stillness, the solitude. After being in the middle of a terrible war, these small comforts are priceless.

Peace is priceless.

"I could fall asleep," I say, snuggling closer to Aydan.

He absently caresses my forearm. "You can rest on the way to L.A."

It's a seventeen-hour drive from Seattle to Los Angeles. I can get plenty of rest then.

"Sometimes I feel like staying," I say.

"Me too."

But we would never do that. We have to go and help root out all the Eklyptors, at least until Kristen and her team of scientists can figure out a way to effectively administer the cure through the air.

Those who were never infected are coming out in droves to receive the vaccine. They are voluntarily adding their names to a global database that checks against pre-takeover records and figures out the totals.

Worldwide, the numbers have been steadily improving in our favor, but we are nowhere near to eradicating the problem. As a matter of fact, James thinks we might never get there, and I tend to agree with him. Because how do you get cure water or even air to every single corner of the world? Eklyptors have gone into hiding and finding them is costly and time-consuming. Already world officials are creating Anti-Eklyptor Forces (AEF.) Their job is what ours has been, except a lot less efficient since they have no built-in way to tell humans apart from Eklyptors.

IDs aren't trusted since Eklyptors can change their appearance. Hence, suspects are subjected to blood tests on the spot. If they turn out to be infected, a cure is also administered on the spot. With a modified formula, survival rates are currently at 95%—not bad considering all the people who died during and after The Takeover. Still, there are those who argue about the morality of what is being done, the power that these AEFs have and the abuses that are likely to ensue.

James says that if world officials expect their plans to work, it will have to be a "constantly changing game." He thinks that once bureaucracy sets back in, and we go back to our old ways, governments will be unable to keep up with the demands. That is why he is committed to the creation of private forces. We are the first, all the IgNiTe cells around the world to whom victory is owed.

Certainly, we have our work cut out for us for a number of years—if not for a lifetime.

"Do you agree with James?" I ask. "Do you think they will always be a threat?"

"I don't know. He's been fighting for so long that I think he has a hard time imagining a world without them. I know it won't be easy finding every single one of them but, with time, I think we'll learn to feel safe again."

I smile, already feeling safer in his arms. I like the way he looks at things, his optimism and faith in humanity.

He says he once lost it and thought of humans as selfish creatures with nothing to give, but this battle, this plight for survival has shown him otherwise. The way we have come together: strangers taking in children whose parents died, people sharing food and clothes when they're in short supply, men and women working as a community to restore their neighborhoods. It all makes him glad to be alive, even if the road ahead isn't as clear as we would like it to be.

I guess I'm glad too.

And for the first time, I have faith in humanity, and faith that I will finally be all right.

I have found something worth living for. The darkness has been shattered. It's time to live in the light.